IMMORTALS: BOOK 2

THE SLEEPER

Published by: Wendiilou Publishing
                                  Wendy Brown
Cover Artwork: © Chelsea Langdon
Line Art: © Andrew Munro
Pointillism drawings: © Theo Wright

To connect with the author, and for more information and resources visit

www.immortalsepic.com

For more copies contact the Publisher c/-
Glenburnie Homestead
212 Glenburnie Road
ROB ROY NSW 2360
Mobile: 0468 998 268
Email:wendiiloupublishing@gmail.com

IMMORTALS: BOOK 2

THE SLEEPER

Andrew Wratten

Wendalou Publishing

Part One:

The Perfect Storm

HOMECOMING

Mannace commanded the captain to set the flying vessel down near the entrance to the bastion of the Grey Dwarves. The captain passed instructions to the Navigator, who gently brought the great iron ship close to the ground, near enough to lower a gangway for Mannace to disembark. Mannace did not have the time or patience for this, but during his last visit to the Oracle, he experienced a disturbing vision that compelled him to travel here.

The big man brazenly strode towards the towering rockface, drawing close enough to the base to run his hands across the smooth steel that capped the bastion's narrow access tunnels. He wondered if the ship's cannons would be a match for the fortitude of this defence, but for all his gusto, he knew better than to try to force entry. When the Grey Dwarves retreated from the land of sun and rain to their dark domain beneath the mountains, they did so on good terms, and Mannace intended to leverage off the alliance of the past. He reasoned that the flying ship, with all its grandeur, noise, and steam, would be signal enough to the Dwarves that he was here. That was if, in this grim location, any of their kin were watching.

The barren landscape felt sterile and cold, like death haunting an old battlefield. Mannace was well used to that, and strangely, it calmed him.

At Mannace's signal, the flying ship retreated to the heavens, where his Ranger guards would keep a distant vigil. Under the shadow of the rockface, Mannace felt isolated, which was a rare reprieve from the constant busyness of his role as General. First, he cleared an area of rubble to pitch his tent. Then, with little choice, the Leader of Nations set about the arduous task of waiting. He was not a patient man, but he reasoned that, of all the priorities facing him, the Oracles warning was more important than the conflict in the North, and he offered a silent prayer to the Light that this would not be a waste of his precious time.

On the second night, a stocky, bearded figure approached, stepping warily out of the dark and into the light of Mannace's campfire. Mannace stood from his chair, and when the burly Dwarf came close enough that he could make out his face in the dim glow, Mannace felt relief and joy to recognise an old comrade.

"Logthar, I am gladdened to see you."

Logthar was apprehensive. "Mannace, my friend, I risk much to be here. I dare not stay long."

Mannace took a moment to collect his thoughts. He hadn't realised just how much he missed the Dwarf until now. He put a hand on Logthar's shoulder, gripping it tightly. Logthar responded with a nod and sigh, acknowledging that he also missed their friendship.

"I visited the Oracle, Logthar. In a vision, I witnessed legions of Dwarves sack the Capital of Galandar. They were killing men, women, and children. It was a ruthless slaughter, not what I would expect of an honourable race. I swear, Logthar, it was deliberate and systematic.

Unimaginable of the Dwarves I have known and have fought beside, *lived* beside, Logthar."

Mannace's words quickly gained heat, becoming accusing. In front of him, Logthar looked down, avoiding the big man's gaze, which already told Mannace much of what he needed to know.

"Since the vision, I have watched the mountains, Logthar. It seems so obvious now that the Icesleepers are coming to life. Over the last decade, the glaciers have melted and withdrawn. The mountains are bare of snow on their middle slopes. It is a thaw and an awakening, isn't it? How long until the armies of the Dwarves sally forth?"

When he looked up to meet Mannace's stare, an involuntary tear rolled from the Dwarf's eye, lost in his white beard. "Mannace, I will not betray my kin. You have your warning; what good it will do you. Take care, my friend." With that said and another thoughtful nod, the Dwarf turned and strode back into the dark.

So that was it! The encounter seemed to Mannace like an anti-climax, even though it was the confirmation he needed. Perhaps he hoped that he might change the future course, though optimism was a rare commodity in recent times, and with so many years embroiled in war, the leader was in the habit of expecting the dramatic. Waiting a short time to let his emotions settle, Mannace waved a burning branch up to the waiting ship. Soon he was aboard, and the great vessel lifted skyward, headed now for Viletri and home.

There were thirty flying ships in the colonial navy.

Mannace would have commissioned more, but the small number of capable navigators limited him. Strangely, the best candidates for the position came from amongst the Goblin slaves. According to the Architect, the Goblin mind was an ideal shape, and once they received the slave conditioning, the selected candidates proved to be capable and dependable students. The Navigator aboard this vessel was a Goblin named Rubal. He was one of the few who could instantly navigate vast distances when needed, although it was a risky business, and Mannace had never seen the feat performed.

The ship he was on was called the Gull. The builders named it after the famous Sea Captain, Urgar the Gull, who was stabbed and killed in a bar fight almost a decade ago. The ship was a marvel of modern ingenuity, with its steam-powered weaponry, clockwork mechanisms, and sleek, elegant design. It resembled a seaborne vessel at a distance but elongated like the blade of a dagger and with a stern section wrapped in iron pipes that occasionally released wispy clouds of steam. The iron hull featured portals of various dimensions along the side that were clamped firmly shut. Three masts stood tall along the Gull's main deck, with lookouts stationed in crows' nests at their top, a throwback to mimic their seaborne cousins. Unseen at its core was the *gridstone*, a device that stored the energy needed to run the burner, which powered the steam chamber and provided the intense energy required by the navigators to move or transport the vessel.

Morgan Cain joined Mannace on the foredeck. It was only an hour's travel to their destination, and both men were glad to be returning to the city. While they embroiled themselves in defence of Veldaan in the North, there was little time for anything else, and they had not visited the colonial capital for over a year.

Morgan needed repairs that would likely require both the Mage-Tech's and Animators. The adventurer had taken a heavy blow from a giant that bent his left arm out of shape, and wizard-fire melted the right side of his face and chest. But here he stood, a man part bronze, part alloy, still enduring. Of most significant concern was, since the wizard's attack, Morgan felt as if his spirit might slip away from his metal form, potentially ending the magic that sustained him. However, the Mage-Smiths were forewarned of his return, and Morgan expected they would have a new body waiting for him. It was an exacting campaign, and this would be his third replacement.

Mannace, too, sent messages ahead, letting the leaders know he would be there for the Council of the Eastern Colonies. It was the first meeting of the Council that he attended for some time. Mannace looked Morgan in his working eye.

"It has been twenty long years since I could call Viletri home."

With his mouth soldered shut by the wizard-fire, Morgan could only nod in response. Mannace continued.

"Times are only going to get harder. The Sleeper stirs, the Dwarves prepare, the campaign in the North has its successes and setbacks. I am not looking forward to this Council Morgan. The Colonial Nations will be wary of war."

Many things ran circles in Mannace's head and gut, juggling numerous challenges. Finally, he shared his growing concern.

"The colonial leaders will be tired of sending their young soldiers to fight and die in a war that has little reward. I was naive to think that the North might break so easily. The Northern conflict is generations old and rooted in deep, bloody history. It is far from finished."

Jayne Azaryn and three other Rangers joined them on deck. Together they watched the distant lights that appeared on the horizon quickly manifest into the magnificent jewel that was the metropolis and outlying towns of Viletri, capital of the Bracadian Eastern Colonies. There was already a flying vessel docked at the city's sky tower. Mannace expected that the other ship would be the Overlord's. He would be glad to see Fitius Angelcry, Overlord of Arenland, but he was immediately agitated at the thought of having to exchange pleasantries with the Overlord's demon bitch. Mannace's mood darkened further as they docked next to the chrome-plated craft. In addition to being sleeker, it was also noticeably larger and infinitely cleaner. It made Mannace feel like a dirty soldier returning home to find that nothing was as he had left it. While he led the war effort far away in the North, life progressed in the colonies.

Below them, the city was spectacular with its magnificent buildings and street lighting. Horseless carriages moved about the streets, and the noise of the nightlife added to the city's character. After a year at the battlefront, Mannace could not help feeling bitter at the comfort of those below, and he reminded himself that this was all his making. It was he who raised Viletri from the ruins. He that united the Blood Sea and Collective nations together under the Bracadian banner. He was, after all, the Governor of the Bracadian Eastern Colonies. He should be proud of what he achieved rather than envious. Knowing his mood was dark, Mannace decided to spend his first night alone, relax at his residence, have a bath, and prepare himself for the busy days ahead.

VILETRI

Fitius Angelcry was Mannace's first visitor in the morning. He came early to share breakfast, and, as always, he was full of energy and enthusiasm. Over the last eleven years, Arenland thrived under his leadership.

"Did you see the new ship, Mannace? Of course you did. It is my gift to you. It has all the latest advances. I will give you a full run-through when you are ready. You will be amazed. I will return to Arenland on the ship you arrived on and upgrade it. Mannace, you must come with me to Antigoth, there is much to see, new things to help with the War. The manufactories, Mannace, the Street of Artisans, they are wonders; what they are doing is incredible."

Mannace smiled. He was surprised when Fitius rose to the position of Overlord when his predecessor passed, seeming weak for such an influential role. He was, however, infectious. Talking to Fitius helped Mannace to remember his passion for technology and invention. After so long in the field, shifting his thinking from General to Governor was not easy. He moved across to Fitius and put his hands on the Overlord's shoulders. "You are an inspiration, Fitius. Thank you for the gift. Show me what this ship is capable of, I need to catch up with what has happened over the last year, and I can't think of a better way to start."

Under the Overlord's fine shirt, Mannace felt the cold steel in place of his right shoulder. The mechanical arm was a clockwork marvel, and Fitius used it as if it were flesh and blood.

As the two men made their way out of Mannace's residence, Kakos Agamos was waiting for them at the entrance. The Lord of Viletri returned to the city a year earlier. Before then, he commanded the legions of the dead at the Northern front. In the furnace of war, Kakos was a Liche of exceptional ability, and his reputation in the conflict was as a powerful and ruthless adversary. It appeared such a contradiction now to see him returned to his position as Lord and Chief Administrator of the Colonial Capital. Mannace pitied anybody that might mistake him for a soft mark, and he could not help but grin at seeing the Liche dressed like a gentleman in his fine clothes. Nobody here, except returned soldiers, would have any idea of Kakos' capabilities, and Mannace doubted they would speak openly of it. The Liche would still be at the front line had the Priesthood of War not insisted that the souls of the dead were their domain. The arguments escalated to the point of fights between warriors loyal to the faith and zombies under the Liche's command. Finally, the High Priestess confronted Mannace with an ultimatum that forced his hand. While Mannace showed reluctance to release the legions of undead, Kakos himself was enthusiastic about returning to Viletri, a city he felt connected to in a way most others could not comprehend. Mannace understood. It was a city powered with the souls of the dead – in its Magetech and animations. Such vulnerability would have been catastrophic if he did not trust Kakos implicitly.

Four Rangers joined Mannace as his guards for the day. Two stayed close to him while the others walked ahead.

Kakos gave Mannace an update of events as they walked

to the sky tower and ascended to the upper deck. As usual, the Lord of Viletri relayed his report thoroughly but concisely. Mannace was surprised that the city's population had reached the four hundred thousand citizen mark. Kakos estimated a further twenty to thirty thousand temporary residents or visitors, more than twenty-five thousand registered slaves, plus twelve thousand undead public servants. In addition, Kakos was commissioning a second undead dormitory, with plans to increase public administration over the next two years. Mannace noted that Kakos no longer asked his approval for such things. It was just another sign of how events were unfolding in his absence.

A zombie cleaner swept the landing deck at the top of the tower. The man was elderly when he died and dressed neatly as if he were fresh from the coffin. The zombie went dutifully about his work and did not acknowledge them as they passed.

Mannace and Fitius stopped short from entering the chrome ship to allow Kakos to finish his account. When done, the Lord of Viletri turned to leave, but not before carefully checking the cleaner's work. Then, satisfied with the sweeper's efforts, he headed back down to the street, preferring the stairs to the lift platform.

Before Mannace crossed the boarding platform, Saska and her bodyguard, Arta, appeared on the deck of the chrome ship and made their way to join them on the landing. Walking past Mannace and his Rangers as if they didn't exist, Saska kissed Fitius on the cheek and whispered in his ear. Fitius smiled, putting his hand on

Saska's waist, and returning a similar kiss. The two women entered the lift without further delay, descending the tower. Inside, Mannace was raging, his hatred of the demon whore growing with every encounter. Fitius was oblivious.

"Isn't she amazing? Could there be a creature more magnificent?"

In his head, Mannace imagined bashing the bitch's skull against the steel of the tower, but to Fitius, he simply stated, "She will be the end of you."

Fitius laughed.

"Quite the opposite, Mannace. I have not aged a day in twenty years, and I am still in my prime."

It was true. If anything, Fitius seemed more youthful. Mannace forced a smile. "Let's see what this fine ship has to offer."

The ship was named "The Bracadian", a title apt for the Governor's Vessel. It was a feat of modern engineering and a tribute to Arenland's artisans' craftsmanship. Every detail was perfect, right down to the polishes on the woodwork, the chrome finish on the metalwork, and painted designs throughout the passageways and rooms. Where pipes ran down corridors or along the ship's outside, they were deliberately prominent to celebrate the industry that enabled the magnificent vessel's creation. Sometimes you could hear the steam running through them, and when Mannace listened carefully, the ship hummed as if it was alive. As Mannace expected, the gridstone was in a metal casing at the rear. It controlled the flow of water that, in turn, produced the steam that powered the ship. There was another casing for the navigation stone, which held the boat in place and facilitated flight. Behind the rock, much of the ship's rear was water tanks designed for cycling the steam so that its water was conserved. Many onboard devices and weapons would draw on this supply, and everything from the privies to the kitchens tapped into the steam power. Mannace was impressed by the banks of steam-powered cannons hidden behind portals below deck, while smaller swivel-mounted guns were attached to the main deck rails. Fitius was particularly proud of the steam vents.

"In defence, Governor, if you are overwhelmed by an assault from the air or ground, order the vents opened. It will blast away the assailants and clear the decks. Choke gas too can be dispersed, it is all-new, and the engineers can explain it best. They are with your captain now. If you are desperate in battle, surrounded, lock down the portals and vents, and nothing will penetrate the seals."

Exquisitely carved furniture was a feature throughout the ship, and even in the crews' quarters, it had the feel of a luxury craft. Beautiful wool carpets lined the corridors and officers' lodgings. In addition, magetech lighting strips illuminated the lower decks. Mannace understood how the Arenlanders despised using technology outside their nation, particularly magetech. Either they had become less fanatic, which he doubted, or the necessity to incorporate the strips must have driven them mad. That made him smile, a reaction that didn't go unnoticed by Fitius.

"So, you are impressed then. I am glad that you like your gift."

Mannace was indeed amazed, even though the technological progress in his absence continued to irritate him. Before becoming so embroiled in the northern conflict, he relished his intimate involvement in such advancements. The truth, which came to him begrudgingly, was that he had never seen anything as singularly magnificent.

"*The Bracadian* is extraordinary, Fitius, as always, Arenland has outdone itself."

DEEDEE'S

Saska met with Deedee at her Viletri residence. It was an annual pilgrimage to travel here and meet with the girls. The brothel, called Deedee's, was famous across the Blood Sea for the beauty of its whores and the extravagance of the parties they hosted. However, the mansion and surrounding enclave were still barracks for the off-duty Blood Legion and a haven for wounded or retired soldiers. The arrangement meant the girls received the best protection, while the soldiers enjoyed occasional rewards for their services.

The girls at Deedee's were exceptionally loyal to Saska, and they were pleased to see her. Through their devotion, they inherited some of their mistress' abilities; to seduce, beguile, and steal a little life to remain young and vibrant. They put their hands on many parts and in many pies. Deedee was perhaps the only person in Viletri that knew more about its comings and goings than its Lord Kakos. Even Mannace's spy, Shylo, frequented their establishment, being as much their informant as the Governor's.

Saska was rich from the profits of her business, but hoarding money never interested her. Instead, she became a patron for those who could not support themselves; widows, women abandoned by their husbands, the growing number of people that came to Viletri full of optimism but since fallen on hard times. It was not stereotypical behaviour for a child of the four hells. Notably, and with satisfaction, her popularity annoyed Mannace. In Saska's mind, with unwavering certainty, she knew that one day she would utterly destroy that man.

A section of the enclave was a refuge for women and their children who needed temporary lodging and assistance for whatever reason. Some resided there for many years, helping with cleaning, cooking, and other duties to keep the enclave running smoothly. They adored their patron, and there was nothing they wouldn't do for her.

Saska's most notorious follower, Jesephine, resided secretly at the mansion. Just three months prior, there occurred an incident at Antigoth where Jesephine drained a prominent businessman of his life essence. It took all of Saska's influence to protect the seductress and her establishment there. Jesephine was safer at Viletri, but Saska knew that her student's appetites would cause further trouble. Although there was no way to be sure, Saska suspected that Jesephine was going through a transformation, a metamorphosis of sorts where she would become more the child and agent of the four hells. There was raw magic in Jesephine that fed her passion and abilities, as there was in Saska. Over the last decades, the seductress was, at times, her pupil and her lover – perhaps the day would come when the student would become an insatiable predator as Saska once was or even a rival. Today, as they sat in the main lounge, Jesephine joined Saska and Deedee in their conversation.

Deedee was talking, but Saska was not listening. She wasn't particularly interested in the update. Instead, she removed her cloak and blouse. Saska looked to Jesephine to help her with the undergarments, horrible things that were the fashion of the wealthy in Arenland. Job done, Jesephine ran her hand from Saska's neck down to her stomach. The touch made her mistress breathe deeply, and the two women came closer so that their bodies touched. Deedee stopped talking. She came forward and ran her hands across the backs of both women. Jesephine turned and reached out to include her in the play, kissing her gently on the lips. Deedee knew from experience that the doors would be closed and barred this evening, and the whole establishment would be enjoying a lady's night indoors.

MAGETECH

The Architect, his Mage-Techs, Animators, and Artisans, plus many of the apprentices, were present to transfer Morgan Cain's spirit from his damaged form into the new avatar they created for him. The Chief Animator supervised the extraction and binding. The specialists incorporated magical defences into the sophisticated design, so it was not a simple process. Three hours passed before the animators stood back so that Morgan Cain could take his first step in his new form.

Although the avatar's shape was human, Morgan did not feel human. His mortal visage was moulded into the face, though as a younger man, beardless and with smooth lines. A symbolic crown adorned his brow, elevating his stature to appear more commanding. He liked that. He also liked that this form was less mechanical and more fluid than previous designs, though fluid to the point where he was unsure of his balance. Morgan waited a minute before taking a second step. With care, he also moved his arms and then other parts. The adventurer discovered an unusual sense of his centre of balance, which he shifted up. Morgan was surprised to be hovering above the crowd who stared up at him with smiles, clapping each other on the backs. He lowered himself back to the ground. "What else can I do?".

Morgan's slurred his words, but the Chief Animator understood, and he came forward to provide further information.

"Your new body has an alloy casing. We call it Animator

Class Ninety-Two. As well as being stronger than steel, AC92 is also a conduit for Magetech Three, which facilitates the addition of the full animation and protection classes. At the central core is a Gridstone and prototype ANS. Um, that's the Assisted Navigation Stone. We filled the entire body with AC4 adaptive webbing and a mercury-based fluid that is a conduit between the grid and the plating."

The Chief Animator, who spent most of his time communicating with his underlings and the Mage-Techs, could see that he was losing Morgan in detail, so he jumped to the main point.

"We didn't know if the navigation stone would work, but you levitated, Morgan. If you can control the stone, then flight should be possible. It is amazing, is it not, Morgan? Your new form has been in development for some years. It is the toughest, most complex thing we've ever put together. Nothing on the battlefield will touch it! How does it feel in there?"

Morgan was starting to feel comfortable in his new form. When he responded, his speech was noticeably better.

"Odd, like I have no bones, but still a firm grounding and a sense for all the parts. It feels right but vastly different. I am grateful as always to The Architect, SOTA, and your crew. And I am done with the battlefield."

The Architect moved away, which was a sign for others to return to their work. However, the Chief Animator and one of the senior Mage-Tech's remained with Morgan. The Mage-Tech fitted a shield disk into a slot in the palm of

Morgan's left hand.

"It's the same one from your old form. Good to go. We suggest you stay close for a few days until you get a feel for the new design. Come back before you leave Viletri, and we'll answer any questions and do a quick check. We are all keen to see how the ANS goes; it could be revolutionary."

Morgan was pleased. Even the blue tinge to the black metal carapace was to his liking. If he was to be a man of metal, at least it came with advantages, and he looked good. Yet, flight was something Morgan needed to think more on. He wasn't sure that he was comfortable with the idea of it, though it wouldn't be the first time he needed to adapt.

COLONIAL COUNCIL

The Colonial Council met every year for a session of three days. It was the most significant event on the colonial calendar, and Viletri was an attentive host. As it had been every year, the city was a celebration of music, performers, markets, and street foods. Visitors came to join the parades and festivities or pilgrimage to the Temple of War, honouring those fallen in battle. There were grand tournaments in the rural areas outside the city, and each town hosted community events. The inns were full. Businesses were at their busiest. On the docks and amongst the market stalls, army and guild recruiters were out in force as always. The technology fair attracted queues of onlookers, and this year, tours of the Sky Tower and Flying Ships were a highlight for many visitors. Everybody put on their best face and their best behaviour for the most part.

The nations' rulers and chief administrators met in the Colonial Hall. Seating was arranged like an arena so that representatives from all forty-four nations could see and hear the speaker at the front. It was Minhouas who ran proceedings. The Viletri Elder welcomed the leaders, paying particular homage to Governor Mannace, who travelled from the northern front. Mannace was surprised to have applause directed at him, and he acknowledged it with a nod. Minhouas' speech in support of the Northern Conflict was rousing. As he looked directly at Mannace, he restated the commitment of the Eastern Colonies of Bracadia to the war effort. The crowd responded with more applause, and again Mannace, surprised but circumspect of the show of support, acknowledged them with a nod. What followed next was a series of updates from guild leaders. First, the Chief Administrator from Yanth gave an account of the colonial treasury and investments. Mannace couldn't remember when Yanth had taken on such a role. Next, the Council broke into smaller gatherings where they discussed all kinds of diplomacy and business. Embroiled in the war, Mannace hadn't attended the Council for a long time, and it was not what he expected. They did not need him.

The Council dedicated the second day to the war effort. Mannace addressed the forum and, using the map that covered the wall behind the speaker's podium, he talked about the territories secured and the size of the armies involved. The Southern forces retained everything South of the Rift, the area of Veldaan except for a small region known as The Aghan, twelve of the sixteen Young Cities, and sections of Southern Sarang. It would have been a remarkable outcome had it not taken twenty years to reach that point. Mannace took the time to show the deployment of the colonial divisions and what role each played. Where he could, Mannace gave examples of how colonial troops contributed to specific victories. He was honest too about some of the defeats, although he was careful to put the colonial units in a good light. Mannace invited questions.

The Prelate of Karanthos stood, "What of the Sleeper?"

It was good to get straight to the point. Mannace considered his response while gulping a glass of water retrieved from a table near him. He placed the glass down firmly, looking the Prelate in the eye.

"The Elves have scouted deep into the territories of the Sleeper." He pointed to the land of Amon Murn on the map. "The people of that land are warlike, numerous and organised. We now know that we fought against them when they attacked the Blood Sea decades ago. The Sleeper is a legend connected to their religious beliefs. We do not know what the Sleeper is, but when it arises from its slumber, we are certain that the armies of that nation and its allies will join the war on the side of the North. When that happens, the number of enemies we face will double."

"Maybe the Sleeper will stay asleep." The Prelate sat back down.

"Why don't you make more progress?" It was the Mad King's daughter, Queen over the Madlands. She stood out from the crowd, with a cloak of fish-like scales that reflected light dazzlingly and resin armour shaped to hug her muscular contours. The Queen wore a necklace of monstrous tusks and teeth across her chest as gruesome trophies. Her hair was uncombed, thickly matted, hanging down her back to her ankles. Threaded through the dreads were bones and colourful feathers. Her features and stance were mannish, and everything about the woman was aggressive. Unsurprisingly, the Queen was loud and her tone accusing.

"My father, the Mad King, would have beaten the North and turned their people to slavery."

"The Mad King hides in his mountain. Perhaps his daughter should come to the Rift, and she might better appreciate what war looks like."

Mannace's words became lost amid the many angry voices against the Queen. The ruler of the Madlands was not a popular figure amongst the Council, and she reluctantly took her seat so that the hall once again became quiet enough for Mannace to continue.

"We would all like to see faster progress, but this will not be a short campaign."

"We remember the invasion from the North. We know that the campaign fought in the North is better than a defence fought in our lands. We are with you, Governor, for as long as it takes. What do you need from us?"

It was Fitius who stood to address his peers. Mannace already talked at length with the Arenland Overlord, so he knew that Fitius was facilitating Mannace to address his needs to the group. From his position, looking at the crowd of leaders, Mannace could see in their faces that there were mixed feelings on the subject.

"Nothing more than you already give: your sons and your full commitment. This campaign in the North is not a war we will win with numbers because the North is much larger than the South. We will see victory through our industry, innovation, and invention. Protect your sons and bring us victories by training your armies, equipping them with modern weapons, and giving them every advantage you can. Where we have thirty flying ships, build me a thousand. Give me the means to roll back our enemy and steer us towards victory."

The applause was enthusiastic from some and measured from others. Mannace could tell that it was in respect for his position as Governor more than his words. He planned to meet with many leaders individually to get to more specifics over the following days.

Mannace hadn't intended to talk about the subject, but as he stood before the nations, he felt a need to say something to them all about the Dwarves, even with the limited information or evidence he collected. He spoke gently.

"Nations of the Colony, be watchful of the Icesleepers. Something stirs within the mountains, do not be taken by surprise."

THE MAD KING

In a bay, at the end of a long fjord, was the City of Colossus, so named for the invincible giants that guarded the sprawling metropolis. Over the last two decades, the city expanded from a small port to being home to as many as half a million Orcs and Goblins. They came from across the Wengo and as far south as Greshnak to live, trade, and be entertained. Central to the city was the grand arena. The massive structure expanded in capacity over the years so that up to forty thousand spectators could gather to watch the breathtaking combats. Some contests were fights to the death, but most were competitions – games invented by the Orcs that pitched tribe against tribe. It was an obsession for the Wengo, and its best combatants enjoyed a life of celebrity and privilege.

Nobody was interested in the war against the South. As the Mad King said, it was not their war. Why should the Wengo tribes die fighting to protect the lands of the humans? War kept the tribes weak. It stopped the Orcs from reaching their potential. The Mad King wanted the Wengo to be strong.

Athose sat with the Mad King. The Elf was spending more time in the city, and he was the only non-Orc that participated in the Games, excelling at all events.

"So, you are famous, Athose, a champion of the people. Why am I so lucky to be visited this day by the mighty Athose in person?" The Mad King was unusually cynical, whose conversation was typically to the point and humourless.

"Because you are bored, and you need company. I know you are sick of waiting for whatever it is we are waiting for. So, we should travel east."

"Why east?"

"The Sleeper is east. Are you not waiting for the Sleeper to wake up? What if he never awakens? What if he does? Is that what you are waiting for? Is that what the others are waiting for?"

"It might be what I am waiting for."

"You don't know? Then why wait? Perhaps if you wait long enough, the people will call you The Waiter, not the Mad King. A Mad King would wait for nobody!"

"I liked you better before you were a champion of the Arena."

"Before I was old enough to know my own thoughts. I'm just saying, I don't think you're a waiter, but you're waiting, just like the others. But you're not like the others. The bell, will it awaken the Sleeper? It will, won't it, but you have the bell. You know the Sleeper will not rise!"

"Quiet! Your mouth is quicker than your brain. Why are you in such a hurry? When the Sleeper awakens, the world as you know it will end. There will be a new Age. And how can we travel east when the Elves watch us. If you, a boy, can figure it all out, do you not think that the Alani may have come to their conclusions."

"I am no longer a boy."

The Mad King "humphed". Then, he poured himself some

water and slowly drank the cooling liquid while Athose slouched in his chair, appearing somewhat deflated. Eventually, the King offered further explanation.

"If the bell is the key to waking the Sleeper, do you not think there are others that are followers of the Sleeper that might also seek the bell. We have not been invisible. We have awoken the Colossi and the Kraken, and here we are in the North, with the bell, waiting."

"They will come for the bell?"

"They have not come yet, but they will come."

Since they were so open, Athose went to another topic previously left untouched. "You are different since the Remman King killed Tyriah."

"Tyriah killed herself", he was snappish in his response. "She chose death over facing a new Age. I intended that she would join me to see it unfold. I thought us like-minded. So now I have only you, boy. Me to see out this Age, and you to see in the new. Perhaps that is how it should be. Us, the old and the new."

"You are not telling me everything."

"I am sure you will figure it out."

"I'm not good at waiting. There is a game tonight. In the morning I will go to The Hand. From there, I will travel east. I have not been to those lands. I will come back and tell you what I find."

The Mad King shrugged as if he cared little for what Athose did. After a moment of thought, to annoy the boy, he suggested, "Why don't you take your father with you."

Athose bit, "I will choose my companions. Vilera will come. If Roanna is at The Hand, she may join me too. She has been east, and she can use the pathways."

The King had a sly look, "Roanna will be there."

"How can you know that?"

"Because the Elves are watching us, and she is their agent. Roanna will be waiting for you at The Hand of Fengal, and she will be free of other commitments. Look at your travels over the last twenty years. Both Roanna and Vilera have always been there when you need them. It is obvious, boy. They are spies for higher powers."

Athose considered. It was apparent now that the Mad King pointed it out. That meant that the Spider Mother was watching him too. "Who else is watching?"

"The Oracle. Possibly others."

"Who is the Oracle?"

"That is a good question, boy. I thought for a time that the Oracle might in some way be the Sleeper or the Sleeper's agent. Now I think that the Oracle is, as it claims, a servant of the Light. The Light and the Darkness both have an interest. It is the Oracle that prepared Mannace and has sent him North. Ask your father about the Oracle and the Darkness. You are a clever boy, Athose. Step back and look at the world for what it is, a game played in an arena."

In the distance, the arena drums started a slow beat. It was part of the build-up to a night of combats and contests.

The Mad King was dismissive, "Best you were away then. The crowds will already be gathering in the streets. The city will want to see its champion."

Athose smiled and got nimbly to his feet. He enjoyed the build-up to the games as much as he enjoyed the games. He liked the attention, the comradery with the Orcs and the rivalry with the other tribes. His people, the Fogmir Elves, were very pragmatic, and they put duty above all other considerations. The Orcs, by comparison, were passionate. They let their passion consume them, revelling, fighting, and fucking as the moment took them.

THE HAND OF FENGAL

The Druid, Ethyraniel, looked down upon the Northern Forest through the eyes of a giant crow. Through the wisps of cloud, he could see that five great rivers cut their way through deep gorges to join into a single spectacular waterway that wound its way north to the distant sea. It looked like an impression of a giant hand against the earth. At that moment, Ethyraniel named the forest region the Hand of Fengal and claimed it as sacred to the god Fengal as a bastion of nature and life. Many wild Elves pilgrimaged from the Fogmir to this wondrous place. Enchanted by its beauty, they made the Hand of Fengal their new home. The Elves built nests in the giant trees, and for the first time, the nomadic wanderers put down their roots. A community formed. The Rhalec made the pilgrimage, too, arriving on ships and navigating as far south as they could down the widest of the rivers. The crocodile people established a port, trading with their Elven allies.

Eya, the mother of spiders, also made this northern place her home and her children infested forest areas, barricading it with their webs. Below the forest, they discovered vast catacombs and underground waterways. Like the Elves, spiders travelled the ancient paths, and in the deep catacombs, amongst the crystal caverns, their lair expanded.

It was not long before the fragile peace between the Elves and spiders shattered. At first, there were minor skirmishes, but as the number of Elves grew, so did their confidence. Finally, in a decisive push, they drove the spiders back so that the creatures were confined chiefly to their underground domain. Preferring a secret war, Eya had the last of the Ra-Anu in her possession, an ancient forest spirit that she had uncovered and subdued. Sacrificing the essence of the spirit, the Mother of Spiders sent ghostly tendrils over a vast distance, infecting the woodlands with her deadly venom. The distraught Elves used all their magic to protect the sacred groves. Other parts of the ancient woods quickly fell to death and decay.

But Eya, for all her ageless wisdom, did not know of the Rebirth of the Ra-Anu. It was a cycle that allowed the spirits to survive the demise of the ancients and persist to this day. Under the protection of the Druids, three Ra-Anu were reborn, slowly regaining their strength. Already the forest was healing, though it would require centuries of nurturing to undo the Spider Mother's destructive work.

Athose knew to be cautious as he made his way through the Hand of Fengal. The healthiest parts of the forest were safest, but where the trees were sick or dead and the forest void of life, this was where spiders might be lurking. As he drew closer to his destination, Athose became aware that Wardens were tracking him high in the trees. Having been a Warden once, he knew their tricks to stay hidden.

The young Elf made his way to the place where he and his sisters first discovered the splendour of this region, and as he steered across the gorge, the view was more spectacular than he remembered. Giant trees on the far bank were magnificent and all along the cliffs, vines, alive with red and yellow flowers, cascaded down to the waterway far below. Other blooms, some larger than himself, filled the air with their wondrous aromas.

"The flowers and scents are the labour of Cheinalya."

Athose turned to face his sister. She was standing next to him, looking down at the chasm. "The Wardens told me that you were approaching, and I knew you would come to this place first."

"You and I are going east."

"I have my duties here. Are you in such a hurry that we cannot have a conversation before you drag me off on another adventure?"

"Sorry, Roanna, I am glad to see you. It is beautiful here, but this place makes me uncomfortable. I feel like an intruder amongst my people."

"Perhaps if you spent time here, you might feel differently."

Roanna unwrapped the fresh food she brought. There was fruit, bread, and cakes. After Athose consumed his fill, he broke the silence, "I know you will come with me."

Roanna didn't respond.

"I am starting to see the world for what it is."

"Somebody needs to look after you, brother. You have a habit of putting yourself in trouble."

Roanna left Athose at the chasm and returned later in the day. She donned a dark hooded cloak and carried a walking staff. Her clothes and dark skin made her look like a creature of the shadow rather than the Druid she was. Only the brightness of her striking blue eyes gave her colour. Roanna slung a knapsack filled with brick-bread and other travelling food over her shoulder. Supplied and ready, the siblings made their way around the chasm and headed east through the forest.

As Athose expected, their sister, Vilera, dropped gently from a tree once they were well away from the Elven territory. Neither Athose nor Roanna saw or heard her in the canopy. Vilera landed gracefully and scuttled ahead without acknowledging them. Her spider-kin form seemed larger since they last met, and Athose noticed she was more muscular in her arms. Finally, after an hour, Vilera turned and came back towards them, "We must stay well clear of the Tangle. The Fen are active."

Roanna added, "Better we head south first, then east, to more easily cross the rivers and avoid the regions contested by the Elves and Spiders."

Taking the advice, it was four days before the siblings emerged from the forest and onto the Saville. The Saville was a savannah, rich with tall grass and wildlife. Roanna, who explored here previously, talked of other areas where there were farms, towns, and large communities. The druids' experience was that the people of the Saville were primarily farmers or hunters. The cities, though, would have garrisons. Roanna broke their customary silence with a warning, "Patrols are likely to be mounted on horses or other beasts. Keep an eye for movement on the horizon. If we encounter hunters, they use dogs as well."

As Roanna guided them through the wildlands, their caution proved to be wise, and twice they took shelter in the tall grass to avoid mounted patrols. The men they observed rode all manner of beasts, from horses to other things like horses but more towering and hairless, and some creatures that were broad, with flat heads that seemed all jaw and teeth.

Once, they hid for several hours as columns of soldiers from the Northern coastal region of May moved across the plains, heading south to reinforce the war at the Rift. There were perhaps ten thousand infantry armed with spears and bows. Some groups were heavily armoured and looked like professional soldiers, while others appeared freshly equipped, mostly bare-chested, and with just enough training to march in a straight line. Vilera commented to Roanna that they seemed a handsome people. All possessed beautiful features, some with trimmed beards, and their bodies were fit and muscular to the point of being sculptured. "I will visit May, one day."

Roanna ignored her sister, concentrating on the enchantments that helped to keep them unseen. Then, when the danger passed, she asked Vilera, "You are part Dark Elf and part Spider. Why would you couple with a man? Why would a man couple with a Spiderling?"

"A man would be fortunate to bind with a daughter of Eya. Am I not beautiful, Roanna?"

The question went unanswered, and they continued east. After another two days, the terrain became a rugged tundra with craggy hills and swampy valleys. It was less populated, but there was still the threat of foragers or patrols. The hillsides meant that the travellers were more exposed, so they hiked at night to stay unseen. Roanna and Vilera's vision in the dark was excellent, guiding Athose, who struggled to keep pace. They were near or possibly even crossed the border into the lands of the Markhon. Beyond was Amon Murn.

ALTHEA

Althea Kane was not an advocate for necromancy. Once a person passed into the domain of the dead, it seemed sacrilege to drag the soul back to the world of the living. The thousands of zombies that ambled about Viletri, to her, were disrespectful of the vibrant, living people they had once been. They existed, and some could even manage a few words, but they lost that spark and compassion that made them human. There were exceptions like Kakos Agamos, who was highly functional, although his moral compass was not always pointing north. She was not as passionate about it as some; she did not advocate the burnings.

As a healer, and the assembly official responsible for the health of all citizens of Viletri, Althea was always considering better ways to care for the sick, wounded, and dying. She was considering an idea that she wanted to run past Render. The animators were easier to track down, but Althea found them hard to talk to and somewhat close-minded. Now that Render was back in the city, secluded at his residence, she wasted no time in booking a meeting. Several days later, they were sitting at a table outside a popular eatery, sharing a platter of fish and shellfish. The food was flavoursome, cooked with spices and drizzled with seasoning and sauce.

"Render, I have been thinking about the way we treat the dead. When some people pass, you restore them as zombies to serve their families and the city. I don't like that."

Render shrugged. People could have their ignorant opinions. He sucked an oyster out of its shell and chewed it before swallowing.

"I was also thinking. We all know the story of Morgan Cain, whose spirit was trapped in a statue, and how it has been moved between avatars when needed. Morgan Cain is coherent, intelligent, and compassionate. Because his spirit never passed into the realm of the dead, he has kept all the characteristics that made him human."

Render shrugged again. "The temple guardians too. The spirits of the chosen became the guardians before they could pass on. Be careful where you are going with this, Althea."

"Why do you say that?"

"Because when the spirit is no longer in its human host, it is no longer wholly that person. It becomes a commodity, usable by the necromancers, animators, and priests." Althea looked uncertain so Render gave her an illustration, "Take yourself as an example. You have control over your destiny and can make choices and decisions. You can say 'no' if I ask you to poke your finger in your eye. When you die, and your spirit is free, I could catch it, bind it, and put it into a statue like the one behind us. With magic, you could move and talk and think and act. But you could not say 'no'. You would be my puppet, my play-thing. I would make your choices, tell you what to think, and decide what is best for you."

Althea felt uncomfortable. The example was unnerving, and the way Render's face lit up when he talked about controlling her was creepy. "But Morgan Cain is a free man. Kakos Agamos is Lord of Viletri."

"Kakos is exceptional. Morgan Cain is vulnerable. A lot of effort has gone into protecting that man from those that would manipulate him. Look at this city. Everything the animators' touch is vulnerable. Don't mess with things you don't understand, Althea."

Althea shifted herself to sit more upright, and she looked Render hard in the eyes. "I understand when a young man's head gets too big for his hat". She poked the Sorcerer in the chest. "You are not the only expert in your field; you might be surprised what the Guild has achieved, what they are capable of doing. The Fesadi Menders, the Temple Healers, and Guild Surgeons have made considerable advances. What if I told you the Fesadi can grow a human form?"

Althea could see Render's interest sparked. That was the bait, and now she would reel him in.

"They call it a Fedling. Each Fedling has a crystal called a Soul Catcher and an empathy stone. They intended to draw the soul out of a dying man to give the form life. But it doesn't work. So, I want you to cooperate with the Fesadi to animate the Fedling. The Fesadi methods are unlike anything tried before. The outcome could be life-changing."

The sorcerer was intrigued, and he could immediately see merit in the project, "Yes, I will help."

"There is only one thing. The Fesadi don't like you. So, the project will be under their strict supervision, and they will want to understand every detail of what you do before you do it."

Render's look soured and he was about to speak when Althea poked him again, "You can handle it. This venture will be revolutionary, Render. Immortality for the commoner, the world will never be the same."

Althea gave some final advice to the Sorcerer as she got up to leave, "Render, shine some light on that big brain of yours. It has been in the shadow for far too long."

A PERFECT STORM

Render was the last to arrive at Mannace's residence. Morgan Cain, Milan Tash, and Mannace were already looking at maps in the study and discussing ideas. On the wall above the map table was a mirror, and from the polished glass, a ghostly face looked down on proceedings. A boy dressed in servant's clothes stood by the mirror with a hand placed on the glass. It was the boy who looked up at Render and said, "Sorcerer, welcome."

"Thank you, Syprus."

The mirror responded with a nod.

As Render peeked over the shoulder of Milan at the charts, Mannace looked up from the other side of the table.

"Milan is visiting. He has brought us new maps. So, for the first time, we can get a proper look at the lands between here and Bracadia."

Render patted Milan on the arm to acknowledge him before moving to a seat to relax. The sorcerer knew that Mannace and Morgan would be engrossed in the charts, and they would share every morsel of information they found that was of interest. Render was more intent to watch from the corner of the room, where he would get a better sense of what the others were thinking. The Sorcerer was curious as to why Milan, who was always so calculated, chose now to share his precious charts.

Render called to the boy stationed at the mirror as the evening progressed. "Fetch me some more wine, boy, the best the Governor has in his cellars." The boy moved quickly to comply, causing Syprus to scowl at the Sorcerer. Render laughed out loud. He enjoyed messing with the old fool. He didn't see what value Mannace found in keeping him around.

Morgan appeared agitated. Render asked from his seat across the room, "Morgan, what's on your mind?"

They all looked at Morgan, who took a step back from the map table to collect his thoughts before speaking.

"I will not be going back to the Rift." After a brief period of silence, he continued, "I am an explorer. I am best employed to investigate these new lands and perhaps other lands not yet charted. I would travel to Bracadia to meet with the Emperor. Through Milan, we trade far and wide, but we have not engaged with the leaders of these other lands. Let me establish embassies and diplomacy. The Eastern Colonies are strong because of the collaboration between nations. Let us extend our influence and broaden our interests."

Mannace asked Milan, "What are your views?"

"It was the Emperor who put pressure on the Guild to open up the seaways. The Empire has expanded in many directions, and the Emperor wants to bring all of the parts together. He calls it a time of unity and consolidation. It will take many years, but when the Emperor looks towards the Eastern Colonies, he will be greatly interested in what he sees here. My advice is to have some skin in the game."

Mannace sighed. "The Sleeper, the Dwarves, and the

Emperor. A perfect storm is brewing, and we are caught at its centre."

Morgan, always an optimist, added, "In the centre, the eye of the storm, it is calm while chaos plays out around it."

"You are right, my friend", Mannace could feel the weight on his shoulders, the tangible pressure of great responsibility. "We will be at the eye of the storm, calm amongst the chaos. Let that be our objective."

The boy, who returned with the wine, was back at his position at the mirror. He spoke for Syprus, "Do not abandon your vision for the North. That is where the fate of the world will be decided."

"Enough, Syprus." There was quick anger in Mannace's voice, enough that they could see Syprus' lips move in response, but the boy standing by the mirror stood frozen, too scared to relay the message. Mannace continued, "We can all see that the war in the North is going nowhere. If the lands loyal to the Sleeper rise, then the enemy in the North will overwhelm us. There will be no final battle to end that campaign in this boy's lifetime."

The boy was horrified to be included in the conversation, fleeing the room.

The others agreed. They all understood that it was complicated and impossible to walk away from the war and return to the North when the timing suited them better. The North, left alone, would again become the aggressor. Without their help, their southern allies would quickly lose ground at the Rift. Also, the war against the North united the Eastern Colonies. It drove their invention and their industry. For now, it was part of the glue that bound the nations together.

From his seat in the corner, Render shifted the conversation, "What do we know about the Dwarves?"

"In my vision, they sacked Rotherdan. Their armies and magic were unstoppable. When I met briefly with Logthar, he could not tell me more, but he did say that the vision was a warning. We know that there are True Dwarves, the Grey General was one of them, and it seems feasible that they have been gathering their strength in the Icesleepers for longer than any can remember. I once asked Logthar if I could meet with the Grey General, but the True Dwarf would only converse with his kind. He showed no tolerance for other races. We fought alongside the Grey Dwarves before they departed the lands of men – we do not want to be facing them and their kin on the field."

The others nodded their agreement. Milan was best placed to discuss the third threat.

"The Bracadian Emperor is ambitious, sometimes fair, and sometimes ruthless. When he casts his gaze over the Eastern Colonies, he will want what you have, particularly your technology and magic. He may be satisfied to learn these things over time, but it is more likely the Emperor will want to bring your industry and modern armies to the capital. If he chooses to, the Emperor has the resources to win the war in the North and possibly deny the Sleeper, but he will only act if he sees that as a priority. The colonies and their challenges are far removed from the Bracadian mainland, so the war here is unlikely to be his primary concern."

Mannace responded, "It has been more than two decades since the Emperor first looked in our direction, and at that time, we did not have the means to seek out Bracadia. Now that we possess the means, we will initiate greater contact with Bracadia and the Emperor. We will share what we have and learn from them what we can. Is that not how we have advanced, through collaboration and embracing new opportunities? We are Bracadian, my friends. We best act like it."

Milan was nodding, "Mannace, you should go to the Emperor. He has not met his eastern governor."

"I cannot afford that luxury Milan; the war with the North is my burden. Until the North is defeated, I will be our First General. I *must* finish what I started. I understand that you must all follow your paths, but when I need you, will you come?"

They all nodded. Milan brought a box with him, and he chose now to place it on the table and pry open the lid. It had nothing to do with what they were discussing, but he thought they would find it interesting. The box contained a long silver wire shaped into a series of loops, with the ends soldered together. A thin bracelet of gold was hanging from one of the circles. Milan flicked the device about and pulled the bracelet free with a sleight of hand. Then, he replaced the bracelet on the loop with a reverse action. Render was sceptical, "Give me that."

The Sorcerer scrutinised the device intently, moving the bracelet between the loops, but there was no way to uncouple it. Mannace leaned over to take it from him, but Render pushed his hand away. He was quickly becoming frustrated. "Go back to your maps. Where's that boy? Mannace, send for more wine."

REFUGEES

Jaal never intended his camp near the Wengo Mountains to be anything more than a temporary base. When the South drove the Northerners out of Veldaan, more than four million refugees fled to neighbouring lands, and from there, to places of relative safety. The refugees assumed that because Jaal camped in the North, he was of the North. At first small groups of civilians settled nearby to have the protection of his soldiers and the Colossi.

The few camps quickly turned into a tent town, then a tent city. Over the space of just a few months, the refugees constructed lumber mills, quarries, and other infrastructure, enabling permanent structures and the building of farms. They were skilled, pragmatic, and determined people.

Jaal was not interested in being their protector. However, his compulsion for order would not let him stay idle and allow the chaos to go unchecked. With so many people under stressful conditions and vying for land and food, it needed a firm hand to keep many families in check. The Colossus and slave soldiers were a sufficient police force, and some of the slaves were capable administrators. So, reluctantly, Jaal helped the Veldaan establish and run their community.

Jaal was surprised that the Wengo Orcs never took issue with the Veldaan refugees settling so close to their lands. He expected it was because they honoured the old Northern alliances. Over time, the two societies mixed more freely, and the growing city became a well-frequented stop for Orc and Goblin travellers. Groups of nomads from the Ryde also visited the town for trade and entertainment. Other refugee communities formed further north, and civilians moved between these, maintaining a semblance of their governance, with guilds re-asserting their presence and Veldaan generals coordinating the ongoing war effort.

Able-bodied men and women continued to be active in the campaign against the South, even though they were losing, and their energy for fighting was diminished. After twenty years exiled from their homeland, some gave up the hope or desire to return to Veldaan. However, their hatred of the South and pride as gatekeepers to the North kept most bound to their purpose. Many clung to the belief that the Sleeper would rise, and Amon Murn would join the war against the South. Then they would have not only their lands returned but also vengeance.

Jaal wondered what Mannace must think of his situation, and it ate away at him that his friends might feel betrayed. He didn't help himself, though; he took a Veldaan lover who lived at his residence, a woman named Matila who was a leader of the Chokra and whose job was to train recruits for the war effort. It seemed to Jaal that life was complicated no matter where he went. The Dark Elf was sure that the damned Oracle was to blame.

There were ten Colossi in the city. Mostly they just stood or sat and waited for Jaal to give them instruction, although occasionally, one might wander off and later return. The Veldaan generals compelled Jaal to lend the Colossi to the war effort, but he ignored them, uninterested in any dialogue. The generals had no choice but to respect his neutrality, though it sat very poorly with them.

Spiderlings arrived at the city to contact their father and trade. Some stayed, preferring the city over their home in the forest, becoming part of Jaal's garrison. Many of his original soldiers were too old to be fighters, so as well as the Spiderkin, Jaal also hired Orcs, Humans, and Goblins to bolster his forces. Jaal was careful to pick candidates loyal to him if circumstances shifted dramatically, which was a constant possibility. He knew he was walking a fine line with both the North and the South.

Part 2:

The Emperor

KRAKEN

There was a buzz about the Blood Sea. Copies were made of Milan's maps and shared amongst the nation's leaders and guilds. New markets, cultures, and open passage to Bracadia were suddenly available. It was like taking the lid off a jar of sweets – everybody wanted to get their hand in there and grab as much as they could.

Merchants were the first to launch new expeditions. They were granted permission from the Colonial Council to trade for the first time in colonial technology – animation, clockwork, steam-tech, mage-tech, and even weapons. The only technology not available to them was the flying ships.

Conversely, the Industrialists, Mage-Techs, SOTA, Animators Guild, and Wizards Conclave were all interested in what technology they might attain. They would be searching for those special people to bolster their ranks – the rare navigators, people with unique talents, the ultra-geniuses. Their agents were upon the first ships to head west.

With similar ambition, Ahmeda, the High Priestess of War, was determined to position the priesthood as a significant player in the coming diplomacy. To achieve that, she planned to take the vision and doctrine of the War God directly to the top so that the message would flow down to others. It required an audience with the Emperor of Bracadia, a man that no leader from the Eastern Colonies had ever seen.

With the invention of the flying ships, the Arenlanders

considered the steel and iron seaborne vessels as ageing technology. So, at Ahmeda's discretion, the priesthood purchased the temple warship, *The Harmsway*, plus two other massive steel ships, from the Overlord. The acquisition and refitting drained the temple coffers, but it gave Ahmeda the means she needed to make such a journey and impress the Bracadians.

In some ways, Ahmeda preferred these magnificent seaborne ships to the flying vessels. She was a traditionalist, plus the steel warships towered over the largest galleons - so intimidating and threatening. Nothing could match the steel ships for firepower or fortitude. The High Priestess quickly assigned crew and marines from the Ostoik and Viletri temples to seize the initiative, leaving those locations with just a skeleton staff.

Amidst all the chaos at Viletri, Morgan Cain received an unexpected visitor. Had he not been made of metal, he would have frowned deeply upon seeing the pirate Kraken at his door, but instead, Morgan stared steely-eyed, and reluctantly he invited the old brigand into his home. It was audacious for the pirate to be here, but they shared a seaman's code, and Morgan gave no thought to summoning the city guard.

Morgan's home was unlike other residences. As a living statue, he did not need the facilities others might require. Instead, he used the space to display things that he found interesting; curiosities from the Blood Sea or objects that he collected in his wider travels. He even kept his old, damaged avatars. Kraken found the displays fascinating, and the two men spent hours looking over the pieces. From their conversation, it was apparent both harboured a passion for exploration.

Later, as they sat exhausted of banter about their exploits, Kraken grinned at Morgan, and he took a deep breath to fortify himself for what he was about to share.

"Morgan, I love the sea and my life, but it has been hard to be an immortal amongst mortals. Over hundreds of years, I have explored the oceans with many crews, and I have watched many fine men grow old and die. It blows, Morgan. I can't do that anymore. I don't want to find and train new blood to replace those lost. I am tired of that life. It is time to try something new."

He suddenly laughed aloud at his thoughts, and the immortal pirate shared with Morgan more of what he was thinking.

"You know, I did have a plan to steal the Overlord's flying ship and Navigator. It would put a wind right up their arses. But then I thought, what next? Another mortal crew and the same cycle. I am always running. Is there an alternative, Morgan? Is there a place for me amongst the immortals?"

Kraken cringed at his own words; it sounded better in his head. Morgan chuckled.

"You make us sound like gods. You might want to lower your expectations. Kraken, you are of the True Men, the old Viletri. Do you want to live again in the city and be counted amongst their ranks?"

"By Ramthos' balls, no! True Men, what a lot of whale-nuts. Sitting in their flash houses looking out their windows and down their noses! I'd rather throw myself in the deep and be done with it."

"What about the Elves?"

"What about them? Oh, because they are immortal. Hells no, pompous cocks!"

"For light's sake, man, you have issues?"

Both men laughed. Kraken was red in the face.

"I feel like an old fool. But look, I can see what you are doing - you know - Mannace and all that - taking on the world. I want to be part of something important. Ramthos guided me here, Morgan. He has a higher purpose for me. It starts here. I can feel it in my bones."

"I like you, Kraken, and I am as much Ramthos' disciple as yourself. I understand his ways and the pull of the sea, the lure of the horizon. We have much in common, but I don't know how far I can trust you. What if you change your mind? What if you want something, like Fitius' ship, so you take it? What if you don't like somebody? How will you handle that? You're a pirate. For hell's sake, you have been a rogue for a long time - is that something you can ever leave behind!"

"What do you want me to say? Look, I'm used to doing what pleases me, but I always do what I say, true to my word, and I say that I will do what it takes to change. I want this. I swear it by Ramthos, Morgan. What more proof can I give."

Morgan instinctively intended to say yes. He had only been immortal a short time, but already he preferred the friendship of others he knew would be long-lived, so he understood the scoundrel's predicament. Both men were dredged from the same seabed. Morgan only challenged Kraken because it was his duty as somebody of importance at Viletri.

"Look, we'll work it out. You'll like Mannace and Milan, and they will accept you if I ask it, though it means that I am accountable for your actions. Understand well that I am not somebody that you want to cross, Kraken. You don't want your head to find its way into my trophy cabinet."

There was a moment of awkward silence before Kraken moved the conversation quickly along.

"Right then. Ramthos protect me. What happens next?"

"Forget about the past. Your allegiances have crossed sides. You're not the first to do so, and you'll have to deal with some people from your past that won't like that. You can handle it, Kraken. *We* will handle it."

Kraken's mind was racing. Morgan looked to put him at ease.

"Stick close to me, and word will get around – then we'll see what happens next. I know that if Mannace comes back from the front, he will want to talk to you about his father."

"Let's hope he stays in the North then."

Kraken gave a nervous smirk. Morgan left it alone, though the sarcasm did little to ease his reservations.

MILAN

Milan was, of course, three long strides ahead of his competition. In Viletri and Arenland, he signed guild contracts to supply many things. Often sealed with a handshake, partnerships established new enclaves or outlets close to the Empire Capital. At the same time, Milan's agents were busy in many cities and ports across the known world, readying themselves to take full advantage of the opening of the seaways and markets.

Milan convinced Fitius Angelcry, Overlord of Arenland, to part with one of his flying ships. The astronomical price was well worth it - what was the purpose of being fantastically wealthy if it didn't bring you the things you desired. As part of the deal struck, Milan agreed to lead an envoy to establish more robust ties between the Eastern Colonies and the Emperor.

There would be three flying ships in the envoy; his own, the Overlord's flagship, and a third vessel intended as a gift to the Emperor - filled with things of the Eastern Colonies that the Emperor would find of interest. The ships were not military designs. Instead, they were the first craft explicitly made to transport leaders and officials of the Colonial Council, focusing on comfort.

Milan handpicked his crew from his most talented and loyal employees. They were a clever and adaptive bunch. Morgan and his new sidekick, Kraken, also joined him. Milan shook his head at the thought of having Kraken, the infamous pirate, on his boat. The man belonged with a rope around his neck swinging off the prow. One foot wrong, and that's where the crafty old bastard would end up. Milan was annoyed at Morgan for his short-sightedness. Although he understood Morgan's disposition toward Kraken, the wealthy merchant had too much to lose to open his arms to such a foolhardy risk.

Milan loved being on the sea. The sway of the ship, the smell of the salt, and the time it gave him to relax and think as he travelled between destinations. Now he relished the sense of freedom from being airborne, and it amazed him how the world seemed so small from high in the heavens. His mind felt rejuvenated and free.

The merchant watched representatives of the Colonial Council board Fitius' vessel; Vas Raylin, ambassador for Yanth, Colotapatl of the Rhalec, Antiel who was Light Bearer for the Alani, and Shepherd of Viletri who returned from Galandar for this mission. Saska also travelled with Fitius. She brought her pet gargoyles, Tamas and Harvor, plus a young hound named Alsa. Her bodyguard, Arta, was close by, although the lofty warrior did not take to travel in the air as well as others. She worried that the ship might fall from the sky. In Arta's opinion, the Navigator who controlled the ship was no more than a troublesome child and would be the end of them all. Aboard Fitius' craft, Rangi was the youngest Navigator in the fleet at twelve years. While he was beyond his age in his ability to steer the vessel, his behaviour was often infantile or inappropriate. Thankfully, Rangi took to Fitius like a son to a father, and he obeyed the Overlord's instructions with an eagerness to please. Saska suggested that the slave conditioning would make him better at his job, but Fitius vehemently denied the request.

It took longer than Milan would have liked to complete the fitting out of the Emperor's craft and other preparations. When they departed Arenland, they were forty-two days behind the fast Steel Ships of the War God. It would be a close race against Ahmeda to see who arrived at Bracadia first.

BRACADIA

Milan need not have worried. He hadn't appreciated how fast the flying ships could travel. After just fifteen days, they spotted the unmistakable silhouettes of the Steel Ships against the ocean far below. Frustratingly for Milan, Fitius commanded the Flying Ships to slow. Orders were passed to the Navigators to keep pace with the Steel flotilla, as Fitius intended to arrive in Bracadia together.

The skyborne voyagers observed other boats and fleets on the sea too, and Milan wondered what they must be thinking as they looked back at them in the sky. He remained amazed by how small the scale of the world appeared from this high vantage. As well as the broad, empty ocean known to Milan as The Deep, the envoy also passed over smaller seas with islands and continents. There were ports and cities, all of which the merchant knew, and he was giving both Morgan and Kraken a lesson in geography as they made their way northwest. Kraken was starting to grow on Milan with his dry wit and seemingly humble character, but he would make a point not to trust the brigand's act so as not to be surprised when the sea snake inevitably turned.

When Bracadia finally appeared on the horizon, it was a broad landscape of hills and mountains, with areas of cultivated land where the rugged terrain allowed for it. They were heading for the port of Dreban. According to Milan, it was the largest city along the continent's eastern coast and the sixth-largest city of the Empire. They could see it spread out along the sea and back across the hills. On drawing closer, the colonial envoy attracted the attention of patrols, and before they made landfall, a

Bracadian fleet intercepted Ahmeda's steel convoy.

Ahmeda flew the colours of Bracadia alongside the banners of the War God. After an initial exchange shouted between decks, she welcomed Admiral Faquis Moldura and two of his officers aboard. The Admiral was a tall man dressed in black pants and coat, with gold buttons and trim. He wore a slightly curved blade in a sheath at his belt. Faquis' look was sharp and harsh, and his words were similarly terse.

"Pull to a stop, lower your boarding gear, and make ready to take on marines for a detailed inspection. Tell your people to signal the other ships to do the same."

"I am not responsible for the flying craft, Admiral. I am sure that the Overlord, their commander, will ascend in his own time."

Farquis gave an exasperated "hmmm", and he eyed Ahmeda suspiciously.

While it angered Ahmeda that the admiral looked down at her, she could not afford a poor first encounter. Reluctantly, she did as instructed, allowing more Bracadians loose about her ships. The marines were thorough, taking several hours, and the inspection ended with the admiral carefully assessing their report.

Despite his surly demeanour, the Admiral was impressed by the metal ships, and once he was confident that the new arrivals did not pose a threat to Dreban, he stayed on board to see them into port. A galleon armada flanked the steel warships as they manoeuvred towards the city. While the War God's ships loomed impressively above the local vessels, the flotilla surrounding them was also an impressive sight that Ahmeda knew not to underestimate.

As Ahmeda and the Admiral stood on the *Harmsway's* prow looking ahead and skyward, she answered his queries about the vessels high above. He appeared frustrated that they were beyond his reach. To distract him, the High Priestess raised the subject of past contact with Bracadia.

"Admiral Mangello D'Austini laid the foundation for the Empire of Bracadia to take hold in the east. It was a foundation built on war with a common enemy. Mangello was charismatic and generous. I liked the man. The Galleons he left with the Governor have ensured the Eastern Colonies security over the last decades. We have copied the technology of the muskets and cannons for our armies. As such, we are indebted to Bracadia and will show the Emperor our appreciation."

"I knew D'Austini, he was a great explorer, and he served the Emperor well. You must have been very young when you met him."

"I am over a thousand years old, Admiral. I am an Elf, a Dark Elf, as you can see. We are an immortal people."

Admiral Moldura looked uncomfortable. He frowned as he processed the information.

"The Emperor is immortal. He is our strength and wisdom, our guide across generations, our commander. He will be interested in your steel ships and your flying craft. There is nothing like these in Bracadia."

"We are of Bracadia, Admiral."

"Indeed."

It was clear to Ahmeda by the man's cynical tone that he looked down on the colonies, which immediately seemed ignorant to her. As she glared back at him, this man of little soul or conviction, the sea breeze seemed suddenly chill. Her words carried power.

"Admiral Moldura, do you pay homage to the God of War in Bracadia?"

If Ahmeda's ruses fazed the Admiral, he did not show it. He was direct.

"No. There were gods and religions in the histories, but they were the catalyst for great discord. Now there is just the Emperor. It is different in the *colonies*, but we do not tolerate religion on the mainland. You would be wise to acknowledge this."

Ahmeda reeled. Who was this man to question her wisdom and show her such blatant disregard? With icy words, the High Priestess was also blunt.

"These ships are the blades of the God of War. Can you not feel his presence here, Admiral, in the steel and the air? His power is undeniable. I am his High Priestess, and these crews are his soldiers. Therefore, I will stand in front of the Emperor as the War God's apostle."

Without raising his voice, the Admiral remained unwavering in his position.

"You will bend before the Emperor as his ward and servant, as are we all."

The Admiral could see that Ahmeda was unused to being challenged. To avoid further escalation, he exposed the palms of his hands, which in Bracadia showed he respected their differences. He had spent time amongst some of the colonies where there was religion, and he knew how fanatic its followers could be.

"I do not doubt that you will stand before the Emperor. Just be warned that he is not a religious man. So, your War God may not be well received."

Dreban boasted a full harbour that was large enough to accommodate a military port and civilian docks. As they drew closer, it seemed even busier than Yanth, with bustling crowds of people everywhere. Many gathered to witness the spectacle of the steel and flying ships. Other locals were hurrying about their work. As Fitius looked down from the heavens, he took stock of this new place, noting the architecture of Dreban was a bit like Yanth, with wood, clay and tiles used in much of the construction. However, it didn't have the precise symmetry. Instead, it seemed a tangle of streets and buildings. There were large warehouses along the front of the piers and districts of stone buildings beyond. It appeared strange to Fitius that there were no walls or fortifications.

The Admiral directed the steel ships to berth at the military docks. Finally, the three flying ships came down to hover above the same pier. Using levitation platforms, the officials of the Eastern Colonies descended to join Ahmeda and her party, alongside the Admiral and his senior captains. Together they walked to a nearby barracks to wait for the Governor of Dreban. Fitius cautiously agreed to allow Bracadian marines aboard his craft.

The Governor of Dreban arrived late in the afternoon. Her

entourage was like a procession, with her six husbands and their attendants walking close behind, followed by at least thirty city officials and a troop of finely equipped riflemen. The Eastern Colonies' envoy knew what to expect after a briefing from Admiral Moldura, and with careful consideration, Ahmeda was their spokesperson. The two women met in front of the barracks while soldiers hurried with chairs so that everybody of importance could be seated. Milan acknowledged the Governor with a nod of his head, which the official returned with a smile. Others sat in a circle around them.

"I am Atrula D'Austini, Governor of Dreban. Welcome to the capital of the East. May the Emperor, in all his greatness, watch over us."

With a smile, the governor added, "I like your ships. I have more, but none of steel or that can fly."

Ahmeda smiled and nodded to acknowledge the compliment.

"Honour to you, Governor D'Austini. I am Ahmeda Ravenborn, High Priestess of the God of War, speaker for the envoy of the Eastern Colonies. I like your husbands; I had enough trouble with just one."

"They are not all my husbands, just the six at the front. I often think I should have stopped at three."

Ahmeda gave a small laugh, and Atrula D'Austini again smiled, more generously this time. Then, with the ice broken, Ahmeda introduced the other colonial dignitaries. Atrula paid attention and seemed to take it all in. The High Priestess could see the Governor was assessing everybody as they spoke, considering their gestures and how they chose their words. She appeared an astute woman, somebody who achieved their station by design. The Governor was perhaps in her early forties and held herself with confidence and authority. Ahmeda had never seen skin so olive and smooth. Atrula's eyes were green and highlighted with a dark shadow. Her hair was oiled, pulled back sharply in a bun, the same as Ahmeda's. Strangely it was a point of similarity that made both women feel relaxed with each other.

Discussions would resume in the morning at the government buildings in the city. Meanwhile, Atrula invited Ahmeda to be a guest at her residence. That night they talked and drank wine. Atrula's mansion was lavish, and the chamber where they lazed paid every tribute to luxury, from the scented candles to the thick carpets and massive embroidered cushions. Ahmeda lived a meagre existence by comparison.

"My uncle Mangello spoke of you and your companion, Casteel. It was one of his favourite stories; how you convinced him to help you rather than conquering you. It changed how he looked at the world. It inspired me to look at my enemies as my allies."

"You have an interesting life."

"In Dreban, life is what you make it. Success finds success. You must live like the rich to become rich. To be governor, you must elevate yourself above others. Why do you think I would take six husbands?"

The reason eluded her, so Ahmeda shrugged her shoulders. She was getting light-headed from the wine and was happy for Atrula to do most of the talking.

"Because others only have one. It sets me apart. It makes me appear potent, dominant. It has other benefits too; my bed is not boring. To control power, you must be powerful in all aspects of your life."

Both women laughed. They were drunk.

"I will gift you a husband for the night. Ahmeda, which will you pick."

Ahmeda laughed again. They could see the husbands relaxing in the next room.

"I will have the tall black one with fire in his eyes." Then, cheekily she added, "And I will have the blonde bearded one with the long hair."

Atrula summoned the husbands, and she instructed the two selected to join with Ahmeda. She picked two for herself. Neither woman was shy. The men also knew their business, immediately settling into the task.

DREBAN

People of different races and cultures crammed themselves into Dreban's narrow streets. The busy port was the centre for trade to the east and north of the Bracadian mainland. Therefore, it was unsurprising that the nations it touched reflected the nationalities encountered in the city's streets and businesses. Other than human races, Orcs and Belg from Charikon were common amongst Dreban's population.

Amid the envoy and colonial crews were Elves, Rhalec, and worker animations used by the colonial sailors to carry supplies. The foreigners were curiosities, and Morgan Cain attracted the most attention. The man of black metal was an oddity that brought people out of their homes and businesses to watch him pass down the street. Although usually one to enjoy a small crowd, the attention he was receiving in Dreban was relentless and overwhelming. For the first time since receiving his new body, Morgan used the ANS, levitating and flying from the city to return to the awaiting sky-ship. That only got people more excited, and from that point on, he dared not go out in public. To the people of Dreban who did not use or understand magic, he seemed like a superbeing.

By comparison, Kraken blended in, spending his time getting to know parts of the city unlikely to be frequented by his new companions. Unknown to the others, in his adventures, the pirate visited Dreban once before, but it was too long ago for him to find familiar faces. Still, he understood the city's underbelly, and it didn't take him long to make new acquaintances. Moreover, he felt invigorated to have his head in the game, to juggle the possibilities.

Ahmeda secured a permanent berth at the military docks. In return, the steel ships joined the Dreban galleons in patrolling the coast. There was even talk of some practice manoeuvres at sea, which Ahmeda knew was a ploy to take their measure. It was made clear by Governor D'Austini that Ahmeda and her charges were not to spread the doctrine of the War God. The spreading of religion by any in the city was punishable by death. All other talk was of trade and tariffs, Milan's domain - with Fitius, Vas Raylin, Colotapatl, and Shepherd all having an active interest. It was hard to tell if the men were happy or displeased with negotiations. Only Antiel of the Alani seemed disinterested. Dreban and its showy Governor did not impress him at all.

Fitius was interested in the rifles carried by the Dreban garrison, but it was another subject where the Governor would not negotiate. As the laws regarding religion, the sale of certain weapons was also punishable by death. Kraken held no respect for rules, and aboard Fitius' flying vessel, he handed the Overlord a gun and ammunition. Even without expert knowledge of its use, the rifle seemed a simpler weapon to operate than a musket. The shot was both the powder and the bullet. It was certainly something to get back to the factories in Arenland for closer examination. Fitius secreted it away aboard his ship.

The Overlord was anxious to move on, but Atrula instructed him to wait for the Emperor's invitation before journeying to the capital. Governor D'Austini was making the arrangements.

THE SHADES

Saska was merely the Overlord's concubine, so like Kraken, she drew little attention and enjoyed the freedom to move about the city. Her disguise was a deep hooded cloak that was big enough to wrap around her body, almost a uniform in the underbelly where she headed. Arta, as always, was at her side, needing no disguise to look like a local brute.

The city was not short of brothels, and Saska expected that some of the brothel owners were amongst the city's wealthiest citizens from the quality of their establishments. However, it was not the high-end establishments where she would make her beginning. Instead, Saska found a humble brothel where the girls were pretty, and the owner lived with them. The owner's name was Tilly, a fine-looking woman with a sharp tongue who ran a tight ship. She employed a brute; an Orc named Scarg, who was large and muscular, though slow and dim.

In the shadow of her cloak, Saska showed Tilly a large sum of coins. It was enough to get her in the door and to start a conversation about partnership. Money, though, was just the lure. Saska would seal this deal with further temptations of body and soul, and by the time Fitius received his Emperor's invitation, Saska intended to have her first followers in this new land.

Saska perceived other opportunities here too. Nowhere was there Nyx for sale or any other pleasure drug. Thog might also do well in dark trade, particularly amongst the Orcs. In Ostoik and Rotherdan, Saska saw what lengths people would go to, to maintain their supply of Nyx. In Ostoik in particular, to control the source of Nyx was to hold the underbelly. It presented a unique opportunity, and the sense of danger was intoxicating.

Saska made her way from her new place of business to the flying ships in the evenings, where she spent the nights with Fitius. Her passage through the city took her along narrow winding streets, with shadowy alleyways between the tall brick buildings. Arta was ever vigilant for an ambush, and in the dark evenings, Tamas and Harvor clambered over the structures high above to watch over their mistress. The gargoyles were creatures of the shadow and exceptional at moving about unseen. On her journey through the city, Saska often stopped to give beggars coins, and in some streets, they would be waiting for her in increasing numbers each night. The demoness rapidly gained a reputation amongst the homeless and destitute for her charity.

One night, as Saska passed through a district known as The Shades, a noticeable absence of beggars made Arta uneasy, slowing their pace to check the alleyways ahead. Too late, a rabble suddenly came at them through doors and from the shadows. Some of the miscreants pointed crossbows and muskets, mostly at Arta. The two visitors were at their mercy.

"Come with us."

They didn't go far, passing behind buildings to arrive at a small courtyard. The assailants bullied Arta back into the shadows and urged Saska forward. A young man and woman, who were kin, possibly even twins by their striking similarity, stood before her. The siblings appeared good looking and clean, which set them apart from the company they kept. Both had loose black hair, soft blue eyes, thin lips, dressing in dark colours, and with daggers at their belts. The woman leaned on a musket while the brother spoke.

"You are careless to travel the shades with such meagre protection."

"You wrong, boy. Arta not here protect me. She protect others *from* me."

With impeccable timing, Tamas and Harvor leapt from high above into the space between Saska and the twins. Their landing was heavy, and its surprise made everybody in the courtyard except Saska jump back. The gargoyles moved to their mistress' side, fanning their wings to protect her from possible missile fire. The sister was first to regain herself and pointed her musket at Saska. She strode aggressively forward.

"Nice trick. Can you dodge a musket ball? Keep your beasts at bay."

Saska hissed, her body tensing, like she might suddenly leap and strike. The sister was close enough to see Saska's long incisors and feel the unnatural heat from her glare, making her take a step back.

The demoness smirked at the reaction, relaxing somewhat, her voice cynical. "What you plan do to me. Rob me? Ransom?"

The sister was not going to let her prey go. She seemed

more determined.

"Ransom. You will come with us."

Saska pulled her hood back, further assessing those about her. They seemed innocent, ignorant, pliable, possibly what she needed. Now her tone carried authority and influence beyond simple words.

"No, will not. You two come me. I have proposal. Bring you wealth. More wealth than ransom."

The brother was going to speak, but he lost his voice. He was falling under Saska's beguiling spell. Seeing his vulnerability, his sister butted him in the arm with her musket. It was enough for him to regain his senses and calm his racing heart, but he forgot what he wanted to say.

So instead, he started a new line of thought.

"I have seen you at the whore house. Perhaps you can earn your freedom."

"Fuck's sake, brother."

The whole group became uneasy, confused about who was in charge and what was happening. Finally, the sister stepped in front of her sibling, assuming control. Unsure of her intent, Harvor rose from his crouch and spread his wings wider, appearing more demonic and intimidating. A crossbow bolt ricocheted harmlessly off the gargoyles stone chest. Saska scolded her guardian.

"Harvor, Leave! Both you, go!"

Tamas and Harvor looked at their mistress, then obeyed, leaping onto the brick buildings, and scampering up into the darkness. They soon blended into the stonework. Beneath in the courtyard, it did little to ease the tension. When Saska spoke, her tone drew terror from the shadow, and the words were laced with arcane energies so that even the brave sister shuddered. It was the Twins that she addressed with her eyes as much as her speech.

"You two come with me. I talk. Others leave."

Saska suddenly glared at the other gangers, who forgot their purpose and smartly fled the way they had come. Arta returned to Saska's side, and at her gesturing, the party of four made their way through The Shades. Saska talked to the sister as they walked, assuming authority, outlining her plan and giving instruction for the selling of drugs.

"I arrange supply. At Dreban, you store and sell. Attract lot of interest. I give money prepare. We discuss Nyx trade at Ostoik, so know what expect here. Split profit; one share you and brother, one share partner Ostoik, two shares me. Fifth share Governor Dreban. Yes?"

The sister seemed to take it all in, though the brother was still too distracted. Saska stared fiercely at the young woman until she got her reply.

"Yes. We will be partners."

Saska handed the sister, who she now knew as Blackbird, a pouch of gems. It was a small fortune, more than a ransom worth of wealth. What the twins did next would show Saska if they possessed the commitment and capability to be the followers she needed. As she left the two, she kissed the brother on the lips. He was a good-looking boy, and one day she might make more use of him than just business. The demoness caressed his soul, too, ensuring that his ache for her would not ease.

SHADOW WAR

Eight days after meeting with the twins, Saska was pleased with Blackbird's effort to expand their gang and extend their influence. So, it was a surprise when Kraken approached her aboard the flagship with a warning.

"The Twins have targets on their backs. Everyone knows that they've come into wealth. It is a race to see who acts against them first, likely the Boots or the Lords."

Saska's eyes narrowed, and her shoulders hunched like a cornered cat. Not wanting a scene, Kraken pulled her aside from Fitius' soldiers to talk privately.

"Look, the Lords are the most organised; they've got lots of members across the city. Not much happens without their authority. The Boots are a rougher crew. They're thugs, operating mostly out of the poor districts. For them, it's about fighting and territory; lots of Orcs and Belg. The other players are all small-time like The Twins. If you've got a play, it's time to use it."

"No understand *play*. I not child, Kraken, don't give nonsense. You know happening, what do?"

"Dunno, I'm just a pirate."

Saska tensed even further, glaring at the pirate as if Kraken earned the brunt of her wrath.

"What pirate *do*?"

Kraken retreated a step. Regretting ever broaching the subject, he rushed a response.

"Shit, I dunno, I guess they'd fight or run. Mostly run. Me, I would cut my losses and make for the deep - better a head on yer shoulders than a full purse. Better to follow your gut than see your guts turned inside out by some sneaky bastard's blade."

Saska was disappointed in the legendary brigand, and she eyed him coldly as she shook her head. Men were so weak. She would not be so spineless. Saska straightened herself and leaned into Kraken, enough that he needed to bend and then step back.

"I fight."

Kraken was genuinely surprised. His gut and brain and every sense in-between united in condemning that notion. This woman of the hells seemed destined to bring him trouble, but despite his strong misgivings, he liked Saska's blatant disregard for reason and the fact that she was true to her nature even if it risked everything. It reminded him of his much younger self. A mischievous glint and wry smile replaced the look of dread.

"Can you do that? Do you want to be responsible for a gang war in Dreban, cause that's what'll happen! In a city where Fitius is talking alliance and trade with the Nobs?"

"I no run, Kraken. You help me."

Kraken sensed that Saska was using more than words to entice him to her cause, though he was no young pup that would jump to her whim. He felt the pull, but instead, he decided with his head.

"All hells, Saska, you are a mad bitch! I'll regret this, but a war in the shadow it is."

To leave The Twins to their fate, Saska would need to

admit she had made a mistake. Saska did not make mistakes. She did not have boundaries either, and it was nothing to her to search through the hold of the Emperor's gift for items that would benefit her immediate need. She would not take it all, as it was not in her interests to see Fitius embarrassed when he presented the gift, but as always, he was overly generous. There were repeating crossbows, enhanced armour, animated workers, and more. The Overlord was too busy to notice her subterfuge during the day, and Saska was confident none of the crew would dare speak out against her. She would tell Fitius when they departed Dreban, and he would forgive her.

Kraken was already helping the twins with their recruitment, but now he doubled his efforts. He was apt at weeding out infiltrators or the wrong kind of miscreants. He was also resourceful and prepared to look at less traditional options. Mercenaries often sought work on ships or accompanying merchant caravans at the port. Some would do any work for pay. Saska had plenty of coin, so Kraken was generous with his offers, and The Twins' gang soon presented themselves as a veteran company.

The Pirate acquainted himself with two other small gangs in The Shades, The Fearless and Del-Gan. They relished the chance to be out of the shadow of the more prominent bands; their alliance purchased cheaply.

The Beggars' Union was his third avenue. Although Saska already paved it with her generosity, that road was trickier. The beggars were not fighters, but they were eyes and ears in the darkness. Strangely, they were not motivated by coin. Instead, they wanted the freedom of The Shades so that they might move about, assemble, and live as they pleased. They wanted protection and respect.

The Twins soon amassed enough members to hold off any rash action from The Lords or The Boots. But Kraken expected that time for himself and Saska in the city was limited and that soon Fitius would move on from Dreban. It was time to act, to seize the day.

The Lords bullied a 'tax' from many businesses in the Shades. Kraken proposed that The Twins would need to stop that to gain respect, so he concocted a plan with the twin brother, Cray, to take control of the situation. Once they were ready, The Twins gang headed to the streets in force so that when The Lords' thugs arrived in The Shades to collect their take, rather than the meek business owners, TT heavies confronted them. Fights ensued, and soon larger groups of Lords entered the territory to enforce their mandate. As the violence escalated, clubs quickly replaced fists, and gangers soon emerged with axes or crossbows.

Responding to the disturbance, city guards entered The Shades in sizable patrols, backed by the largest gang in the city; the Dreban garrison of twenty thousand strong. It did not end the sudden conflict between the rivals, but it moved it back into the shadows where it belonged.

The Lords employed their spies and informants, so that the Baron, their leader, learned of the relationship between The Twins and Saska, and he devised a clear message to Saska that the Lords were not to be trifled with. When Saska and Arta arrived at Tilly's in the morning, city troops were stationed outside the establishment, blocking the entrance. Not wanting to disclose her interest, Saska withdrew to a tavern within

The Shades, and the beggars were her eyes. The news they brought fuelled primal anger in Saska. Enraged, she vowed payback a hundredfold upon the Lords for the eleven bodies reportedly taken from the house. With her powers fuelled by hatred, the seductress immediately rallied the men about her, beggars, gangers, patrons of the tavern, and even passers-by. They all hurried to obey. The humanity in Saska evaporated, and the demon was apparent for all to see. Her lust for retribution fed a passion in others, and the rapidly forming mob could not help but share her vengeful purpose. It replaced all sensibility or caution.

Escalating quickly, the crazed mob was rampant as it moved about the streets, dragging Lord's gangers out of houses, executing them, slaying those that defended them, and becoming fanatical where they met stronger resistance.

Amid the rampage, Arta kept pace with Saska. The revealed demoness wielded flames as if they were weapons, setting Lords on fire and reducing some to ashes. As she moved about, Saska drew more unwitting men, Orc's, and Belg to her cause. Looters followed behind. The maddened crowd took on a life of its own, splitting into parts that headed off to different locations in the city. "Kill The Lords" was their mantra.

In desperate response, the Baron summoned all his soldiers. At his instruction, The Lords hurried towards the docks, increasing in numbers, and gaining confidence as members came running. Soon, more than a thousand Lords prepared their defence in an empty lumber yard behind Warehouse Three. At one end of the yard, Lords with muskets and crossbows broke into a brick building and took positions on its metal balconies. Others ducked behind makeshift defences or in the shadows, while groups with shields spread out to bear the brunt of any assault. Bashing in a door to Warehouse Three, the Baron and his elite thugs grabbed more empty crates and barrels to use in the lumberyard for cover.

Kraken did not join the mob. Instead, he organised TT members as they rallied at the gang headquarters. There seemed no better time to hand out the unusual equipment they kept stored. Kraken had experimented with the weapons over the last days, giving instructions as he passed them out.

"Repeating crossbow, point and shoot. Eight shots. Don't leave your finger on the trigger."

"Stun hammer. Any good contact will put a man down."

"Take that metal man over there. Tell it to follow you, then tell it to attack the Lords when you see them."

"Repeating crossbow, point and shoot. Shit, not now, you idiot. NEVER leave your finger on the trigger."

"Body armour. Put it over your shirt. Put this on your arm and your hand in the fist; release this leaver when the straps are tight. Practice over there."

The enterprise was reckless and utterly irresponsible, so much that Kraken, who found joy in such madness, held a permanent grin. He offered one last instruction for those gathered.

"Show those bastards who's in charge now!"

Shortly after, with word reaching them that the Lords

were making a stand at the docks, Kraken took the band of TT thugs in that direction. Blackbird joined them, quickly assuming command, spurring the ragged crew into a run. So much for a shadow war, it seemed that every hooligan and gangster in the city was running about in broad daylight yelling and pointing weapons. Kraken, chuckling at the bizarre scene, imagined that Fitius and Morgan, if the truth was discovered, would not find this the least bit entertaining.

Saska, and the mob that followed her, were not the first to arrive at the timber yard. Casualties already lay in the open, while armed rioters were returning fire on the Lords from around corners or behind cover. Saska's rage demanded a massacre, urging the crowd forward. They responded with berserk fury, charging at The Lords' position.

Kraken arrived in time to see the mob surge toward the barricaded gangers. Some were immediately victims of the bolts and bullets fired into their mass, but others clashed with the Lords' defenders and the bloody brawling ensued. Blackbird and her lot ran around Kraken, also charging into the fray.

The old pirate clambered onto an empty cart to get a better view. At first, it seemed as if the mob might be pushed back by the organised defenders, but then he saw Saska at their fore and the big barbarian Arta defending her. Around Saska, Lords burst into flame, and brutes threw themselves at the enemy like fanatics. Another mob was arriving at the far end of the yard to join the onslaught.

Closer to Kraken, the weapons he handed out were having

an impact, particularly the repeating crossbows that, when used well, were devastating. Unfortunately, he did not think to hand out extra ammunition. Fighting alongside The Twins, metal animations smashed apart defences, easily throwing men about. Kraken cheered for them, then he clapped as three Belg assaulted the Lords, bashing a bloody path with their clubs. Picking out the large targets, gangers with muskets on the balconies aimed, and one of the Belg staggered, clutching his shoulder.

By Kraken's quick estimation, at least three thousand ruffians bashed it out in the confused brawl. Some had no business in the gang conflict, but they fought just as desperately. Around the outskirts, crossbowmen and those with muskets continued to shoot from cover positions. The Lords were losing, and the mob was relentless. From his vantage, Kraken witnessed the moment it became hopeless for the Lords, their resolve snapping. Where they could, many tried to flee. Even the Baron and his elite henchmen retreated into the warehouse, but it was not the haven they hoped. Saska joined the assault to flush them out, and soon the whole building was an inferno as the demoness unleashed blasts of flame with careless abandon. Nothing was going to escape her.

Through Saska's eyes, everything became a red haze. Inside the blazing building, there were only the dead and those few who still burned. The screams of the dying and heat from the inferno reflected her passion, and she let it consume her. Gradually, however, with no enemy in sight, her fervour ebbed, and Saska's body became heavy with tiredness. Depleted and dazed, the taste of blood on her lips was distracting. She needed rest, a dark place to lie down. Ignoring falling debris, Saska followed steps leading into the floor, discovering an open door, and then entering the tunnel beyond. Through a narrow corridor was a room full of things. Clambering amongst them, Saska found a place that seemed safe, collapsing to the floor, and drawing a tattered sack to cover her. Exhausted, her mind welcomed the relief of unconsciousness.

Kraken watched the throng in its relentless pursuit of the fleeing Lords until they disappeared from his view. In their place, the first unit of city guard emerged from a side street and deployed into the lumber yard. They aimed their rifles and shot at any thug that presented a danger. Their accuracy was much more precise than the indiscriminate shooting he witnessed earlier. Kraken hopped down from his vantage and slunk into an alleyway. Making his way back to the gang's headquarters, he was determined not to delay there long, supposing that a safe place much further away would be sensible. Time was needed - to think and devise new plans.

AN INVITATION

The Emperor's invitation to journey to the capital could not have arrived at a worse time. Fitius was furious and distressed at how events were unfolding. Foremost, Saska was missing, though he knew her to be alive in his gut. The Gargoyles were in the city searching for her. Arta was wounded with a bolt to her chest and might die. What made him livid was that it was a bolt from one of his repeating crossbows, stolen and misused. He was not good at anger, but it was impossible to be calm with so much fuel on the fire. He ordered Ahmeda to make the best of it with the Governor while he dealt with the discipline of his men and commanders. The plundering of the Emperor's gift was unforgivable to Fitius.

The damned pirate was missing too. Milan was on the lookout for him, and it would be hard for Kraken to weasel his way out of the city by ship or road. Moreover, Milan was sure that the pirate was intimately entwined in what occurred. If his agents were to find Kraken before Morgan did, the bastard's fate would be an unpleasant one.

Morgan was responsible for Kraken, and he worked with the city guard to locate him and Saska. The Shades, and districts surrounding it, were placed under military lockdown so that the streets were empty except for soldiers searching alley to alley and door to door. While they uncovered no sign of Saska or Kraken, there was no shortage of miscreants that the soldiers dragged away for further interrogation.

Elsewhere in the city, Ahmeda accompanied the

Governor, who seemed unfazed by what had occurred. They were walking through the corridors of the City Hall.

"It is important to always appear in control, Ahmeda. Always stand above current events, deal with them with pragmatism, seldom with passion. It is we who decide if this is just a little craziness between rival gangs or a diplomatic catastrophe."

They entered through a door into a large chamber. Four officers were standing at a table looking over items that were familiar to Ahmeda. Even worse, two metal workers stood idle in the corner, one with a bent arm. The High Priestess' heart sank, seeing Atrula's ambush for what it was.

"We can skip the part where I embarrass you with questions. Instead, let's talk about how you make this right. I have already given it some thought. The men of metal are unique. Your gift to me will be one thousand of these."

"It is not possible. Atrula, they are not that simple to produce."

"You are resourceful, Ahmeda; you will make it possible. It is the price to be paid for such blatant disrespect."

"An alternative, Atrula, if I can arrange it, is an Animator. A person capable of making steel men and other things. Why settle for the creations when you can have the creator."

The Governor was unsure of the offer; she knew what she was getting with the steel men. What if the Animator did not meet her expectations? She was impressed, though; it was an excellent counteroffer.

"Two Animators and five hundred steel men."

"Two Animators, one senior and one apprentice. I will guarantee their service for one year, and then they will be free men. Ten steel men."

The Governor appeared happy with that arrangement, though she toyed with a few things on the table and looked closely over one of the metal men before giving Ahmeda her response.

"Make sure the Animators are attractive, Ahmeda, and tall. I appreciate your gift. Until the gift is delivered, I will enjoy your company. It has been a busy time - yesterday, a blood feud between two rival gangs brought violence into our streets. The city's garrison was quick to react, and through their capable efforts, more than a thousand criminals are dead or awaiting execution. Do you see, Ahmeda? We can make good of any situation."

As the priestess nodded, Atrula's expression darkened, and for a moment, she was not the calm woman Ahmeda thought she knew. Her eyes were piercing. Her words were slow and deliberate. There was a rage trapped behind the visage, that threatened to escape.

"Ahmeda, you are indebted to me. I have made this easy for you now, but the favour I require in the future will not be so trivial. Do we have an understanding?"

Ahmeda was unused to taking a backwards step, but Atrula surprised her. She met the stare, and in the same chilly tone, the priestess responded.

"In the future, I will show you the same favour you have shown me, Atrula. We are allies, are we not?"

The question went unanswered. Instead, Atrula's normal mantel returned, and she lightened the mood.

"You will join me at my home. Tonight, we celebrate."

That night, Fitius commanded Rangi to transport them to Viletri. They arrived moments later near the city at a place the navigator kept in memory. Their first stop was to see Render, and with the Sorcerer's help, it still took Fitius most of the night to find an Animator and apprentice prepared to toss their gear in a bag and move to a foreign city. In his rush, Fitius was overly generous with their compensation. They loaded the Animator's belongings and tools onto the Overlord's ship along with ten animated workers. Fitius was back above Dreban before dawn, and the surprised Governor received her gift soon after.

Ahmeda and the Emperor's messenger boarded Fitius' ship late morning, and the three flying vessels departed the docks to head West across the Bracadian mainland. The route they followed was well-defined in the invitation. Behind them, the War God's steel ships remained dockside, and Fitius hoped that somewhere in the sprawling city was Saska. His heart would ache until they were reunited, though he dreaded that the ache might fade and signal his dark angel's demise.

Saska awoke from her long slumber. It took her time to regain her wits, long enough to stand and then stumble her way through the passage to the ruins of the warehouse. In the fighting, she expended vast amounts of energy, and even after sleeping, she was struggling just to breathe. Saska looked down at her arms and hands. Her skin was wrinkled and dulled to a putrid grey. As she came out of hiding, it felt like there was a cat in her head, clawing from the inside, made worse as she squinted in the daylight. Best retreat to the darkness for now. During the night, she would feed.

THE BLUE LAND

As the ships travelled a high trajectory above Bracadia, the envoy marvelled at the beauty of the landscape below. At first, it was mountainous, with fertile valleys and plateaus. Beyond was a stretch of wooded hills and forested lowlands. Swamps and tangled jungle filled the lowest points, with small rivers winding their way amongst the terrain. Gradually, the land became less forested and more cultivated until, laid out before them was a patchwork of farms, crops, and orchards that reached beyond the horizon. Long, straight roads connected villages, towns, and cities. Fitius and his navigator were following the same route travelled by the mighty river Bracia that wound its way gracefully west across the landscape. There were ships on the river and magnificent bridges, on a scale larger than any civilisation Fitius had witnessed before. It inspired him to build similar edifices in Arenland, and for Antigoth to be a pinnacle of grand design.

After two days, the river took a sharp turn south, and at this point, they diverged North, away from civilization and followed a road that, like the others, drew a straight line across the land. The thoroughfare was yellow and shone as if it were gold. Milan confirmed that the region they entered was the Emperor's demesne.

Below them, the forest and grassland portrayed a determined sense of symmetry, as if great care went into its design and maintenance. Beautiful lakes were dotted across the scene, held in place by sturdy stone dams. The mirror surfaces of the lakes reflected the bright blue of the sky, providing the envoy with a spectacle of vivid colour. At a high point in the land, encircled by hills and with enormous dams that blocked the valleys, was the largest of the human-made lakes. The road they followed became a bridge that crossed the water to an island. Three other crossings, following the points of the compass, led away from the sanctuary. Milan informed the others that the highways led to different regions of Bracadia. He shared that they were at the centre here, the centre of the mainland and the centre of the Empire. On the island was the Emperor's palace, rectangular at the base and perhaps eight to ten stories in height. Some parts were taller than others, capped with high domed roofs. The most elevated section boasted a magnificent open space with gardens and balconies under its dome. Splendid towers stood at each corner, tall and commanding. Like the roads leading to it, the palace was golden, with the roofs painted turquoise blue and flecked with silver, glistening like jewels. A small number of residents occupied the roads and the island. They were the gardeners and caretakers going about their maintenance. The splendour was serene, and it left the representatives speechless.

A great lawn surrounded the palace, and they came close to the ground near the front entrance as instructed. The dignitaries were lowered on levitation discs to stand on the golden road. On close examination, the paving was a yellowish stone with a fleck of metal that shone. Antiel's look was smug, as if the stone that resembled gold were evidence that all they saw was fake.

"There is nothing here that compares to the brilliance of the Light. Only the Light can create. The industry of men cannot compare with divine design."

The palace doors were immense, big enough that a flying ship could pass through them with width to spare. As they took in the magnificence of the scene, two massive Belg pushed the portal slowly open. With the task complete, the creatures assumed a position next to the doorway until needed. The hall beyond the doors was huge and grandly decorated with banners and tapestries. A troop of soldiers marched out and positioned themselves on the grass, standing stiff and alert. Their uniform was dark blue with black trimmings. Each carried a rifle and kept a rapier at their belt.

The Emperor emerged next, with just two guards flanking him. Milan immediately stepped forward and went to one knee, bowing slightly in reverence to the leader. The other dignitaries followed Milan's lead. They waited for the Emperor to come closer and speak.

The Emperor was a handsome man, tall and fit. He appeared in his thirties, although as an immortal, he was much, much older. He had dark hair to shoulder length and wore a thin golden band that sufficed as a crown. His eyes were also dark, and his gaze was penetrating. The Emperor was dressed in a blue cotton robe, drawn in at the waist with a plain black leather belt. It was bold to come out of the palace to stare up at the metal ships. It could have been a trap.

"I wanted to see these flying ships. They are magnificent."

Milan stood, still bowing.

"The one in the centre is a gift to you, Emperor. A tribute from the Eastern Colonies."

The Emperor seemed pleased but said nothing. Instead, he gave attention to the delegation, which included races he had not seen and a man of metal. Milan took the initiative and introduced the delegates. As they all rose, The Emperor approached Colotapatl.

"I look forward to learning more of the Rhalec."

"Tiss will be an hon'r, Emperor."

"I look forward to talking with each of you over the coming days."

With that said, the Emperor smiled politely and withdrew into the palace. In his place, other servants and soldiers approached. First, the guard captain required the ships and visitors to be searched and interviewed. Next, men came to take possession of the Emperor's ship and navigator. Once the crew were transferred to the other craft, the Emperor's gift was guided through the entrance. The hall beyond was large enough that the parked craft was well out of the road of people moving about. Immediately, a maintenance detail was assigned to clean and polish the vessel.

Like the other dignitaries, Morgan stayed within the palace. The explorer found the Emperor's home much like his own, yet on a far grander scale. Like him, the Emperor was a collector, and the halls and passages displayed items of interest from across the Empire. It was fascinating and illuminating. Morgan was getting a picture of just how diverse the Empire was, and it provided an insight into what it meant to be a piece of something impossibly gigantic.

After a day of waiting, Ahmeda was the first to have an audience with the Emperor. Summoned to the upper gardens and standing together on a balcony, they looked over the island and lake. The Emperor's voice was calm, his tone mesmerising. He surprised Ahmeda with his opening comment.

"I have always been one to speak plainly, Ahmeda. When I met the delegation at the palace entrance, only one thing truly caught my attention; your beauty is compelling. I would let you know that I am attracted to you."

"Thank you, Emperor. What of the flying ships? Did they not meet your expectations?"

"Indeed, they did, Ahmeda. But ships on the sea or in the sky are just things. I see a lot of amazing things, Ahmeda. But I find people to be more remarkable."

Ahmeda was not good at small talk, preferring to get to the point. She was uncertain what to say next, but she needn't worry as the Emperor raised the topic.

"I do not want religion to be a barrier between us, Ahmeda. Tell me about your War God? Take your time. Start at the very beginning and leave out no detail."

Ahmeda did as asked. The Emperor was an attentive listener, posing questions that showed he understood the nature of belief and the power of conviction. He deviated at times to better understand her role as a leader and a warrior. In the end, he allowed Ahmeda to sum up her case.

"Why, Ahmeda, should I embrace the Doctrine of the War God when I have decreed that all religion is forbidden?"

"The Doctrine will strengthen your nation, not divide it. It is strength for your armies. It is protection and reward for your soldiers. The Doctrine has a simple premise; Faith in the God of War, loyalty to the Emperor, loyalty to Lord or officer, loyalty to fellow soldiers, glory in battle."

It was a slightly different Doctrine to the one that had inspired the soldiers of the Eastern Colonies. Ahmeda was satisfied at being heard.

"I will take this into consideration, Ahmeda."

Servants brought food and water while they continued to talk. The Emperor asked questions about the Eastern Colonies, its people, the war with the North. He dug deeper into her opinions of what was right and lacking in the colony. He was interested in her ideas about the future. When they finished, Ahmeda felt good about what had been discussed and valued for her insights. She did not resist when he gave her a bold kiss on the lips before departing.

The Emperor spent time with all dignitaries, although he was sometimes interrupted to guide his aides. Each night he dedicated time to dine with Ahmeda, asking more questions. She quizzed him on his life and the Empire. After each dinner, he kissed her gently on the lips before saying their goodnights.

Morgan Cain was the last to be seen. He enjoyed his time at the Palace, exploring the halls of artefacts and talking with the palace staff. Morgan learned about the massive underground network below the lake and the tunnels linked to nearby cities. There was much about the Empire that fascinated him. When he talked with the Emperor, he was enthusiastic with his questions. It was a different type of conversation than the others, as Morgan carried no agenda other than sharing knowledge. If Morgan's appearance fazed the Emperor, he did not show it. Like the others, Morgan came away from the meeting inspired. The Emperor was a man to follow.

When it came time to leave, the visitors met together with the leader a final time. He summed up what some already knew, and he gave them his decisions on other matters. His reasoning seemed considered. The most important things he left to last.

"I will not provide troops for your war against the North. I will gift you what is in the armoury beneath the palace; two hundred thousand rifles and ten artillery. They will be made ready for transport. It is a concern that the prophecy surrounding the Rift War predicts the end of the Age of Men, but there is insufficient evidence that this is more than a local phenomenon. Greater evidence may warrant greater priority. I will require updates. It has highlighted that while our fleets dominate the seas, our armies are not sufficient to meet potential threats on the land. Over the next five years, I will increase the standing army by one million soldiers each year."

The Emperor paused, drawing a deep breath, considering

his words carefully.

"Most importantly, tell our people in the Eastern Colonies that their Emperor decrees this new age will be the Age of Empire, the Ascent of Man. A prophecy to counter prophecy. The Emperor will support them in their time of need."

The leader looked each of his visitors in the eye, as if testing their commitment.

"Two of you will be staying here at the palace. Morgan will enter my service. He will assist me with the consolidation and integration of the colonies. Ahmeda will construct a temple beneath the Palace, and the Empire will embrace the Doctrine of War. The doctrine aligns with my intent to consolidate and strengthen our position."

Ahmeda, puffed out her chest, her eyes gleaming, proud at having attained her ambition.

"I thank you for your travel here and your inspiration, loyalty, and service. I give to you, in return, *my* loyalty and service. Together we will conceive and accomplish great things, we will defeat these false prophecies, and we will witness the true Ascent of Man."

Part 3:

The Dwarves

EaJa-KulAmani

The First Dwarf, old as the mountains, sat next to the Diamond Throne. He was once vital, thunderous, and wise, but now his bones ached, and his mind wandered. Nevertheless, he was still an important symbol and revered by the Dwarves, who put great value on lineage and tradition.

On the other side of the throne, SinKayLas was an imposing figure. He was tall for a Dwarf and decked in the red robes of the KinRa-KluerKinBar, with a peaked hat that made him seem even loftier. In his right hand, he held the staff of JolRek-AsnakTorWervak that cracked with the white energy of the Core. Like others of the KinRa, SinKayLas' eyes were just the whites, which only made his glower more intimidating as he scrutinised the waiting throng.

The Generals stood to attention. They filled the hall with their numbers, male and female, side by side, dressed in their formal armour to honour the landmark occasion.

Amongst them was the Grey General, military commander of the Grey Dwarves. He was one of only two generals whose army was not the immortal True Bloods. Deep in the histories, the blood of some families, mixed with the blood of humans, had become tainted. Their lineage, though long-lived, now aged and died. Such was the burden of the Grey Dwarves who lived in isolation for so long - kept apart so that their pure-blood kin would not share their fate. The KinRa decreed mortality part of humankind's curse, a genetic flaw of the young races that contaminated all it touched. It was the reason that so many millennia ago, when the young races first infested the world, the Dwarves chose the sanctuary of the Icesleepers for their abode.

Now though, the KinRa sensed the end of the age of Mankind, so they ordained that it was time for the old races to reassert themselves upon the world.

EaJa-KulAmani, revered BruEkNa of the Dwarves, entered the room from an entrance at the rear of the hall. As she moved towards the throne, the generals thumped their chests in time and intoned the mantra; "BraYel Ank Novik GarGyak, BraYel Ank Novik GarGyak, BraYel Ank Novik GarGyak".

EaJa-KulAmani raised both hands, and the multitude fell silent. She remained standing, appearing short alongside SinKayLas, but broader and commanding. Her gaze scoured the room, connecting with each Dwarf and conveying a bond of both blood and steel.

The BruEkNa acknowledged the families and paid respect to the KinRa-KluerKinBar. She thanked the Core for giving them life and making them strong. Her speech covered much that was already known of the history and events that brought them to this moment. Then the BruEkNa promised her audience the end of the Age of Men. She described the cycle of the Ages and predicted the rebirth of the Age of Dwarves. Finally, EaJa-KulAmani told her people that the way was open to the land of the light, the ground walked upon by the first Dwarves, their land.

To conclude the address, the BruEkNa beat her chest and repeated the mantra "BraYel Ank Novik GarGyak" back to the Throng. Then, raising her voice, she added, "UrakJa Nahil Aka FerAltol HeManJuri Tos Varel Aka NatooVaTar"; "The way is open, go forth my champions".

THE YOUNG CITIES

Mannace, his fleet of flying ships, and the Brula hurried to the city of Toomb. Fifteen of the Young Cities were now under the military control of either Roundhome or Cavalere, and the Roundmen of General Harold of Toth surrounded this final bastion. With Mannace's help, the allies breached the remaining defences, and Roundhome infantry cleared the desperate defenders from the walls and streets. It would be a short time before the region was utterly subdued. The occupation of the Young Cities was another landmark moment in the war with the North.

The victory also reinforced the value of the flying ships with their ability to strengthen any part of the Northern conflict quickly. The Southerner's dominance of the sky continued to be a decisive factor in coordinating the ground forces and keeping a step ahead of their enemies.

During the siege, the first reports came to Mannace and the other Southern Generals of a storm brewing in the region of the Icesleepers, of black clouds enveloping the mountains and rolling north across the plains. Then, as he feared, the reports spoke of a Dwarven host issuing forth under cover of darkness, legions attacking outlying towns then marching in force against the cities of Roundhome.

The Southern Generals met aboard the *Bracadian*. Their flying vessels were docked alongside, joined by gangplanks. The ship's war room was not large, but it had maps and clerks assigned to keep track of troops and logistics. The generals were quiet as the clerks gave an account of confirmed and unconfirmed Dwarven movements. Harold paced back and forth.

"We're fucked!"

None of the others disagreed - the latest reports suggested an attack of vast proportions. However, Callos Reylor, the General of Galandar and Supreme Commander of the Southern Armies, wanted to be optimistic.

"We always find a way. The people will look to us to be the light in the darkness. We have never failed them."

"Aw, fuck off! - Hundreds of thousands. No, millions of Dwarves. Millions! That's a lot of fucking Dwarves! Shall we just tell the millions of fucking Northerners 'we're sorry for driving you out of fucking Veldaan so you can have it back, and we'll just head back south and call it even'? We're fucked!"

Otheygo, the elderly Knight General of Cavalere, never showed his emotions, and he did his best to ignore the Roundhome General's ranting. He understood that Roundhome bordered the Icesleepers, so their cities were the first to be assaulted. But they all knew of Mannace's vision of the fall of Rotherdaan, Capital of Galandar, and that prediction seemed more likely to be real now.

"Do we have any idea what motivates the Dwarves? Can we negotiate with them? Is it just Roundhome that is under attack?"

"The Horseclans too, but the Dwarves will encounter nothing there until they reach the capital in a week … if they keep marching." Callos added his own opinion, "I anticipate they will."

Mannace voiced his concerns, "There is no news yet from south of the Icesleepers. I expect it goes poorly for the Iron Jaw. They live up against the Mountains, and it is hard to imagine they would not be a target? If the Dwarves march south from the Icesleepers in large numbers, only the sea will defy them. Render and Kakos are at Viletri; perhaps that will make a difference."

Greygor, King and General of the Horseclans, knew his course.

"Our armies will return to the South. The commanders already have their orders. Dwarves are fat and slow. We will meet them on the plains and rout them back to their holes."

Hymal Aktul, the young Apostle of the Holy Lands, commented, "I have never seen a Dwarf. Are they fighters?"

Mannace gave an involuntary "Hah!" and then felt the need to back it up with "Yes, Hymal, the Dwarves are fighters."

Rakor, the King of Remman, was another to have never seen a Dwarf, but he often shared stories and knowledge with Mannace, so he knew the gravity of their situation. The Remman did not fear death and fronting against this new foe grabbed Rakor's interest. He knew what he must do, what his people would expect of him.

"I will call the Ja'Toh, the Absolute War. All will take arms, all of Remman will march. The Remman will join the Horseclans on the tundra to make a stand."

Greygor slapped Rakor on the arm.

"The Clans and the Remman will send these Dwarves scuttling. Or perhaps we will go to the gods together. Hah, we will drink together at the Horse God's table."

Harold calmed somewhat, but he was still at a loss, "How will that help Roundhome?"

Callos took control of the gathering.

"If the information we are receiving is accurate and the Dwarves intend to have Roundhome, then it is lost. Get your people out of there, Harold. Learn from the Veldaan; a nation is its people, not its land. Withdraw to Galandar, where we will decide together if Galandar is the place we make our stand. If not, then we move north to the Veldaan. In the meantime, let's plan how we hold the Veldaan and Young Cities and the Southern Sarang, and at the same time send troops south to make a defence at Galandar. Mannace, you will command the armies in the North. Do what it takes to hold the Northern side of the Rift. Ironic as it is, that may become our best line of defence."

NORDAN

Nordan appeared out of the sea. As he stepped toward the beach, the water hissed about him, and steam rose like a cloud from his shoulders and torso. He flexed and looked about.

Other shapes appeared out of the water nearby; dark Colossi gathered on the shore, awaiting instruction from their master.

When Nordan moved off the beach, a wyvern landed nearby and squawked. Looking up, Nordan could see a cluster of creatures circling high above. He moved to the one on the sand, stroking its scaled neck. It responded with a gurgle and another squawk. Then with a leap and powerful thrust from its gigantic wings, it was again airborne and returning to join the others of its kind.

Nordan leaned forward and scooped up the sandy dirt with his massive hand, putting it to his nose and taking a deep breath. He let the dirt fall through his fingers. The land was not how he remembered it; wild and alive, the elements battling for control, a forge of chaos. This was a dead land, or a land asleep. It seemed odd that this was where the Age would be reborn.

He purposefully left his armies behind. They did not have the means to travel the vast oceans. Not that it mattered, the war against the relentless Surg-Ta was a way to pass the time; something to do while he waited for the Age to pass and the ordained Age, an Age of rebirth and rejuvenation to begin.

Nordan wondered what others would come. The remnant of an Age past.

THE SIEGE OF VILETRI

The storm came suddenly, rolling down from the mountains, across the land, then out across the Blood Sea. There was rage and power in the tempest, and Render understood it to be a thing of elemental magic, heralding the coming of the Dwarves. It crackled and boiled, but it held tight to its lightning and rain for now.

The next day, Lord Kakos received a warning from the Spiderkin that the Dwarves were collecting on the plateau. They formed into armies, marching quickly east into the lands of the Iron Jaw and south towards Viletri. a day later, other reports came from the Fallen and Silos that Dwarves entered their territories. Many people from Silos fled east towards Arenland, while the Fallen retreated to their secret places.

Farmers and townsfolk from the rural areas near Viletri hurried to the city, bringing livestock and possessions. With them came news that Dwarves were crossing the border close behind. There was no doubt that the Dwarves were a hostile and possibly overwhelming invading force. Kakos forbid sending messengers to the fleets to request assistance with evacuation. Abandoning Viletri was not a possibility he would entertain. Instead, Kakos closed the port so that none could depart, and envoys hurried to Yanth and Fremen for reinforcements.

Titus Kane commanded the garrison at Viletri. Three thousand soldiers were available to him, equipped with the best modern weaponry, including repeating crossbows, choke gas and new stun hammers. Also under

Titus' command were two thousand animated statues and a similar number of animated workers, which varied in size from human-like to gigantic. Nineteen massive temple guardians and perhaps thirty War Priests would join in the defence. Moving about the city like frantic ants and readying themselves for the conflict were more than thirty thousand trained militia, plus a similar number of other residents capable of taking up a sword.

On the walls were the stone lobbers, ever vigilant and battle-ready. Kakos joined them to look across the outer city and to prepare mentally. With his mind, he reached out and connected himself to the metropolis about him, tapping into the life magic that powered it and taking control of the multitude of souls as he had done on the Northern fields of war. Kakos and the city, *his city*, were as one.

North of Viletri, SinKayLas marched alongside the Dwarven general GyinToth and his VenGuan elite. Some of the VenGuan were amongst the first Dwarves who fought in wars during the Age of Legends. GyinToth selected other soldiers during the trials, for their courageous nature, as much as their sword arms. The VenGuan wore thick grey coats over chainmail armour, with metal helmets, and deep hoods to keep out the light. Even with the stormy darkness, his soldiers were sensitive to the brightness of this world above the earth. The VenGuan carried tall shields strapped to their left arm and spears in their right hand. To complete their armament was a wide-bladed sword at their belt. Next to his broadsword, GyinToth bore a long-handled ice-pick tucked into his girdle. It was an artefact gifted to him by his father, worn with immense pride.

SinKayLas felt connected to the Core and the storm. In his hands, the staff of JolRek-AsnakTorWervak crackled with furious energies that urged to be released. SinKayLas, the mightiest of the KinRa, raised the staff so that lightning arched from it into the brewing tempest high above. The black clouds responded with bolts of their own that arched down to scorch the earth and light their way. Thunder rolled across the plains, and in the flashes of light, SinKayLas could see the city of Viletri outlined on the horizon. The Dwarves looked to the sky, beating their chests, "BraYel Ank Novik GarGyak."

Render joined Kakos on the wall as he watched the lightning through gaps in the outer city buildings. He caught glimpses of the Dwarven host, though it gave him no particulars of the number of the enemy. As always, Render's soul-bearing statues and several apprentices were with him. The demon, Fek, and his cult followers were in the shadows. Gax, Ruu, and more cultists waited back from the wall where they could still see the Master. The other apprentices, potent wizards in their own right, were elsewhere as part of the defence.

As far as Render could see in the darkness, garrison troops, militia, and stone lobbers defended the city walls. Although they were not trained to be fighters, Kakos also ordered the city's zombie workforce to the battlements. While some undead were supplied with weapons, others made do with what they had to hand. Render smirked when one passed him by, armed with a broom.

In another bold move, Kakos ordered the animated statues and workers deployed before the city wall. Looking down, Render watched them taking up their positions. A temple guardian waited nearby. It was an imposing figure, the height of the wall and sculptured to the likeness of a past champion. The tactic made sense to Render; the animations would be more brutal to get past than the walls, and they were possibly the only thing more resilient and relentless than Dwarves.

The battle would soon be upon them, and Render raised his magical defences. His apprentices prepared other enchanted shields, needing to be vigilant against attacks from the physical world and different dimensions.

Dwarves were more visible now at the city's outskirts, and thunder boomed, but not from the clouds. Instead, the noise came from the Dwarven lines. Behind where Kakos and Render stood, a large building exploded. Timber and stone blocks hurled in all directions, and a wave of force washed over those on the wall. Render could see huge missiles arching out of the sky to impact other parts of the city. Where they hit, the destruction was immense. Already there was at least one colossal breach in the wall.

Unexpectedly, Kakos stepped up and over the crenulations. He dropped like a dead weight, landing on his feet in front of the wall, then marching through the outer city towards his enemies. From his vantage on the battlements, Render observed the air about the Zombie Lord become thick with spirits, like looking through distorted glass. The city was answering Kakos' call, and as Render glanced about, he saw trails of spirit power being drawn from the city to follow in the Liche's wake. Statues positioned outside the defences marched forward, and along the walls, zombies dropped to the ground, then picked themselves up to amble in the same direction as their Lord. Strangely, rats were everywhere. Render hadn't thought the city to have so many vermin. They scampered over the walls and from hidden places to swarm through the outer city streets and join the undead and animated in their advance.

Render commanded his demons to follow, then summoned his levitation disk. When it arrived, he and two apprentices boarded the floating platform. They hurried forward to catch up with Kakos, who was already halfway to the enemy. Behind them, the explosive missiles continued to assault Viletri. Not wanting to leave it too late, Render ordered the light globes deployed. Instead of releasing the orbs high into the atmosphere, his apprentices cast them low over the outer city rooftops so that they came to pause directly above the enemy lines.

At the outskirts of Viletri, SinKayLas was content to watch the mortars go about their work. Concerningly, balls of light appeared in the distance, gliding towards them, then hovering overhead. Everywhere Dwarves pulled their hoods over their faces and looked downwards to avoid the harsh illumination. GyinToth prodded the KinRa, to spur him into action.

"Do your job, KinRa!"

SinKayLas scoffed. He had battled magic users before. Shaking his staff, he sent a bolt into the sky. Forks of lightning arched down into the city, answering his summons. As SinKayLas controlled the elemental forces, he directed other bolts at the light globes. While a few of the lights diminished, others grew in intensity, and only one exploded in a shower of fire and sparks.

Not to be outdone and ignoring GyinToth's glower, SinKayLas let his mind relax, searching out the globes with his thoughts, feeling their contours and drawing the moisture from the air to embrace the light. He shaped the vapour, and he gave it substance. When he focused again in the real world, the globes were still hovering overhead but encased in ice. The light dimmed to be little more than a dull nuisance. Satisfied with the result, SinKayLas turned his attention back to the storm and intensified the lightning assault, targeting areas he expected to be the inner city and walls. Thunder became a constant roar, drowning out all other noise.

A giant form manifested out of the cityscape and charged at a unit of Dwarves. Soldiers scattered as it impacted, and with a broad sweep of the guardians' blade, the field was littered with tumbling bodies. More giant shapes and many smaller ones appeared. Responding quickly, Dwarven infantry manoeuvred to form defensive lines, while scurrying crews aimed their cannons. GyinToth expected that combat would be challenging in the glare, and once he understood that many of the attackers were stone, he sent the hammerers and VenGuan against them. To other troops, he issued orders to fall back and stay in support. As he expected, the fighting was bloody, and the statues were formidable. GyinToth was relieved to see one of the giant stone creatures collapse, shattered by a direct cannon hit.

Zombies and rats assaulted GyinToth and his legion. A powerful undead was amongst them. As the liche came out of the city, the buildings near him broke apart and came back together in a whirlwind of debris, flying at the Dwarves and battering them. Other invisible forces tossed dwarves in the air or crushed them where they stood. The Dwarves were hapless against the Liche's wild assault.

Render joined Kakos. He arrived on the levitation disk with his apprentices just in time to shield the Lord and himself from lightning that arched down from the storm, scorching the area about them. While Render maintained the magical defence, he scanned the field. It was not easy to see anything in the poor light or with the flashes from the storm, but he soon discovered motionless forms of Viletri statues drained of their magic, knowing at least one enemy wizard was nearby.

Trusting his apprentices to shield him from the tempest, Render laid down a barrage of force and fire, aimed at the adversaries he could see and anything beyond. Dwarves were knocked off their feet, crushed, and some set aflame.

One Dwarf stood unaffected, staff in hand, defiant among the carnage. When Render focused his magics against the Dwarf, they were brushed away by his rival's arcane defences. Abruptly the figure was hidden by the storm that descended and coalesced in thunderous human shapes - gigantic and raw in their power. The formidable elementals advanced, meeting Kakos' tornados of debris head-on. The battlefield became lost in a clash of titanic forces.

Render reached deep into his well of energy, drawing on the souls held within the obsidian statues; then, harnessing the light globes, he released a mighty spell. The ice encasing the globes disintegrated in a piercing hiss of steam, and spears of light momentarily dominated the landscape. Some rays reached spectacularly into the sky, shooting towards the stars. Where the rays struck the earth, shocked Dwarves were blinded, and some knocked senseless. All were disoriented. Only the stone statues and zombies went unaffected about their work. Amongst the enemy, the Dwarven dead were rising at Kakos' command to stab their kin, adding to the terror. The few Dwarves unaffected by the light rallied and guided their companions, but their stalled assault was becoming a desperate defence.

SinKayLas was unaffected by the light, and he, like Render, possessed enormous reserves. Wanting to end this now, he re-focused his mind and concentrated on the area around the enemy sorcerers. Everything he held in reserve, and the potent power from his staff, was channelled instantly into that space. When he focused back to the real world, he could see his work completed; a gigantic wall of ice where the enemy once stood. He mouthed a blessing to the Core, turning to retreat to a safer place.

SinKayLas sensed a movement to his left and stepped away just in time as a shadowy creature swung its long talons at his neck. The beast was quick, surging forward, raking his arm with its claws so that he dropped his staff, and with another slash, the creature tore a deep gouge across his chest. In desperation, SinKayLas stumbled quickly backwards and reached into a pouch on his belt, grabbing at the device there, which he activated with a flick of his thumb, and instantly the Dwarf disappeared.

As SinKayLas reappeared in a chamber under the mountains, he berated himself for his cowardice. Immediately he knew there were more honourable actions he might have taken, even if it meant risking death. He looked down at the device Logthar gave him, and he cursed the Grey Dwarf. The KinRa's left arm was in tatters, and blood flowed down his chest. Nevertheless, the magic he maintained kept him alive, and he used that magic to begin the healing. For now, regrets and new plans would need to wait. SinKayLas sat in a chair and retreated into a spiritual, regenerative state.

Render was not protected against the ice that formed instantly around him and the others or the raw power that scrambled, almost pulverised, his brain. Too late, he used the last wisp of his senses to slip into near-space. Free of the icy prison, his body was shockingly numb, and he watched one of his fingers snap off as he slumped then fell against an imagined floor. With his last vestiges of consciousness slipping away, Render noticed Fek approach out of the nothingness that was near-space and reach down. He sensed himself being pulled. The floor he imagined was evaporating, becoming an expanding pit. Amongst the Wizard's scattered thoughts was a sudden, helpless panic. He was at the demon's mercy. As Render's mind let go its fingertip grip on the edge of the abyss, he felt dizzy as if he were spinning, plunging helplessly into all-consuming nothingness.

Kakos, though hampered by the Ice, was already dead and cold. Strangely, the frozen trap cleared his mind of physical distractions and focused him on the task at hand. The storm creatures dissipated with the exit of their master, leaving him free to assault the Dwarves. He did not need the movement of his body or clear vision. Instead, he saw the energy in everything about him, and as the manipulator of energies, he was in total control.

Units of soldiers and militia from Viletri joined the combat, using their crossbows, and attacking where they had superior numbers. The Dwarves struggled under the fierce skylights, and GyinToth ordered a withdrawal. His army was blinded and battered, but they recovered more of their senses once they retreated from the light globes. Today's battle reminded GyinToth of the time of Legends and the magnificent creatures and magic he faced then. He knew that this campaign would have its peaks and valleys like in the Ages past. This was the first conflict for many Dwarves in his army, and it was good for them to learn what war was about.

With the Dwarves withdrawn and Viletri fortifying its defence, the next day did not herald a new attack. Instead, orders from EaJa-KulAmani commanded GyinToth to reinforce operations against other human cities and await the arrival of the VengTan-AsTenRey, with their mighty earth breakers and drills.

JA'TOH

The Ja'Toh, the Absolute War, was called, and the Remman responded as their King knew they would. Across the rugged terrain that was their home, the Remman gathered at rally points or in the cities. They chose leaders and formed into units. As the Remman departed their homeland, only those too young, in the care of those too old, remained behind. It was a great honour for the women who trained alongside the men to march to war. For old veterans that never thought they would have the opportunity to raise a blade again, and for those young but eager to be blooded, it was a hope made real. King Rakor joined them; the Ja'Toh was his to command. The King and other experienced warriors arrived on flying ships. In all, a select eight thousand fighters journeyed from the front lines at Veldaan to join eight hundred thousand of their kin as they marched in a long procession towards the territory of the Horse Clans.

On the tundra, garrisons of foot soldiers from Thunderhome and Gaidon joined them, and for the first time in many generations, the slim Vostov walked to war. The Vostov were a strange people, dark-skinned and small-boned, with sharp features. When they spoke, it seemed in riddles, and they quipped and laughed amongst themselves, though their humour was lost on the Remman. The Vostov wore simple clothes and carried weapons of bone and wood, carved and imbued with their magics. The last to come was the soldiers of Eck. Like those of Thunderhome and Gaidon, they were infantrymen with leather or chainmail armour, and their units were equipped with a variety of armaments. The combined force was perhaps a million strong and contained everything the makeshift Easterners could muster.

It took almost a month to arrive at the conflict, and ahead they could see the storm on the horizon. All knew from reports that the dark clouds heralded the armies of the Dwarves, who were creatures of the cold and darkness. Upon seeing the wild power of the roiling tempest, even the stoic Remman became uneasy.

Before they reached the storm, their scouts brought them first to the forward camp of the Horseclans. Rakor was surprised to see the Clansmen arrayed in units of footmen, but when he met with Greygor, the King of the Clans explained.

"Rakor, we have been fighting the Dwarves since they came to the tundra. You would think that half a million Dwarves would be easy pickings for a million horse on the flatlands, but they're determined, and they're winning. It's the storm that aids them and the sorcerers that control it. The horses panic when they use the lightning against us. See what we are reduced to, Rakor. But you are here, and we will fight with the earth at our feet if that is what it takes for us to stand together."

Greygor's usual bravado was gone as he gripped Rakor by the arm.

"The Capital fell in the first week, Rakor. They killed all those that did not flee. They are possessed, these dark Dwarves. They will persist until we all are dead."

Rakor looked at the clansmen without their horses. It was not a sight to inspire him, not what he expected when he committed everything to the conflict. It was not the same men that rolled like thunder across the tundra and were like lightning when they struck.

"Ja'Toh, my friend."

The storm and the Dwarves were headed directly for them. As the allies formed ranks, the Remman took up the centre, while the clansmen deployed infantry on the flanks and archers behind the front lines. The Thunderhome, Galdon, and Eck troops were in reserve to reinforce any line breach.

Vostov fighters moved about in small groups, placing themselves at the back of the Remman units. Rakor heard that the Vostov were quick and fearless. Like the Remman, the Vostov were not afraid of death. They called themselves the Blessed People, although he did not know why.

As the two armies drew close, Rakor watched the Dwarves form a line similar to their own except stretched thinner, possibly six ranks deep compared to their fifteen. Even in the darkness, the Dwarves appeared to be heavy-set creatures, well armoured and carrying tall shields. They stopped out of bow range, and at their beckoning, the storm unleashed its lightning and gale against the Human host. It was a terrifying spectacle with barrages of electrical energy sweeping through the Remman and Clan ranks. The blinding blizzard seemed to last for an eternity, and when the assault died away, enough for the allies to look up, the enemy was almost upon them. The Remman quickly reformed their shield wall, shaken but resolute, and the Clansmen rallied and charged. Clan archers fired over the front troops, but it did not bother the Dwarves as arrows clanged off armour and shield. In return, the Dwarven mages battered the archers with more lightning and swirling winds.

The charging clansmen contacted with the Dwarves, leaping into their shield defence. Ferocious warriors pushed the enemy a step backwards, but the advantage was short-lived as the dwarves surged forward with their shields and stabbed with their weapons. The Dwarves were strong, stout, and tough to kill. They outclassed and outmuscled the Clansmen who were experienced and fierce but made meagre infantry. The unrelenting Dwarves edged forward at a steady walk, forcing the clansmen ever backwards so that their defence quickly took on a desperate appearance.

With the most experienced warriors in the front rank, the Remman met the Dwarves in a clash of steel, at first giving better than they got. But in the slow crush, the Dwarven fortitude was undeniable, and their metal armour impenetrable. So, for every Dwarf to fall under the blade, unbelievably, it seemed that two or three of the Remman met their deaths.

Somehow the Vostov soldiers worked their way through the Remman ranks and just as easily slipped between Dwarven shields. Even now, amongst the Dwarves, most Vostov eluded any attention. They calmly slunk their way towards the Dwarven spell casters, and of the three mages, only one noted their progress. The wily mage directed other Dwarves to intervene, and once they paid proper attention, they made easy work of the Vostov infiltrators. Where the other casters remained distracted in their storm-work, the Vostov sidled up to them. With quick stabs, the spellcasters were victim to bone knives, and only then did Dwarven guards scramble to the defence. After the advantage of surprise, the Vostov were no match for the Dwarves in open melee. Incredibly, a few of their numbers escaped through the Dwarven lines.

The soldiers with King Rakor were his most elite but even they were matched blow for blow with the Dwarves as their shield walls ground against each other. The heavy cloaks worn by the Dwarves were good armour, but the chainmail and breastplates beneath the covers were even tougher to penetrate. The only vulnerability appeared to be the open-faced helms which the elite Remman did their best to exploit. Rakor himself sheathed his sword. Instead, he grabbed up a hammer taken from the belt of a dead Dwarf. As the Dwarf in front of him stabbed at him with a spear, Rakor easily deflected the blow, then with his shield, he pushed against the defence of the Dwarf who matched his strength. Using the advantage of height, the King struck over the protection at his adversary's head, connecting with the helm and momentarily stunning his foe. Rakor pulled his dazed enemy down, clambering over him, and throwing his weight at the Dwarves to either side to disrupt their line. Other Remman were quick to react, several bashing their way into the small gaps that briefly appeared in the defence. While two Remman near Rakor were stabbed and fell, others leapt into the widening breach, continuing to break up the structured Dwarven resistance. To Rakor's surprise, Vostov warriors appeared amongst the enemy, adding to the chaos. With momentum turning in the allies' favour, the breach quickly became a wedge that broke apart the Dwarven line. Behind the Remman, fierce warriors from Thunderhome gathered to take advantage of their success. Armed with heavy two-handed axes and mauls, they were most effective with space to wield them. Suddenly there was a glimmer of optimism amongst the allies' ranks.

With only one of the three Dwarven mages surviving, the lightning harassing the allied lines diminished. King Greygor, whose clansmen were having little success in holding the Dwarves at bay, ordered half of his units to make haste for the distant base camp and return with mounts. He knew they would not be seen again for at least an hour, but it was apparent to Greygor that to fight on foot was a terrible mistake. His men were fierce and skilled, but they were no match for the Dwarves on the ground. Only where the infantry from Gaidon and Eck aided them could they mount a worthy defence. He would have withdrawn all his men on another day, but Greygor understood that the Remman would not give the centre, and their Ja'Toh was to face death. He would occupy the Dwarves as best he could on the flanks and provide the Remman with their chance for success. Even with many of his troops departed, the Horse King commanded enough numbers to outflank the enemy and harass them from the side and rear. Greygor issued the command to surround the Dwarves. While he might not beat them, he would stall their advance.

Rakor, and the Remman about him, burst through the last rank of the Dwarves then fanned out, forcing them to fight on two fronts. As he hoped, the combat at the breach lost its structure, breaking into skirmishes. Now the Remman benefited from their speed and agility.

Amid the battle, Rakor smashed a falling Dwarf with a second sharp blow to ensure his work, and then with a moment bought, the leader looked about. As he turned, it was in time to see flame erupt from a long tube carried by two grey-cloaked Dwarves. Rakor brought up his shield in defence, but the flame swept over him, and where it contacted his body, the fire spread and burned. Consumed by the fierce heat, Rakor felt the skin peeling from his scalp and face. Courageously, he raged against it, screaming as if his fury might cheat the fates. But his roar ended with his last breath, and the bright light in his eyes twisted agonisingly into darkness. The Remman King's burning body slumped to the earth.

Other Dwarves of this new type rushed to the breach. They aimed repeating crossbows, firing into the Remman and Gaidon mass, bolt after bolt issuing from the devastating weapons, quickly clearing a path. Amongst them, Logthar of the Grey Dwarves hurried two other flamers forward. The Remman, women and young amongst them, fought fearlessly, but with more of his kin gathering about him, Logthar was confident of restoring the breach. He left his kin to their work so that he could focus on the entangled flanks. He hoped the same tactics would drive the raging clansmen back.

Greygor had never witnessed a battle so bloody. When combat was close, usually, the resolve of one side would triumph over the other, and the bulk of troops would withdraw to fight another day. However, both the

Remman and Dwarves showed no intention to leave defeated. The Remman still outnumbered the Dwarves, but the woman and old veterans were now at the front of their ranks, and he could see youngsters entering the fray. As competent as they were, they did not have the experience to endure this ordeal. The Dwarves, whose troops were also male and female, suffered significant losses, but their line held firm and resolute. Even when surrounded, they kept their discipline and composure.

It was clear to Greygor that the allies were losing, and it was agonising to watch the Remman fight on – them and his men who should have retreated but stayed for honour. There were no more reserves. He looked over his shoulder at the tundra, hopeful of the miracle that he would see cavalry coming to their aid. He realised, though, that they would still be far away.

THE PRINCE

At the base camp, Prince Malakai, son of Greygor, collected his horse and rode hard, back towards the battle on the tundra. Tens of thousands of other clan members did the same, and it felt good and right to be back on their mounts. There was optimism that the conflict could take a different shape with just one mage to face. Now, the storm and the enemy were in their sights.

As he came closer to the conflict, Malakai passed groups of his kin hurrying in the opposite direction. Some were retrieving horses from the clansmen who brought them for that purpose. A battered unit of Gaidon soldiers also passed by. They didn't turn back. Their heads were low, plodding on, defeated.

When the prince arrived at the battle, its shape was very different. It was broken into skirmishes between units rather than the long battlefront he left. There were far fewer soldiers on both sides, and the bloody carnage strewn about the tundra was like nothing he witnessed before. To Malakai, it seemed that the Dwarves were victorious this day and were pursuing the defeated enemy to seal their victory. Gone was the lightning from the sky. Losing no time, the prince raised his spear to rally others to him, and he sped to attack.

Already the Dwarves saw the danger of the arriving cavalry and were breaking off combats to regroup and defend. The horsemen, though, came in great numbers, crashing into units of Dwarves and scattering them. A few foot units joined the horseman in the renewed attack, though most infantry were too exhausted or broken to contribute further. The Dwarves were also tired, and it took all their endurance to gather in a circle and reform their shield wall. Malakai estimated perhaps a hundred thousand Dwarves remained. There was twice that number of clansmen and other allies still making a defence, though most survivors were fleeing, and he could see no Remman standing. With the Horse Clans strength regathered, Malakai was at the vanguard of at least a quarter of a million fresh cavalry. It was enough to secure the field and protect the wounded. He sent out riders to look for his father, the King.

King Greygor was amongst the many injured. He nursed a broken leg and severe concussion. For now, that put Malakai in charge, and he knew his course. Summoning his kin, the prince raised his spear, setting off at a canter, hooting and calling others. He rode directly at the enemy then abruptly changed course to circle them. As others joined him, they also raised their war cries, and some fired arrows into the Dwarven throng. The growing mass of cavalry whooped and jeered mockingly at their enemy. As their frenzy peaked, Malakai turned again to charge at the Dwarves. From all angles, the Clansmen assaulted the Dwarven defence.

At the last moment before impact, Malakai used his knees and momentum to launch his horse into the shield wall. The magnificent beast smashed between two Dwarves, knocking them sideways to land amongst others. Malakai reined in his fierce mount before it stumbled on the bodies, and he stabbed down at a stunned Dwarf. As the Prince took a moment to look about, he was satisfied to see the Dwarves scattered by the charge. As solid and enduring as Dwarves were, the clansmen knew how to bully them with their horses. This battle would end with the enemy utterly decimated.

Distant from the battle, a unit of Grey Dwarves hurried as best they could across the tundra. On a stretcher made of spears and shields, one of the KinRa lay wounded, near death but in a state of regeneration. Logthar expected they would need speed and luck to get back to the mountains.

WE THREE

With the Dwarven storm covering the lands of the South, it was taking longer for messages to reach Mannace in Veldaan. Finally, however, welcome news arrived of a victory against the Dwarves on the tundra, although it seemed less a triumph and more a great tragedy as he read the detail of the message. Now it was his job to tell the Remman that their people had perished and that their King, his close ally, and friend, was dead. The Remman troops were the backbone of the southern allied armies. He knew enough of their character to understand how they would react to this news; they would want to travel south to take what vengeance they could against the Dwarves. They would throw themselves at the enemy until this last generation of proud Remman soldiers were no more. Mannace sighed. He could not allow them the honour of such a death. They were essential in the North.

Messages arrived from Viletri that the city and other communities south of the Icesleepers were at war with the Dwarves. Render was missing in action. Mannace knew that Render was resourceful, but the news made his gut tighten. He reminded himself of Render's vision at the Oracle, giving him confidence that the sorcerer would still play his part in the events ahead. Mannace drew strength from his vision and higher purpose at times like this. He felt intensely alone.

The other generals were busy south of the Rift. After the evacuation of Roundhome, the allies made their defence at Galandar. None of the reports from that conflict carried good news. Where the allies fought, the storm scattered their cavalry, and the Dwarven infantry scored victory upon victory. Mannace thought of sending the flying ships to assist, but they would be vulnerable to the storm and lightning. If he were to send the Remman, it might slow the tide, but it would mean giving up the North. As hundreds of thousands of refugees flooded into the North, he knew he must focus on his assignment.

Mannace's enemy was aware of the invasion of the South by the Dwarves. Sensing a turn of fortune, it was not long before the Northerners increased the frequency and determination of their attacks. With just his Colonial forces and the Remman, even with his flying squadrons, Mannace was hard-pressed to counter the aggression. He relied more on the fortified cities to help slow the Northern momentum. Mannace was losing ground in Veldaan. Without the numbers of troops to cover the vast expanses of captured territory, he was unable to prevent the Southern Sarang from being retaken.

Mannace received a visitor. After showing up unexpectedly at the allies' base camp, Jaal was brought immediately to his command tent by the Rangers. Glad to see each other, the companions' estrangement didn't matter. Mannace was sour at Jaal for his refusal to be involved in the war in the North, while Jaal resented Mannace for insisting he played his role in the Oracles games. However, the last two decades showed the companions that life was not so simple. As they stood face to face, it was grounding for them both.

"The fates must be laughing at us now, Jaal."

"Laughing at you, maybe. And that ridiculous uniform."

"A bit of colour looks good on a man. You have no sense of style, Jaal. Little does it matter - I am starting to believe that the Age of Men is coming to an end."

Jaal shrugged. Perhaps it was not a bad thing that Men ended their time. He came here for other reasons.

"I heard about Render from the Spiderkin. I don't know if we need to search for him. Do you have word?"

"Only that he is missing after a siege at Viletri. It's Render; if he's hiding, then it probably isn't in this world. We would need a Wizard to find him. If he's dead, that won't slow him down too much. His apprentices are likely taking action."

Jaal was not one to leave a task to others.

"We owe him more than that. We three, we are in this together. Mannace, give me a flying ship, and I will travel south and do what is needed."

Mannace was hit with mixed emotions. Jaal saying that they were in this together was an affirmation he longed for. He wanted nothing more than his companions to support him in the challenges ahead. It irked him, though, that his friend talked about togetherness, yet his actions in recent years set them apart. He drew a deep breath and composed his thoughts before responding. Mannace wanted to make a bargain, but that would risk putting Jaal back offside.

"Yes. Of course, you can take a ship. The Gull has just arrived; it has been refitted and refurbished. The Blood Legion is providing crew. They still see you as their patron."

Jaal was surprised that Mannace was so accommodating. He expected to argue or at least have to bargain. But, instead, the ship and crew couldn't have been better, and he appreciated that Mannace had made it easy.

"Good."

"Good."

"I have brought some soldiers."

"I heard that you live with the Veldaan. What soldiers did you bring?"

"Just ten. They should make a difference."

Mannace knew that Jaal was referring to the Colossi. He wasn't expecting that, and yes, they would make a significant difference. He felt emotion swell up inside, but he pushed it back down. It meant a lot to have his friend back on side.

"Good."

"The Veldaanian's aren't that bad. They are just like any other men. They hate you, though!"

Mannace laughed. What a ridiculous situation. He wasn't sure what to say to Jaal, so instead, he took him to the camp of Casteel and the Blood Legion. From there, he would show him the ship, and then they would need to talk more about the Colossi. As he walked about the camp, Mannace could see the Colossi at a distance, their oversized silhouettes black against the sunset. The massive creatures drew the attention of many others, and Mannace took a moment to explain the situation to one of the commanders, who hurried to stop anybody doing something stupid.

A day after Jaal departed on the Gull, there was another significant event. In the camp of the Rhalec divisions, a fantastic stone artefact mysteriously appeared. It was rooted in the earth and formed a massive arch of stone in the shape of a rainbow. It was of a size that, if the arch were in Viletri, its ends would have reached the city's western and eastern edges, and its height would easily be twice that of the sky tower. But, again, Mannace was frustrated not to have forewarning. The air within the arch shimmered, like a portal.

Soon after the arch appeared, Rhalec warriors stepped out from the shimmering air, hundreds of them pulling on ropes attached to some object not yet revealed. Rhalec priests walked amongst them, strutting proudly and ceremoniously swinging their tails. The priests carried staves and wore bands of silver and gold studded with large gems around their arms and necks. One, who appeared to be their patriarch, sported a wild headdress of colourful feathers and a cloak to match.

Out of the portal appeared a tower. Mannace could see why the Rhalec strained on the ropes and was amazed that they could transport something so immense. He noticed then that the tower floated slightly above the earth, like other levitation devices he had seen. The spire was stone, square at the base and tapering to a small platform at the top. It was perhaps as tall as three galleys laid end to end. The tower's stonework was new and functional, with decorative carving around its base. When the Spire was clear of the arch, and everybody's attention was on the Rhalec High Priest, he cast his arms high and screeched in the Rhalec tongue. The tower responded with crackles of power that sparked from base to top, quickly drawn to the upper platform where the energy exploded skyward in blasts of electrical force. Now activated, even when the lightning dissipated, the top platform continued to spark and glow.

A second tower emerged. This time the Rhalec dragged it well clear of the Arch so that another two spires could follow. Over the next three days, two entire divisions of Rhalec and fifty towers joined their kin on the plains. The Crocodile People always proved themselves to be good allies, and it reminded Mannace that he was not a leader standing alone – that he stood at the front of a dominion that shared his vision. While that bolstered his spirits, it also made him worry for the Eastern Colonies under assault from the Dwarves. He hoped that the colonial nations rallied for them too.

THE GULL

Aboard the *Gull*, Jaal was glad to be reunited with Casteel. There were few others amongst the Blood Legion crew that he recognised; an old campaigner named Rusuck, Rey the large Belg, and a Daglari called Refonsa who winked at him when he looked her way. Refonsa hadn't aged well, her fur was matted, and some of her teeth were missing down the left side of her long jaw. She was bulked up and broad as well as tall. Rey was also grey at the temples. He put a big hand on Jaal's head and ruffled his hair. Casteel laughed.

Unlike the blood legion, the *Gull* was pristine. Its decks and fittings were polished, and when a crewman ushered Jaal to his cabin, he noticed that the ship's interior was ornate and functional. For Jaal, who lived in the remote north for many years, it seemed like he stepped into a different world.

Back on deck, Jaal chuckled to himself as he watched Rey finish tying a piece of rope between one of the masts and the deck railing. Over it, he hung washed clothes so that they caught the soft breeze blowing across the deck. When he finished and turned away, another legionnaire was quick to grab down a colossal pair of underclothes which he took to the front of the ship and, clambering far out, placed them over the prow, which was shaped like a gulls-head.

Jaal left the legionnaires to their business to meet with the captain and the Navigator. Casteel listened in.

"Set course for Viletri."

The captain was an Arenlander named Dantain Gerbals. Gerbals was short, with delicate features and an oiled moustache. His sharp blue uniform was pressed neat, and his buttons and boots were polished. The crew, mainly below deck, were likewise military and formal, appearing very diligent and efficient as they worked. The Arenlanders and Blood Legion seemed to mix well despite their apparent differences.

"Yes, Sir, how would you like to travel? To come here, we skirted the storm to the east. Chimchum is a Class A Navigator; he can take you to Viletri instantaneously if required."

Chimchum was a Goblin, dressed in plain shirt and pants and with a slave-ring about his neck. He was lean, his body bending oddly to the left. Chimchum's expression was dim, with a prominent brow that made him appear dull. His eyes were thin and dark. Jaal questioned the Goblin directly.

"You can get us there in an instant?"

"Yes. No. Yes."

"How is that possible?"

The Goblin seemed agitated, so the captain answered on his behalf.

"Apologies, Sir, but explanations are not Chimchum's strong point. He is, however, exceptional at his job. Chim can move the ship to any location he has been to before instantaneously. He does this by imagining the ship in both places, then allowing only one of those locations to be true. The Navigation Stone and the Grid Stone are below deck. Chim draws on the power of the Grid to command navigation. It's all a trick of the mind. It is not done often because of the risk that something else might occupy the same space we are travelling to."

"Do it."

"No. Yes. No. No. Yes."

"Yes, Sir."

Jaal was distracted. Four Legionnaires manoeuvred a table from the crew quarters onto the main deck, and others were joining them with chairs and drinks. They were making themselves at home, joking and laughing. Jaal missed the camaraderie.

As he watched them, the sky darkened behind the group, and when he focused back on the ship and its surroundings, Jaal was amazed that they were in a different place. Above them, the sky was dark, with clouds that crackled with power. He'd never seen anything like it. On the horizon were city lights that he assumed was Viletri. Moving to the rails at the side of the deck and looking down, Jaal observed a familiar coast, with a blood-red sea and gentle, sandy beaches. It was dusk in the Veldaan. It was hard to tell with the darkness created by the storm overhead, but he assumed it was dusk here too.

The captain was cautious as he pulled alongside the Viletri Sky Tower. Jaal stayed at the rails, looking down. Below him, the city seemed as alive as it had always been. It was possibly more so, with bright streetlights and crowds of people moving about.

Jaal, knowing where to go for information, was impatient to get on with his mission. Legionnaires joined him as he descended the Sky Tower and headed for DeeDee's. Casteel instructed the soldiers to be back at the *Gull* by dawn.

DeeDee's was once his residence. Even now, it stirred things inside him - to remember his time there with Saska. Tonight, he approached the doors as a stranger, although he was surprised to see so many familiar faces once inside; familiar and ageless, perhaps even prettier than he remembered.

DeeDee met with Jaal in her private rooms. The two were intimate before, so DeeDee assumed this encounter would be no different from the past. She seldom serviced customers herself anymore, but this was no ordinary patron. Jaal remembered DeeDee fondly; she was imaginative and uninhibited. He was pleased to be here.

It was still the dark hours of the morning when Jaal awoke. He knocked over and spilt the contents of a jar of ointment as he stretched his arms. Then, absentmindedly, he righted the pot and took a deep breath. The smell of scents was still in the air – aromas that scrambled his brain, even more so than Nyx. Nevertheless, he felt adequately relaxed for the first time in a long time.

DeeDee was now awake too. She ran her hand down Jaal's chest and abdomen, stroking his cock gently. It was a whore's way of saying "good morning". Jaal was not going to stop her, though his sense of urgency about his mission returned. He took another deep breath to clear his mind, then started with his questions.

"I came here to find Render. Do you know where he is?"

DeeDee kept up her handiwork; it gave her a sense of control. Like Jaal, she took a moment to collect her thoughts. Information was power, and in this sense, DeeDee was perhaps the most powerful person in the city. That didn't mean that she possessed all the answers.

"OK, sweety, I only know what others know. Render escaped the battle. He was encased in ice by a Dwarven wizard, but they didn't find his body when the Ice melted. His apprentices have been searching for him, though he is in none of the places they might have expected. The cultists don't say much, but I expect it's because they don't know much. Everything is a secret for them, sweety. Kakos does nothing. He is a creation of Render's, as are many of the animations and other things in the city. A question asked in many circles is what happens if Render dies? If he were dead, would his magic die too?"

"I don't know. That sounds like Render, a way of ensuring others are interested in keeping him alive. Why did the Dwarves stop attacking?"

"There are several schools of thought on that one, sweetie. Many people believe that Kakos drove them back. He led the defence against the Dwarves. Stories of what he did during the war in the North are the talk of the city. By the light, the tales will send prickles up your spine. But you're a big boy, aren't you, sweetie? That kind of thing won't worry you."

Jaal was quiet, waiting for DeeDee to fill the silence. She didn't disappoint him.

"With Render gone, the city looks to Kakos as their

protector, and they believe that the Dwarves fear him. He likes the attention, though it's hard to tell what zombies think. Some people are more pragmatic. They believe Viletri was tougher than the enemy expected and that the Dwarves will be back when they have gathered more strength. The last school of thought is that Kakos killed the enemy wizard, and the Dwarves can't take Viletri without magic. I think there is some truth to all these theories, but the last one feels right."

DeeDee anticipated Jaal's next question.

"The Dwarves hold all the land from the Icesleepers to the Blood Sea. Only Viletri still stands. New Hindas evacuated. The people of Silos were either rescued by ship or fled east towards Arenland. They wiped out the Iron Jaw. I know they're just Orcs, but you've got to feel sorry for them. You know what I mean, sweetie. The Spiderkin are underground. News is infrequent, but some of the Iron Jaw are with them – not a fate I would wish on anybody. There have been no signs of Dwarves moving towards Arenland, but if they do, that is where the Colonies will make a stand. The fleet is off the coast of Viletri. They keep their distance as they are wary of the storm. The storm has been quiet since the siege at Viletri. In my personal opinion, darlin', we will see Dwarves at our walls again soon."

DeeDee sat up, then got off the bed and draped a soft cotton robe over her shoulders.

"If you want a starting point, talk to the Fallen. Render is deep with them, and the Cultists don't talk much outside their circle. If you want to deal with them, go in hard. They have no respect for softness. Those living at his residence are your best hope."

DeeDee was ready with questions of her own.

"What is happening North of the Icesleepers? What have you been doing for the last twenty years, Jaal? Sweetie, tell me about Mannace. You have his ship, so you must have at least seen him."

Jaal stood from the bed to get dressed. DeeDee moved over to him and pushed him back down. He was going to get up again when he felt her hand around his balls, threatening but also promising. It took away his strength to resist.

"Don't think you are leaving until I have something interesting from you. I expect you have plenty to tell!"

Jaal respected that he must provide information in return for the information given. So, he answered the three questions, giving the details he knew would interest her. When Deedee asked more questions, he put a finger to her lips.

"Enough, once I have found Render, if I can, I will return before I travel North."

He finished dressing, kissed her passionately, then departed.

FEK

Jaal went to Render's Viletri residence as suggested, where two women and a handful of slaves ran the household. The women were cultists, one bald and both heavily tattooed. Neither were beautiful, although they both possessed a wild charisma. Jaal had a penchant for bad girls, and as they made small talk, he flirted with them. They told him little of relevance, but he understood which one possessed the dominant character. There was a single door to the chamber they were in, which Jaal shut. The girls seemed none the wiser to his intent, and they were both surprised when he used his speed to throw the bald one backwards and push her violently against the wall. He drew his knife and put a gash across her face before holding the knife to her neck.

"Where is Render?"

The bitch spat at him, so he kneed her hard in the guts. Jaal let her collapse to the floor, and he stomped down at her head, causing the woman at first to cry out, then moan as she struggled to stay conscious. Jaal intercepted the other cultist as she dashed for the door. He pressed her firmly against the wall, too, and with his knife resting on her cheek, Jaal repeated his question. When she hesitated, the Dark Elf let the knife tip work its way up to her eye so that she could see the metal almost touching the pupil.

"We don't know where the Master is. So we wait for his return."

Jaal tensed to thrust the knife, and the desperate woman responded.

"Fek is missing too."

She knew she shouldn't have said it. It was a betrayal to speak of the demons to one outside the cult. She was weak. If others found out, the price paid would be much worse than an eye. Jaal tightened the grip on her arm.

"Where do I find Fek?"

The Cultist surprised Jaal.

"Kill her first."

The woman on the floor wanted to talk, but it came out as a gurgle as she choked. Then, unceremoniously, Jaal used the knife to slit the bald cultist's throat. Blood quickly pooled on the floor, running down the grooves in the tiles. Jaal looked back at the other woman. He was confident that she would be more forthcoming now.

A day later, the *Gull* was moving Northwest over the lands of The Fallen. Even in the darkness of the storm, Jaal could see units of Dwarves moving about the landscape below. There seemed to be thousands of them, and now he understood why the Fallen fled or were hiding. He didn't expect that the flying *Gull* would go unnoticed by the Dwarves, but he hoped that the speed of the ship would hamper any pursuit from the ground. Jaal searched for the landmarks that the woman described, and it soon led him to a barren landscape where there was a narrow ravine between two low hills. Although there was a darkness to the chasm that may have hidden its contents if Jaal were on the ground, it was not hard to discover Render's secluded tower from this high vantage. The navigator carefully lowered the ship into the crack in the earth so that the rear deck drew in line with a balcony at the spire's upper reaches.

Jaal was wary of the Fallen and harboured no desire to fight demons. Already, he sensed being watched. Jaal gave Casteel a nod, keeping his blade sheathed, then stepped onto the balcony. There was a movement in the shadows, and he remembered DeeDee's words; to show a strong hand.

"I am Jaal. Companion of the Master. You will show me the same respect that you show him."

Alone he opened the door to the tower, entering. It was a far larger building than he expected. The rooms in the tower contained the type of junk Render might find helpful but held no interest for him. At the base of the structure, there were living quarters for a small garrison, lived in but vacant now. Below the ground was, by all appearances, a temple, including a small arena. Exploring even deeper, Jaal discovered catacombs, not extensive but challenging to move through and with a stink of death. As he progressed, the Dark Elf never lost the sense of being watched and scrutinised.

Render lay in the nest. It was not a nest of twigs and leaves. Instead, about the Sorcerer were carcasses and limbs. Some were old and stinking, some new. Render was playing with a face that he held in his hands. The skin was still bloody, and he was fascinated by the long beard. It had rings of gold platted into it. He liked the feel of the

153

round metal. When Render heard somebody entering the room, he pulled himself up to look. With effort, the Sorcerer dragged his legs to be in a position where he could see. His eyes adjusted enough to the dark that Render watched a shape come forward. It seemed to speak, but he didn't understand. The figure reached down and pulled him up. He couldn't much resist or help. It was the most he could do to keep hold of the face with the smooth rings.

Jaal heard fighting as he climbed the tower stairs. Render was a dead weight over his shoulder, but he still drew his sword into his other hand and summoned his reserves to run the last few steps and charge out onto the balcony. On the deck of the *Gull,* Dwarves engaged with the Blood Legion. Jaal could see more Dwarves jumping down to the ship from the edge of the ravine above. As soon as Jaal crossed to the stern, he placed Render on the deck, calling the captain to depart. Jaal sensed shapes moving about him, and he caught glimpses of skin and weapons. A solid form bumped him aside, and he momentarily saw the outline of a demon; Fek.

Fek materialised behind two Dwarves. He was taller than they were, and he reached over them to put his arms about their necks. While he looked gaunt, his strength was substantial, and he squeezed until he heard bones break and the bodies go limp. He was more cautious when other Dwarves faced him with shields raised, but now cultists were also revealing themselves and stabbing or grappling with the enemy.

All of a sudden, they were in the sky over Viletri. Jaal

hadn't expected to jump locations in the way they did, but it was a welcome shock.

The stranded Dwarves battled hard, but the Blood Legion and cultists outnumbered them. It still took time to overcome the last fighters. When the combat ended, Rey came to Jaal. He held a limp Dwarf in his big mitt.

"When this one wakes up, we can ask it questions."

"Good idea, strip it down and hang it over the side by its feet. Did we take many casualties?"

Another legionnaire, Jesso, approached. The man possessed mad eyes and a permanent grin. He was always the joker, but like the others, he transformed into a soldier when it was time to go to work.

"We gave much better than we got. We should get down to the healers before we lose more."

Jaal watched as the wounded lying on the deck received treatment from their comrades. Some were in a dire state.

"Make it so."

The Dwarf that hung over the side started to call out in its strange language. Rey laughed. So much for his plan to interrogate it. He looked over to Jaal and pointed his knife at the rope.

"No, leave it there. It will stop yelling soon enough."

Some Blood Legion took a wager on how long the unfortunate Dwarf would last. A few baited it and laughed when it responded. Casteel shook her head disapprovingly, but she smiled at some of the banter. It was only three days, and already, Jaal was leading the legion astray.

A THRONE IS NOT A CHAIR

EaJa-KulAmani, revered BruEkNa of the Dwarves, marched in the front rank of the Dwarven host. By her command, three armies came together here at Rotherdan to deliver the decisive blow of the campaign. EaJa-KulAmani drew the humans into the fight, knowing they would not forsake their capital.

As it was during the conflicts of the time of legends, the storm-sky was alive with the power of the Core, and its magic licked the battlefield like a dragon's tongue, causing great carnage and terror. Behind the Dwarven infantry, the boom of mortars joined the cacophony of thunder in a great discord that broke both the enemy's walls and spirit.

The KinRa-KluerKinBar insisted that she remain under the mountain, too important a figurehead to risk in the chaos of war. But a throne is not a chair; it is a purpose. The BruEkNa is not a figurehead; she is the executioner. The KinRa were wrong to think that their methods might be more vital than the old ways. As always, wars would not be won from a chair but on the field and with blade in hand. EaJa-KulAmani yelled "BraYel Ank Novik", and the call was taken up by those around her and spread so that the armies of the Dwarves took power from the chant as they marched forward.

The enemy was not without resolve and ingenuity. In the outer city, they used the buildings and barricades to break the Dwarves' line and force them into smaller skirmishes. In response, the Dwarves were patient and systematic.

Where they needed to, they took their time to overcome defences, and they regrouped to push their line slowly forward. The mortars caused devastation all that time, so when the Dwarves came to the city wall, large sections of it were in ruins. The fiercest fighting was at the breaches. Here, ballista and massed archers fired down from walls and towers while heavily armoured defenders met the determined Dwarven attack in kind.

In places, the magic of the KinRa clashed spectacularly with human magic, but the mortal wizardry could not withstand the limitless power of The Core. The human wizards and their arcane champions did not have the unwavering, absolute certainty of purpose as the KinRa. They could not stop the storm from battering their walls and decimating their troops, and when they faced the possibility of death themselves, the mages were quick to run.

The relentless Dwarves pushed back the defenders from the city walls, securing and clearing the rubble, so that their forces moved freely through the gaps. Once in the city proper, fighting fragmented into smaller battles, scrapping over blockaded streets, or fortified buildings. Human soldiers set traps or used fire canisters to slow the Dwarves and wound them. Some groups employed lanterns to blind the Dwarves. Other bands of determined defenders took a high toll on the attackers with heavy crossbows, mainly when they could get behind them to bypass their shields. Again though, the Dwarves were systematic and relentless. They adapted quickly to counter any new attacks and were ruthless in their slaughter. Rotherdan would fall, just like the other cities they vanquished.

The BruEkNa was already considering her next move. Roundhome was in ruins, and across Galandar, her armies and smaller bands of Dwarves secured strategic targets, burning and purging. Hundreds of thousands of displaced civilians hurried toward territories not yet under siege, although most fled to the Rift, where they waited to cross into Veldaan or the Young Kingdoms. EaJa-KulAmani expected the Rift would be the next battleground. Even if outnumbered and outclassed, humans would rally to protect their people so that they might escape into the North.

A BASTION OF LIGHT

For now, the Dwarves did not return to the Tundra of the Horse Clans or venture further East. With the respite from conflict, Prince Malakai rallied the Clans, sending them to aid the defences in Galandar and protect the roads leading to the Rift. The young General divided his horde into six armies, each roughly one-hundred thousand horse. They all had the same orders; to harass the larger forces of Dwarves, engage with smaller bands, and disrupt communications and supplies. After discussions with the Galandar General, Callos Reylor, Malakai also tasked two armies to target mortars and cannons that often travelled behind the main forces. All the clan commanders understood, by instruction and experience, not to commit to combat where the Dwarven wizards controled the storm.

The clansmen were at their best harassing the enemy and using shock tactics where they encountered troops they outnumbered. The cavalries' raids soon slowed the Dwarven advance and forced them to consolidate into larger groups. Moreover, it gave the desperate Roundmen and Galandarians the time they needed to cross the Rift into the Veldaan.

While the Horse Clans employed their tactics, so too did the BruEkNa. Believing the timing to be correct, she commenced the fortification of the lands taken. At strategic locations across the landscape, significant earthworks commenced. Soldiers transformed into engineers, excavating the first holes for what would eventually be a vast network of garrison bunkers and tunnels. Where Galandar bordered the rift, engineers destroyed bridges. Finally, at the site where both sides of the split touched, the KinRa gathered to summon an icy blizzard of such ferocity that it would make the location inaccessible to all.

In the following days, the nation of Cavalere offered little resistance to the Dwarves, and in the face of overwhelming odds, the Cavals, and what remained of their armies, crossed the rift into the Young Kingdoms. The Holy States were a more challenging target, and when the Dwarven storm roiled above the Capital city of Imazaran, light broke through the cloud so that the city and its vast surrounds bathed in the sun's warm glow. Defiant, Imazaran became a new rallying point for the Southerners. Straggling soldiers from Galandar and Roundhome regrouped there, and the Horse Clans, too, shifted their base camp to this rare place of light and refuge, away from the storm and rampaging enemy.

Imazaran was the only major bastion remaining of the Great Southern Alliance south of the Rift. Once the Dwarves focused their attention east, they easily defeated Remman, Gaidon, Thunderhome, Vostov, and Eck. The population of the Havens fled to sea, while in Mongier, the people dispersed and hid amongst the hills, fighting from shadow. The inhospitable Demonswar mountains became another refuge for the Wain and their wagons, plus small bands of survivors from all nations. The Demonswar was blessed with inherent magic, old magic, that also kept the Dwarven storm at bay.

EaJa-KulAmani, triumphant BruEkNa of the Dwarves,

was satisfied that the cleansing was complete. The storm extended as far as the Core would allow, and on the ground, the Dwarves reclaimed as much land as they might realistically hold. It was time to consolidate and fortify. Then, her people would return to the earth and comfort of the darkness.

EaJa-KulAmani now appreciated the danger of cavalry; how their mobility and variety of weaponry allowed them to fight a different kind of war - one where they dictated the battleground and tactics. The Grey Dwarf, Logthar, warned her of this, and he even proposed solutions. Amongst other knowledge shared, the mortars and cannons were his design, and it was time to reconsider some of his other proposals. EaJa-KulAmani gave GarRamMon, her Mastersmith, instructions, and she summoned Logthar. While it might be too late to influence this campaign, she was determined to learn and better prepare for further conflict.

Malakai sat amongst the Clansmen and their horses - which were always close to hand if needed. A vast camp stretched out in all directions. He was waiting for scouts to return with information so that he could decide their next move. The Dwarven generals were wiser in their tactics, and it appeared that the conflict in the south might be drawing to its conclusion. Looking up, Malakai saw the same dark clouds that always filled the skies, but something was different. Holding out his hand, a snowflake landed on the palm, quickly melting. Other snowflakes soon swirled about him on the light breeze. Malakai sighed. He instinctively saw the cunning of his enemy's plan.

THE AGHAN

Within the Veldaan was a small province referred to as The Aghan. None who entered the region returned. Amnicles investigated it and confirmed that its border, marked out with white stone cairns, was protected by magic, though the enchantments were beyond Amnicles talent to decipher. Mannace ordered a stone man sent into the Aghan, but as the tales warned, the animation did not return. He sent a squad of Brula to scout the territory from high above, but even they were lost. Now Mannace stood at the edge of the region with his Rangers and a Colossus. He ordered the indestructible Colossus forward, but the creature turned to him, then it walked away.

Mannace felt the anger building within him, though he could do nothing to compel the Colossus to obey his order. Instead, he let out a frustrated "aargh!". He hated having this mystery on his doorstep.

Unexpectedly, when Mannace also turned to leave, a figure manifested nearby. It was a trick Render used many times, so he was wary but unfazed. The figure was a dark-haired young man with beautiful features, likely in his early twenties. Looking stern, he waved his hand toward the Colossus.

"This creature. Why does it walk upon the earth?"

The Colossus turned to face the young man. Mannace sensed tension and was cautious with his words.

"It protects these lands, as do we."

"It is from an Age past, with no place here. Who would be so reckless as to set this creature free?"

"I am Mannace of the True Men, Governor of the Eastern Colonies. Who am I addressing?"

The young man smiled. It was not in any way a friendly smile. He paced about and looked more closely at the Colossus and the Rangers. Finally, he came to stand before Mannace, too close for Mannace's liking, and he examined the Governor's features.

"I, too, am from an age past. And like this creature, it would be best to leave me be. It is a time for the mortal races, for Men. Savour your time, do not open the way for the past to also be your future."

The figure disappeared, but it reappeared a little further away a moment later. The young man seemed annoyed.

"We were enemies, this creature and me. I put this enemy in a place where he should have stayed. I put him there so that the mortal races might have hope - a chance to have their time in the light. I will not raise my hand again. Your choices, your hand, will decide your fate!"

With that said, the young man disappeared and did not return. Mannace looked up at the Colossus, who stared blankly back.

The Aghan proved an interesting distraction - another piece in the puzzle revealed. Once returned to base camp, Mannace was immediately back to the role of General. Reports from Brula scouts revealed new enemy movements just north of Veldaan, and Mannace sent orders for the army at Angorok to intercept the invaders. In support, the flying fleet hurried to reinforce them.

The most significant threat to his forces was from the

horsemen of the Rhyde. Over the last decade, they were mostly dormant. Recently, however, large numbers of their troops forayed into the Veldaan, attacking civilian migrants and refugees fleeing from the south. Millions of refugees from Roundhome, Galandar, and the territories of the Horse Clans claimed the empty cities and farms of the Veldaan as their own. It presented an easy target for raiders, and the protection of the people was an ongoing challenge for Mannace and his commanders. It helped that many Galandar and Roundhome troops were re-joining the defence. What he needed most was the warriors of the Horse Clans to return North, to bolster his cavalry.

Mannace was uncertain how best to deploy the Rhalec and their towers. For now, they protected the base camp on the Palainth, the entrance to the Capital of Angorok, and the vital road in-between.

The loss of the Southern Sarang was a necessary sacrifice. Mannace could not fight on every front with reduced forces. Now the Elves reported a massing of northern troops near the Sarang Capital. From experience, Mannace anticipated he had about thirty to forty days to prepare before this Northern force appeared at the edge of the Veldaan. He wasn't sure he could hold off a major offensive, at least not without forsaking all other defences.

He required different strategies.

Part 4:

The Sleeper

THE DRAGU

Athose, Roanna, and Vilera passed beyond the highlands of Markhon. Travelling through Amon Murn, they found it to be a beautiful landscape. It was lightly wooded, and through the open canopy, they caught glimpses of steep, snow-capped hills set against a bright blue sky. They planned to move directly east, but the terrain slowly turned them south along a forest track. The deviation brought a chilling transformation to their surroundings.

Roanna was first to sense a corruption of the woodland. Soon after, Athose and Vilera observed blackness on tree trunks and disease scarring the leaves. Then, as they continued, there was total absence of noise: chirping birds, insects, or even the rustle of leaves to ease the haunting stillness. But that was only a prelude to the dead landscape that followed, where rotting vegetation clung desperately to the smallest vestiges of life. The increasing struggle for survival was palpable so that Roanna became anxious and nauseous. It didn't help that a soft wind started from the east, swirling the dust, and carrying the stench of rot and decay.

After ascending to the top of a sharp rise, the trio faced a craggy and desolate valley. Manmade, it had the look of a quarry, carved out of a rocky landscape, and angled into the steep hills along its eastern edge. The siblings watched teams of people dig and cart dirt or stones along roads headed further south. There were deep pits from which orange steam leaked, dissipating quickly into the air and likely to be the source of the forest's corruption. It stank, and for Roanna, who was already unwell, she stepped away from the others to vomit. To Athose, who frequently lived with the Mad King, there was a familiarity to the scene. The people were slaves, some chained and others free to move about unchecked. Small shelters were scattered amongst the rubble, shaded with heavy covers, and guarded by slave soldiers. Although he could not see into the tents, Athose was confident that there would be Molemen lurking there – everything he saw showed their hand at play. The young Elf walked and slid down the sheer valley side without hesitation. His descent immediately drew the attention of slave soldiers, that ran to intercept him.

Roanna cursed. She and Vilera stepped back from the tip of the rise to remain unseen. Their brother was always rash, seldom considering the possibility of a poor outcome or seeking the counsel of others.

However, because Athose marched confidently towards the closest shelter, the slave soldiers fell in beside him rather than stopping and interrogating him. Then, because he was escorted, the Moleman sheltering under the tent treated Athose as an ally rather than a threat. Athose was around Molemen enough to know how they greeted one another.

"Na vesche ta-semae Dragu-las el-efor tusom-atay. I am Athose of the Wengo. I have come east to seek the Sleeper."

The Moleman came closer and sniffed the air. Athose was used to having his scent scrutinised. He knew that amongst other things, the Molemen could sense fear and deception, but he carried neither of these. There were chairs, so Athose sat in one. He drank deeply from a cup of water brought to him by a Slave.

Under the shelter, Athose could see that the Moleman was brewing a concoction. There were five large cauldrons, of which two held orange crystals. In one vat, where the Moleman added other substances, a light orange mist swirled about, and every so often, the rocks would split. Finally, it made a loud bang, with fragments ricocheting about the metal pot. The Moleman checked the cauldrons, sniffing and adding more ingredients. After a timo, he sat and was provided with water by the slave, which he sipped rapidly.

Four slaves stood outside of the tent, idle. The Moleman directed them to their next tasks, except for one he ushered inside the shelter. Then, after looking over the cauldrons again, the Moleman turned to Athose, giving him another precautionary sniff.

"You speak old tongue - no more Dragu-las. Now we Dragu. This dig-fetch, take you to Imbor. Send-return. Atay-tusom."

The Moleman seemed agitated at being distracted from his business, turning abruptly to go back to its work. It huffed and sniffed before calming enough to pour a black liquid into a cauldron at the back of the shelter. There was a gurgling noise from the pot, resulting in a foul stench that filled the air. From the distressed reaction of the Moleman, it was not the expected result. The creature was frantically adding other ingredients to bring the concoction back into balance. Athose decided it was time to depart, commanding the slave to take him to Imbor.

Leaving the Moleman, they followed a well-worn trail through the rubble before joining a road headed east and back into the dead forest.

Other slaves travelled the road, and occasionally a covered wagon or cart carrying stone would clatter past. The woodland returned to life the further Athose moved away from the valley. Then, when the corruption was well behind him and night fell, he stopped to camp. Roanna and Vilera re-joined him.

"You're such a shit, little brother. You will be the end of us."

Athose ignored the complaint. He was glad to have made it apparent that he was his own master. He would follow his mind and no other.

"We have a new friend. This man is Dig-fetch."

Dig-fetch maintained a blank look. He seemed more like furniture than a person. It was probable that he was conditioned and possibly even born into slavery. Roanna considered slavery abhorrent. She ensured that their guide, who was emaciated, drank and ate.

After discussing their options, the siblings decided to stay on the road they travelled. So far, nobody challenged them, so it seemed plausible that they might pass for a northern envoy.

IMBOR

The journey to Imbor took them eight days, during which the siblings travelled through three large towns that were crossroads leading to cities or places of importance. They seemed to be at the heart of Amon Murn, following a route through a central highland flanked to the north and south by more populated lowland provinces. The road was busy with merchants, civilians, and soldiers going about their business. Most watched them with fascination, particularly Vilera's spider form, but nobody challenged them. The siblings were similarly surprised by the variety of races that made up the population of Amon Murn. There were tall men with pale skin that wore colourful robes and hats that made them seem even loftier. Some dark-skinned men and women rode on horses and always seemed to hurry. One large group of travellers they passed had pale skin but black hair and were heavily bearded. The majority of people that shared the road were much like men of the Eastern Colonies, perhaps a little taller and broader at the chin and shoulder.

Twice they passed giants on the road, wisely standing aside to let them pass, and once Dragu led a large troop of chained slaves. It seemed that everybody made way for the Dragu, and by the reaction of other travellers who dipped their heads to avoid eye contact, the creatures held an elevated status.

Much of the land the siblings passed through was cultivated or cleared for farms. It remained cold, but the skies were clear and bright, making for pleasant walking.

Imbor was a temple city set against a steep hill with religious buildings commanding the slopes. Residences and businesses spread out in the damp shadow below. It felt primeval; perhaps its foundation was laid by the servants of the ancients themselves. To the people of Amon Murn, it was an important and sacred holy site.

The three siblings were not the first to travel here to seek the sleeper. Pilgrims of many nationalities moved about Imbor's streets and gave offerings at the multitude of shrines. As envoys, as the trio claimed to be, they stayed as guests of the Priesthood in the lower dormitories while they waited for an audience with the High Satar. Both Roanna and Vilera felt uneasy, sensing power in the city's old stones and more profound energies within the hill. They could believe that the sleeper lay within.

Athose, though, was unconvinced. After hearing so much about the might of Amon Murn and Sleeper prophecy, Imbor did not meet his expectations. He imagined finding the Sleeper would be much more complicated. So, as he always did, the young Elf ignored the rules and chased his intuition. While the others waited to be summoned by the High Satar, Athose searched for the leader. It seemed evident to him that the most important man in the city would live above all others, and he was not wrong to head to the top of the hill. As he climbed the many steps, Athose received odd looks from priests as they sat in front of their temples or went about their rituals. Temple law forbade those not ordained to climb the hill. It caused the priests to wonder, "What makes this young man with the blonde hair and pointed ears so special that he might ascend?"

At the top of the hill was a vast temple with gigantic stone blocks for its walls and a canopy of silver leaves for its roof. On entering the building through a gap in the stonework, Athose was amazed to see the trunks of eight gigantic trees, large enough to rival those at the Hand of Fengal. Their upper branches fanned out to form a natural ceiling, through which there were flickers of sunlight. In a city so bleak, he hadn't imagined seeing something so beautiful. The floor of the building was a garden with paths and shrines, and near the entrance was a large block of dark stone. It was roughly hewn with moss around its base. Athose imagined dark priests placing a sacrifice upon the slab, with other priests gathering to plunge their knives into the hapless victim. With his minds fantasy running rampant, Athose was startled when a hand came to rest on his shoulder.

An old priest in plain robes smiled at his reaction. Athose recovered his composure quickly.

"Are you the High Satar?"

"I am, boy."

"This temple - it is surprising. I didn't expect anything so magnificent. It is almost enough to make me think that the sleeper might indeed be here. But he isn't."

"Hah, could a boy be bolder! Where is the sleeper if he is not here?"

Athose perceived an intuition in his gut, and his mind leapt ahead of itself. He tried to stop the words coming out of his mouth, but they leaked through his lips as a whisper.

"You don't know!"

If Athose's revelation provoked the High Satar, he did not show it. On the contrary, the man reminded Athose of the Mad King. He even possessed the same plain face and wise eyes. It put Athose at ease, but it also made him wary of underestimating this priest.

"Nothing is that simple, boy. You know, boy, I have been the High Satar for more than two thousand years. Millions of pilgrims have passed through Imbor to pay homage to the Sleeper during that time. But *you* are the first to break tradition and climb the hill."

The High Satar smiled, but his eyes were malevolent. A chill ran up Athose's spine.

"Explain to me why you are here. But beware that this is no time for games. The penalty for climbing the hill is death by stone."

Athose knew he must collect his thoughts, pull together the pieces of information he had gathered and present a reasoned perspective. It seemed so obvious once all the details shifted into place. Then, he was able to speak confidently.

"I have been sent here to tell you that the bell will awaken the Sleeper."

"Who sent you here, boy?"

Athose doubted that the High Satar would know of the Mad King - at least not by his title.

"A man much the same as yourself."

"Why did he send this message?"

"Because he wants the sleeper brought to the bell. Brought to the Wengo. To the city of Colossus."

That revelation, at least momentarily, appeared to give the High Satar some angst. Then a look of resolve replaced the holy man's frown. It was his turn now to put the pieces together.

"Boy, I will have further questions. You will remain in the city."

Again, Athose's mouth was quicker than his sense, "I will not. I will go where I please."

"You would defy me?"

"I would be true to myself."

The High Satar was surprised by the answer. There was something unique about the boy that stayed his executioner's hand. This boy was more than a messenger. He was one to watch.

"Go, boy. Be quick before I change my mind."

THE SLEEPING NATION

Vilera would not leave Imbor without uncovering the dark magic within the hill. While the chill sensation gave Roanna a sense of dread, it was a lure to Vilera that she felt compelled to pursue. Nevertheless, her investigation was something best done alone. Besides, why should her brother be the only one to have his fun?

At night, under cover of darkness and a veil of shadow magic, Vilera moved about the city unseen. With most of the priests gone to rest, one temple on the lower hill was still guarded, with fire pits set to light its courtyard and entrance. Clambering lightly across the temple roof, Vilera appeared at the archway behind the armed priests and slipped quietly through the tall arch and onto the hall ceiling beyond. There was no trouble moving quickly along the rough stonework, and at the far end of the room, Vilera lowered herself on a thin web to the tiled floor. A broad stairway led down to a poorly lit basement chamber, empty of trappings. From there, a single broad passageway steered deeper into the hillside. Proceeding with caution, Vilera encountered doors, nooks, and rooms off to the side, but mostly the corridor was a straight line leading deeper into the hill. Eventually, the passage widened further, and a glow of red light guided her to a massive cave at its end. The cave was roughly circular and carved into a dome. Much of the floor formed a bottomless pit that emanated a red, fiery glow. There were no other exits.

As she made her way up the ceiling of the dome, Vilera marvelled at the carving covering the rock surface.

Amongst the chiselled shapes and runes were tiny warriors with creatures attacking them, overwhelming them. From the high point of the ceiling, Vilera could see directly into the pit. Partway down, a red, glowing smoke swirled about, obscuring the walls but still leaving a hole at its centre: a bottomless void, possibly a portal to another place, or even the entrance to another world. Being so close to the magic within the hill, Vilera no longer connected to it. Instead, it repulsed her, and as she examined the pit with her arcane perception, she could see dark shapes and eyes staring back. Famished, the beasts craved to taste her body and blood. Vilera fought back mounting terror, ending her magic, focusing back on the mortal world. Closing her eyes momentarily to seek comfort in the darkness, Vilera took a deep breath before opening them again. The pit and the swirling red mist were still there, but the watchers were gone, and her calmness returned. Vilera headed back to confide what she had found to the others.

It was a mounting need within Athose to know where the Sleeper slumbered. The Mad King, the Bell, Mannace, the Sleeper, Amon Murn - it was a puzzle that would frustrate him until the final pieces were in place. Yet, when he looked about him, it amazed Athose how people were so content to go about their everyday business when important and climatic events were in play. Even the pilgrims and emissaries who visited the High Satar were ignorant, going through the motions and waiting for others to act. Athose was determined not to be a spectator.

The young companions uncovered no leads as to where the Sleeper might be, and they were on their own in a hostile country they did not know. The only advantage they possessed was the truth. Armed with that truth and the intent to flush out the Sleeper, and against the advice of both sisters, Athose shared with those who would listen, everything he understood about the Mad King and the bell so that it was soon the fiery topic debated between emissaries, pilgrims, and the clergy. Many pilgrims immediately insisted the priests fetch the bell to Imbor, while others demanded the sleeper be rushed to the bell. Some were sceptical of the story, but when people desperately wanted answers and action, the sceptics were a dwindling few.

The High Satar was suddenly under siege. After his conversation with the boy, he made subtle inquiries and hastily pulled together a plan. Now the boy was forcing his hand, and he needed to act quickly before the situation got beyond his control. So, priests, armed with the truth of the bell, were dispatched to the cities of Armon Murn and remote temples. It was a call for the Sleeper to emerge, ignite the prophecies, and for Amon Murn to rise.

It became unsafe for the young companions to remain at Imbor. Priests and others wanted to know more about the Mad King and the Bell. At first, the power of the truth was their ally, but its detail would put them in grave danger and reveal their association with the South.

After learning something of these foreign lands, Athose desperately wanted to travel north to the capital of Regnorak. He heard that there was an arena there and games like those he enjoyed. Reputedly, the city was so large that it took three days to cross from the eastern to western gates. It was home to giants as well as men. Athose pitched the idea to his sisters, who agreed that it was time to depart.

However, guided by her wisdom, Roanna decided on a different course. While Roanna supported Athose, she realised they had gone too far. She never considered that people would be so fanatic and was surprised at the pace at which events were unfolding. When they packed their things to leave the city, Roanna used her magic to open the ways, and without warning her companions, she transported them back to a place of familiarity, back to the Fogmir and well away from the drama at Amon Murn. Athose was incensed. He felt betrayed.

"You have no right to decide for us that we were finished in Amon Murn."

"You have done enough, brother. You have been the Mad King's agent, and we have helped you execute his plans. Together we have awoken the Sleeper. There are great consequences to that action. We must warn the Elves. They will tell the alliance of the South."

"The Sleeper is not woken. They don't even know where he is. He might not even exist!"

"Do you not see it, brother. The sleeping nation, Amon Murn, is roused. Prophecy is unfolding."

A WAR OF TERROR

The armies of the North gathered near Katandul, the capital city of Sarang. The combined forces elected a Marshal, an intelligent though cruel man named Domas Tanquinon of Koln, who now rode through the camps on his chariot to take stock of the Northern host. The nations arrived in strength; the proud Men of May, the Islani with their chariots and wagons, the dour soldiers of the Sompher Gris, the legions of Yan, Orc hordes from the pits of Granash, Tubul's swordsmen, the Markhon, the strange Mago, the Sarville with their beasts, Ekos who brought their women and children to war, plus those of the Veldaan that fled east from their homeland and now resided in Islan.

Domas' personal army, the stalwart Sarangese, were close. But, sadly, the giants of Rockhome, who suffered so many casualties when the Veldaan was lost, were absent except for the few giants that were mercenary contingents of other armies. Domas dispatched messengers to the Wengo and other nations of the west, but he did not know if they heeded the call.

The Dwarves laid waste to the Southerner's homelands to the south, breaking them and pushing survivors into the North. There would be no better time than now to deliver a final, decisive blow. It would bring an end to the countless generations of conflict. Domas would do it without Amon Murn, Churlamen, and the other nations to the east; let them sleep and let history pass them by.

Domas ordered his driver to slow the chariot. Around

him, soldiers pointed skyward. Enemy flying ships appeared above the horizon, perhaps as many as fifty craft. It frustrated Domas that the enemy commanded the skies. Unless they came close enough for archers to be effective, the Northern forces could do little. He lacked the magic and technology to counter such a threat.

Soon after sighting the ships, a mounted scout came charging through the crowd, seeking out Domas to relay a message of an attack; the enemy Colossi were engaging with the Islani and Markhon. Domas once witnessed one of the Colossi in battle, so he knew the terror and destruction they caused. But, again, although the Colossi were very few, he possessed no apparent means to defeat them. Was the enemy's plan to harass and delay him?

The flying ships came in low. As they did so, enemy Brula lifted from decks into the sky. With darts and bombs, they mercilessly attacked targets on the ground. The ships themselves drew close enough to come under fire from Northern archers, but the arrows and bolts were ineffective against the ship's metal hulls. When the Southerners found their targets, hatches opened on the side of the craft, and cannons fired into the camps, creating chaos. Too late, Domas realised they were attacking the command tents and leaders. He could see a ship come low over the field in his direction. With the banners on his chariot, Damas might as well have been waving a torch to get their attention. He commanded the driver to turn the chariot, making a hasty path for Katandul. The capital city was in the distance, and Domas hoped to keep ahead of his pursuer.

When Domas drew closer to his destination, the capital was under siege. Two colossi tore apart the city wall and eastern gatehouse. The creatures threw chunks of rubble at the hapless defenders who could do little against the immense creatures. After assessing his options, Domas diverted towards a farm with several large buildings. As he passed by some of his regiments including a unit of Sarangese cavalry, the troops rallied to him. Together they arrived at the facilities and dismounted, running inside. Domas handed his cloak and helmet to one of the horsemen. The man knew the intent, and he put the gear on, giving his cloak and soldiers cap to Domas. Other troops were hurrying to their aid and helping to prepare a hasty defence. Archers took up positions to keep the Brula from getting too close.

With a crack of timbers, the pursuing flying ship crashed into the first of the farm buildings, toppling it. The hatches on the ship's side opened, and cannons let loose a volley that tore apart other structures. Desperate, Domas ordered those about him to run, joining them as they scurried for their lives. The metal hull of the ship passed directly above, then past him. He could see the shadow of it catching up with the man who wore his clothes. There was a loud grinding of metal and then a thunderous hiss as steam erupted from vents on the metal ships underbelly. Away from the full impact of the blast, Domas turned his head and ducked just in time to save his face from the scolding water. He screamed as the skin on his arms and neck blistered under the intense heat. After scuttling away, he looked up to see the enemy vessel already moving on. Domas, the Marshal of the North, yelled at troops nearby to pour water on his burns. He was angry and humiliated. The bastards would pay.

Back from the action, Mannace stood with his captain and the navigator as they observed the scene from a shielded window beneath the flagship's prow. The enemy numbers were endless, and their camps spread over the plain and into the distance. The attack of the ships could not hope to defeat the Northerners, but it would disrupt them. Moreover, if they successfully targeted their leadership, it would cause confusion and panic.

Mannace planned for the flying ships to retreat to base when evening came but return as soon as they were re-supplied, and the navigators rested. Some navigators could travel instantaneously between locations, including Mamohan, who stood near him now. Mamohan was born of the Keshik and was a seer amongst the tribesmen. They respected his ability to predict the weather and omens. He was in his middle years, with black hair and beard. He liked to talk, and even when he was quiet, his lips would mouth what he was thinking.

Mannace ordered the captain to take the ship higher, well out of archer range, where they could view the scene below from the ship's main deck. From this clear vantage, Mannace watched the flying ships target the tents of the enemy leadership. Already, as the enemy caught on to what they were doing, the desperate leaders took steps to make their positions less obvious.

Suddenly, creatures covered one of the ships below, insect-like in their movements and perhaps the size of a horse. They were leaping onto the boat and scuttling about it. Then, a great puff of steam engulfed the vessel, clearing away the pests.

Elsewhere, the Colossi were devastating and relentless. Mannace watched them rampaging amongst the mass of enemy on the plain and at the edge of Katandul. They would need no rest at night, permitting the Northerners no slumber. Mannace wondered what he might do if he were the enemy general. It made him laugh, which amused the captain and navigator. As general of the Southern forces, Mannace felt no need to explain himself, but he took a moment to gloat.

"Those poor bastards. They have numbers beyond counting, but they have nothing that can touch what we have thrown at them. I do not envy their predicament. Captain, take us back to the Palainth."

BLOOD ON THE RYDE

Gathered on the grass plains of the Ryde were all the Ryde horsemen and a large host of displaced Veldaanians. Joining them were units from the coastal nations of Kampatan, Churos, Anglan, Ulo, and Greshnak. There were even patriots from the Wengo, although that nation turned its back on the old ways.

Overall, it was a great host of Orcs, Goblins, and Men. Even the Asari resurfaced to join the Veldaan troops, sensing that a final triumph over the South was imminent. The potent Asari and their apprentices were fewer, having been hunted by the demons they summoned during the infamous siege of Angorok, but who Render set free.

The gathered force was confident and cocky, expecting that west of Veldaan, an even larger Northern host was ready to strike. They were already in a celebratory mood.

Mannace risked everything in taking the attack to this Northern contingent, and he depended on the flying ships and Colossi to keep the other Northerners out of play. His plan also relied on the Dwarves not attacking across the rift or against the Holy Lands. Finally, Mannace's tactics required the Rhalec and militia to defend the occupied Veldaan territory. The lives of a great many civilians depended on him getting this right.

When considering his strategy, Mannace was mainly concerned that the Asari's magic, unchecked, would ruin his plans. Amnicles, foremost of his Battle Wizards, joined him on his ship to make final preparations. Meanwhile,

Brula scouts and messengers were constantly landing and taking off from the boat's deck. Mannace employed a staff of clerks and advisors to handle the communications and keep his maps up to date with troop movements. When he was free of their attention, Amnicles approached him.

"General, we have placed enchantments on your vessel, but it may still be vulnerable. I suggest keeping well back from the front lines when the fighting starts. The Asari will be formidable, and they will target the flagship if they have the chance."

"What of the Galandar and Roundhome wizards. Where do they stand?"

"They are soon to arrive with the other reinforcements from the Holy Lands. I will talk to them tonight. It is likely they will play cat and mouse with the Asari – the first to find the other will have the advantage."

Mannace relaxed. It seemed the Asari would be kept in check, and he could feel some of the tension release from his neck and shoulders.

"Good, we will be their match then."

"Possibly, General. It is rare for magicians to face off across the field of battle. They are too invested in staying alive. The Asari may not know that Render is absent. They may think he is lurking, and therefore, they may be cautious."

"Thanks to the War God that his priests are not such cowards. If priests and soldiers were like wizards, they would wield pens from behind their desks and wage war with messages. Is Render the only wizard to keep his balls?"

"The Sorcerer picks his battles, General. Are we not all playing the same game? Today, we fight because we have drawn the enemy out and outnumber them. If they knew our ruse, they would retreat to fight when the odds are in their favour. None of us can afford to throw our lives away. We must all have a longer-term strategy and be ready when the final battle comes."

Mannace was attempting to lighten the mood, but Amnicles did not share his sense of humour as Jaal and Render did. He missed the presence of his friends. So instead, the leader sighed and ended the conversation.

"Very true, Amnicles. May you serve the War God well."

Amnicles was going to move away, but he hesitated, to raise a final point.

"I am a Battle Wizard, General, trained for war like all Hindassians. Most of the wizards that fight for the South come from a variety of occupations. They are forced to war, by circumstances and patriotism, like other militia. They give their all into the conflict."

It was a sobering thought for Mannace and he nodded at Amnicles to acknowledge the distinction before the wizard departed.

Mannace commanded enough Brula at the Ryde to own

the skies. The winged men brought information about the enemy's position and helped Mannace keep his opponent ignorant of his troop movements. On the ground, the Alani hunted and eliminated enemy patrols.

Overnight, allied garrisons from the Holy Lands completed the long journey to his camp. Cavalere and Roundhome were also marching to the south, joined by the Horseclans. Finally, Mannace's trap was set, and with all the allied armies moving into place, he delivered final instructions to the generals.

The Ryde was another immense and flat battlefield with just a scattering of trees and gentle rises. It suited both sides. Mannace did not want to scare his enemy away, so at first, he presented only the army they were expecting. It was a long front line with the elite Remman in the centre, flanked by battalions from the Colonies, and with infantry and cavalry from Galandar on the flanks. Mannace watched his troops take their positions from his vantage in the sky. Out of sight of the enemy and beginning their flanking manoeuvres were the majority of Galandar forces and their allies, plus mounted units from the Holy Lands. He could not see the Roundmen, Clansmen, and cavalries from Cavalere, but the Brula assured him that they were hurrying to attack the enemy from behind.

The Northerners deployed a mix of cavalry and infantry at their centre, with goblins swarming to their right and more human and Orc infantry from the western coast to the left. Stationed behind the main force were the Veldaan infantry and Chokra. Mannace expected their job was to relieve the line when needed. However, he could see that most horsemen from the Ryde were also behind the main force, undoubtedly intending to swoop around the flanks. There were some giants amongst the enemy ranks and units of creatures that might be Belg. Monstrous champions fronted the attack, and Mannace recognised a Manticore by its red mane and scorpion tail. Mostly the battleground was too far away to see the true nature of what his soldiers faced. As veterans of many campaigns, the enemy appeared organised and formidable. Still, the rival hoard was a third the size of his combined forces once he brought all elements into play. Mannace drew a deep breath and exhaled to relax. He was achieving his ambition of commanding the Southern host.

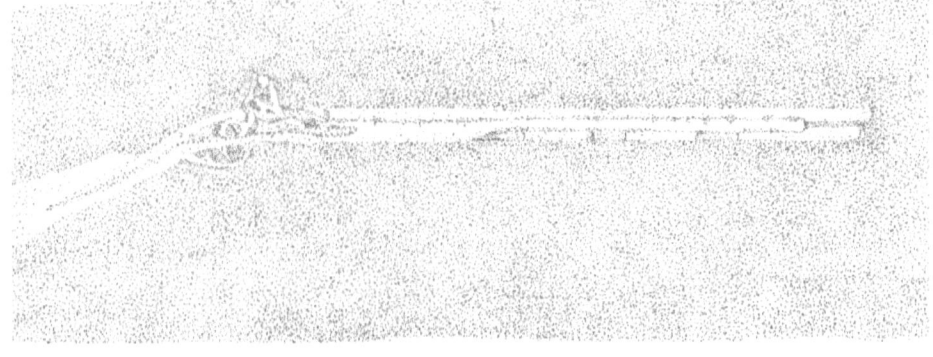

Both sides marched steadily towards each other. Goblins scuttled ahead, and their skirmishers were the first to be in bow range, releasing their arrows at the Southern lines. The Southern forces stopped their advance, holding their positions while the colonial musket men and longbowmen from Roundhome aimed. The Goblins died in their hundreds, and the survivors sent scampering. Veldaanian Chokra moved up through the enemy ranks, and as they did in previous battles, they formed a wall with their tower shields to protect the Northerners as they advanced into musket range. Soon bullets and arrows filled the air. As the armies drew closer, javelins also arced between the forces, most clanging into shields.

Amnicles was wrong about the Asari. They came to fight, and swirling fireballs exploded amongst the Southern units. Magic blasts targeted the revealed mages in retaliation, and wizard combat commenced in earnest. From what Mannace witnessed from his high vantage, the Asari were right to be confident, quickly taking the upper hand.

When the armies were close, warriors charged across the gap. While some yelled and ran at their enemy, others, like the musket men, took up their firing formations. Mannace was apprehensive as the neat battle lines lost their shape and the melee commenced. Frustratingly, he was too far away to know who claimed the better of the first contact.

As predicted, the Horsemen of the Ryde manoeuvred around the flanks, sooner than Mannace hoped. In response, he hurried orders to the commander of the reserves to counter the horsemen. Fortunately, he could see the Roundmen, Clan riders, and knights from Cavalere appear in the distance behind the enemy position as planned. More than ever, Mannace needed his fighters to keep their order and composure until the other parts of his force arrived. However, the enemy Asari acted freely, invoking all hells down on the elite Remman and musket men. Mannace gripped the deck railings tightly, willing his men to hold fast against the devastating onslaught, wishing he was amongst them to do more. His warrior spirit sensed his soldiers' hopelessness and pain.

The Ryde cavalry created mayhem. With the speed of their mounts, many avoided the reserves Mannace sent. Instead, they attacked vulnerable troops from the side and rear. While veteran units adjusted to fighting on two fronts, less experienced troops panicked, making their situation dire. It was fortuitous that Mannace's second wave of soldiers was arriving, at first the heavy cavalry of the Holy Lands, and soon after, the legions of Galandar came at a run. The fresh troops trapped the Ryde horsemen. But so too, Mannace's front-line units were surrounded, some of whom became overwhelmed. The fighting was desperate and chaotic.

The Clansmen and Cavalere knights quickly covered the distance to attack the enemies' backs. Mannace watched them charge across the plains and into the frantic melee. Where the enemy reserves were prepared, the Clansmen were cautious, using their bows while waiting for the Roundmen infantry to catch up. Where the riders and knights surprised the enemy, they used shock tactics to smash their foes.

Like any prey caught in a trap, the Northerners fought with tremendous tenacity, and for a brief time, it looked like they might overcome the odds. In places, the front line was a brawl with no shape and barely enough room to swing a blade. By the time the Roundmen entered the fray, it was a ragged and disorderly scrap. Their arrival, however, cemented the enemies' fate; they were outnumbered, outclassed, and had no means for a retreat.

Now that his victory seemed imminent, Mannace willed the Northerners to give up, concerned that casualties were mounting. Finally, exhausted, the enemy lifted their weapons and hands in surrender. In the chaos, it seemed to Mannace to take an Age before the combat ceased, and enemy contingents stood silently, seeking terms.

With the other Northern army on the Sarang still a threat, Mannace could ill afford to waste time on a lengthy negotiation. He and the Southern Generals met on the field with their Northern counterparts. The Northerners did not have somebody to speak for them all, so each nation chose its negotiator. They gathered in a semi-circle facing Mannace while the leader explained to them his terms.

"I ask for peace with Kampatan, Churos, Anglan, Ulo, Greshnak, The Ryde, and those that were once Veldaan. I desire peace with the Asari. To have peace and to save your armies, you must put aside your oath of allegiance to the North and, in its place, take a new oath that your nations and the South will live side-by-side. You must welcome the South into your territories, and we will welcome the return of the Veldaan to their lands."

Everybody went quiet, hanging on Mannace's words.

"What I require, to prove commitment to an alliance, is that one in five soldiers here today will become part of the Southern Alliance armies. One of the Asari must join our ranks. Know that we will leave from here to conquer the armies of the North that threaten the eastern Veldaan."

Eerily, crickets native to the Ryde started their chirping. It bemused many of those standing or sitting about. Mannace ignored the racket, staring at the faces of the enemy commanders - knowing they must despise him, and they would hate the alliance he was forcing upon them. But, to avoid more bloodshed, which he could poorly afford, he placed his trust that these enemies were honourable.

"These are my terms, and you will find that I am a better friend than an enemy. The alternative is that we finish what we have started - I cannot leave an enemy at my back as I move further North. You have until sunset to give me your answer."

It was an odd scene to have the soldiers remain in place while their commanders considered Mannace's terms. Most warriors stood, some sat, and a few, exhausted, slept. The wounded that received treatment lay in a torturous state, while some died. The battlefield dead remained where they fell, already attracting flies. It was disheartening and ghoulish to be sitting amongst the corpses. The Southern and Northern forces talked, although Mannace could not imagine what they might be discussing. He could hear laughter from one group. If it came to it, picking up the combat where they left off would not be as simple as charging into the enemy from a distance.

Mannace need not have worried. The Northerners, facing utter defeat, agreed to Mannace's arrangements. Warriors swore new oaths, and Mannace wasted no time taking his one in five new allies and incorporating them into the

Southern ranks. It seemed to him to be the right balance – there were enough new troops to make a difference and set in stone their new allies' commitment. However, if they were to have a change of heart, he could deal with the number of potential turncoats. Aides assigned the new troops to the generals.

A great pyre of the dead was set ablaze, and the War Priests fuelled the inferno with divine blessings, gifting the souls to the War God to mark the epic conquest.

THE POWER OF THE SLEEPER

News reached Mannace that the Sleeper was awake. Although the reports contained no evidence, the rumours changed everything. Amongst his new allies, it immediately divided loyalties between those that honoured the North and those that respected the new oaths. Closer to the Rift, uprisings among the conquered Young Kingdoms needed a heavy hand from the Cavalere soldiers and Roundmen to keep the disorder in check.

The revelation of the Sleeper awakening gave renewed confidence to the enemy camped on the Sarang, east of Veldaan. Battered by the Colossi and Flying Ships, the host dispersed, withdrawing to their home territories to await instructions and the anticipated reinforcements from the east.

The Northern armies' retreat was a poor omen for Dumas and the Sarangese. While the troops of Cavalere and the Horse Clans remained to keep the peace in the newly occupied territories, Mannace sent his other forces into the Sarang, quickly conquering the besieged Katundul and expanding into surrounding lands. It was Mannace's second time occupying the embattled region, and he showed the populace no mercy.

For all his victories, Mannace could not quell the panic that the rising of Amon Murn caused amongst his own populace. Millions of southern civilians that took refuge in Veldaan, having already fled from one homeland, began a new migration with the Rhalec's help.

The mysterious Rhalec portal that remained on the Palainth was an escape to the home of the Crocodile

People within the great Fogmir. The dense forest became a staging ground for relocation to the thriving cities of the Eastern Colonies. Many native Veldaanese also opted to migrate rather than rebuild their homes in the troubled North. It was a boon for the Eastern Colonies, whose cities swelled with the influx of skilled workers. But, on the other hand, the exodus was another closing chapter for the nations of Galandar, Roundhome, and Cavalere. Their leaders were giving up hope of a return to their southern homelands.

In the South, where the Dwarven storm still engulfed the land, the snow fell and settled for long enough that the landscape was white and desolate. Abandoned cities rose out of the snow like old ruins, and it was impossible to imagine that their inhabitants would ever return to resettle. The Dwarves were thorough in their dark work. Now the creatures were hidden away in their bunkers and mountains, satisfied that the weather would complete what they started. Only the Holy Lands and the Demonswar provided sanctuary south of the rift. At the southern tip of the continent, Viletri stood defiant, coated in snow but adapting to life in its new climate.

EaJa-KulAmani, revered BruEkNa of the Dwarves, judged the cleansing of the land to be complete. In her wisdom, she decreed that the final bastions of resistance at Viletri and the Holy Lands were not worth the cost it would take to dislodge them. Many of the Dwarves were free to return to their usual occupations. Logthar answered the BruEkNa's summons and arranged for the knowledge of the Grey Dwarves to be passed onto the Mastersmith and his chief craftsmen so that he was given new devices and techniques to consider. It was much for the Mastersmith to ponder as Logthar's concepts defied tradition. EaJa-KulAmani told the Mastersmith that Logthar's ways were the ways of the future. Some of the Grey Dwarves, the Clockmakers and TechSmith's, joined his extensive workforce.

Logthar proved himself loyal in battle. He had gifted his kin the design for the mortars and cannons. His daring enterprise saved one of the KinRa. The Grey Dwarf brought concepts that would ready the Dwarves for the new Age. Now Logthar brought a request to the BruEkNa. He had earned the right to ask such a question.

"BruEkNa, I ask your permission to return to the lands of the humans. So much of what I have learned has been in partnership with men. They will continue to invent new things. It is in their nature to change and evolve. If they accept me back into their clan, I will learn what they learn."

EaJa-KulAmani acknowledged Logthar's dedication. His loyalty was unquestionable, and she believed he would continue to put kin above all other things.

"Logthar, always remember that the Core is our strength. Loyalty to kin our armour. I release you from my service, Logthar. Choose your passage wisely and return to us when you are ready."

"I will forever be in your service, BruEkNa."

RENDER'S BANE

Render stretched his body, sighing as he relaxed. He felt calm and unburdened. Despite the snow in the gardens and ice around the eaves, the Viletri Temple of Healing abounded with life, colour, and fragrance. The patient Fesadi Menders brought Render back from a very black place. Their ongoing labour was to replace the darkness infecting his mind with light. He could now do most simple things without help, and he sensed the latent magical power within himself, although he could not access it. Nevertheless, Render harboured no desire to return to wizardry.

The Sorcerer's missing digit was growing back, but it was not a finger of flesh. Instead, it was like many tiny vines interwoven and alive. The vines tapped into his nerves and bloodstream, becoming part of him. The repair resembled a finger, as nimble as its predecessor, restoring Render's function completely. Althea Kane came in the morning to visit him as she often did. She seemed to enjoy the new Render, and everything he said, she found funny. Today Jaal came with her. Render raised his hand slowly and gave Jaal a soft wave, smiling to see a familiar face. Jaal scowled at the healer.

"What have those Fesadi freaks done to him. Have they replaced his brain with apples? All hells woman, he behaves like a child."

Althea laughed. Even when she tried to stop, she giggled each time Render smiled, which he did often and for no apparent reason.

"Are they putting apples in your head too? For hell's sake, woman, tell me he will improve."

When Althea shrugged, it pushed Jaal's patience too far. He struck out at Render and knocked the Wizard to the ground. As Render struggled to get to his feet, Jaal grabbed him by the arms and threw him against a wall. Loose clay clattered to the cobbles.

"Wake up, you brainless ball-bag."

Jaal pushed Render hard again, breaking away more of the clay. Then, picking a rock up from the garden, he looked to give the wizard a whack to the side of his head. Before he could complete his strike, Jaal's vision went black as he received an invisible blow to his chest and face, throwing him back so that he rolled across the ground and impacted with the opposite wall. There was blood on his lip and a trickle coming from his nose. It took him some time to regain his wits and stand. Looking across at Render, the dumb smile was gone, but he was still not of his senses. Althea interceded.

"Enough, Jaal, some things take time. Healing the mind is not simple or quick. Render is not in control. He could kill you."

"The Fesadi are changing him. He does not need curing of his darkness, Althea. He needs the shadow to be who he is. I should not have brought him here; the cult would not have meddled like this. Perhaps they will have a better way."

"Jaal, you would put his fate in the hands of the Fallen. I suggest a little more light will do him no harm. He was not in balance."

"He made his choices Althea. It does not serve him to be balanced. He is a sorcerer, a man to be feared, a harbinger of death, a weapon of war." When Althea seemed unconvinced, Jaal fell back on an adage, "Even the most pious of champions casts a shadow, Althea. He was your friend too."

Althea took a deep breath. Perhaps she shouldn't be laughing at the Sorcerer, although even thinking about his behaviour made her want to giggle again. Nevertheless, she empathised with Jaal and would help him as best she could.

"You got him to use magic. That is a step forward. You were right to think that stress can bring back memories. The Fesadi have done good work, but if you want faster results, it will help to stimulate him in a way he will respond. We could put him on a horse or take him on a boat. Perhaps for a Sorcerer, stronger methods are needed. If he were to return to the front, to be close to the battle, it might remind him of who he is. You know him best, Jaal."

Jaal was suddenly distracted. An object that he assumed was a plant pruned to the shape of a man moved across the garden. Althea laughed at his surprise.

"That is Hestor. He is meditating."

"Hells, Althea! You are a strange woman. But look, I have an idea. I will be back soon."

It took longer than he anticipated as the guards at

Mannace's home were reluctant to let him enter. It required authority from Althea's husband, the garrison commander Titus Kane, before the sentries allowed Jaal inside. After finding what he needed, Jaal returned to the temple. He passed Render the device. Render snatched up the thing of metal wires, and he felt the smoothness of the Golden bracelet looped through it.

"That will do it. We called it Render's Bane. If you want real laughs, watch him with that thing!"

A day later, Render exited the temple. He seemed in a mood, stomping up the street and throwing aside the mess of mangled wires he scrunched in his hand. He was hungry too. Now that he had regained his senses, they told him he needed meat - how the bloody Fesadi survived on fruit and vegetables eluded him. After that, he was going to blow something up. And what was with all this fucking snow!

LAST OF THE ANCIENTS

Nordan took up residence in a fortress. It was in the hills near a forest. It provided no strategic value for Nordan, who vanquished it more out of habit than need. There was no challenge in such a feat, giving him no sense of satisfaction. The previous residents were either dead or fled. He intended to keep some of them, but they talked so fast he could not understand them, so instead, he let his wyverns feast. Now the fantastic beasts slept wherever they could find a space to curl up. The Colossi stood stationary on the fortress grounds or amongst the trees nearby.

Nordan stood unmoving in the fortress' great hall and, after a time, closed his eyes. Emptying his mind of thoughts, Nordan melded to the rock about him. While his physical form remained motionless, his being was now traversing the land, expanding through darkness and light. He was stopped eventually by the oceans. They were a void he could not cross. Nordan absorbed data as he travelled, and once he returned to his body, he allowed himself time to process through it. When he eventually opened his eyes, Nordan considered what he now knew; of all the ancients, only Eya had come. Churgwarthos and Grengal left their mark further east, but perhaps that was just a residue of the past. He also sensed lesser beings that were familiar; the Ra-Anu, other Colossi, the Kraken, the Servants – but they were all of minor consequence. The Enemy was here as well. Good, that was how it should be. There was another, masked so he could not tell its nature other than those about it called it *The Sleeper*. Nordan decided that when the wyverns were rested, he would send them out so that he would have eyes upon this changed land.

Eya was aware of Nordan's arrival, and she sensed that he was searching. Was he merely inquisitive, or was he hunting? She did not want Nordan as an enemy, but she would not back down from a fight if he were to seek her out. For Nordan, she would need to make special preparations and devise a trap worthy of the invincible ancient.

Concerningly, Vilera disappeared from Eya's vision, and with that, Athose and Roanna too. Perhaps the boy, Athose, had now played his part, although he was quite the Mad King's student, so Eya expected that drama would continue to follow him. All three young ones were worthy of observation.

Unaware of Eya's search, Vilera and Roanna both enjoyed the distant tranquillity of the Fogmir. It was good to relax after their adventure in Amon Murn. However, Athose no longer felt comfortable amongst the forest and other Elves. He continued to be sullen and was mad at his sister, who betrayed him with her magic. They were in the territory cared for by Roanna's mentor, Ulalyyarwherri, and it was not hard for Roanna to search out the Druid. While many Druids travelled to the distant Hand of Fengal, Ula was content to care for her Fogmir birth-home.

Roanna and Ula talked at length about the young Elf's time

with the Alani Elves, including what occurred at Amon Murn. Ula was wise about many things, but politics was not a skill or interest. She could not advise Roanna on how to deal with the unfolding events, but she could still guide her apprentice in simpler things.

"Roanna, you have many paths in front of you, and you must take care which of those you will follow. The further you travel one path, the fewer opportunities you will have to diverge down another. Eventually, the route that you choose will take you to your destination. If you know the destination you seek, it will aid you to choose the right path."

"Ula, why are you telling me this?"

"A good question, girl. I am telling you this because I can see in your stories that those about you would choose your path and destination for you. The Alani are guiding you down a path. Your brother, Athose, would lead you off the trail and into the wilderness. I am proud of you to have ended the mischief and returned here. It is the first step to choosing your rightful journey. Now, look up from your feet and see into the distance. Where is it that you are heading, girl? How are you going to get there?"

"Ula, what I want seems out of reach."

"Why?"

"Because I am only young. Because it is beyond what I can do."

"What is it that you want to do?"

"I want there to be peace between the Elves and the Spiderkin. I want to bring about that peace. Among the Druids and Wardens, others take the opposite view. They want the Spiderkin eradicated."

"And what about after that, when there is peace with the Spiderkin?"

"I want the Elves to be at peace with the Fen too."

"And what will it achieve, having peace with the Spiderkin and the Fen?"

"It will mean that there is no conflict in the forest at The Hand. That the races can work together like the Rhalec and the Elves here at the Fogmir."

"Why is that important?"

"It is respectful to the forest. The forest suffers when there is conflict; it will grow stronger with peace. It is shocking to see the damage already done. We must follow the way of Fengal. There must be balance and harmony."

"Is your current path taking you towards this destination of balance and harmony, Roanna?"

"No, Ula, it is not."

"Let yourself be powerful, Roanna. You have it in you. But, most of all, gift yourself the right to walk the path that will bring the harmony you seek."

A COMING OF AGE

There was not a particular age when a child became an adult among the Elves, but Roanna knew in herself that she was making that transition. So, before returning to the Hand of Fengal, she first called a congress with the Alani. In the meeting of minds, Roanna relayed to them her final report. She was blunt with the Alani elders that she would no longer serve as their eyes and ears.

Soon after, Roanna opened the ancient paths so that she, Vilera, and Athose, returned to the forest where their adventure started. Athose set out immediately for the mountains of the Wengo. Vilera planned to update the Spider Mother, but Roanna waylaid her.

"Sister, come with me to meet with the Druids. You can tell them about the demon portal."

Vilera looked at her sister as if she were mad.

"They will kill me as an enemy?"

"I will not allow it."

Roanna spoke with such confidence that Vilera trusted her word.

"Then I will come with you, sister."

As Roanna and Vilera entered the territory of the Wild Elves, both knew that Wardens were watching them from the trees. They stayed close to each other, so it was clear that the Spiderkin enjoyed the protection of the Black Druid. When they finally arrived at the tree city, there was animosity from the Druids that the Spiderkin had travelled so far into their domain – an unimaginable trespass only tolerated out of respect for Roanna's occupation. Roanna reminded the Elves that Vilera was present at the discovery of the Hand of Fengal, long before any of them ventured there. It did little to appease the prosecutors.

At Roanna's insistence, the Elves arranged a night-time conclave to discuss Amon Murn. Elves from the Hand sat on the ground or in the trees surrounding a glade. Included amongst them were other Druids. Roanna addressed the group, providing details of their journey into Amon Murn and the awakening of the sleeping nation. When Roanna gave an account of their time at Imbor, Vilera spoke of the demon gate. They both answered questions.

As the conference ended, a brown-skinned doe emerged from the trees, tiptoeing gently between those seated to stand in front of Roanna. It nestled its head into her abdomen, and she stroked the creature down its neck and brow. All those present could see that the doe carried the spirit of the Ra-Anu and its presence emboldened Roanna to speak her heart further. With her deep blue eyes, the Black Druid looked into the faces of those around her. She talked frankly of peace that might lead to unity, healing the forest, and honouring Fengal and the Ra-Anu by achieving balance and harmony. It was a speech that resonated with some but was unwelcomed by others. Finally, a male Elf, a Warden, came out from his standing place amongst the trees. He confronted Vilera.

"Your kin are a stain on the forest. You poison its roots from below the earth. There can be no lasting peace between us. The Spider-Mother murdered the Ra-Anu, but they are reborn, and when they are mighty, we shall purge the forest of your darkness."

One of the other wardens called down to his emboldened comrade from his perch, "Tooth and Claw". A few of the other Elves took up the call, but most remained silent. It was the right to challenge; they wanted to see the Elf and the Spiderkin fight.

Roanna moved to be in-between the Warden and Vilera. She started to speak, but the Ra-Anu nudged Vilera. It nestled at her side. The Ra-Anu was the spirit of the forest, and you did not need to be a Druid to understand its intent. That small action hushed the dissidents back to silence. All present looked at the Dark Druid in a new light. Roanna earned respect by travelling to Amon Murn and speaking her mind. It carried significant weight to have the Ra-Anu stand at her hip. Roanna captured the Elves ' attention in a society with no formal leadership aside from reverence for the Druids. Ula would be proud; it was a positive first step down her chosen path.

It was nine days before Athose arrived at the city of Colossus. The Colossi and the Orcs were glad to see their champion return. He felt energised to be back amongst the Wengo, which quickly evaporated his dark mood. Still, Athose was finished with Elves and with sisters.

If the Mad King was happy to see Athose, he did not show it. They sat at a table facing each other, and Athose relayed what happened on the visit to Amon Murn. An old human slave brought them water, and there was a bowl of apples already on the table. Athose picked one of the fruit and ate it as he talked. The Mad King found the chewing while talking impossible to tolerate. He put his hand across Athose's wrist so that the boy could not take another bite.

"Did the Sleeper awaken?"

Athose finished chewing the apple that was already in his mouth.

"I told you, the Sleeping Nation has awoken."

"They are not the same thing, boy."

"The High Satar commanded the Sleeper to emerge. I would have stayed to learn more, but Roanna brought us back."

The Mad King seemed happier with that answer. It appeared to flick his brain into a more positive frame.

"The city has missed you, Athose. I think that even the Colossi have been looking forward to your return."

BLACKBIRD

Six months after the brawl at Warehouse Three, soldiers still patrolled The Shades, and arrests were common. It was not bad; it brought stability to the district and gave the Twins time to consolidate their position. They used the wealth Saska gave them to grow their numbers and influence. Blackbird led the gang now. Her brother was a hollow shell, most of the life sucked out of him by the demon bitch. She left just enough essence for him to breathe and eat and shit. He was not like her many other victims buried about Dreban who were lucky enough to be properly dead.

Despite that, Blackbird saw the wisdom in the bitch's plan. The gang did not need to operate outside the law; brothels and drugs were not illegal enterprises. Ambitiously, Blackbird partnered with business owners and merchants, quickly finding that her reach could extend far beyond the Shades. With patience, she would have the associates she needed in Ostoik to the east and The Hemens to the north. The Hemens were much closer, with alchemists able to enhance the mind and bring about visions with their odd concoctions. Saska's earlier enterprise helped her to understand the value of such a commodity.

Strangely enough, the gang was like a private army, allowed to operate with relative freedom within the city. Blackbird learned that city officials and commanders could also be allies. Her new investments were well protected with a bit of coin wisely shared.

Because of Saska's powers over men, Blackbird hired female mercenaries for her protection. Six lived at her headquarters, including a Belg named Beck, who she kept close whenever she moved about the city. They were given orders to kill the demon on sight if she were bold enough to show herself. Until Blackbird knew the bitch was dead and her brother avenged, she would have little peace.

Blackbird needn't have worried. Every five days, a flying ship appeared above the city of Dreban and took its berth at the military docks. Agents of the Overlord checked in with Officials before searching the streets of Dreban. Unknown to Blackbird, they returned home with their prize on their last visit. Saska was restored to her old strength, though not wholly to her evolved self. There was a wildness about her, a bubbling fury in her eyes and demeanour. After boarding the flying ship under cover of night, the agents returned Saska to her residence at Antigoth. With her were her pets. The Gargoyles had found Saska soon after her disappearance and were her protectors. Her other guardian, Arta, never recovered from her wounds. Instead, the big bodyguard convalesced at the Dreban infirmary under the Governor's protection.

Governor Atrula D'Austini visited Arta whenever she could spare the time, to learn more about the Eastern Colonies or to ask specific questions. Arta had travelled widely with Fitius and Saska so that she could answer most of Atrula's queries. After several months, when Arta was fit to walk, she accompanied the Governor as she moved about the city. Atrula saw potential in the experienced bodyguard, and even in her poor state, she was still looming and formidable. Also, it was rare to find somebody as trustworthy amongst her people. Arta was loyal, observant, and discrete.

Following a communication from the High Priestess, Ahmeda, the impressive *Harmsway* took up a permanent berth at the Dreban docks. The War Priests operated a temple from the ship's main and second decks. Mercenaries, marines, and soldiers from the city garrison visited the temple, fascinated with the great vessel and its divine magic. Some, particularly young warriors, immediately connected with the doctrine and the priesthood. With the Governor's approval, it was not long before the priests trained their first Bracadian initiates.

In the Blue lands, beneath the Emperor's palace, Ahmeda established a second temple and barracks, already full of soldiers allocated to assist her. She showed them the doctrine and inspired them with demonstrations of the power of the War God. These soldiers would be Ahmeda's agents to spread the religion. Vitally, as promised, the Emperor proclaimed that Bracadia would embrace the War Gods doctrine, and the military dutifully honoured the Emperor's will.

At the Emperor's palace, of the hundreds of soldiers that Ahmeda tested, eight possessed the potential to join the priesthood. Because they were experienced with rifles rather than hammers and swords, Ahmeda invested more thought into their development. She hoped that her divine patron was ready to become a modern God.

Ahmeda's relationship with the Emperor moved to the bed-chamber. He continued to be affectionate, and they talked easily about all things. It was not a passionate affair, but it worked well for them both. As an immortal, the Emperor at last found somebody he measured to be his equal.

The Emperor considered Morgan Cain another immortal peer. He assigned the adventurer to be his envoy to the Northern Colonies, equipping him with the gifted flying ship and crew. Morgan was easy to respect and trust, sharing the Emperor's curiosity and sense of duty. He reminded the Emperor of the late Admiral Mangello D'Austini, who he once considered a close ally and loyal servant.

The Northern Colonies, also known as the Island States, were an endless expanse of shallow seas, with broad and deep trenches that divided groups of allied territories. Those states closest to Bracadia were civilised and industrious. However, some of the cultures Morgan encountered further afield were primitive and isolated. His first tour consisted of travelling between the islands to scrutinise the colonies and make his authority known. During inspections, Morgan witnessed a constant naval presence from the Bracadians who were policing their trade routes and enforcing an easy peace.

Supporting the Emperor's desire for greater unity and consolidation, Morgan took a lesson learned from his time with Mannace. He conceived the Island Colonial Divisions. It required men from each Island State to support the Emperor's expansive military plans. Morgan expected he would need help from the Bracadian military to design a uniform, train officers, and equip such a force. As the Emperor's envoy, he carried all the authority he needed.

THE NEW ALANI

Mannace could not prevent the uprising of warriors from amongst his new allies. The insurgents journeyed from the cities near the western coast to Northern rally points outside his controlled territories. Mannace's officers estimated half of the fighters in the region were moving across the Ryde into the highland north of Veldaan. Thankfully, just as many honoured the Ryde agreement, and those bonded to his armies remained loyal, for now. Perhaps he should have finished them properly when given the chance. What was most frustrating to Mannace, was knowing that he would have proven to them that the South made better allies with more time.

The Veldaanese departed the North in increasing numbers through the Rhalec Portal to lands free from war. After being at the forefront of the Rift War for so many generations, it seemed ironic that as the final campaign approached, it was they who lost the will to fight.

More families evicted from the South joined others escaping through the gateway. At the insistence of Rhalec officials, Mannace limited the flow of civilians travelling to the Fogmir, giving the Rhalec and Colonial navy time to transport them to locations where they could have a new beginning. As a result, many refugees found their fresh start in the vacant territory surrounding Karanthos and Lapthos. Soon, settlements were appearing on every speck of land south to Yanth and west to the Footsteps. Fishing villages popped up in bays along the coast, with every means needed to feed the swelling populace.

Fitius brought Mannace a gift from the Emperor; one hundred and fifty thousand rifles and the decree that they approached the Age of Empire and the Ascent of Man. It was a significant boost to the troops to know the Emperor acknowledged and supported them. Mannace distributed the new rifles amongst the Eastern Colonial Divisions. Because they did not have an endless supply of ammunition and the rifles sometimes jammed during training, the riflemen also kept their muskets. The advanced weapon's rate of fire was exceptional, and the bullets packed a powerful punch. Notably, the guns arrived aboard twelve new flying ships from Arenland.

Mannace reorganised the Southern forces into six armies. His generals thoughtfully allocated Troops and leaders, and now each force was training together. In reserve, civilians willingly practised with the militia. With the awakening of Amon Murn, nobody questioned the urgency and importance of the preparations.

Talks were held each day with the leaders of the Elven Congress. Their scouts tracked the progress of the Northerners in Amon Murn and its allied nations. Indications were that the gathering horde might number several times the allied host if combined with the warriors the South already faced. The same fearful news was delivered with dreaded gloom each day. Frustrated by the pessimism of those around him, Mannace wanted to understand better the makeup of troops he would face. He hoped that if they could measure the enemy's strengths and weaknesses, they might find ways to negate the disadvantage in troop numbers. The Elves launched ambush attacks to reveal more about the enemy. Such aggression would also show the enemy that they were vulnerable, even deep within their lands.

The Alani were masters of near-space, and they understood how to navigate the pathways. Other Elven nations could travel the ways, but mostly this was restricted to the paths that the Alani showed them. While, to other Elves, the travel through the pathways was instantaneous, the Alani moved about and existed in near-space as if they were parallel to the real world. With the aid of their spellweavers, the Alani slipped between worlds as needed. They could move whole armies or communities into near-space with the proper preparation. Near-space was not solely their domain; Render knew how to utilise near-space, some demons could exist in the parallel world, and it also contained rare denizens who were often monstrous and solitary.

The Alani divided into units of one thousand warriors, carrying ornate muskets, finely crafted to give them great distance and accuracy. With them travelled Wardens from the Fogmir and The Hand. Spellweavers and champions led from the front, plus, in some contingents, there was a scattering of Dark Elves. Jayne Azaryn was amongst them at Mannace's request to be the leader's eyes and ears. Jayne took up his bone rune-bow, a favoured weapon, in which he was highly adept.

An Alani champion named Ansal Orenly led Jayne's troop, although his troopers called him Sally. Sally was bold to the point of being reckless. The force had two spellweavers who were proficient at moving them about and keeping them safe. Jayne was impressed with the trooper's audacity, and today would be no different. The attack they planned was in the streets of the Amon Murn capital itself.

Inside the Eastern gate of Regnorak was a rallying point for the Northern army. Regular troops, including armoured giants, maintained a strong presence in the streets and garrisoned the gatehouse. Nobody expected an attack here, even with news of ambushes elsewhere in the region. Already by midday, more than two thousand recruits were gathered, answering the summons to war. Some came with weapons and armour, while others were armed only with enthusiasm. Spears and shields were distributed to those who needed them, while officers allocated men into units and organised them into formations. As they stood about in lines and talking amongst themselves, archers suddenly appeared, and bangs accompanied objects whizzing through the air. Many were dead before others understood what was going on. Wild Elves cleared a space for themselves and engaged in close combat with the stunned recruits.

Further back, where there was more room, Alani Elves aimed their muskets at the regular troops and giants, most of whom showed the good sense to scamper for cover. In a short time, the attackers caused devastation, and the paved courtyards and streets were running thick with the blood of dead and wounded. But then, as quickly as the Elves appeared – they were gone.

Jayne and one of the spellweavers remained behind. During the confusion of the ambush, they grabbed an enemy officer and dragged him into a nearby building.

Jayne commenced his interrogation while the Spellweaver secured their hideaway with his magic. With little time, Jayne put a knife into the Officers leg, twisting it. The man screamed, but thanks to the Spellweaver, only he and Jayne were witnesses to his agony.

"I will make this simple for you. I will ask you a question, and if you do not answer to my satisfaction, I will put this knife in you and twist it. If you answer my questions, you will live."

Jayne started with something simple that he knew the officer could answer.

"Who commands the Armies of Amon Murn?"

"Vestig Gozer."

"Good. How many men do you command?"

"Six hundred."

"How many are giants?"

"Six."

"Good. When will the Armies of Amon Murn travel east to attack the South?"

"When they are ready."

The man screamed again as Jayne dug the knife into the same leg and twisted. The Dark Elf did not give the officer time to recover his wits.

"When will the Armies of Amon Murn travel east to attack the South?"

"When The Sleeper arrives at the capital."

"And ..."

"He is expected to arrive soon."

"And ..."

"We will move east. I don't know more."

"Tell me something that will save your life."

The officer looked panicked, his eyes darting about as he tried to find something to satisfy Jayne. He appeared like he might lose his sanity and his bladder. Seeing they would get no more, Jayne gave the man a quick death, and the Spellweaver moved them to near-space, where they re-joined the other Elves.

It was now the Spellweaver's turn to be surprised. Turning and scanning the void, the mage sensed an invisible but powerful foe. Jayne and the other Elves could see the wizard's panic, but they were otherwise confused about what was happening. The Spellweavers opened a gate with urgency, drawing the troop through it to safety. They were back in the Veldaan, shaken but unharmed. The Spellweaver that accompanied Jayne addressed them.

"We were being examined. The presence was powerful and a traveller of the paths. It was cautious this time, but its intent was murderous. I would name it demon."

The other Spellweaver was frowning and nodding.

"I too sensed it and would name it beast. It desired to

devour us. All of us together in its great maw."

Jayne was dubious as he had not seen or felt anything, nor could anything be so immense. It seemed a drama and exaggeration. However, the Alani and Wild Elves took the spellweavers at their word, and they were reluctant to return to Amon Murn. Commander Sally ordered the troop to make camp and rest.

On hearing the Elves' report, it was one more thing for Mannace to manage. In response to the Elves' concerns, he sent a messenger to Viletri to summon Render. Demons were the Sorcerer's domain, and Render enjoyed solving problems. In this case, Mannace suspected Render would relish an opportunity to accomplish what the Elves could not. The General of Generals needed his friend back at his side.

ROCKHOME

North of Veldaan, in the highlands nestled amongst the mountains, were the settlements of the Giants. It was a rallying point for warriors awaiting the armies of Amon Murn to march. Mannace's Brula reported as many as two hundred thousand enemy soldiers encamped.

Thag was Chief in the region, and as such, he took command of the ragtag host. By his order, the Giants also made their preparations for war. They suffered terribly in the Veldaan defence, and even with two decades behind them, Thag could call upon only a quarter of the forces he raised in the past. The Giants of Rockhome learned from that conflict, and now his warriors carried massive wooden shields. Some had rocks in baskets on their backs that they could throw from a distance. Like the Chokra of the Veldaan, Giant warriors trained to fight as units and presented a shield wall that the enemy muskets and archers could not assail. Thag imagined the giants descending upon the enemy like an avalanche rolling off the mountain. Nothing would stand in their way. Moreover, it gave the chieftain a great sense of pride.

Thag's imagining was interrupted by a lone scout returning hurriedly to camp. The panting man brought warning of approaching enemies. It surprised Thag that only one of the many scouts watching the countryside came with such news, but perhaps that was a failing on his enemies' part to allow this one man to escape their net. Thag ordered the horns to sound, and in response, he heard other horns in the distance. As he moved about the camp, the big giant encouraged warriors in their preparations. The enemy would not be so dominant with their guns in this hilly terrain. As practised, the Northmen took positions behind prepared cover, and archers and rock throwers scurried to high points where they benefited from the best vantage. There were roughly a hundred giants at the camp, many of them forming a shield wall at the top of the valley from where they expected the attack to come. Already, warriors in the highest lookouts were yelling to others that enemy troops were in sight.

Southern riders with bows appeared in the valley and on ridges. The most advanced swooped close enough to release a volley at his warriors then scuttle away to safety. Thag laughed aloud when some of the horses stumbled and fell. It was naïve of the enemy to think him such an easy target. The beasts thrashed about with broken legs and wounds while their riders ducked for cover. The surprise of the traps was enough to keep other riders from being as bold, and it allowed Thag's archers a moment to find their mark and give a good account of themselves. Perhaps this was no more than a raid.

Soon after, however, long infantry lines came into view, cautiously advancing up the vale. The lookouts were indicating other enemies to their flank and rear. Then, in the sky, Brula and flying craft came into focus. That would be interesting; Thag chose this location because of the aerial threat. Almost immediately, he could see four great Rocs appear in the sky to the east in response to the invaders of their domain. The giant birds were still small on the horizon. Thag hoped that if they came in large numbers, it would be enough to drive off the Brula and give the ships trouble.

Thag perceived musket shots in the valley, and arrows arched through the air from both sides. Having learned there were traps, the enemy was testing the ground as they approached, both forces not charging until they were almost upon one another. Across the hills, units collided. The din was deafening as metal clashed and shouts of the fanatic mixed with the howls of those wounded. At the centre of the defence, the giants' shield wall was already under vicious assault by units of muskets and pikemen, supported by winged men who threw missiles and bombs.

Thag was large, even for a giant. He made a tower shield for himself, and now he put his arm through the strap, gripping it tightly. In his other hand, the Chieftain clasped a great maul. The two giants with him followed his lead. Thag raised his weapon to point at a heavy cavalry unit positioning themselves on a ridge. As the three giants charged the long distance, the cavalry responded with a canter down the slope that increased at the last moment to a gallop. Waiting until they were almost on him, Thag swung the massive shield to knock horses and riders aside, sending them sprawling and rolling. He stepped into the next rank and took the heavy weight of a charging horse on the shield, staggering backwards a step but then pushing forward so that the beast was upended and fell on its back, crushing its rider. As another horse galloped past, its rider aimed his spear at Thag's side, but the giant showed remarkable agility to angle his body away from the thrust. He countered with a swing of the maul, launching his assailant into the air, colliding with another horseman and taking them both down.

The giants with Thag likewise absorbed the cavalry charge, and now the three cohorts ran a path of destruction, stopping only when they achieved the top of the slope. Here at the ridge, they looked down on a unit of surprised musket men who stopped marching to turn and take aim. All three giants raised their tower shields and retreated under a hail of bullets before facing the regrouping horsemen. Thag and his companions attacked, leaping onto their foe.

Above the battlefield, the Rocs disappeared momentarily from the distant sky but reappeared overhead, diving at great speed. Where they fell upon the Brula, they knocked them out of the sky and caught others in powerful claws, crushing them before dropping them to the earth. The riflemen aboard the flying ships shot at the great birds, but they were fast and had tough hide. The cannons also fired when the birds crossed their path but failed to hit the fleeting targets. However, the noise of the guns and the danger of the cannons were enough to send the Rocs back into the clouds, where they circled and watched. Risking a glance skyward, Thag estimated more than a dozen of them now, with others rising from their nests on nearby peaks.

Bollo, son of Rollo and champion of Galandar, skirted the battlefield. He already blooded his axe, and from a distance, he watched the big giant fight, knowing he must test himself against that foe. His blood raced as he manoeuvred, passing by a unit of Galandar spearmen who he called to his side. Not waiting to check with their commander, the soldiers fell in behind the Half-Orc, and together they picked up their pace to a run. After a short ascent, they charged over a rise and down the slope beyond to join combat. Ahead of them, three giants were destroying the remnant of a cavalry unit. Two of the giants used massive shields to defend and attack. Next to them, the largest of the monsters put aside his protection. In its place, he held the body of a heavily armoured man by the legs and was using the corpse to bash the outclassed cavalry. In the other hand, the gargantuan warrior accomplished the same thing with a massive maul. Soldiers of different types from both sides fused with the combat, which lost any sense of shape. Everywhere there was killing and yelling.

The spearmen accompanying Bollo relieved the beleaguered horsemen, charging in-between them and joining combat with the giants and others. The Galandarians were a veteran unit, and as they charged, the three giants fell back so as not to be surrounded and overwhelmed. Then, sensing the time was right, Bollo, accompanied by six spearmen, sprinted at the largest of the giants, who readied to defend himself.

As strong as Bollo was, he knew that his advantage would be speed in this melee. He drew a sword from its sheath on his back so that he held his axe in one hand and sword in the other. Darting forward, he hoped that the big giant would take time to swing his weapons. But his opponent surprised him, and rather than swinging the maul, the giant thrust it forward. Bollo took the blow on his chest, somersaulting him backwards. It was the most the champion could do to keep a grip on his weapons and scramble to his feet. Now the dead body, wielded by the giant, caught him on the side. Bollo spun to deflect most of the impact, nimbly keeping his balance and squaring up with his foe.

At the same time, three spearmen thrust at the giant's torso, drawing blood with their stabs until the creature, with another swing of the body, sent the spears flying out of their hands. That presented Bollo with the opportunity he needed, ducking under the improvised weapon to strike at the giant's leg with his axe, chopping through leather pants and giving the creature a deep gash. As the giant stepped back, roaring in anger, the axe was ripped from Bollo's grasp. Instinctively, Bolo slashed upwards with his sword, but the attack bounced off armour. As Bollo took a moment to grab up another blade from the ground, the giant used that instant to throw the limp body in Bollo's direction. When Bollo ducked, the giant grabbed his maul in two hands, swinging it with all his massive strength in an uppercut at the Half-Orc. Had it hit, Bolo's skull would have been shattered and brains cast through the air, but he deftly leaned back just in time so that the wind of the metal head whistled past his face. In quick response, Bollo lurched forward and thrust with both blades so that while the giant was able to sidestep one, Bollo drew blood again with the other. The giant leader was bleeding heavily, and the mounting wounds made him stagger.

The two giants with shields bore stab wounds too, but they did not suffer as severely as the spearmen they bashed, whose survivors retreated from the fierce onslaught.

Gifted a brief reprieve, the giants withdrew to their leader, and one used his shield to block Bollo's relentless assault. The defence was so formidable that it seemed to Bollo as if he were fighting a moving palisade. Reluctantly, the champion backtracked and let more spearmen take up that challenge.

Bollo smashed his way around the giants, killing two enemy fighters and pushing others aside. Finally, he achieved a position where he could renew his assault from the flank. The giant Bolo ran at was unsurprised by the ruse, quickly turning to face the danger and swinging his shield. Bollo crouched, so that the shield rim passed over his head, close enough to wrench a patch of his hair. Then, as the giant loomed above him, Bollo thrust upwards with both swords. One blade caught on a leather belt and tumbled from his grasp, but the other sword slid neatly into his enemy's abdomen. Bollo twisted it before the giant's weight hit him, bowling him over. A massive foot stomped on the Half-Orcs face as the gargantuan fighter crashed past and tumbled to the ground clutching the fatal wound. Bollo, momentarily stunned, could feel his nose broken and possibly his jaw. Spearmen swarmed over the dying giant, while Bollo regained his wits and clambered to his feet.

The two other giants wisely retreated, standing in a creek with water to their knees, joined by fierce men and Orcs on the far bank. Across the hills, the circle of Southerners was closing in on the remaining Northern fighters, and soon they would have no option but to make a last stand.

Without warning, the giant chieftain was plucked from

the field. The leader screamed as the beast's talons pierced his shoulders, and he was lifted skyward. Thag was quickly high above the battlefield, so striking at the bird or twisting free would do him little good. Shots from one of the flying ships whizzed past, but the danger was soon left well behind.

The Roc dropped Thag as gently as possible on a grassy knoll. Another giant was standing there; Gurad the Shaman. Thag was bleeding down his shoulders and chest, so Gurad moved to help the leader remove his leather hauberk and tend to his wounds.

"Gurad, what have you done?"

"The battle is lost, Thag. It is not your time to die. We must get the tribes to safety; they will follow you. A hundred giants will die this day. There are thousands more who will die when the Southerners attack our homes. We have bled enough for the North. It will fall to Amon Murn to see the war to its end."

"I saw Filli fall, and Kerak will die too."

"It is an easy path for the dead, Thag. It is the living who carry the burden of sorrow and duty. I will take their place at your side until our people are safe and this war is ended."

THE MUSTER OF WAR AND MAGIC

It was a risk to take the war into Rockhome without the magic users and War Priests but cleaning out the northern rally point and territory meant fewer troops Mannace would face in the battles to come. Most warriors at the rally point were amongst those he fought and had beaten on the Ryde. There was no mercy for the oath-breakers, with prisoners escorted to the city of Colossus for transportation aboard the Ark to Tarash Gormoth.

Scouts reported that the Giants of Rockhome were withdrawing to the east, abandoning their settlements to avoid further conflict. Mannace let them go. If they stayed, then he would have dealt with them ruthlessly, so he was relieved to have one less bloody massacre staining his hands.

With the Ryde occupied and an armistice with the Veldaan, the way was open to the Wengo and Mad King. The Mad King did not speak for the Wengo, but they always looked for his wisdom. He said to them that the Southerners would bring the Wengo wealth. It was true; already, they were paying generously for access to their port. The Southerners were also showing interest in the arena and games.

For the Iron Jaw Orcs that no longer had a southern home to return to, the Wengo seemed familiar and welcoming. Mannace encouraged the association, allowing the Iron Jaw Battalions to camp close to that region. With the Elves of the Hand and Spiderkin also in proximity, the territory appeared secure. The Islani to the east of Veldaan would be his next target.

While Mannace continued his plans of conquest, the War Priests and the Wizards gathered at the Veldaan capital of Angorok. War Priest, Dekon Ruel, organised the meeting, calling it The Muster. The best ships and navigators were provided in support.

All the War Priests and their initiates were there. Only the High Priestess and the priests she took west to Bracadia were absent, not expected to return. So, as his first order of business, Dekon appointed himself High Priest in Ahmeda's absence. He also named twelve Deacons to be his council and to lead the priests in war. The Deacons all wore the God Armour and were devout champions.

Render attended. With the Sorcerer were the Fallen Summoners and the ghoulish demoness Ruu. It was certain that Fek and Gax were nearby. Render remained the patron of the Wizard's Conclave at Viletri, but he was no longer active in the society of the mages. It now fell to Amnicles to lead the Conclave and its magicians. All were present, even the newest students.

As the Muster called their first session to order, Dekon looked about the room. Most were represented; Alani spellweavers were standing tall and arrogant. The Galandar and Roundhome wizards with their underlings. Two Fogmir Druids. Althea Kane came for the Healers and Fesadi. It was the same for the Animators and Mage-Techs that only their senior Guildmasters were present. Four

Asari were there with their novices, curious to see what magic the Southerners offered. Dekon would have liked to see the Spider Mother attend, but at least two Spiderkin Weavers stood together at the rear of the room.

Dekon cordially welcomed the other Gods to the muster. The Iron Jaw Shamen with their Great Spirit. The Priests of the Holy Lands were the bringers of The Light. The Rhalec Priests with their many animal deities and the Prophet of Kampatan from the recently subsumed nations. The Prophet was unknown until he appeared at Angorok, so his abilities and motives were unclear.

Kakos Agamos was notably absent. Render suggested to Dekon that the Liche Lord was unlikely ever to leave Viletri. He was no longer sure that he could make him.

They all knew they were here because the final campaign was upon them. With the southern lands lost to the Dwarves and snow, the northern campaign was now a fight for survival for most. For those with old loyalties to the North, it seemed likely to Dekon that they were still considering which side they would take.

Dekon prepared his words carefully ahead of the muster. He was a fighter rather than a diplomat, and everything he knew of leadership was from watching Ahmeda and Mannace. He drew on the War God's grace to assure him. Now was a time for fighters.

"Blessings upon you."

Dekon gave the crowd a moment to feel the blessing wash over them. He saw it raise their shoulders, and some took a deep breath of it in. Even the priests of other religions welcomed the War God's gift.

"We muster here at Angorok because we begin the final campaign in a war that has spanned many generations. It is a campaign that will mark the end of an Age and a New Age of empire and ascent. We must win the northern campaign, and it will need the strength of those here to see it done. We represent darkness and light in this room, spell and prayer, death and life. We have the authority of magic, technology, and the Gods. And we will face the power of Amon Murn and their magic and their Gods. We are strongest in partnership to finally see this war done. Now is the time we must collaborate, put egos aside, give our full selves to this cause so that we will assert our victory and ensure our ascent."

There was a lot of murmurings and voices raised about the room. The Muster was not a crowd to cheer. Instead, they assessed Dekon's words, and they would take time to decide their minds. With such an abundance of chatter, Dekon could not decipher what any were saying, so he called the muster to order, and he invited those wishing to speak to join him on the podium. The first to do so was Antiel, Light Bearer for the Alani.

"I have glimpsed the new age and have seen the path to it. Across the path is a barrier that we must overcome: the Sleeper. The sleeping nation has arisen. It can be defeated if the Sleeper, its ancient king, its essence and soul, its slumbering demigod, does not rise to lead them. Light shows us the way."

After a period of uneasy quiet, the Prophet of Kampatan took the podium. He was a middle-aged man with a simple look about him. He dressed in an orange robe with an orange hat. He scratched behind his ear and cleared his throat before talking.

"I was not trained to be a prophet. Rather I started having dreams from a young age, and I soon learned that at least some of those dreams came to be true."

The room was silent. Many wanted to know what this prophet was about – whether he was nobody or somebody of importance.

"I predicted the coming of the man you call Mannace, your leader. I foretold that the Veldaan would be defeated. I knew that the army of Kampatan, alongside our allies, would be overcome on the Ryde. Nobody wanted to believe those things, but they were true. So now I tell you what you already know; that Amon Murn will rise and that there will be a great battle. However, this battle will not decide how one age ends and a new age begins. Others will decide; players in the game, active for as long as there has been conflict between North and South."

Antiel, standing beside the platform, stepped up again and interrupted the speaker. He was agitated.

"The Mad King. I have seen his darkness too upon the path. He is the chaos that clouds the outcome. Eliminate him!"

That got a mixed response from the room. Dekon put a hand on Antiel's shoulder to suggest that the Prophet be allowed to continue. Antiel pushed Dekon's hand away, and he "hummphed", looking down his nose at the High Priest. The room quietened, waiting to see where the sudden tension between the two Elves led.

Before they could act, the prophet raised his arms and held his hands together. Then as he moved his hands apart, an apparition appeared between them. It was like looking through a bird's eyes, perhaps from a tree looking down at a scene. The muster fell silent as they watched giants carry a great sarcophagus through a city gate. The giants placed the massive coffin onto a six-wheeled wagon that took up the width of the road, and a team of draft horses strained to move the cart forward. Lining the street were soldiers that fell in behind. Now, as the bird launched from its perch and climbed higher into the sky, they could see a military procession of armed men on the road and more gathering at the city gates. It was evident that they saw the sleeper and the march of armies from Regnorak. The Prophet closed his hands, and the room erupted into confusion as the muster discussed what they witnessed. After a time, Dekon called them to order, and he asked the Prophet the question on many lips.

"When? Is this a vision of the past, the present, or the future?"

The prophet shrugged. He knew that would not be enough, so he gave his best answer.

"From my experience of visions and what I feel in my gut. I would say that it is imminent."

"Who is the sleeper?"

Again, the Prophet shrugged, but a voice rose above the others from the floor. At first, it was hard to hear against the din, but once people realised it was one of the Asari, they stopped their chatter to listen.

"The Sleeper is from the time of Ancients. Defeated and entombed because he could not be killed. The priests of Amon Murn, the Eternal, are his protectors, and they wait patiently across generations for his restoration. They believe that Amon Murn will make slaves of all other nations under his leadership. They will own the world."

"And that is what you want? It is what the North desires?"

It was Dekon who asked the question. His tone demanded an answer.

"Amon Murn is the North. All other northern nations were born of it. It has always been the way."

Dekon scoffed, "It is no longer the way."

The room was quiet. The Asari took the opportunity to raise a topic of great concern to him.

"We, the Asari, are hunted by demons."

Render snickered and shook his head. Were they seriously about to ask for help? It cemented his opinion that they were weak. He climbed onto the podium.

"They are a problem of your own making."

"If you can remove the threat, we will be in your debt."

"What of your allegiance to the North. When the time comes to fight, which side will the Asari fight for, or will you be hiding in the hills."

"The Asari follow the Veldaan; we will see the fighting

done."

"Huh!"

"We had loyalty to Tyriah, not the Sleeper, not to Amon Murn. We are not in a hurry to be the puppets of the Ancients. Those days should stay in the past."

Dekon expected that managing such a large and wilful group would be challenging, but he often worked with initiates, so he knew how to focus them on the work at hand. He raised his arms in blessing and let the power of the War God wash over the crowd. The invisible force was invigorating, and it made them feel powerful. Those not used to it were suspicious, and some secretly put up their shields. Others who fought alongside the War Priests and understood their ways soaked it in.

"We will work as one. Those that can free the Asari of their demons go to the throne room. Those that want to learn more about the Sleeper and his minions go to the entrance hall. Those that remain here will prepare for the campaign. Forget what was important before today. Until Amon Murn is defeated, the work we do here is your priority. It is the priority of all those that you represent."

IN THE KITCHEN

Whenever he was free of other duties, Jayne Azaryn could be found in the kitchen supervising the evening meal for Mannace, his chief aides, and generals. Tonight, he managed to purchase a fat sow, so juicy pork would be on their plates. First, he seasoned the meat, and now that it was roasted, the smells were delicious. Helpers took vegetables out of the ovens and flavoured them with onion flakes, salt, and butter. A large pot of apple and berry sauce was on the simmer. Simple things cooked well.

Jayne was preparing the plating when a group of men entered the kitchen's back entrance. Armed with crossbows, they pointed their weapons at the cooks and put fingers to their lips to indicate they wanted silence. All, including Jayne, complied. Then, more men entered; some Veldaanese, but most were Islani. As he watched them, it made sense to Jayne that they would seek to chop the head off the snake. However, it was a mistake for them to pass through his kitchen. Jayne picked two long knives off the bench and launched himself at the closest crossbowmen. Two of the assassins fired hasty shots, but Jayne was adept enough to dodge the bolts, covering the distance to them quickly and stabbing them in the chest and throat.

Not wanting to lose the element of surprise, many of the cutthroats rushed toward the door to the dining room. Jayne, unable to prevent them, grabbed a stack of dirty pots and threw them, so they clattered across the floor. It was sure to get the attention of the diners. Jayne dodged another bolt. Two cooks that were not so deft lay dead on the floor, but the others were hiding behind their stations, throwing anything that came to hand. The sauce was a cruel missile, causing several assassins to scream curses as the boiling liquid splattered across their faces and chests.

Once amongst the attackers, Jayne was a whirlwind of death. He seemed untouchable even with his kitchen knives against swords, outclassing his opponents and killing with ease.

The Galandar general, Callos Reylor, appeared at the dining-room door, looking cautiously, then drawing his sword and joining the melee. Mannace and others came close behind. The Generals were all seasoned fighters, and they efficiently dealt with the remaining foe. However, it would have been a different outcome had Jayne not been amongst the staff.

Jayne was astute enough to capture one of the men, and there was another wounded that he stopped Callos from finishing. Pork would not be the only meat he would put on the grill tonight.

Before the two men died, Jayne knew all he needed about their operation. It was a collaboration between a freedom faction within the returned Veldaan and the Islani, whose agents were spying and planning sabotage. The freedom faction kept two safe houses in Angorok that Jayne knew how to find. He asked for help from Jaal, and knowing they must act quickly, together, the Dark Elves cased the residences and coordinated an attack.

Jayne commanded the Rangers. They were all experienced fighters, skilled with bow or clockwork-crossbow and sword. The troop swarmed out of streets and alleys to assault a two-storeyed home. The rangers executed ten traitors in the skirmish and took another four prisoners.

Jaal faced a larger challenge. Casteel and fifty of the Blood Legion broke into another two-storeyed complex. Extending from its basement was an old network of tunnels that connected other homes and businesses. Jaal could not assume that every linked home and business were conspirators. Instead, he questioned the families and made his arrests where he saw fit. In one basement, the legionnaires uncovered a vast arsenal of weapons, and after searching the home above it, they soon held six Islani men in custody. As a precaution against other manoeuvres, Casteel placed the city under lockdown and assigned extra security at the gates.

After the arrests, the *Gull* parked above the two-storeyed building seized by the Blood Legion. The upmarket dwelling sported a flat roof with trapdoor access to the lower stories. In their typical fashion, by nightfall, there were kegs of ale rolled in the front entrance and music and laughing attracted the interest of people outside on the street. Jaal enjoyed how the Legion lived for the day, and he was pleased to put his lot in with them for now.

The legion made further arrests over the next three days and uncovered new plots. The conspirators were not a professional crew, loyal to the North and hateful of the Southerners they fought for so long. Jayne previously served Tyriah and was unaware of any Veldaan shadow guilds. When required, Jayne had always been Tyriah's dark blade.

It was not surprising to Jaal that the Veldaan would not bend so easily to Mannace's will. He lived amongst them and knew their character well. While the majority of their race appeared conquered, some would never give up the fight for reasons of pride and principle.

During the turmoil, Mannace left Angorok and travelled with his forces as they moved east to lay siege to Islan. Jaal expected the Islani would flee further North.

ISLAN

Islan was a large and populace nation set amongst rolling hills and broad plains, similar to the Veldaan. However, its culture was remarkably different for two countries that existed side by side. The Islani were a passionate people and made for a fierce and relentless foe. They were light-skinned but dark-haired, and the men grew long pointed beards and braided their hair. Islani women wore bright colours, also with braided hair or wigs. Their style was to drape themselves in loose-fitting clothes, and the soldiers often swathed sashes or scarfs over their chainmail armour. Conical helmets made the soldiers appear taller, while curved blades rested inside scabbards, with colourful stones or intricately carved bones set in the pommels.

Jaal was wrong to think they might give up their territory without a fight, but Mannace was wiser to their character. He expected organised, determined resistance, though he was surprised to find so many cavalries from the Ryde defected to the enemy. Moreover, Islan harboured many other dissidents, unhappy with deals made with the South. But, at least now, these rebels were apparent and could be dealt with.

The horsemen, combined with the chariots and war wagons of the Islani, meant they were a well-appointed and mobile force. Islani's footmen were also versatile troops, lightly equipped with short bows, curved swords, and small shields.

Of more significant concern to Mannace was that the first

troops from the northeast were appearing – not of Amon Murn, but barbaric fighters from Churlamen that came by ship. The Brula reported that the Churlamen forces brought flying creatures with them; large vulture-like birds. Like the Keshik, they employed elephants, too, with war towers upon their backs. While they were still few, it was a prelude to invasion.

Mannace deployed his six armies so that they operated independently but stayed close enough to one another so that they could combine into a more significant force if needed. Because Islan was such a broad landscape, the furthermost armies were about three days march apart. When the Islani sent raiding parties to bypass his troops and strike into the Veldaan, Mannace's military intercepted them, but only just. Once confronted, the enemy avoided contact and withdrew. The tactic forced Mannace to commit two of his six armies to defend.

Meanwhile, his forward troops faced ambushes and nuisance attacks as they advanced through the border hills. The enemy defended their homeland tenaciously when they held the advantage but fled when outnumbered. Mannace was cautious, although news from the muster and the wisdom of his gut were telling him that he was running out of time.

The cities of Islan were large and sprawling, with central defences often set upon strategically defensible positions. As they approached the metropolis of Kesevak, the two armies that converged there met an evacuated city but a heavily defended hill fortress.

Likewise, the city of Skon was next to a river. The river's

course flowed around the city, lapping against its outer walls. The buildings inside the walls were many stories high to fit the population. Their roofs were flat to be used as part of the defence, with archers and siege engines positioned there.

Scouts reported to Mannace that the land surrounding Kesevak was cultivated plains, ideal for cavalry and the enemy's chariots. By comparison, the landscape neighbouring Skon was forested and wild. To understand Skon's terrain better, Mannace headed to the river city with his flying ships and Brula. He decided to take personal control of the siege.

On his arrival, Mannace was awed by the beauty of the Skon valley. Tree covered hills surrounded the broad vale, and deep green forest carpeted the valley floor. A wide river passed slowly through the glen, splitting to wrap itself around the city island. The riverbanks were thick with foliage along its length, including smaller trees that grew in the shallow water. A road north led to distant farmlands, and another headed south to other districts of Islan. Mannace's troops camped along both roads and in the woods. As told to Mannace, the city was indeed a great fortress, and he marvelled that the residences were built so tall. He expected there must be tens of thousands of people crammed into the island sanctuary. There was no central keep. But from his high vantage, some buildings stood out from the others; government and military structures of stone, decorated with statues and colourful mosaics. Like the outer residential towers, these buildings were also tall and equipped with siege machines. Some weapons he saw seemed designed to deal with his flying ships. Scouts reported enemy infantry in the wooded hills to the east, and skirmishers were already harassing his encamped force in the valley. Mannace could not be sure of the enemies' numbers but expected as many as twenty thousand soldiers nearby. There were possibly another ten thousand fighters defending Skon, including sightings of the strange Mago. The Mago were tall and with long arms so that their soldiers stood out from the humans around them. Their oddly crafted carapace armour and helmets gave them an insect-like demeanour.

Mannace commanded eight hundred thousand troops present or arriving. Accordingly, all cavalry units diverted south to assist in the siege at Kesevak, replaced with legions of Fogmir Elves and fierce Two-Face Orcs better suited to the Skon terrain. There was good reason to be confident.

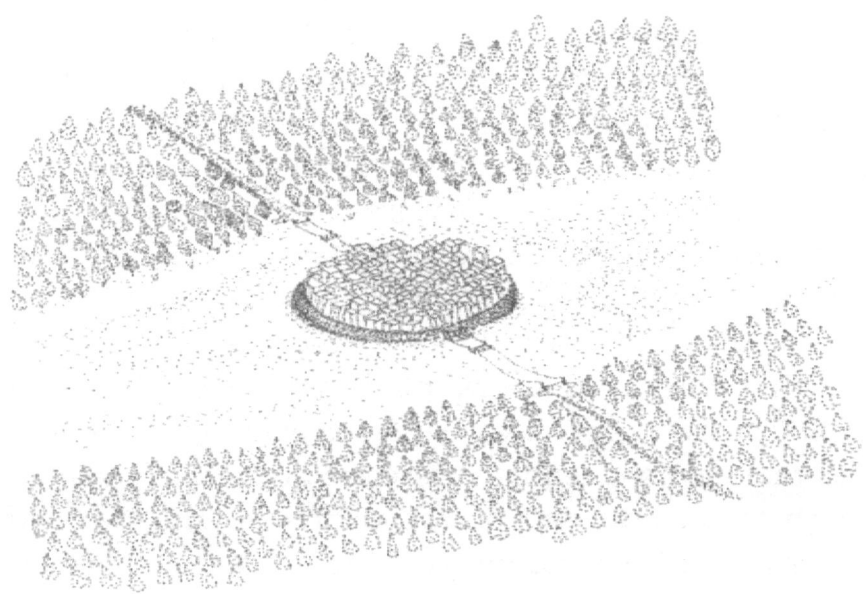

When his troops were ready, Musketmen, deployed along the riverbank, harassed the Islani who waited on the walls. Flying ships came in low across the forest and drew in line with the enemy artillery, exchanging fire. Cannonballs ripped into towers and tall houses, causing mayhem and carnage. The city garrison returned fire with stones or massive bolts. Where the enemy missiles hit, mostly they deflected off the flying ships armoured plates, but occasionally they pierced the wooden frame, causing clouds of steam to hiss out of the breaches. High above Skon, Brula dropped missiles and bombs, ruthlessly targeting crews, and setting defensive platforms on fire. The enemy had no response to the flying men except to yell curses and stay ready with their bows.

On Mannace's order, three ships came in low over the river at both the city's northern and southern entrances, concentrating their firepower on the gates. The entries could not withstand such a modern onslaught, and both portals were soon in tatters. On the south gate, however, the doors abruptly rightened. Although the cannonballs continued to hit them, they were steadfast as if rocks and dirt were suddenly piled at their back. Soon after, green vine-like tendrils appeared over the top of the battlements and reached quickly out to the nearest ship, latching onto it, and wrapping themselves around the hull. The crew hacked at the plants, but they thickened so fast that soon the tendrils were the breadth of a man, too tough to damage with a sword or axe. The two ships nearby withdrew and targeted the vegetation. But as the vines continued to grow, soon, even cannonballs caused little impact. Mannace expected this was the magic of the

Mago.

The creepers wrapped around the trapped ship tightened their grip as they expanded. Onlookers could see that the vessel's hull was buckling, and its timbers screamed. Then, spectacularly, an explosion of metal, wood and steam filled the air. Water discharging from the ship's rear tanks sprayed across the river and walls while the fore and aft of the boat plunged into the waterway. A few surviving crew yelled for help as they were swept downriver alongside the debris.

The three flying ships at the other gate blew apart the shattered doors. Then, joined by other vessels, the boats manoeuvred side-by-side to provide a bridge for ground forces to cross the waterway and enter the city. Animated steel workers led the way, with the elite Viletri troops close behind. With their enhanced weapons and armour, plus metal and stone men amongst their ranks, the Viletri made easy work of the defenders that rushed to prevent their entry. The shield disks provisioned long ago by the Grey Dwarves protected them from intense missile fire from windows and the battlements above.

Meanwhile, in the nearby forest, the enemy's local knowledge gave them an advantage, dictating the course of the fighting. They were significantly fewer than Mannace's southern force, but the defenders concentrated their attacks and retreated wherever southern reinforcements arrived. Mannace intended to secure the valley by late afternoon, but the Mago again spoiled his plans. Along a section of the valley, amongst the trees, animated vines entangled themselves around the foliage to present a wall of vegetation that his troops could not pass. In one location, the enchanted tangle reached out and grabbed at soldiers, wrapping around those they caught and crushing them. Then, the Mago's insects came in a great rush across the wall. Green like the forest, some lighter shades, and others dark. Some of the dark ones were as big as a horse, and old scars on their shells marked them as veterans. Each creature had six legs, with the rear being larger, allowing them to leap long distances. The insects propelled themselves across the ground or through the trees where they overwhelmed Men and Elves, teaming over units and crushing soldiers with powerful mandibles. They were tough to kill, being of a shape that the soldiers were unused to fighting and their carapace shell was hard, like metal. Thousands of the creatures ran amok forcing Mannace to withdraw his forces to present a stronger defensive position.

A second wave of insects did not come. Whatever sentience controlled the beasts now held them at bay, possibly content with the carnage caused and satisfied for now with the status quo.

Above Skon, the flying ships and Brula were winning their fight against the city's artillery and archers. Gradually, they drew close enough that musketmen amongst the marines could concentrate fire on engine crews or crossbowmen stationed at the windows. Bolder captains were landing marines on rooftops before returning to the forest road to transport more troops into the fight.

The Mago Dreyac, who saved the southern gate and destroyed the flying ship with her vines, made her way across to the northern entrance, but too late to repeat her magic. The Viletri troops already held the gate district and fought locals and soldiers in the houses and narrow streets. Behind the Viletri troops, other infantry units crossed into Skon, mostly Galandar pikemen or crossbowmen. The crossbowmen fortified captured homes, stationing themselves at windows and roofs. Islani archers and crossbowmen returned fire from bridges that joined many of the houses at the higher levels.

The Dreyac had only one seed left. She would save it for a defining moment in the battle or perhaps to aid an evacuation when the situation became desperate.

That defining moment did not come until the following day. Overnight the fighting continued to be fierce in the streets, although the southerners pushed the Islani ever backwards until there were only isolated pockets of resistance. The last formidable bastion for the Islani was a rectangular courtyard at the entrance to the town hall. In the yard, the Dreyac battled alongside the garrison commander and his elite Ravista. The Ravista wore chainmail coats that hung to their ankles, and all wielded a long, curved sword in one hand and an oddly shaped blade-catcher in the other. They bore surcoats and sashes of blue, lined with silver. At the top of their conical hats were ornate silver fish. The commander's uniform was similar, though his cover was a darker blue, and he wore no helmet. Alongside the Ravista, a smattering of other fighting units and militia were defiant. Archers and Ballista provided deadly support from balconies above the town hall entrance.

Mannace looked down at the city from the deck of his flagship. In the courtyard in front of the town hall, he could see his Viletri guardsmen meeting determined resistance. The First General ordered the captain to move closer so that the riflemen on deck provided needed support. It was the first time Mannace witnessed the rifles used in combat, and their dominance emboldened him to order the ship even nearer. The long courtyard was the only space large enough to get close to the ground. By manoeuvring downwards, the cannons targeted the balcony defenders. Mannace liked being amongst the noise and chaos. Once he subdued the archers, Mannace would reinforce the attack with Brula that waited on the rooftops nearby. This siege would soon be over.

As Mannace watched from the foredeck, vines suddenly appear from the enemy ranks. It was a circle of vegetation with a few figures at its centre, but it expanded rapidly so that the soldiers nearby scampered out of its way. Then, as he immediately feared, the vines arched up toward his flagship, and within moments there were already green tendrils gripping rails and running across the deck. Having witnessed the ship's destruction at the gate, Mannace would not let that happen here. Already the vines were the width of his arm. The leader shouted to his rangers as he dropped out of sight over the side of the craft.

At first, Mannace clambered down a vine, but it was soon

too wide to grip and instead, he slid down it and dropped the last length uncontrolled so that, as he hit the ground, he bowled against the legs of those below, knocking them over. His right side hurt, but his adrenaline brought him to his feet, instinctively pulling his sword from its sheath on his back. He felt another pain in his side as a Ravista stabbed up at him from the ground. Mannace reacted instinctively, jumping away to avoid a second fatal stab. Swinging his blade down, he severed an arm raised in defence. Then he and others fell again as one of the Rangers descending the same route tumbled amongst them. Another Ranger landed close by; his skull crushed as it struck the cobbles.

Mannace could tell by her insect sculptured armour that one of the enemies near him was a Mago. As they both got to their feet, Mannace struck at the Mago's head, but the swing deflected off the helm, sending the strange woman staggering back. The Ranger tackled the Mago, upending the woman and pinning her to the ground. It left Mannace to face an assault from the garrison commander and another elite Ravista. The shrinking space amongst the vines became too small for Mannace to wield his two-handed sword effectively. Instead, he parried and kicked the Ravista hard in the knee so that the man staggered and fell. It provided him with enough room to hack at the commander, who deftly snagged Mannace's broad sword in his blade-catcher. With the sabre in his other hand, he slashed at Mannace's neck. Mannace leaned backwards, enough to save his life but leaving him with a biting cut under his jaw. He ducked the back-slash before throwing himself at both the commander and the guard who was back in the action, taking them to the ground. With his size and strength, Mannace grappled the commander so that he quickly had his arm about the man's neck. He wrestled a dagger from the officer's belt and held it to his throat.

"Yield."

The man did not reply, and when Mannace looked over at the Ranger and the Mago, he could see that the Mago grasped the disarmed Ranger firmly. However, it did not change his terms.

"Yield."

As the Mago looked at Mannace through small holes in her helm, she began transforming. Up close, the creature's armour was not crafted metal but revealed as some form of natural shell. The Mago's legs sprouted roots that embedded themselves in the ground while her arms melded gruesomely into the ranger; both of the figures rapidly enveloped in vegetation. As Mannace looked on in horror, he was astounding how quickly their human forms disappeared, mutating into a giant pod, and rooted firmly in the cobblestones and earth. The Pod hardened so that it looked as rigid as granite. Mannace tightened his grip on the officer's neck, preparing to end him with a quick twist.

"Yield."

The man was helpless.

"I yield."

Mannace snatched the officer's blade as he made it available, and he waved it to indicate for the two wounded soldiers to toss their weapons aside. Once they complied, Mannace relaxed and let the commander withdraw to the others. They were trapped by a ring of giant vines, with nothing for them to do but wait. Risking a glance up, the leader was glad that his ship was still present and intact. His prisoner spoke.

"You are Mannace, ruler of the southerners. It is you who has awoken Amon Murn. Hah, you are the dead living. The Razzak will come, and they will feed off your darkness."

Mannace took another glance up. A smaller flying ship was alongside his flagship, and men descended towards him on ropes. A Brula also circled downwards. The commander continued to harass him.

"They will hang you down the pit of Ur so that the Drakhan will finish what the Razzak have left of your carcass. They will clean their fangs with your bones. And they will raise you and kill you again and devour you the next day. They will eat you every day …."

Soldiers landed on the ground next to Mannace and the Islani. One passed their rope to Mannace while the other secured his prisoners. The Ravista with the severed arm lay on the ground, now silent. His comrade was allowed to help him, though they could all see it was too late. One of the other arriving soldiers beat on the Mago Pod. It was as hard and impenetrable as it looked.

The ship lifted Mannace over the vine prison and lowered him to the ground using a rope. Southern soldiers were in command of the courtyard and hurried in and out of the Town Hall. There was still the noise of fighting in the distance. A Fesadi healer rushed to care for Mannace's wounds, while the leader stared at the vines and his ship, knowing himself fortunate to be alive. Forty years ago, he would have risked the same feat but with more skill. The thought made Mannace give a small laugh. It was the first time in his soldiering career that he had been cut this badly, and the scar he would have under his chin would be a good reminder that it was now the job of others to leap into danger.

That night, animated workers and soldiers with axes hacked the vines away from the ship and the courtyard. The Mago pod unexpectedly cracked as they worked near it, causing the soldiers to scuttle back. The crack widened as if pushed from the inside. Once the gap was broad enough, the creature within emerged. Jumping into the air, then hovering there for a moment, was a gigantic bug - hornet like but with a greenish carapace and multi-coloured wings. The wings buzzed as they beat, while the creature's bulbous eyes took in the surroundings. Then, with incredible swiftness, the incarnation was suddenly much higher, again hovering and watching, before disappearing into the night.

The following day, reports arrived detailing the battle at Kesevak. There too, the southerners celebrated a victory on the field. Then, the siege of the city-fort commenced. Mannace expected the Colossi would be impossible for the enemy to hold back, and the defences would fall quickly.

Elves brought other news from Amon Murn. The armies of that land and their allies were on the march, and the final campaign would soon be upon them. Immediately, Mannace hurried to Veldaan to prepare.

Part 5:

End Game

THE WENGO

Athose spied emissaries from Amon Murn visiting the Mad King. They tried to mingle with other travellers, but he recognised their look after spending time amongst that nation. However, the Mad King was dismissive when Athose asked him their intent. Athose was smart enough to know for himself that there were two things they would be interested in: the Wengo and the Bell. Over the last decade, the Wengo Orcs lost interest in the war between the North and the South, so it was most likely the Bell. A Colossus carried the Bell into the fjord during the visit, guarded in the deep by the Colossi and Kraken. It was a statement that nobody would get to the ancient artefact without the Mad King's consent.

The Mad King was dismissive about other things, too, acting more withdrawn than usual, not interested in the city of Colossus, the games, or anything that was happening.

Athose was keenly interested in the war. Because he once fought in the campaign against the Collective and travelled with the Blood Legion as a peacekeeper, Athose was certain the Blood Legion would have him back and that they would welcome Hu too. Perhaps he could collect Vilera along the way. Vilera lived amongst the humans near the Wengo mountains. Because of her lineage and capability, she would fit well into the legion.

Although he expected another moody reception, Athose visited the Mad King before he departed the city of Colossus. As always, they sat at a table, and an old slave brought them water. The servant was so ancient and frail that he struggled to lift the jug. It was good that the Mad King was acquiring many new slaves, including some giants, which the Molemen conditioned.

Athose sat upright to avoid the King chastising him about his posture. He expected it was best with the King to get straight to the point.

"I will take Hu, and we will join the war against Amon Murn."

"Huh, are the games too boring for you?"

"The games are games. Who can call themselves a champion in the arena when there is a battleground to test their courage and skill? The games do not compare to war."

The Mad King surprised Athose with his reply.

"Others would follow you. The Wengo can be convinced to march with you to war. They are a warrior people."

"But you have told them not to go to war. The Orcs do what you say. So why get them excited about war now?"

The Mad King shrugged, so Athose answered the question for himself.

"Because now they would fight with the South. You want the South to win."

"Huh, I want you to reach your potential, Athose. You cannot stay a boy forever. They would follow you."

"I have no interest in leading the Wengo. I will fight with

the Blood Legion."

"You may take Hu. Why don't you take some of the other champions of the arena? The Blood Legion would welcome them."

The idea instantly appealed to Athose. He had friends amongst the game's elite.

"Not all, but Argo and Felack might be accepted. I will ask them."

"Do as you see fit. Never let another tell you what you should do."

For the moment, the Mad King seemed to have come out of his apathetic mood. Rather, he looked serious as he sat next to Athose, resting his hand on the Elf's shoulder as was the custom amongst the Orcs when saying farewell.

"You have been a rare pleasure, boy."

Without waiting for a reply, the Mad King stood and departed the room. Athose sat quietly before getting up and returning to his home. The old man's increasingly glum mood and parting words concerned Athose. Conversations with the Mad King often left him confused.

As the Mad King suggested, Argo and Felack were easily convinced to go with him. Argo was a massive mountain Orc, while Felack was of the Long Jaw valley tribe. Both were excellent fighters and long-standing champions of the games. Although Athose asked them to come alone, both arrived with other warriors when it was time to depart the city. It was still a small group, although Hu added a considerable presence. Athose knew that the legion would not accept the additional followers, though it seemed likely there would be a place somewhere in the army for them.

As they travelled through the city, other Orcs approached them. Fans put an arm around their heroes' shoulders and talked passionately about the games. Sometimes bull-Orcs picked fights, and just as often, she-Orcs would be eager to rut. They were attracting considerable attention.

Again, while Athose instructed those accompanying him to keep their destination to themselves, the Orcs made no effort to comply. Instead, they boasted that they were off to war and beat their chests to show their strength. Athose was glad when they were finally free from the city.

That night as they camped in the valley of the Long Jaw, Orcs armed and armoured for war began to arrive in groups. More were still joining them in the morning, and now it was a long procession that wound its way through the mountain valleys to the fortress overlooking human lands.

At the Veldaan Camp-City, Athose met with Vilera. The city was much smaller now that most Veldaanians were returning to their homeland, but it was still a busy centre for trade and travellers. Vilera was always glad to have her brother's company, quickly agreeing to travel with him.

Several thousand Orcs collected at the city's outskirts when they set out across the Ryde in the morning. There was even a Chief amongst them. Whether he liked it or not, Athose was leading the Wengo to war.

By the time they arrived at the gathering point in Veldaan, news arrived ahead of them that the Wengo were marching. The Brula reported large groups of Orcs all making their way across the Ryde to join the southern host. It was a surprise to Mannace, and he summoned their leader to his command tent. It was even stranger to see Athose in front of him, an Elf, the son of Jaal, commanding Orcs. The young Elf was honest with Mannace that the Wengo simply followed him and that his intent was not to be their leader but to re-join the Blood Legion. It was a great coup for Mannace to have the Wengo fighting for the South. As well as their numbers, it would also encourage his reluctant allies from the north-western coast to cement their commitment. As such, he did his best to make the Wengo and their reluctant leader welcome.

Mannace decided to combine the Wengo with the Iron Jaw and the Two-Face contingents. He called them the United Tribes, which they liked. The Orc leaders immediately transformed the rabble into a cohesive military force. Mannace assigned the Blood Legion to work with the United Tribes, as they naturally integrated with any race, and it ensured that Athose continued to play his part.

Argo and Felack were accepted into the Blood Legion by Casteel. She accidentally called Argo, Agro, which the Blood Legionnaires found amusing, so the new name stuck. Agro seemed happy with it. As founder of the Blood Legion, Jaal assisted Casteel in the assessment, and Athose harboured mixed feelings about seeing his father again. He was his own man now, not needing tutoring or advice.

On the other hand, Athose was delighted to reunite with Rey. The Belg was just as happy to see the boy, and he helped Athose assimilate into Legionnaire life. Athose shared a cabin with his old friend aboard the *Gull*, which also meant more time close to his father, but it was a price worth paying. Agro, too, was assigned to the flying ship while Felack joined the Legionnaires on the ground.

Vilera did not have the chance to be tested by Casteel. Instead, Casteel sent her immediately to join The Muster.

PALAINTH GAMES

For the Orcs, the games were a way of life. As they formed into their army regiments, it was natural that they immediately developed a rivalry between the contingents. Soon each company boasted their colours, slogans, and teams. The Orcs organised competitions every evening, with the entertainment running late into the night. It was so loud that the United Tribes camp was moved to the opposite side of the Palainth. Above the field were hills where the Orcs used the slopes like an arena. In some places, they even carved seats out of the earth.

Some games involved whole regiments, such as "last Orc standing", which was as simple as it sounded. The only rule for all the games, set by the human generals, was no permanent injuries or deaths. On the rare occasion of a fatality, the Orcs worked together to cover it up. Usually, that meant there was more meat in the evening stew.

Individuals and teams from other races started to join them. Bollo and a group of Galandar soldiers were amongst the first. The Half-Orc quickly made a name for himself, and from his past exploits, they revered him as "The Giant Killer". Rey was another crowd favourite. He and other Legionnaires became regular participants. Agro and Rey were both unstoppable at any game that required brute force. Athose though, was their champion of champions. In the games that relied on agility and skill, he remained untouchable. In response, he was cocky and always played up to the crowd to give them their thrills.

There was one game called *Cabbage in a Basket* at which

Athose excelled. Each team was given a cabbage carried by the players, and a basket left stationary on the ground. Athose's task was always to get the cabbage into the other team's basket. His comrades helped to clear him a path or were defenders. There were variations of the game using different objects, and Athose's favourite variant was where the players' hands were tied behind their backs. Back in the city, the crowd would drink rukk and roar. Here on the Palainth, there was no rukk, but the roar was deafening.

Tonight was "Horsehead in a Basket". It was a massive crowd with many soldiers coming across from the other camps to watch. The Roundmen entered their first team, and even though they were novices, they brought many supporters with them. Each team put their name-stone in an oversized helmet, and Jaal, the Master of Games tonight, drew the first two stones out. It was The Spikers versus The Bloodless. His assistant yelled the names to the crowd, who cheered and whooped.

The Bloodless was Athose's team. He was disappointed to be going first. The first game was often the warm-up for the crowd, and things usually got livelier as the night progressed. There were a lot of teams, so this night each could only be drawn from the helmet once.

The Spikers was Bollo's team. For Bollo, this was a chance to face off against other champions and prove his dominance. He had watched The Bloodless, and their big men were the best in the competition. It was Athose, though, that consumed his interest tonight. Bollo possessed a secret weapon; his carrier was from Vostov, and the strange young woman would be a lot for their opponents to handle.

The horse head was perhaps two days old and stunk. As the game started, Athose's picked the thing up, and he was surprised by how heavy it was. Taking a tight grip of the mane with both hands, he immediately moved forward with Agro and Felack as his wingmen. There were six other legionnaires to protect him, busting open a path to the opponent's basket. Eight defenders hung back, including Rey, who would ensure their rival's carrier did not complete her task.

Usually, teams focused on attack, but today the Spikers had twelve on defence. As Athose advanced across the playing field, six of them, including Bollo, ran at him, while six others fanned out to intercept the other Bloodless attackers. Often Athose would cut left or right to move quickly around them, taunt them until a gap appeared, but today, like Bollo, his ego pushed him toward confrontation. Soon the opportunity to avoid contact was gone, and his wingmen, Agro and Felack, stepped forward at just the right time to take the brunt of the Spikers assault. They grabbed and wrestled the determined Galandarians that double-teamed them. It was as Bollo planned, and now the crowd were on their feet, eager to know how the match-up between Athose and The Giant Killer would play out.

The two champions charged at each other. The horse's head burdened Athose, so at the last moment, he threw it at the Half-Orc and slid low to avoid Bollo's fists. Bollo instinctively put a foot out to prevent the Elf from pushing past, and he was quick enough to catch the head in one hand. Athose was faster, and after impacting with Bollo's leg, he reached up behind the Half-Orc and grabbed the collar of his leather armour. He pulled down hard with all his weight so that Bollo swung backwards, his legs tipping into the air. Just as nimbly, Athose let go of Bollo before the Half-Orc landed, and he grabbed at the horse head mane. Clasping the thing in both hands, he yanked with all his strength as Bollo impacted the earth. But Bollo kept a good grip of the mane, and despite the fall taking the wind from his lungs, he did not let go. Bollo grabbed Athose by his waist belt with a free hand and yanked him, stumbling to the ground. In response, the Elf kicked him in the chest, and Athose's other boot landed repeated blows to the Half-Orc's face. Bollo could smell blood and feel it running down his jaw. Fired up by the scent, he lifted Athose by his waist with a mighty effort, then smashed him face-first back to the earth. Athose caught a mouth full of dirt, and he was partially pinned by the Orcs bulk, though he continued to lash out, twisting desperately and using his elbow to strike heavy blows at Bollo's head. It was like pounding rock.

Agro appeared above the two as they wrestled, ripping the head from Bollo's grasp. In a desperate attempt to win the game, Argo heaved the head toward the opposition basket. It arched high, and the crowd went quiet as they watched it descend. If he were successful, the throw might go down in games legend, but it hit the side of the basket and sent the wicker tumbling back. When Agro turned around, Rey looked back at him across the field and shrugged his broad shoulders. They had already lost.

Agro and some of the other players pulled Athose and Bollo apart. Both were bloodied and still looking at each other with fury in their eyes. When Rey came over, he hauled Athose aside and ushered him into the team area.

"Not our day, boy, let's get you cleaned up."

"Don't call me boy, Rey. I should have run around them. They all came forward. It was a rookie move."

"Next time."

"I let him beat me."

"Looked like you gave as good as you got. He's a mean one, Athose. Once he got hold of you, it could have been much worse. I would hate to see your pretty head bobbing up and down in the pot."

"I don't like losing, Rey."

"Move on, boy. It is your ego that got hurt. At least your body is intact."

"I said don't call me boy."

"Then don't act like one."

After a period of silence, Athose asked Rey a question, "How did the girl get through, Rey. They put everything into defence. Their attack was weak."

"She just walked past - a bit of a sidestep. I'm pretty sure she winked at me. I don't know how she did it. Expect we'll hear more about it in the morning."

Athose was not one to let something go so quickly. Once

his bleeding stopped, and he received the all-clear for breakages, he looked for the young woman in the players' area. When he failed to find her, he didn't feel like joining the crowd on the hill. Instead, he headed back to The Gull. He sensed somebody next to him as he walked and was startled to see the young woman keeping pace at his side. She was dark-skinned and slight. Her features were delicate and pointed, presenting large eyes with bright whites but dark pupils. Her clothes were pure white fabric tailored to hug her body tightly. The stranger was shorter than him but walked with the same quickness.

Athose stopped and turned to face her. He had many questions, but she surprised him again by reaching up and kissing him. It was much gentler than an Orc kiss. At first, he didn't feel that he was in the mood for celebrating, but the young woman was confident and persistent. She kissed him again, this time with more passion. He returned the favour, but before he could continue, it seemed that something needed to be said."

"Athose."

"Yuriki."

It was good that the long grass was dry and made for a soft bed.

THE BLOOD LEGION

As was its way, the Blood Legion integrated quickly into the United Tribes army. Of course, it helped that amongst the Blood Legion, there were Orcs from the Two-Face and Iron Jaw, plus the two recruits from amongst the Wengo. It meant that, although they were only one thousand in number, the Legion was an accurate representation of the collaboration between all races. Moreover, the Orcs respected war-skill and strength and the Blood Legion represented both: a gathering of elite champions.

Casteel led the Legion, even though Jaal returned to their ranks. That suited Jaal as it meant he could come and go as he pleased, unburdened by responsibility. As the leader of the Legion, the United Tribes initiated Casteel into their council. It was an assembly of all the Orc chiefs, who met every day to discuss their readiness for the war to come. Preparations included manufacturing of Thog and training in the Rage. At Mannace's order, the Wengo equipped themselves with metal weapons and armour sourced from the armouries and forges across the Blood Sea.

More than half a million warriors from the Wengo journeyed to the Palainth. It didn't seem to be an issue for them that they came to fight for the South. The South embraced the Wengo, made them stronger, gave them gifts for war. They quickly forgot the battle twenty years ago on the Veldaan where the South defeated them and their northern allies. The Orcs rallied now to the prospect of bringing Amon Murn, the ancient and arrogant overlord of the North, to its knees.

Training in the Rage gave the Orcs a sense of pride and purpose. During the training, they received small doses of Thog to become familiar with its effects; know how to channel and control the fury and strength it bestowed on them. Used in the way the Two-Face prescribed it, it helped build muscle and endurance.

Mannace arranged the Remman to train with them when the Orcs felt they were ready. It wasn't kind, as the Remman shield wall and the elite skill of their soldiers efficiently handled the Orc brutes. However, it made the ashamed Orcs more determined, and they devised hooked weapons to pull down the Remman shields. They focused on the Rage so that strength and ferocity would match the Remman's skill. Many Orc units equipped themselves with axes and clubs to throw as they charged into combat. Such was their passion that Mannace dared not put the Remman in front of them again.

The Elven Spellweavers stopped aiding the scouts, preferring to join the Muster, and it seemed to Jaal that, with their change in focus, nobody was effectively tracking the movements of the North. So, he took it upon himself to learn the enemy's progress and plans. Because only the Elves and the Spiders could travel the ways, Jaal gathered twelve Elven legionnaires, including his son Athose, and he took them first to the Hand, then into the lair of the Spider Mother. It was more than a decade since he last visited Eya, but he needed her help to provide them passage and guides through the ways.

As his small troop trekked through the Spider Mother's domain, a Spiderkin patrol appeared, staring menacingly down from the trees, while their leader boldly approached Jaal on the ground.

"Father, you have been absent. Have you forsaken the mother?"

The Spiderkin understood order and authority, and because of that fact, it was always best with his children not to tolerate such nonsense questions. Instead of answering, Jaal was direct.

"Take us to the Spider Mother now. These Elves are of the Blood Legion, and no harm is to befall them."

The leader looked hard at Jaal, scrutinising him. Thankfully the Dark Elf's authority amongst the Spiderkin still held, and the scuttling creatures led the party to a clearing in the thick woods, where they waited in silence. The Blood Legionnaires peered nervously up at the spiders and their tangle of webs high in the trees.

Jaal was anxious, as he always was when he had not seen the Mother for some time, unsure what reception to expect. In his thoughts, Jaal couldn't help but play out the sexual interaction he hoped for – the elevated anticipation and ecstasy he relished in the past. The danger, the intense sex, the primal energy that no other partner could provide or even imagine. Was this the true lure that drew him here? Of course, it was selfish, but he didn't care, and even though he knew the perilous risk of such a plan, his mind raced in dread and anticipation.

Eya came late at night when the forest was at its blackest

so that even the Elves could not see the movement amongst the trees. Instead, the legionnaires perceived the scuttling of spiders that filled the blackness around and above them. The arachnid's animosity and hunger were palpable, making the air difficult to breathe. Athose, who never experienced fear, suddenly felt like prey, as good as naked before the monstrous predators, a pounce away from mandibles gripping his throat and rending his flesh. A chill ran across his body, settling itself in his mind and assailing his normal self-assuredness. As the terror intensified, fed by arcane witchery that was also palpable, wetness trickled down the inside of his pants. When the air became intensely colder, Jaal knew that Eya, the Mother of Spiders, stood in the blackness before him. Her displeasure was like icicles that prickled his skin. Even he struggled to speak through the malevolence that threatened to overwhelm them. His sexual desire was forgotten.

"Eya, the end of the age draws near. I come to ask for your aid against Amon Murn."

"You should not have come here, Jaal."

There was a scream in the forest, some distance away, that sounded like Eldash, an Alani Elf that travelled with him. The cry was cut short. Jaal could hear the others with him shuffle closer together, and some drew their weapons, no longer caring what consequence such an action might incur. Two stabbed at the darkness but connected only with air.

"Have things changed so much? I am the father of the Spiderkin."

"You have brought creatures of light into my domain."

"There must be a balance in all things. Darkness and Light, they need each other to exist."

There was a commotion behind him, then silence. Jaal reached out in the darkness, and he found Athose and one other figure, Semril the Dark Elf. The others were gone, without combat or screams. Eya's voice cut the air.

"No more Jaal. There is no peace between dark and light. Darkness will ascend, and light will become shadow."

Jaal wondered why Eya spared Athose. He was not of the Darkness. Then, as if sensing his question, Eya provided an answer.

"The boy will serve the Darkness. One day he will be its champion. Your seed is the foundation of that darkness, but it is the fates that groom him and shape his path. They have a place for him and a destiny that he will fulfil."

Athose was too terrified to hear what was said. Instead, he waited for his turn to die. Hours passed, and he was still standing there, paralysed by fear, when the first rays of morning entered the clearing. It was enough light that he could see about him. The legionnaires, his father, the spiders, all were gone. Overwhelmed with a sense of dread, Athose fled back the way they came.

Eya led Jaal and Semril through the catacombs beneath the Hand. Once returned to her sanctuary, Jaal sensed the Spider Mother relax, and the overbearing darkness abated enough that both Dark Elves breathed more easily.

Semril was left with the Spider Mother while Spiderkin took Jaal to their garrison. Once away from Eya, the Spiderkin talked more freely with Jaal. They treated him as the father returned and expected him to resume command.

URATH'A'THARACK

The Sleeper had a name, Urath'a'tharack. He was first amongst the Giants; powerful, invincible, and indestructible. It was the muster that uncovered the history of it, but once the name was spoken, it spread quickly so that all carried it upon their lips. He was not an Ancient, but he was their equal. Urath led the lesser races away from the ancients, and it was he who founded Amon Murn.

Nordan opened his eyes, clearing his mind of visions. Urath'a'tharack; another enemy revealed. The ancient spread out his arms to soak in the day's warmth, take energy from it. The data he gathered gave him a sense of purpose. He was rooted in this one spot since taking the fortress, but now he took his first step. The nearby Colossi turned to watch their master, and as he moved through the fortification's broken gates, they strode to keep pace with him.

Eya, too, awoke from her meditation. Urath could not be allowed to reach the bell. The pieces of the puzzle were coming into place. It was not the final piece; she still did not know how the Age would end, only that those of darkness would survive and that a Queen of the Night would ascend.

Jaal assumed command of the Spiderkin. He could see that he was given little choice, and it might even suit his purpose. The Spiderkin Weavers were knowledgeable in the ways, often guided through the secret places by the Spider Mother and given the keys to unlock untapped paths. However, as he saw in Eya, Jaal observed blackness in the weavers too, given wholly over to the darkness and sewing that darkness into others. He knew that there was no going back once the weavers embraced oblivion.

The darkness was in no way a cloud upon the mind. Jaal still knew his purpose and continued to make his choices, at least for now. With his new authority, he assumed the role of spies for the southern armies, using the spiders to travel the paths and watch the northern enemy. Sometimes his scouts captured prisoners for interrogation. They quickly learned, though, that races such as humans or even giants could not survive a journey through the ways; it stripped their essence so that they were left dumb and lifeless.

As the Spiderkin reported back to him, from what Jaal could tell, the body of Urath moved deliberately slowly so that the horde of the North could gather about it. Armies arrived from nations south and west of Amon Murn. Ahead of the horde, loyal troops from the north-eastern territories waited for Urath's procession to arrive. Jaal used the Spiderkin to relay information to Mannace's advisors. He knew Mannace would find every detail meaningful.

Jaal expected Eya to take issue that he was using her armies to spy for the South, but she surprised him by ordering the operations increased and that a great store of food was to be collected. Jaal responded with a war of terror, striking at military and civilian targets at night.

The catacombs below the Hand of Fengal quickly filled with paralysed victims, stored, and cared for by the spiders. Jaal trusted the Spider Mother's instincts, also making other preparations by disguising entrances to the catacombs, setting sentries, and strengthening the web curtain over their territory above the ground.

Contact was re-established with the spiders still residing in their old abode near Viletri. It seemed to Jaal that as long as the ways remained open, they would always have the option to retreat to that place if the Hand became unsafe. One of his Spiderkin offspring named Xinzan commanded there. Above the underground lair, the spider forest was covered in deep snow and abandoned. The spiders now lived exclusively alongside refugee Iron Jaw in the expansive network below ground. Jaal instructed Xinzan to gather his arachnid horde to join him on the raids into Amon Murn. The marauders quickly became experts at overwhelming enemy positions and plundering their lands.

An entity travelled the pathways that the Weavers opened into Amon Murn, a monstrous creature, immense and powerful, felt but unseen, that lurked menacingly amongst the swirling light and shadow. It was a thing of darkness, allowing other darkness to pass. Therefore, it was no enemy to the Spiders, and they came to name it The Creeper, paying it reverence by lowering their eyes when they sensed it nearby.

THE ROAD

Mannace knew the tombstone of Urath'a'tharack was moving towards the bell. But, again, it left him wondering what game the Mad King played. He was grateful to the King for the Colossi and the Wengo – both of those gifts helped unify the Southerners and gave them confidence that Amon Murn could be defeated. Mannace liked and respected the Mad King, but it was a leap to trust a man who used such indirect methods and consistently left chaos in his wake. Mannace's agents already informed him the King was taking the slaves destined for Tarash Gormoth as his own, but that was of little importance – a fair trade for all the good the King did.

There was much to consider. Perhaps the Mad King did him another favour to lure Amon Murn out of its northern hold? Finally, Mannace would have the decisive battle he spent these last forty years preparing to fight. It was not hard to see the path that Urath's cavalcade would take. It followed the East-West Road across the Markhon, through the valleys of Rockhome and would wind its way through the territories of the Wengo Hill Tribes. The major trade route skirted the Northern Ryde before diverging into minor paths that serviced the continent's western nations. Once at the Wengo Mountain range, it would be a short journey for the forces of Amon Murn through the pass to the city of Colossus where the bell awaited them, secured by the Mad King in the depths of the fjord. Mannace did not doubt that if the armies of Amon Murn made it to their destination, the Mad King would provide them with their prize for whatever price was agreed. What would it matter anyway if Urath's tombstone arrived there? It would mean that the South, and Mannace, were already defeated.

Mannace's forces held Rockhome, and the Wengo Hill tribes were amongst his new Orc allies. He planned three primary defences; first, he would harass the enemy as they passed through Rockhome, then defend the location known to the local Orcs as Bald Hills. If Amon Murn defeated them there, they would retreat and wait for the Northerners on the plains of the Ryde. If needed, a fourth defence at the entrance to the Wengo Mountains was possible. By then, the most they could hope to achieve would be to delay Urath from reaching the city of Colossus while the South regrouped. It seemed likeliest to Mannace that the Ryde would host the final confrontation.

Other routes were possible. The Northerners could come down from the Markhon, through the Gap and Islan, to attack the South in the Veldaan. He would welcome that tactic, which is why he thought it unlikely. Another alternative was to take a path through the Hand of Fengal. The wildland would not be an easy route for such a large force, and the forest was a fortress for the Elves and Spiders, who would be challenging for the Northerners to dislodge. If he were the leader of the Northern hoard, Mannace would not take that path.

The Brula were Mannace's best scouts, but they no longer dominated the skies. They encountered giant vultures, and flights of demons were becoming common where the Northern army gathered in strength. The hell-spawn were black-skinned, so near impossible to see in the night. Humanish, twisted, hairless bodies sporting sharp claws and fangs. The fiends swooped and screeched like flocks of crows, sometimes fighting amongst themselves.

Mannace relied more heavily now on the Spiderkin to bring him information. The latest reports confirmed that the Northern vanguard forces were active in the Markhon. Mannace suspected they would secure the roads and valleys for the more significant forces that followed.

An Iron Jaw bull rider, one of the First Orcs, brought other news of ships from the enemy nation of Churlamen, landing troops in Sompher Gris and gathering in eastern Islan. It wasn't until Mannace sent spies and scouts to investigate that the Southern commander learned that other enemy nations were also gathering there; armies from Jirdas, Daras, Xu, The Free States, and the Dead Wastes. Joining them were warriors and militia from nations bordering Islan that they had already fought. Every fighter in those lands was taking up their swords and spears. Finally, Mannace was getting a proper sense of what it meant to take on the full might of the North. Even with the alliances and progress made, it appeared overwhelming.

Another name was now on all lips within the captured cities of Islan; Churgwarthos. People whispered that Churgwarthos journeyed with the armies from the west. The news met with a mixed reception. Some thought him a ghost, scoffing at those excited by rumour. Others in the conquered cities were quick to embrace Churgwarthos as a saviour, taunting the southern garrisons with the terror that would soon befall them. Some seemed afraid themselves, as if Churgwarthos was the stuff of their nightmares. When the Muster was informed, the Asari provided further background, naming Churgwarthos, Necromancer; a Sorcerer of great power that stood at the side of Urath'a'tharack and enforced his will. The great Magus was unseen in the North for over a thousand years.

No wizard wanted to look down the finger of a more powerful magician, and Render could see the Asari waver. Their innate cowardice fuelled the fear and concerns of other wizards amongst The Muster. When they met to discuss the topic of Churgwarthos, Render took control of the forum, and Dekon nodded to him knowingly as he stepped up to the podium to address those gathered. Dekon understood that the rising of the Sorcerer was not a problem for the priesthood – Render needed to take charge of the Wizards – put a hammer to their egos and remind them that like the priesthood, the mages, too, had a hierarchy.

Before he spoke, though, Render set darkness upon the hall, and he drew on the powers that came to him so quickly now, dampening any other enchantment and allowing him to channel his magic unfettered. Behind the crowd, Fek appeared, then Gax and Ruu. The two Drutha were with them, bound to Render and forbidden to vent their wrath upon the Asari. The demons blended with the darkness, and they moved unseen amongst those gathered, bumping against the humans and other kin, breathing across their necks, caressing them with their tongues and claws. While they enjoyed themselves, Render spoke, using small sentences to make his points.

"Churgwarthos is mine. No other is to touch him. It is the way with a new age that the old will fall and the new will rise. Churgwarthos has come here to die, and I will see the task done. You will call *me* Sorcerer. There will be only one."

Render wanted to be clear with the Asari and others who harboured doubts.

"Cowardice will not be tolerated. Cowards and traitors will have the Drutha at their backs. They will face my wrath. I will not stand for weakness or disobedience."

Render expected disobedience would be a bitter word for some of those present to swallow; it meant acknowledging him as a higher authority. One of the Asari choked and was coughing. It made Render smile at his analogy.

When the darkness faded to light, the demons and the Sorcerer were gone.

THE COUNCIL

Despite the busyness of the campaign preparations, Mannace needed to trust his generals to oversee the detail while he returned for a brief visit to Viletri. It helped that the travel aboard *The Bracadian* was instantaneous. The flagship pulled alongside other ships using the Sky Tower, dwarfing the civilian vessels. Below, the city of Viletri was white with snow on its rooftops and along the streets. It didn't stop people from moving about and starting their day. Decorations and banners were flying to mark the week of the Colonial Council. Mannace was apprehensive about being back at the capital after another year away.

It was the second day of the Council meeting, and as custom dictated, the war effort in the North was the focus of the day's agenda. Mannace understood from experience not to get into the detail too early. So instead, he started with a high-level summary.

"As you know, the Dwarves hold all lands north of the Icesleepers, all the way to the Rift. The only exception is the Holy Lands, which the Dwarven tempest cannot touch. There are also refugee settlements along the Demonswar, and resistance in Mongier. It has been eight months since the last Dwarf attack."

Mannace pointed to the locations on the map painted on the wall and ceiling. It helped him to focus. He circled the extensive area of the North that his forces now controlled.

"While our main base continues to be in Veldaan, the Southern Alliance controls The Young Kingdoms, Western Islan, The Ryde, and the territories along the west coast, including the Wengo. In addition, we have occupied The Sarang and Rockhome, where the Northern populace has fled. Here on the Palainth is the Rhalec Portal. South of the Palainth is a camp of more than two million refugees waiting to resettle in the Colonies. They are a mix of southern nations, mostly Galandarians. In addition, as many as a million Veldaanians live in camps here and here, also waiting their turn to migrate."

Mannace could see mixed views regarding immigration on the faces and in the nervous movements of the Colonial leaders. He imagined most of the day would be covering the topic in more detail. In relaying his next message, Mannace didn't want to panic his audience, but he needed them to know the gravity of the battles to come.

"Amon Murn is marching across here into Markhon, and then their armies will pass through Rockhome. If they reach the western coast, they will attempt to restore the Sleeper, Urath'a'tharack, first of the Giants. Urath'a'tharack is bound in stone, but the Mad King's bell will restore him. The bell is secured at this point, here at the city of Colossus. We will attack Amon Murn and the armies of the North along their route. We will not allow them to reach the western coast."

As Mannace took a slow, deep breath, the councillors remained silent, though some leaned forward, eager to know more.

"Another northern force gathers here in Eastern Islan. It consists of these western nations of the North, Churlamen foremost amongst them, plus local contingents. The Sorcerer, Churgwarthos, leads them. The host of Amon

Murn and the host of Churgwarthos have collected about them the full strength of the North. An epic campaign is at hand; the final fight in this war that has crossed so many generations."

He did not want to worry the councillors about the numbers. So instead, Mannace gave an overview of the alliance deployments.

"We have three primary forces. The largest contingent is in the north of Veldaan, and it will face Urath'a'tharack's horde. Another significant group is here in Islan and patrolling along the Sarang. Based at the Palainth is the third force. We will commit those troops when we have better information about the armies gathering in Islan.

The Lord of Karanthos stood and asked a question. Naturally, it was of interest to many others present.

"Are the colonies protected from attack by sea?"

Mannace was uncertain, but he spoke with confidence.

"We are not expecting an attack by sea. We believe that past attacks originated from Amon Murn and their allies – from independent city-states. Now those states march with Urath'a'tharack. They no longer have the fleets to launch a major offensive by sea. Our fleets patrol the waterways of the Eastern Colonies and remain our best line of defence."

It was Ramon of the Merchant's Guilds who stood next. It was the first time that guilds attended the Council.

"It is more than twenty years since the Veldaan was

defeated, and we are still fighting across their borders. If we defeat these hosts of the North, will the North finally be ours?"

"That is a good question, though not easily answered. It is our goal to defeat the North in the coming conflict utterly."

"Then it could go on for more generations?"

Mannace could see in the faces that his audience wanted a decisive answer.

"It ends here. All those with the sight are gathering. They can see that the Age ends. The upcoming fighting will decide the future."

Speaking with such firm conviction, many nodded at the leader's words. Fitius stood. He performed many of the Governor's duties in Mannace's absence and was the Emperor's voice.

"It will be the Age of Empire, the Ascent of Man."

Mannace would not compel the nations to provide more support for the war. It was too late for that. Instead, he gave the podium over to others and spent the morning discussing the detail of immigration and the war effort amongst interested groups. When the opportunity presented itself, he ushered Kakos into a private chamber.

"Kakos, as a friend, I need your help to end this war. So, return with me and see this conflict done. I ask this as a personal favour."

"No."

"Consider it. You know the war in the North, what we face. You are needed there. Viletri will still be here, and you will still be its Lord."

"No, Mannace."

Mannace was not used to hearing "no". He knew Kakos' preference to remain in Viletri but expected him to do as he asked. Despite Kakos's changes since his death, Mannace still considered him a close ally and friend.

"I am Governor, Kakos, and I need my Lords to stand at my side when needed. It is not an order I give lightly. You will come back to the North."

"No. I will not. Mannace, I will not leave Villetri."

The Liche's rejection was the first time anybody outrightly refused Mannace's orders, and if it had been anybody else, he would not have tolerated such defiance. Mannace could not afford Kakos as an enemy. Instead, he turned and stormed out of the chamber.

In the corridor beyond, Fitius was there, and his bitch was with him. Saska looked different, less composed and with a fire in her eyes. She hissed at Mannace and showed him her fangs.

Mannace had enough. It was time to put her in her place. As his eyes narrowed and his hand tightened into a fist, he could feel the darkness descend over him. He let it fuel his wrath towards the demon whore. Fitius was quick enough of mind to see Mannace's intent, but he was too slow to intercede. Mannace easily knocked Fitius aside, and with his free hand, the big man pushed the Overlord of

Arenland hard enough that he collided with the corridor wall and fell. Then, he landed a punch in the bitch's face with his other fist that sent her tumbling. It was a great release to strike her down. But as others came to watch, he could see from the horror on their faces that they perceived it very differently. Fitius was bloodied and struggling to stand, and when an onlooker came to help Saska sit to regain her wits, the elation Mannace felt quickly evaporated. Too angry for words, he stormed away.

Now everything was pissing Mannace off. He could see people talking about the war but not understanding it; how could they when they were so removed from the conflict. Here in Viletri and the Colonies, the Rift war was news to discuss as they went about their regular business, ate cakes, and sipped their bloody tea. Mannace could not stomach any more of it. Boarding his ship, he returned in an instant to the North. Before the upset, he planned to visit the Oracle and release Logthar, who languished in a Viletri dungeon, but those things would now need to wait.

Perhaps this upset was what he needed, to draw on his darkness to face the darkness ahead. Possibly Angry Man would be the one to give Urath'a'tharack and Churgwarthos a bloody face, rip their fucking heads from their shoulders, and end this damned, light-forsaken conflict.

CHURGWARTHOS

Mannace was no longer satisfied with his strategy of defence. It seemed weak, and he could see now that it gave his enemy the initiative. Why wait when his forces were as prepared as they could be, and the enemy were still gathering their strength. Immediately he moved reinforcements into Islan, and he sent Render there to lead the attack. It seemed the right thing to do, to pitch his Sorcerer against theirs. The young Prince of the Horse Clans, Malakai, was the Sorcerer's military advisor and general. It surprised Mannace how few Wizards Render took with him into the west, leaving him much of the Muster to deploy. Acting decisively, Mannace took them and his armies north into Rockhome, then east to where the valleys opened onto the plains and hills of the Markhon.

General Callos Reylor was left in charge of the defence of the Veldaan, with instructions to send half of the Rhalec towers and sufficient militia forward to Rockhome to protect the passage through the mountain valleys.

In Islan, Churgwarthos was not ready to face the armies of the South, and he shrewdly moved his host back to the coastal provinces of Sompher Gris, where reinforcements continued to arrive by ship. The fortified capital of Tarnac was an ideal location to make ready his defence. Within days, the Belarch would come, and he would have all he needed to sweep the enemy from the field. In the meantime, he used vultures to keep the skies clear of spies, and packs of demonic hounds scoured the land in search of southern patrols or other easy targets.

Render and his armies marched to be close on Churgwarthos' trail.

The region of Sompher Gris was mostly flat woodland with forested knolls and more prominent hills that the locals dared to call mountains. The low area around the city of Tarnac was rich farmland with a scattering of orchards. From the capital, it was half a day's walk east to the coast and the port of Highcliff.

When Render finally caught up with the sorcerer at Tarnac, the city's walls appeared unspectacular, low enough that attackers could see the roofs of the homes and businesses it protected. However, the main gate boasted a broad tunnel under a formidable fort, towering above the wall with a spectacular vantage over the city and surrounds. As well as archers and siege engines, Render expected that Churgwarthos would command his defence from the fort's battlements if he were equal to his reputation.

From a long distance, there appeared to be a black haze about the city, and when he drew closer, Render observed wisps of darkness polluting the land it touched, blackening grass, and putrefying other vegetation. He couldn't imagine how the people within the city could survive. When Render ordered scouts to investigate, the fog expanded to consume them as if it were a conscious, predatory thing. The unlucky men did not return.

Alarmingly, outriders hurried back from the surrounding lands with news that the armies they were tracking were gone. It frustrated Render that they disappeared, eluding him, as if they were a ruse. Was he tricked into following ghosts, or merely outmanoeuvred? Fresh enemy troops continued to land along the coast, and Render's spies reported a sizable contingent amassing near Highcliff.

While Render took a day to assess his enemy's strength and the mystery of the darkness, Brula arrived with messages from Islan of the enemy besieging allied cities. Sightings of other enemy troops on the borders of Veldaan followed. With the Northerners active behind him and confronted by the darkness consuming Tarnac, nothing was how Render envisaged it.

Malakai did not wait for Render's command. Instead, he gathered the Horseclans and other cavalry from their host, making haste toward Veldaan. Malakai realized that without his help, when the enemy attacked the Southern occupied lands, the civilians there would be easy targets.

Uncertain how best to use the remaining military forces, Render cautiously divided the army into three parts. One force he sent to secure the coastline and waylay arriving troops. Another part he sent back to Veldaan on Malakai's heels. The third, a much smaller contingent, stayed with him at Tarnac. Render was compelled to know what tragedy happened there.

CALLOS REYLOR

Callos once commanded the Southern Armies, but since the fall of Galandar, he felt inadequate in that role. So instead, he let Mannace be the leader, and like others, Callos hoped that the immortal General would be the one to lead them to victory over the North. For him, it mattered much less than before the Dwarves sacked and desolated the southern lands, but it would still be gratifying to see the Rift War ended in his lifetime.

As the host of Churgwarthos crossed from Islan into Veldaan, Callos mobilised the militia and sent word to the broader populace to take refuge in the cities. But, for those hundreds of thousands of civilians still camped near the Rhalec portal, he sent instructions to make haste through the gateway to the safety of the Eastern Colonies. These were desperate times, and the Colonies would have to cope.

The Veldaan Chokra made up the majority of troops available to him. They were well trained and disciplined. Of the other militia, some bore armour and crossbows, but just as many armed themselves with whatever they could bring to hand. Each city in Veldaan was garrisoned and boasted formidable defences. Civilians who could not make it to the cities or portals ran or hid. To buy them time, Callos marched his capable Angorok militia to face the wrath of the Sorcerer and the North. The one hundred and eighty thousand Capital fighters under his direct command had trained together for the last seven months, presenting a professional force as they approached the Veldaan border. The ploy to lure the enemy was successful, and Brula scouts reported to Callos that three marauding forces were converging to surround them. Callos stopped the march at a large town, and the Capital militia busied themselves with preparing makeshift defences, blockading roads, and positioning crossbowmen at windows or on top of buildings. Chokra, with their large shields and Galandar spearmen, worked together, presenting a prickly defensive wall. The militia brought wagons with them, distributing caltrops, barrels of Thog, fire flasks, flame sticks, and extra ammunition. When the wagons were empty, crossbowmen used them for elevation to fire over other troops. Callos was the South's chief general for over twenty-five years, and he knew the business of war. His militia leaders were well versed in his tactics and plans.

Enemy riders appeared, seeming content to watch from a safe distance. They were relaxed and confident, talking and laughing amongst themselves. Callos expected they had every reason to be cocky; by his scouts' account, more than half a million troops were arriving soon to back them up, possibly more, if other armies were to appear out of Islan. Vultures, perhaps as large as a donkey, were circling overhead. Seeing the danger they presented, Callos deployed more spearmen to protect the crossbowmen and counter any attack the birds might make. The militia shared their first sip of Thog at his command, putting metal in their backs and hearts.

The first enemy to arrive was a rabble of wild-looking men, long-haired and tattooed. Some wore leather or metal armour, although just as many chests were bare. Their armament was not uniform, but they appeared to know their business and were keen to get to it. In a great wave, they came across the farms and past outlying buildings toward the town, screaming their war cries and slapping each other on the back. At first, the slapping seemed to be for encouragement, but Callos saw there was more to it – it drew them together as they ran so that they presented a formation of sorts. Those with shields raised them to defend against arrows and bolts, while others ducked and weaved. Soon they were upon the barricades.

Callos expected his militia to appear as a rabble to the enemy, but they soon learned that the defence was determined and capable. In places where caltrops fronted the barricades, the charge of the wild men faltered. The small spikes scattered over the ground caused men to stumble, and others pulled up short of their target. In those locations, the crossbows drove the wild men away. Combat resounded from other areas, though the town parameter held firm, and the organised militia proved themselves deadly and steadfast. Rather than back off, the wild men used the barricades and buildings as cover, throwing weapons through the defences. Callos could see that it wasn't in their nature to give up easily. Even though they were only a spears length apart in some places, the enemy contented themselves to shelter in the refuge, and the battleground became deathly quiet. The Galandarians amongst the militia started up a song. The "Bloody War Song" was most commonly heard in taverns or around campfires. It was as good as Thog for the spirit of the defenders, and even Callos raised his voice to it.

More wild men and regular soldiers approached. Some wore military surcoats, and Callos observed infantry, archers, and cavalry units. They sported the same long unkempt hair and beards, giving them a mean disposition. There were designs on the armour similar to the wild men's tattoos. A commander amongst them was a large brute, outfitted in heavy armour and a two-handed blade on his back. His long hair was white and skin pale, giving him a deathly presence. The warriors about the leader were also heavily armoured, most wearing helmets decorated with animal horns or in the shape of beasts. At his order, the wild men resumed the attack, and he moved units of archers up in support. Heavily armoured footmen assaulted the barricade at the eastern end of the town's main street while warriors with axes hacked through buildings to bypass the organised defenders.

Callos issued orders to use the flame sticks. Even though the Dwarven devices were single-use, the enemy commander would not know that. Flames soon drove back the armoured warriors and cleared other barricades. The axemen coming through the buildings was now of more concern, and the militia would not survive long once the enemy bashed a door through their defences. In response, where the axemen were breaking through, Callos ordered the buildings set alight. It was inevitable that either his forces or the enemy would put a torch to them at some point. At least this way, he had control over the inferno.

To Callos, it seemed that these initial attacks were testing their strength. Nevertheless, he was proud of his troops that the enemy found no easy gaps or routes into the town.

The townsfolk were encouraged to flee their homes, but as

many as half stayed. Despite their terror, they did their best to aid the militia in the fighting. Men from the town took up what arms they could to assist, while their families carried water from the well to the defenders, and some found employment distributing ammunition or Thog.

Around the village, the defence remained resolute, and as night approached, the enemy withdrew to make camp nearby, close enough that Callos could hear them drinking and enjoying themselves. Fair enough, he thought, a final drink. Tomorrow many of them would die.

A fourth army arrived in the morning, but it soon moved on, taking some of the wild men with it. Then, mid-morning, the attack on the town, which Callos only just learned was called Riesenberg, recommenced. The Capital militia sipped their ration of Thog, putting a little madness in their eyes.

This time the enemy deployed troops at all the town's entrance points, approaching at an orderly pace rather than a charge. Enemy archers targeted the crossbowmen, and their numbers were such that they forced the defenders into cover. Soon their opponents were once more pushing up against the defences, and Callos could hear the din of clashing steel and shouts in all directions. The general deployed his reserve militia where most needed, and as he moved about, he could see the defences holding. Where fire flasks were thrown over the barricades to disrupt the attack, the horrific screams of enemy burning rose above any other noise.

The heavily armoured fighters succeeded at pushing the

Southern militia back, enough that they were clearing the barricades in some places. Where that happened, enemy cavalry joined the assault. The defence would have come undone without the Thog, but Callos' militia were tenacious, and their formation held. Fierce spearmen dealt with the riders, surrounding and killing them, or driving them back. The dead from both sides littered Riesenberg's streets.

Callos was a veteran of many battles, and in his gut, he was confident that here at Riesenberg, they would see another day. Every hour he waylaid these rampaging armies protected civilians fleeing the region.

SORCERERS

Tarnac had been under a cloud of darkness for some time. Possibly for as long as the troops from the northeast had been arriving. There were no people in the city, no life at all. The roiling night that consumed Tarnac was magnificent. As Render passed through the streets, he felt it swirling about him, observing him, caressing him. It was demonic and dark, beyond normal darkness, as if summoned directly from the four hells. Render was in awe. He would need to rethink how best to defeat Churgwarthos. He did not expect the Sorcerer to be this powerful.

The military commanders understood their business better than he did, so Render messaged the officers that he was departing. He also trusted Malakai to chase and deal with the forces that already slipped past them, grateful that the war leader grabbed the initiative to hurry to Veldaan. Conveniently, that left him to focus on Churgwarthos.

Render chose just four hundred soldiers as his guard. The remainder of the army joined those troops patrolling the roads through Sompher Gris and along the coast. The wizard and his contingent moved quickly into Islan then veered east towards the border with Veldaan.

Malakai was well ahead of Render. His cavalry moved boldly along the roads through Islan and into Veldaan, where Brula scouts brought him news of enemy forces rampant across the territory, killing and destroying. There were at least four rival armies of considerable size and many smaller groups of raiders. Carefully considering his tactics, Malakai split his army into two to seek out the main forces and destroy them. From what the Prince could discern, his opponents hadn't brought or built siege engines, so the well-fortified cities were not at risk. However, the camp cities near the portal were exposed. Taking one of the armies, he immediately hurried towards that location.

As Malakai rushed across the plains, the Brula returned from their forays with increasingly disheartening news. As well as massacres at the hands of the marauders, the town of Riesenberg and the impregnable fortification of Adash were both awash with Churgwarthos' darkness. Malakai refrained from sending his scouts to warn other communities. If the mighty Adash was defeated, he was unsure what action others might take to ready themselves anyway. It seemed that nowhere was safe.

When Malakai's cavalries arrived at the Rhalec Portal, a battle was already in progress. Many experienced Chokra and Militia were amongst those gathering near the gateway. The brave men and women did their best to defend against the wild men and other Northerners. Across a vast distance, Malakai witnessed hundreds of thousands of troops manoeuvring and fighting. In places, surrounded civilians were trapped and mercilessly butchered, while at the portal itself, the bulk of refugees pushed through in a panicked rush. Rhalec troops were helping the desperate families as best they could, and the Rhalec towers deployed to protect the portals wreaked havoc amongst the enemy that came close. Priests atop the spires directed divine lightning with theatrical movements of their arms, hissing as the bolts obliterated multitudes of enemy troops. One of the towers was dormant, its priests fallen to enemy arrows, and those civilians under its protection lay dead around its base.

Malakai's horsemen outnumbered the foe and outclassed them on the open plains. With the advantage of surprise and the momentum of his charging cavalry, they broke the enemy units so that the Northerners were soon fighting a desperate defence. Wedged between Malakai's horsemen and the militia, there was no escape, though there were heavy casualties to both sides before the last of the enemy was overcome.

A chill wind suddenly gusted over the battlefield. It had the stink of magic to it, and Malakai immediately feared the darkness might be upon them. Indeed, the enemy Sorcerer was making his presence felt, and Malakai didn't need to give an order for people to flee the growing gale.

Although the magic wind intensified, it did not manifest into the same darkness that consumed the doomed cities. Instead, it built steadily so that soon the sky was filled with clouds, and heavy rain fell across the field, turning it to bloody muck. As Malakai and his guardsmen came closer to investigate, the rain swirled about and drove into their faces. The deluge did little to dampen the sensation of magic in the air, and their horses moved about nervously. Finally, one close to Malakai panicked and bolted despite its rider's efforts to control it.

From the mud and muck, the dead lifted themselves on

hands and bent knee, clambering awkwardly to their feet, heads downcast. Then, incredulously, the risen dead began a deathly procession towards the east at a slow walk. Malakai dismounted and braved the blizzard to see more of their nature. One close to him turned and hissed, and the shocked leader could see all hells in its eyes. It frightened him more than any mortal creature could. Malakai shifted quickly away, back to his horse and kin so that they hastened to re-join the others. The surviving civilians were his ward now, including those here or further afield. He would see to their safety until they all passed through to safer lands.

Render's scouts brought him the same fearful tale of the desolation of Adash, and with fateful anticipation, he hurried toward that location. It was easy to avoid enemy marauders under the shamans' cloaking shroud as he sped through Islan and into Veldaan. When his small force drew closer to Adash, he encountered the undead gathered on the plains, a grisly host standing idle amongst swarming insects and flies. Hundreds of thousands of the risen, many dressed in civilian attire alongside dead soldiers from the South and North. Rotting, stinking corpses. Render waved them aside, and they obeyed his command, ambling mindlessly, then slowing, and again standing, staring blankly into the grotesque crowd. It was not a type of undeath Render was familiar with, and he could see the swirling darkness in their open mouths and soulless eyes. It was the same depth of blackness he witnessed in Sompher Gris, and Render sensed that it controlled their bodies and minds. It did nothing, though, to heal their open wounds or protect them from the decay of death. Concerned, Render stopped and commanded two undead to attack each other. Both screeched and lashed out with their hands, tearing at faces and skin. When he told them to stop, they returned to an inanimate state. Render suspected that through their eyes, all their eyes, even the empty sockets - the darkness was watching him. Its master was watching him. High above the horrific scene, giant vultures circled and observed.

The undead were not an immediate danger to Render, but he could not be confident about the safety of the others with him. He ordered the wizards, shamans, and soldiers he brought to wait further away on the plain. He would have liked Jaal or Morgan at his side – somebody fearless and competent that he trusted. Instead, he moved alone through the nightmare horde until he stood before Adash's open gates. The darkness was like a mist inside the fortress city, and its black tendrils leaked out through the gates to create wispy pools of darkness over low-lying areas of the plain. Render walked through the gloomy haze and into Adash. Like Tarnak, the streets were empty, with no sign of life, body, or blood to indicate a siege. There were demons here; he could feel it in his bones. They were powerful and menacing but not brave enough to escape their hiding place. Render laughed, but he did not goad them. They were wise to stay away from him. But, of course, his demons were with him, Fek was always nearby, and the two Drutha were experts at being unseen.

Adash was not a large city, though its streets were cramped and narrow. Render was ascending as he made his way towards the central keep. Even with his magic, it was hard to navigate in the darkness, and the slope helped him keep his direction. Eventually, he came to the citadel. Its massive doors were open wide, and heat radiated from within. Render did not hesitate before walking through the entrance into the welcome light.

Churgwarthos was a master of darkness but, like Render, still a creature of flesh and blood. The entry hall to the keep was warm and illuminated with the glow from fireplaces and torches burning along the walls. At the back of the large room, a huge vulture perched on the shoulder of a massive statue. The statue depicted a giant bird with its head held low and wings outstretched as if it were about to take off. The vulture squawked and was constantly lifting and stomping its right leg.

Under the head of the statue was a chair carved from stone. It was the seat of the Lord of Adash, solid and formidable just like the city. In the seat sat the enemy sorcerer. Churgwarthos appeared relaxed. It surprised Render that the sorcerer's physique was that of a fighter and metal armour covered his body but exposed his head. The armour was ancient, like its owner, with runes inscribed into its design. In his right hand, Churgwarthos grasped a long sceptre with a pick like head so that it might be a weapon. By comparison, Render wore dark robes and a sword at his side that he had not drawn from its scabbard in over two decades. In his left hand, Render clenched the Dwarven staff of JolRek-AsnakTorWervak, perhaps the mightiest of all weapons.

Now that Render was here, the Belarch entered the hall

through side entrances, positioning themselves along the walls. There were nineteen of them, looking much like their master with heavy armour and ornate weapons. Render learned from the Asari that each was a potent caster. Like the sorcerer, they wore no helm and stared maliciously at him. The faces of Churgwarthos and the Belarch were fierce; meanness was etched on their brows and painted onto their eyes. They looked down on Render, and the enemy Sorcerer sniggered.

There would be no dialogue today. To plan, Alani Elves appeared, filling the room, and launching themselves at the gathered enemy. Taken entirely by surprise, four Belarch went down before they could react. Their armour or mental agility saved others. Magical shields manifested to deflect attacks and push their assailants back with quick hand gestures. Elven champions danced around the Belarch while bullets slew two more. Render was joined by the spell weavers and their assault immediately brought a pillar of purifying light down upon Churgwarthos.

Churgwarthos was unaffected as the magic washed over him in a spectacle of pyro-techniques and noise. He did not expect an attack from the Elves, but he was prepared for Render to strike. Next, Antiel, the Light Bearer of the Alani, appeared near the throne, pointing his sword at Churgwarthos. A ray of vivid white light pierced the enemy Sorcerer's defence and struck him in the chest. Churgwarthos' armour glowed, the engraved runes took on the brightness so that the sorcerer appeared like an avenging Angel as he launched himself forward and struck down at Antiel with his raised sceptre. As the weapon impacted Antiel's shoulder, the light from the armour transferred onto him, enveloping, and rapidly consuming the Elf, utterly, until he ceased to exist. At the last moment and just in time, Render reached out, grabbing Antiel's soul, saving it from obliteration.

The Belarch unleashed the four hells on the Elves, who returned in kind with sun-blasts and ice. Just as many spells were unseen, as the casters surrounded themselves with invisible wards and shields. Those Elves most used to moving between real-space and near-space did so to avoid attack and launch assaults. Although the throne room was large, it was crammed with magic and combat, and as Alani perished, others appeared to take their place. Spellweavers and Belarch put all their might into their attack, screaming with ferocity and hate. This battle was fuelled by deep history and heavy grudges beyond Render's understanding. Render, at least, knew his role today, and he gathered his strength and wove his magic, waiting for his opportunity. Above him, Churgwarthos' pet circled, but as the magic below intensified, the creature dived low across the heads of those fighting and disappeared out the open entrance. At that moment, Render gave a fleeting thought to the demons that would be battling outside amongst the darkness.

Churgwarthos cast a spell and struck at a silver armoured champion who ducked the swing and stabbed back with his spear. Then, letting the stab bounce off his armour, Churgwarthos touched his sceptre to the ground so that the stone in the floor blasted upward. The Elf disappeared to near-space in an instant.

At that exact moment, Render sent forth his magic at Churgwarthos with the unfettered strength of the Core drawn from the Dwarven staff to give his spell immense power. The throne and giant bird behind the ancient Sorcerer glowed white. Still, an invisible shield absorbed any light that was to consume Churgwarthos, who haughtily brushed the incantation aside and countered with swirling darkness. He looked directly at Render and, with a cruel smile, pointed his sceptre at him.

Above Churgwarthos, there was a piercing squawk, and the surprised Sorcerer looked up. He was not quick enough to duck the great stone beak that swallowed his head and chest. The Sorcerers skull was crushed in a spray of blood, and his body tossed back and forth, eventually released to clatter against a wall. The great stone bird took a step forward, clambering over the throne and squawking again. As Render watched the imposing animation, it transformed, becoming a thing of flesh and feathers. That was not his doing; it must be Antiel letting his magic flow into the stone and draw from the power Render fed into it. The great Roc spread its wings and flapped them once for practice before launching into the airy spaces of the hall and taking the same path as the vulture through the exit and into the persisting night.

The battle was not done, and Render assisted the Alani against the diminishing Belarch. Without their Sorcerer, they were becoming desperate, but there was no escape except death, and now Render was vigilant to capture their souls so that even that avenue was denied them. Unfortunately, he was not able to catch Churgwarthos'

310

essence. It was too powerful. In his gut, Render could foresee the ancient conjurer seeking him out for revenge.

By the time the last of the Belarch fell, Render harvested eight souls, which he stored for safekeeping. Knowing the artefact's worth, he was quick to retrieve the Sorcerer's sceptre, although he was disappointed at its weight, far more cumbersome than he could properly handle. The Alani Spellweavers joined him near the throne, and he let them take the weapon from him. They stripped the body of the crushed armour, and then more Elves came to carry away the dead. As they stepped back to near-space, Render could have joined them, but chose to stay. Despite Churgwarthos' departure, the darkness consuming Adash remained, and there was an army of undead at the doorstep that would need a Sorcerer to give them commands.

Fek appeared at Render's side. There were gouges torn from his arms and thigh, but it didn't seem to inconvenience him. Render was fond of the demon, and he left the creature to lick the bloodstains on the floor. It was a climactic day, and it felt good to have his part in the war concluded. There was much to learn from studying Churgwarthos' methods. Render was haunted, though, by the Oracle vision from so long ago, and reluctantly he conceded that before he could investigate the magic at Adash, there was one more battle to fight.

THE FEN

In her gut, her woodland being, Roana felt drawn toward the Fen. The Fen lived in the northern forest, in a wild stretch known as The Tangle. The Fen were not elves, but they were not human, either. They looked like both but possessed animal traits in their mannerisms, wild nature, and sensitivity to the environment. The Fen were territorial, with a pack mentality in defending their lands, so they were largely left alone by the May and other civilizations on their borders. Nobody except the Fen entered the tangle until now.

Roanna drew her cloak about her as she crossed into the thick wood. A Ra-Anu trotted beside her. The delicate fawn attached itself to the Druid since the Council and followed her as she travelled. At night it would sleep on the ground, nestling into her for warmth. Roanna knew it was not seeking comfort but was there to give her the strength to travel her chosen path.

The Fen had been watching the Druid since she traversed their borders.

When they chose to reveal themselves, it was a surprise to Roanna. Figures stepped out of cover and dropped from trees to surround her. It was her first glimpse at the Fen, and the young Druid was amazed at how tall they were and the fierceness in their round faces. Two Fen ran at her with staves raised to strike. Instinctively Roanna summoned the forest to intervene. At her command, vines lifted themselves from the forest floor to catch and trip the attackers, and as they fell, more vines grabbed at arms and weapons to quickly pull the two Fen to the ground. Even though Roanna withdrew her spell, the vines tightened their hold and the forest floor folded over the struggling fighters until the earth covered them and all that was left was two leaf-covered mounds. That was not Roanna's doing; the Ra-Anu was also defending itself.

Several more Fen came forward. One waved his staff at Roanna and spoke some words she could not understand. However, the intent was clearly for her and the Ra-Anu to depart. Before journeying here, Roanna knew little of the Fen and hadn't anticipated language would be a barrier. Still, during her apprenticeship in the Fogmir, she learned other ways to pass on messages. So, reaching into the mind of the talker, she put there the thought, "Do not fight. Put down your weapons."

Taken aback, the affected Fen recovered quickly, and he yapped to others of his kin before waving his staff at Roanna again, even more aggressively than before. Roanna reached into all their minds.

"I am Roanna of the Elves. My companion is of the Ra-Anu, a spirit of the forest, and servant to Fengal. All here are creatures of the wild."

The antagonist pointed his staff, but another Fen stepped forward to calm him. He addressed Roanna more respectfully, and his tone seemed conciliatory. Roanna placed a thought of thanks into his mind. She felt his curiosity as she did so, but it was beyond her fledgeling skill to make greater sense of his thoughts.

Roanna sat and, with a gesture, invited the speaker to join

her. He did so, and the Ra-Anu acknowledged this stranger with a touch of its head to the Fen's arm. Then, reaching out, the Fen stroked the fawn down its neck and back. Roanna tensed, sensing a moment of darkness in the Fen as he considered grabbing at them both now that he was close, but his curiosity stayed his hand. Roanna smiled and introduced herself again using the common tongue. It was a beginning.

The Fen lived like the Fogmir Elves, travelling The Tangle, and spending the nights in trees or amongst their roots. Roanna quickly adapted to their routine, although her distrust of some of the Fen kept her awake the first night and plagued her sleep as they travelled. The tribe she adopted was more than two hundred men, women, and children. The curious man, Ernak, was one of several patriarchs, and Roanna was under his protection. It was odd that the two Fen that died at Roanna's hand drew little attention from the clan, as if death were not important, or was purposefully left unmourned. The Fen were a primitive people leading simple lives, and like the Elves, respected the forest around them. They coveted their isolation.

Most days, other tribes crossed their path. They traded and briefly socialised, then moved on. Roanna and the Ra-Anu were a curiosity to them. Each tribe had its differences; one kept large hunting cats, another wore only bear skins and grasped weapons that mimicked a bear's claw. Learning their culture and language required more time than Roanna could afford. So, when she felt the need to return to the Hand, she arranged with Ernak to make a trading place at the border of their territory, where Elves and Rhalec would come to exchange goods. Roanna promised to talk to the merchants she knew.

When Roanna left the tribe, the Ra-Anu stayed. The Fen embraced the forest spirit and its enchantment. In the brief time the fawn was amongst the Fen, a sickly child grew in strength, which the Fen attributed as a great blessing. After that, everything good; a successful hunt, a warm morning, even the appearance of a child's first tooth – were all attributed to the Ra-Anu. The Elves at The Hand would not be pleased to lose possession of the spirit, but it would give them greater motivation to embrace the arrangement she made with their neighbours.

Roanna expected that her second objective, making peace with the Spiders, would be more complicated. The arachnids were fortifying areas of the forest, often those expanses most impacted by the disease Eya spread, shutting themselves away behind a maze of webs. It seemed to Roanna as if the Spiders and Elves wanted to keep the feud alive, giving them a reason to hunt each other and test their courage.

The Elves of the Hand were aware that Jaal led the Spiders in raids against Amon Murn. Both nations were on the same side of the war, and to Roanna, it seemed outlandish that they could simultaneously be enemies and allies. But, while the thought gave Roanna hope, she was wise enough to appreciate that the path toward unity would be long and filled with obstacles.

THE HIGH SATAR

The High Satar mingled around the demon portal with his many priests. They prepared carefully for the summoning, and there was a nervous tension as the final ritual commenced. The men poured water over the floor when all was ready. As it touched the side of the dark hole, it hissed, turning crimson and thickening to a bloody consistency. The multitude of priests chanted the words of the ritual in unison. Although they whispered, the collective sound echoed eerily about the large chamber.

Clawed hands appeared at the pit's edge as three dark shapes pulled themselves onto the lip, shuffling through the muck and examining the priests. As the High Satar witnessed many times before, the demons were emaciated, and their sunken eyes seemed dim and lifeless. They were like dried husks. The creatures searched amongst the priests with great care, sniffing and caressing the holy men with their long nails, tasting them with extended tongues. When they selected the one they wanted, the chosen man was grabbed by the other priests closest to him before he could run. Forced to his knees, the desperate man struggled and screamed. Initially, the demons scratched the man in the neck and back so that he bled, and then they climbed on top of him to open the wounds and drink his fluid; at first sips, but then gulping his blood as they tore larger gouges in the flesh. Finally, the other priests let their comrade go, stepping well back to allow the creatures to complete their messy work.

These were the Portal Keepers, and refreshed, their demonic eyes glowed with primal energies. Even their wrinkled skin was smoother and took on a glossy sheen. Ready, they leaned over the pit and screeched, calling on their diabolic magic. Immediately, there was a distant wind, and soon after, the room filled with flapping shapes, demons that were clustered around the portal exit waiting for their opportunity to escape. But the Portal Keepers bound them, and as they always did, they passed command over to a waiting priest.

The priest followed the demons out of the underground cave and into the light of the temple city. Some fiends lost their enthusiasm in the sunlight, perching on temple roofs and cowering, while others found places in the shadow. Raising his staff and shouting the phrase of command, the priest ordered the demons to come closer so that they glided to be near him on the ground or crouched on the stone wall nearby. One bat-like form came too close, and the priest scolded it, causing it to scuttle backwards into others of its kin who hissed and pushed each other. The demon's part-human head glared back at the priest with malicious intent. The priest incanted the last of the ritual, sending the demons into the air where they circled above. Together, they scuttled and flapped down the hill of temples and through the town. Behind him, more priests were bringing other flights of creatures to heel.

When the day's ritual and summonings were complete, the High Satar stood alone in the empty chamber. The priests were all departed, and the Portal Keepers slunk back into the pit. He would send the initiates to clean up. The dead man on the floor was a priest he had known for many years, Figal, not a good man. The initiates would be glad to see him gone. It seemed such a small price to pay for the cooperation of the four hells. He remembered first opening the portal and the mass sacrifices that left the whole hill covered in gore. The High Satar recalled the blood seeping down the hill and along the gutters of the city streets below. With pride, he recollected Urath'a'tharack bending the greater demons to his will. It was a time of unparalleled majesty. Under his breath, the ancient priest muttered a blessing in Urath'a'tharack's name.

The High Satar accomplished all that he could; Urath'a'tharack was on his way, and the armies would have enough demons to fill the sky. He gave them prophecies too, but he was as blind as all the others to how the age would end. They would all know soon enough.

VESTIG GOZER

Vestig Gozer gathered the Thran, a meeting of his many generals, the Wurn, and the Hunga. The Wurn set enchantments, while the Hunga placed sentries to protect them from spies or the Spiders. Vestig commanded the Armies of Amon Murn. He rose to that position after the bungled invasion of the Blood Sea over two decades ago. During that campaign, under his leadership, the soldiers of Eymar sacked the city of Hindas. He would have taken the prize of Viletri too, if not for the interference of the Bracadians. Fortuitously, the Bracadian fleet killed his predecessor, who would never again have his name spoken for the shame of his defeat. The Thran elevated Vestig to be the Efate: General of Generals.

But in that last campaign, it was just the twin cities that had gone to war. Now, every town in Amon Murn and their allies gathered to follow Urath'a'tharack's tombstone east. Of all the leaders of all the generations that fought the Rift War, it would be Vestig Gozer that would see the South finally defeated.

Vestig was waiting for Churgwarthos to join them. The Sorcerer and his minions would be vital in the battles to come. Now the Wurn told him that contact with Churgwarthos had ceased, they were concerned. Concerned! Within, Vestig was seething, but he appeared calm as he always did to those about him.

The Hunga brought him better news. He sent them abroad to re-unite the North, and only the Veldaan and Wengo defied them. The Veldaan was not a surprise. That nation was broken and rebuilt by the South. He knew the lands of Veldaan was their refuge after the destruction of the Southern strongholds by the Dwarves. The Wengo, though, disappointed him. He sent the Hunga to set an example of the Orcs; show other nations' leaders the consequence of disloyalty.

The enemy, Mannace, intended to draw him into battle on the Markhon. The Markhon was primarily flat land that would aid both forces as a battlefield. His adversary set up his pieces as if inviting him to a game of H'ru. For now, it suited Vestig to gather his troops in the hills near his enemy's location. Then, if Mannace and his minions grew impatient and attacked, the high lands where Vestig gathered his forces were defensible. He possessed no patience for H'ru or those that played it, but this game suited him. The North would have its full strength soon, and then the contest, the generations-long conflict, would finally be concluded.

Urath'a'tharack's tombstone would arrive the next morning. It was an important symbol to the soldiers, and Vestig gave the artefact appropriate reverence. The massive sarcophagus was the heart and soul of his force, so he understood the importance of protecting it, keeping the legend and prophecies alive. But, of course, he was a cynical man himself who would not rely on myth to end this war, though cynicism, like any emotion, was best kept secreted away.

Vestig Gozer, Efate of Amon Murn, nodded to his speaker to address the assembled Thran. A thin, supple-looking man in loose-fitting clothes stepped forward. He was blessed with a handsome face, kind eyes and blonde hair that was cut short on one side and hung in braids to his waist on the other. In a lively tone, he welcomed the gathering and paid homage to Urath'a'tharack. The speaker's job was to give the Efate's report and issue orders to each person assembled, verbal and written. A small squad of aides ran papers back and forth.

Vestig prepared the orders over many days. Reygan, the speaker, boasted an impressive intellect and exceptional memory. Most importantly, he made the process feel personal for those involved so that they understood their part was vital to the campaign's success. The gathering listened so that everybody knew each other's business, where they would fight, their role in the conflict, and any unique details. When Reygan finished, heads were nodding.

The Efate turned over a crate used to hold papers. He stood on it, addressing those present. Unlike Reygan, his voice was coarse, and he could see the generals close by cringe at its deep tone. It made them seem weak.

"You have your orders. You know the signals. Do not fail me. Do not fail Amon Murn and Urath'a'tharack."

The Thran was quiet as Vestig stepped down from his box. He liked that the generals and others took a moment to consider the consequences of not doing their part. Vestig left them to their thoughts and made his way back to his tent. With the battle planned, Vestig could focus on getting himself ready. Back at his quarters, the Efate removed the chest plate of his armour from its stand, and he sat with it on the floor. Taking up an oiled rag, he caressed the metal with gentle, round movements. Vestig relaxed into the task, letting his mind empty of the planning that consumed him. Instead, he focused on the fighting to come, the hacking and slashing, the familiar business of murderous combat.

THE MESAH LONG

Markhon was a wildland. Most people lived in the northern reaches, in towns and cities by the sea. Here in the east of Markhon, the territory was often windswept and inhospitable. Today though, the breeze was barely noticeable, and the sun was pleasantly warm. Mannace sent Brula with orders to adjust the lines. The armies of the South had been in place for five days, and each day Mannace moved troops in response to new information coming from the winged men.

The southern forces camped along the eastern edge of the Mesah Long, a narrow but lengthy plain bordered by hills to both the east and west. It may once have been a great lake, flat and with pebbly earth. Vast expanses of grass and copses of trees grew on the plain, and an unimpressive creek wound its way from south to north. Patches of red blooms gave the plains some colour and life. From high above, Mannace observed the prairie to have a crescent shape, thickest at its centre and curving gently back around the eastern hills. The western elevations were higher and steeper so that the Northern army that camped there enjoyed a slight advantage in defence and with its lookouts. The land dipped into a valley with a small lake and sparse forest to the northeast, while the Mesah Long converted into a narrow ravine with steeply sloped hills on both sides at the south-eastern end. Behind that, a range of towering bluffs known as Meype Blight dominated the skyline.

Mannace would have liked the battle to commence

sooner. Instead, he would be patient while Amon Murn continued gathering its full strength. He expected they would not come down onto the Mesah Long until they were confident of victory. The extra time was helpful to him as well; the Rhalec towers and the War God's Thunder were brought through the valleys of Rockhome and set up behind the southern camps. Also, Render was bringing reinforcements. His army of undead hurried through the hostile territories of Islan, Tubul, and the Gap to be in time for the conflict.

Jaal ceased the spider raids and re-joined the Blood Legion. After that, it was up to Eya to decide if the spiders committed to aiding them on the Mesah Long.

The Alani returned and joined the camp of the Fogmir Elves. Together, the Elves were one of his elite divisions, equal to the Remman and Colonial Riflemen. Mannace was proud of his southern host.

Mannace's long-ranging Brula did not return from their missions the following day. His spies observing the northern camp came under attack from squads of winged creatures shortly after. The outnumbered Brula were surprised and overwhelmed, not fast enough to escape their attackers. Suddenly, Mannace was without eyes in the sky, losing a significant advantage. As more time passed, the flying demons, as Dekon Ruel identified them, increased in number so that they swarmed above the northern camp. Their movement reminded Mannace of the flocks of Loretts that gathered in their thousands at twilight over the Veldaan, swooping madly back and forth.

Mannace received news of enemy troop movements to the north and south. He was not surprised that they would want to surround him. However, the discovered troops were patient, positioning themselves perhaps half a day's ride away. Worryingly, other news came from the lands under the Southerner's control, The Young Kingdoms, the nations along the western coast, the Ryde. The Northern rulers hadn't forgotten their old allegiances to Amon Murn, and they were reneging on recent agreements made. It would make the defence of Veldaan much harder for the Southern garrisons and militia left behind, but Mannace refused to be distracted, and he kept that news from the soldiers of those nations that made up his armies. More than ever, time was his enemy's friend.

Mannace sat at his desk aboard his flagship, scrutinising the numbers and deployments. The scribes made lists in the way he liked it, detailing the mix of troops in each division. It was like reminiscing, to peruse the Eastern Colonies roster; it proved a long journey to establish the Colonial Divisions, but now there were two hundred and fifty thousand modern soldiers equipped with rifles and muskets. Mannace ran his fingers over the entries for his other troops; Keshik war elephants, Brula, Belg, the Furi skirmishers, the brave Fesadi, heavy cavalry from Cavastock, the magical Alani, the Two-Face berserkers, Orcs from the Iron Jaw and Black Valleys, the wild Madland's troops with their slave soldiers, and likewise the slaves from Tarash Gormoth. As he reflected, Mannace realised the Charikon mercenaries served in the army for more than twenty years. It made him laugh out loud for no particular reason, attracting the clerks' attention as they scurried about his command tent.

Mannace was quicker to glance over the summaries of other nations; three hundred and fifty thousand Remman – the last of their kin. He took a moment to reflect on Rakor and their friendship. He expected the king-general to be standing next to the War God, looking down on them and giving his frank critique. There were fifty thousand infantry and cavalry from the Holy Lands. More than ever, they were the carriers of the Light in this time of darkness. Six hundred thousand soldiers made up of men that once called Galandar, Roundhome, and Cavalere home. Mannace was rushing over the list now. He laughed again as his finger settled over the entry for more than five hundred thousand Orcs from the Wengo hills and mountains. What a coup that was to not be facing the savages over the battlefield. There were over fifty thousand troops from the northern lands that knew nothing of their leaders change of loyalties – at least as far as he knew. It was a sobering thought, replacing Mannace's smile with a deep frown.

The clerks counted and assessed the enemy too. He studied those entries long enough to have them in memory; almost eighteen divisions of one hundred thousand troops each, compared to his fifteen divisions. Mannace realised that the comparison would have been much darker if the South hadn't persisted and triumphed against Veldaan over the last decades. He should be proud rather than worried.

As he stood, leaning over the table filled with papers, a clerk approached him and cleared his throat to get Mannace's attention.

"General, sir, lookouts are reporting the enemy is coming down from the hills. They are forming their line."

"Thank you, Erwin. Enact the plan."

FIRST BLOOD

Mannace stood with his generals on the slope, giving them their final instructions. The last of them now hurried to re-join their divisions. Taking a deep breath, Mannace took time to look around him and further afield.

The number of demons was such that the Brula could no longer be used to carry messages, and instead, some of the Alani were waiting nearby to assume that role. Mannace was concerned that it would not be as effective, but it was vital for him to have a way to control the ebb and flow of the battle. At the top of the slope, Rhalec hauled two of their towers forward. A contingent of crocodile warriors with muskets followed in support. Turning his gaze to the stony field below, Mannace noted that the War God's Thunder was ready on the plains with its entourage of cranes and ammunition wagons. Once in place, the great mortar seemed vulnerable to attack from the sky. Mannace called an Alani to him.

"Tell commander Tilkatea to bring three towers down from the hills to protect the mortar. Then go to Rhumas and tell him to send two thousand muskets there. Be quick."

The *Bracadian* was nearby, but it was unlikely the skies would be safe enough to use the flagship. Mannace watched as some of the other flying ships moved low over the battlefield, staying close to the musket men as he instructed. Other flying craft would be cloaked, waiting in ambush. He squinted to see further north, hoping to make out the *Gull* that travelled with the Wengo. Jaal was issued his instructions too, but the leader expected his friend was more likely to follow his intuition.

Mannace made every effort to appear confident, though his heart was racing. With the last of the Generals arriving at their positions, it would soon be time to commence the attack. Lastly, as tension escalated, Mannace waited until the Towers and musket men moved to protect the mortar as instructed. Once in place, he turned to Jayne, always near his side.

"Put out the green smoke."

A puff of green smoke filled the air behind the command group and rose skyward. Rangers piled the fires with extra sticks and dried grass, as well as the powder that turned the smoke bright and green. An Alani wizard, Amelia, standing next to Mannace, enticed a light breeze that pushed the smoke upwards and away from the gathering. Mannace was momentarily distracted, watching the graceful movements of Amelia's tiny hands as she wove her incantations. Then, a thunderous boom broke his miasma and brought him back to the scene on the plain. The War God's Thunder fired the opening shot of the war. In the distance, near the enemy's formations, there was a great puff of dirt and dust as the giant mortar shell exploded. Mannace couldn't tell if it landed amongst troops, but he expected any close by would be cleaning out their pants. A cheer echoed up from the plains, and Mannace watched the soldiers on the slope celebrate what they assumed was first blood.

The southern armies moved forward until they were a quarter of the way across the plains, where they reformed and waited. Skirmishers hurried ahead, but not far enough that they would be vulnerable to the swarms of demons. The Southern reserves, including the few units of cavalry and the mighty Colossi, stayed back on the hills. It was how Mannace envisioned it.

At the southern end of the valley, shapes swarmed over the hills, massing and moving onto the plain. Mannace was relieved to see Render finally arriving. Everything was now in place. The enemy was also ready, and Mannace watched them step into the open in a long line. Behind the western hills, the sky turned orange, more intense than a sunset. When Mannace looked at Amelia, she waved her hands again, pulling some invisible force towards herself.

"General, I believe the orange sky is an illusion, used as a signal to the armies of the North, much like our green smoke."

"I think you are right, Amelia. Impressive, don't you think."

"Spectacular, General."

Mannace left the command group and walked a short distance along the slope. Around him, magically cloaked soldiers became visible and made way for him. Finally, he came to a gathering of casters. Here, a Shaman maintained the shadow cloak, surrounded by others of The Muster and their guards.

"Are you ready, Wizards?"

"Yes, General."

"Begin."

The first fireball rose into the sky from where the wizards hid, arching over the southern forces and gaining speed as it descended across the gap separating the two armies. Like the mortar blasts, a cloud of dust and dirt rose from the plains where it impacted. This time the smoke had a tinge of red, and a column of fire rose out of it, moving about until it was suddenly snuffed, replaced by a patch of darkness. Other magic arched out across the plains, landing amongst the enemy. Balls of fire and magic were returned across the battlefield, most colliding with unseen forces and exploding or vanishing in the air. A few landed amongst the southern troops causing carnage. Mannace closed his mind to the distant screams as he made his way back to his command position. He knew this was just foreplay for the magicians – testing each other before the armies collided and the actual duelling began.

An Alani appeared next to him. It was one of the Spellweavers that travelled with Render.

"The Sorcerer has arrived, General. He asks for his instructions."

Mannace smiled.

"Tell him to get on with it. He should stay on the right and make his presence felt. Tell Render to show them what a Sorcerer is capable of."

Mannace smiled as he looked down at his hand. He had drawn his broadsword from its sheath at his side without realising it. It reminded him that he was still a warrior, and the steel felt good in his grasp. He used the sword to point at a mass of giants moving behind the enemy lines. Then, he spoke to another of the Alani messengers.

"Tell Khing to take eight Colossi and make that horde of giants his business. When they come forward, I want the Colossi in the defence."

"Yes, general."

The Alani shifted into near-space. It was as if he stepped behind a wall.

Amelia touched Mannace on the arm. She pointed skyward to shapes circling far above, much higher than the demons or Brula. Mannace could tell from the sighs and comments around him that everybody was surprised and concerned.

"What are they?"

Amelia did not know, though one of the Alani messengers was bold enough to give his opinion.

"Wyverns general. You can see that they have a fork in their tails. They exist in the ice wastes to the northeast of Amon Murn. They are typically a solitary race."

Mannace squinted to see more, but his eyes were not as good as the Elf's, and he certainly could not see the tails well enough to tell they were forked. He could count, though.

"There are at least thirty of the creatures. That does not sound solitary to me. Make sure the towers are aware and prepared. Make it clear to the Rhalec that the Wyverns are not ours."

Mannace raised his voice so that those about him could all hear.

"Perhaps they have come to witness the battle of this Age. Today that Age ends, and tomorrow the Age of Empire will begin."

As if triggered by his words, the rumble of musket shots echoed across the Mesah Long accompanied by a haze of gun smoke. Soon after, arrows arched in both directions, most coming from the ranks of the Northerners. For a long time, it seemed to Mannace that the fury of the muskets stalled the Northern advance, but in places, through the din of the rifle and musket fire, came the roar of charging warriors and the steel-on-steel clash of units colliding.

THE UNITED TRIBES

Jaal was at the prow of *The Gull* with Casteel, Athose, and two Orc Shamans. The Shamans placed the ship in shadow as it hovered low over the Blood Legion gathered below. Accompanying the Legion were the Orcs of the Wengo, a gathering of Two-Face, and an elite cluster of Iron Jaw. Jaal looked ahead at the formations of the enemy. Mostly they were the heavily armoured legions of Amon Murn, but behind them were auxiliaries with bows and a horde of wild men. There were a handful of Giants amongst the troops, but Jaal's eyes were on the legion of Giants further back from the combat forming into ranks.

He enjoyed a spectacular view of the Southern line from the ship's deck, which appeared endless in both directions. Absentmindedly, Jaal placed his hand on Athose's shoulder. The young Elf shrugged off the gesture, moving back to join Rey, Agro, and others at the rails. Agro was pointing and laughing at something below.

Arrows whizzed through the air. Jaal watched the Orcs respond with a roar and then charge, barely holding their loose formation as they sprinted forward. He could see the Two-Face swilling their Thog and rushing ahead of the others. Jaal's experience told him that the berserk Orcs would be a handful for the soldiers of Amon Murn. Nevertheless, the Blood Legion on the ground kept pace, and *The Gull* jolted slightly as the Navigator, Chimchum, manoeuvred the sky-ship forward.

Jaal was disappointed at Athose's reaction to his touch, and he was surprised in himself that he couldn't shake that small rejection. All of a sudden, he no longer felt comfortable aboard the *Gull*. Even looking at Casteel, he realised that his presence undermined her. He adored the Elf, and perhaps with all that happened over recent decades, she understood him better than any other.

"You have done well, Casteel, to prepare the legion. They respect you. You have earned the right to lead them."

With that said, Jaal stepped up on the prow rail, and picking his moment, he leapt from the ship. With skill and an element of luck, Jaal landed on his feet and between two legionnaires. One caught him as he stumbled and pulled him along so that he was soon keeping pace with them. They seemed glad to have him there, and he drew his blades, hooting a battle cry. Then, using his fantastic speed, Jaal surged forward and was soon at the Legion's fore.

In front of Jaal, Orcs were already engaging the footmen of Amon Murn. They employed the Rage and threw themselves against the enemy ranks. While many were pushed back, just as many broke through the defence to make way for others. It quickly turned the front line into a messy brawl. The legion flowed into the gaps the Orcs created.

Jaal was suddenly amongst the combat. The two Orcs in front of him bashed past their opponents, relying on him to protect their flank. Immediately, Jaal faced two heavily armoured swordsmen. The Dark Elf was precise with his parries, thrusts, and cuts, letting time slow to help guide his blade. He dispatched the soldiers, caught up with the Orcs, and ran ahead. Mercilessly, Jaal slashed a bloody path. He had never extended his abilities so far or experienced so much control, ducking an arrow, and accelerating to stab his blade in the archer's neck. Two more fell as he spun past them, slicing their throats, and then leaping at more armoured men. It was such a release to lose himself entirely in the combat. Jaal was no longer sure what direction he moved, but as he cut through the enemy lines, Orcs and Legionnaires filled the space he created.

Amongst the disorder, a veteran unit of Amon Murn infantry closed their ranks and raised a determined shield wall against the Orcs assault. The Orcs charged boldly at the infantry, screaming their taunts, but their rage did not break the tenacious defence. Swords poked back at them, taking a bloody toll. Finally, a Two-Face berserker ran past Jaal and pushed aside a retreating Wengo. He launched himself at the shields, swinging his two-handed maul. A blade cut a trail of blood down the Orcs side, causing him to drop his weapon, but it did not stop the beast from reaching over the protection and bashing an enemy soldier with his fist. The Orc grabbed the man's shield with his left hand and pulled it down, giving him momentum to wrestle his victim to the ground. Jaal was into the gap, stabbing at a shield-bearer's exposed side and parrying a thrust from another foe. With his unnatural quickness, Jaal pushed more soldiers out of his way to widen the breach, and then he resumed his bloody dance. Wengo brutes piled in behind him, while others arriving with shield-hooks pulled down more of the defences. One of the Blood Legion was beside the Dark Elf, a lanky Keshik dervisher who danced his own path of whirling blades. It encouraged Jaal to increase his effort until he was a blur of cuts and thrusts.

A giant loomed to Jaal's left, bringing his axe down hard to split him in half. With time slowed, it was not difficult to dodge the blow, but his counterstroke bounced off an armoured thigh. The giants were formidable without armour. Clad in metal, they were an impenetrable fortress. Then in the chaos of melee, an ally bumped Jaal from behind. He recovered just in time to duck under the giant's shield as the creature looked to crush him with its rim. Again, Jaal's blades clanged off the gargantuan's defence, unable to find a vulnerability.

Without warning, the giant lurched forward, crashing down toward him. To avoid being crushed, Jaal dived, and as he recovered his feet, he could see an Iron Jaw Bull Rider on the giants back. The bull was slipping after the collision, beating its enormous wings to give itself balance. The Orc atop the bull pulled back on the reins, and with a great thrust, the beast leapt back into the air. Moments later, a shadow blocked the sun as bat-like demons swarmed close overhead to pursue the Iron Jaw champion. The fiends' high-pitched screams drowned out all other noise of battle as they passed close above. Jaal stood stationary as he watched the demons pass. Orcs clamoured past him, so again, he let his energy surge, racing back to be at the fore of the action.

Behind the enemy, more giants loomed. This time they marched in large numbers and were formed into orderly ranks. To Jaal, they seemed like a wall of steel stretching as far as he could see to his left and right. The giant infantry edged forward, pushing up against the melee so that the Orcs moved quickly backwards while the soldiers of Amon Murn were allowed to pass through the monsters' ranks. Even the maddened Two-Face backed off, confused. A trumpet sounded when the battlefield was clear of the withdrawing Amon Murn troops, and the giants quickened their pace. The outclassed Orcs retreated, and some fled, terrified at facing such an impossible foe. Where the giants chased them down, the Orcs turned and desperately slashed or stabbed, but it was futile, and they were bashed or crushed underfoot. The blood legion fared no better, and it was not until *The Gull* came forward and showed the rampaging giants its broadside that the beleaguered infantry escaped. Jaal, who withdrew alongside the others, watched the barrage of cannon fire, killing some giants, but others roared and came at the Orcs faster. *The Gull* climbed higher to be out of reach while continuing to unleash its incredible firepower. Other ships appeared alongside the Legionnaire's vessel, and Brula came in numbers to throw their flaming bombs. One ship foolishly ranged lower than the others, and Jaal watched giants grapple onto it, pulling chunks off its hull and smashing it with their weapons. He saw one giant shoot a bolt into the ship's side, so large that it poked through the hull.

A colossus stepped near enough to Jaal that he could have touched it. He was too distracted by the smoke and noise of the cannons to see the titanic creature approaching. Now that he looked more distant, other colossi were advancing to intercept the enemy. They were few, but they were massive, and they were invincible. Jaal yelled to be heard over the noise.

"Turn, you bastards. Follow the Colossus."

Legionnaires nearby responded, and together they moved in the shadow of the colossus to benefit from its protection. More allies joined Jaal, including Wengo and a remnant of Iron Jaw. *The Gull* was directly above, with demons hanging from its rails, swooping, and clawing at her hull. A Brula crashed into the ground ahead of him with two demons attached. He accelerated, stabbing at the creatures while running past, moving on without knowing the winged man's fate. Jaal realised it was insanity to return to this fight, but he was not afraid of death. Instead, he laughed and charged to meet it head-on.

The Colossus towered above the giants it was fighting. It threw the creatures about, and one that landed heavily near Jaal looked to rise to its feet. Instead, Jaal and others swarmed over it, hacking, and stabbing between the armoured plates. Death was everywhere, friend and foe, a desperate frenzy of gore and blood and killing. Jaal felt elevated by the carnage. It was as if his power fed off the darkness. With time slowed down around him again, Jaal ducked an infantryman's sword, and he stabbed at others, surging forwards, wounding and sometimes killing. Then, unexpectedly, an immense weight hit him from behind; another giant tossed aside by a Colossus sent Jaal tumbling and colliding with other soldiers. They all rose, a little more battered, and charged back into the fray.

Casteel returned to the bow of the Gull once the steam vents cleared demons from the decks and hull. She ordered the ship lower, knowing that the cannons were more effective against the giants when they were at their level. Next to her, Rey leant over the side to dispatch a solitary demon, hanging on despite a scolding. Athose clambered onto the *Gull's* head, loosing an arrow that bounced off a giant's helm. Rey laughed.

"Good shot, boy."

After releasing its volley of cannon fire, The Gull lifted higher again, shifting slightly to starboard to pass by a colossus. Seeing his opportunity, Athose ran along the rail, and he leapt out into space, deftly landing on the colossus' shoulder, and stumbling forward slightly before regaining his balance.

"Hu. I have missed you."

The colossus could not respond, but it let go of the broken giant it held and straightened to its full height. The action made it easier for Athose to perch, but it restricted Hu's ability to fight. Other Colossi entered the fray. Athose did not recognise the new arrivals, but they fought the giants just as fiercely. The young Elf was curious that one of the Colossi was made of a different material, black like the others, but reflecting the sun so that it shone. Athose fired another arrow. It struck a giant in the face, causing the creature to stagger back as it pulled the missile from its cheek. Blood flowed out its mouth and down its chin, making the creature cough and choke.

Casteel also watched the new Colossi arrive. They came

from the north and were intent on throwing themselves against the giants. The wyverns that circled high above seemed allied to the group. Occasionally one of the enormous flyers would swoop down to harass the giants, raking their heads with extended talons, before climbing back to the skies. They were fearless of the demons, quickly scattering them if they swarmed nearby. The majestic creatures were magnificent and terrifying.

From her high vantage, Casteel was optimistic that the battle between the United Orc Tribes and Amon Murn forces swung in favour of the South, for now. There were still thousands of giants, and legions of other infantry rejoined the conflict too, but the Orc hordes were reclaiming lost ground with help from their allies. While the flying ships helped slow the giants, the rampant Colossi broke and scattered them. The Colossi were indeed indestructible, and even the most potent of magic washed over their towering forms.

Several exhausted Brula landed to rest and treat their wounds on the deck behind Casteel. Further afield, the skies seemed safe for the moment. Other ships were flying in low to reinforce the conflict, and casters on one of the vessels added blasts of magic to the chaos. The scene was both macabre and spectacular.

THE WURN AND THE HUNGA

Vestig Gozer ascended the ranks of the Hunga to be their commander and the General of Amon Murn and all its allied forces. He felt at ease amongst the Hunga's ranks, and as they marched, he reached out to push the man to his right. The shove caused a chain reaction to others as they bumped and then righted themselves.

"Ha, you are weak. Vestig will show you all what it is to be mighty."

Each warrior of the Hunga was hugely built, fortified with the Mole Men's science, and fully plated in thick metal armour. Only Vestig wore no helm, letting his matted blonde hair hang in knotted locks down his back. He looked down the long line of warriors and back through the deep ranks. The time felt right, and he roared to ensure those nearby paid attention, then he jogged slowly forward.

Ahead of the Hunga, the battle raged. The Mago, with their insects, swarmed over enemy soldiers, but Vestig could see they were too few now to sustain their onslaught. At least they completed their job to bloody the enemy and break apart their formations.

As Vestig ran, those closest to him took position behind, with others following so that the Hunga surged forward as a great wedge. It was their way, Vestig's way, that their champion would be at the fore of their attack. Above him, the fire spells of the Wurn arched overhead and landed to clear him a path. Above that, the demons gathered in a great swarm. Then, at the command of the priests, they set out ahead of the Hunga to assault the defensive positions on the hills.

It was not Vestig's intent to trample the Mago, but where they did not leap out of his way, Vestig knocked the insects aside and kept his line. He stabbed at a southern soldier and knocked aside the musket of another. It was simple stuff, and the Hunga wedge was unimpeded as it broke through the scattered ranks and into open ground. Not far away, more Southern units were readying themselves for his assault. These enemies were more to his liking, and a champion amongst them strode forward. Vestig increased his pace, and he heard the Hunga shout their war cries as they charged. The approaching hero was unphased, encased in a fantastic contraption, like armour but much bulkier than that worn by the Hunga. Power radiated from the enemy warrior, and with an outstretched hand, an invisible wave of terror enveloped Vestig and the warriors behind him. But terror was nothing unusual to the Hunga and would not break their spirit. Rather, it fed them, adding to their frenzy. In his other hand, the enemy champion swung an enormous hammer that Vestig only just avoided, running wide to prevent losing his momentum. He looked over his shoulder in time to see the champion slam the weapon into one of his warriors, creating a wave of invisible forces that sent some of the Hunga tumbling. The magic was not enough to stay the momentum of the wedge, and at its fore, Vestig drove into the enemy ranks. Such was the Efate's bulk and strength that the impact did not slow him, and the point of the Hunga's formation bore deep into the Southerner's ranks. As the spearhead of the wedge pushed harder, the Hunga warriors overwhelmed their foes and caused others to retreat hastily. Those few that stood defiant were stone rather than flesh, fighting statues, fearless and unbreakable. Vestig left his soldiers much further back from the tip of the wedge to deal with them.

Once past the infantry, Vestig again had open ground before him. Adrenaline peaked, he ran, and always, the Hunga followed. As the Efate drew close to the foothills, a horde of beasts hurried across the stony plains; They were four-legged and much larger than a horse. Enormous tusks protruded forward from their heads, and on their backs were shielded platforms with archers. Elephants, not unlike those of the Dead Lands. Vestig could see Frain, one of the few giants amongst the Hunga, break away from the wedge and move towards the beasts. At Frain's call, many other warriors changed direction to run with him, forming their own wedge.

Magic arched towards Vestig's troops from the hills, roiling missiles of flame and ice and darkness. But, before they struck, they met with invisible forces, exploding into incredible pyrotechnics in the sky. The Wurn were at work, and shapes grew from the brilliance; birds of fire that circled the field and shrieked. Their noise was an assault on the mind, though not the Hunga. Vestig could see that it confused the tusked beasts causing some of them to collide, encouraging the Efate to laugh at their feebleness.

Across the hills ahead, balls of fire and acid rained from the sky, exploding along the slopes - also the Wurn's doing. The hills appeared black in places, not just from the magic, but where whole flights of demons lay dead. The few surviving hellspawn swooped at the gathered enemy. Unexpectedly, behind Vestig there was a tremendous boom. As he glanced back, a blueish glow rose from the field, well back from the Hunga. With that, the missiles stopped falling from the sky, and the screeching birds were suddenly gone. Vestig roared, picking up his pace, focused on the hills ahead and the enemy troops gathered there. To his left, however, cavalry rapidly approached. The noise of thousands of hooves drowned out all other sounds. Vestig was frustrated that he would not cross the Mesah Long in time, and his demons had not distracted the enemy as much as he hoped. Without the Wurn at their backs, the Hunga were vulnerable. Cursing, he changed direction and ran towards the galloping horsemen. Behind Vestig, the wedge lost its shape as the Hunga turned and charged to meet the swiftly closing foe.

The Hunga and the cavalry forces collided with great violence. Even Vestig was knocked back by the bulk of a galloping horse. But keeping his feet, and with a mighty sweep of his blade, he took the legs out from beneath another as it charged by him. The cavalry's momentum drove the Hunga back, trampling or scattering them. Quickly recovering, warriors soon reappeared around Vestig, using their unnatural strength to push and panic the horses or stab up at their riders. Like the Hunga, the cavalry was heavily armoured and seemed experienced. So be it, let the generals on the hills see what the Hunga were capable of, what fate they would soon share. With that thought, Vestig let his wrath loose on the enemy, cleaving and bashing. He loved to kill.

COMMANDER

Mannace understood the danger. Below on the field, the enemy broke through the centre of the Southern line. Only the Cavastock horse and Keshik with their war elephants were between his command on the hill and the rampaging enemy. He knew they were the Hunga, the elite of Amon Murn, and he could see that they deserved their reputation. Across the Mesah Long, the battle remained in balance. It seemed the action would be won or lost here at the centre.

Mannace sent messengers to the Remman units to halve their ranks and send reinforcements to the middle, to aid the defence of the slopes, and assist where other enemies were streaming through the breach the Hunga created.

The towers and muskets along the ridges proved devastating against the demons, and the South were again masters of the skies. Mannace called for his flagship, and soon *The Bracadian* was positioned to take the command group aboard. Before clambering up the rope ladder, Mannace addressed those that remained behind.

"Keep our positions secure along the hills. Justus, you are in command here. I will need the Brula and the casters. The Hunga will have no reason to assault this position once they see us depart. Stay the course."

Once aboard, Mannace walked to the prow, where there was a commanding view of the battle scene below. Although the casters were aboard, it was still too great a risk to approach the combat at the centre where enemy Wurn might still be lurking. So instead, Mannace commanded the captain to take them right and high. Instantaneously, the ship was on the flank and well above the combat.

"Bring her low, slowly, but be ready to move to safety."

"Yes, General."

From the prow, Mannace could see a mass of troops fighting below him and even amongst the steep hills where the Mesah Long converged into a twisting valley, skirmishes abounded. As the *Bracadian* drew closer, it seemed to him that the dead were fighting the dead. All types of ghouls and horrors crashed against one another, clawing and slashing, while more of their kin crowded behind, driven by human masters. Render was there amongst the carnage and other casters with him. Even an Iron Jaw waved his staff and rattled bones. Mannace was close enough to see the magic users lay waste to all that came near, adding flame and noise to the mayhem surrounding them.

The leader called a Brula officer to him. The creature was large for his race, with mean eyes. Although his glare was malicious, Mannace was used to it, and he matched the winged man's glower. Jayne, who was nearby, put a cautionary hand on his sword hilt.

"Gather the flock. Bring all you can muster and put an end to the necromancers."

He pointed to the men he wanted to eliminate. There were possibly sixty of them behind the enemy's undead horde. From the prow of *The Bracadian*, they were easy to make out in their colourful robes, and each carried a bone staff that they swung around as they cast. Units of soldiers, dressed similarly in bright colours, protected the Necromancers, and fought alongside the enemy undead.

It was the first chance for Mannace to assess the undead that followed Render. They were a shambling mob, mostly lifeless until they drew close to the combat. Then they, too, grew in vitality and were throwing themselves ferociously amongst their opponents.

Back from the action, riflemen reinforcements waited. Mannace could not afford soldiers to be idle, so he summoned another Brula to him.

"Tell the commanders of those units to move back and towards the centre. Tell them to run. They are urgently needed there."

Mannace was satisfied that the flank would hold.

"Captain, go higher and move along the line."

The enemy they passed consisted of many races of men. Some, like the Islani, were familiar enemies, while others Mannace had not seen before. In this melee, the Colonial riflemen and Remman seemed dominant. Moreover, the unit of men from Kampatan and the Manticore that led them stood out. The Manticore was spectacular as it used its enormous wings to batter the enemy it faced.

A lookout yelled.

"Demons above."

Mannace steered up, but where the lookout pointed, the glare of the sun obscured his vision. Before it could adjust, he was looking up at a clear sky. *The Bracadian* shifted position. Far below, the two undead armies were still locked in combat. Brula gathered, perhaps hundreds, which was alarming compared to the thousands they could muster when the battle began. Mannace would join them, ordering the Captain and casters to prepare. After dealing with the necromancers, he intended to keep the flying men with him and return to the conflict at the centre.

In the hills at the end of the Mesah Long, Giants were clearing the slopes. Mannace recognised them as the Rockhome tribes. But strategically, the hills were unimportant. It would only be a factor if the giants descended and attacked Render's undead in the flank. Then, without the riflemen to cover them, they would be vulnerable. Reasonably, Mannace felt less concerned about losing undead than he did his living soldiers, plus Render was always at his best under pressure.

THE GAME

Nordan summoned the Colossi to him. That included those who travelled here with him, plus the others who were his servants until *The Enemy* entombed them. It was a moment of rare pleasure to enter the battle and fight the giants, but like other mortals, they were no match for the power of the ancients. Now Nordan grew impatient to get to his business, to find Urath'a'tharack. He cast his gaze over the enemy from his elevated vantage, reaching out with his mind.

Athose watched the Ancient from Hu's shoulder, anticipating Nordan's intent. He knew from listening to Casteel and his father talking on the ship, where they thought the tombstone to be.

"Behind those hills, where the road comes onto the plain."

Hu and some of the other Colossi started moving where Athose directed. Nordan did not notice the young Elf until now. It was a curiosity. The Elf was right, though, and Nordan set out in the same direction.

Behind them, the giants of Amon Murn regrouped. They regained confidence with the Colossi and wyverns gone. Unfortunately for the battered Orcs and Legionnaires, the absence of the Colossi and resurgence of the Giants, put them immediately on the defensive. The poor change in fortune would be paid for with their flesh and blood.

Behind the battle lines, the Northern reinforcements scampered to let the gathered Colossi pass, except that when Nordan's troop came to a road between two hills, a line of armoured giants and priests formed a determined barrier. In support, demons launched themselves from the ridges, filling the air, swooping, and screeching. Nordan looked up and signalled. Wyverns came immediately like bolts from the sky at his summons, sweeping aside the demons, breaking, and scattering them. Other wyverns landed upon the giants and priests, crushing their opponents, and chasing down the few to escape their initial assault. Athose was wide-eyed and open-mouthed at the breathtaking display. As he stood, awestruck, with one hand on the side of Hu's head for balance, he raised his bow high in his other hand and hooted a shrill war cry.

Not waiting for the violence to finish, Nordan strode toward the revealed wagon that carried the massive tombstone of the first-giant. Summoning his power, he raised a fist and brought it down upon the stone. There was a deafening crack as the granite split. Magic from it sputtered with blue sparks before fizzing. Nordan reached his hands into the divide, pushing the two pieces apart. The ancient casket was empty. Urath'a'tharack, the Sleeper, was not within the stone. Nordan immediately understood that the stone and its enchantment were a ruse. In a sudden fury, he kicked the cart so that two of its massive wheels broke, and the casket slid, ending with one side on the road. The Ancient was not usually quick to anger, but now his temper was ablaze.

Urial, Acolyte of The Eternal and partisan of The Wurn,

sensed the dispelling of his enchantment. He acknowledged the discovery of the ruse he and others of the faith planned. Not that it mattered now; they were at their destination, and Urial's gigantic ship berthed next to a handful of smaller vessels. First, warriors from Amon Murn made landfall and secured an area outside of the city of Colossus. Then, using ropes, armoured giants shifted a great slab of granite from the ship to the shore. Upon it was carved a depiction of the sleeper, Urath'a'tharack, held within. A small army of giants and men were disembarking through other exits along the vessel's side. They were an elite group befitting of the task entrusted to them.

Several Colossi watched the preparations while Orcs gathered at a distance. Finally, a single slave came forward from the city, walking casually to join the visitors. The slave smiled warmly and spoke in a soothing voice.

"Welcome to Colossus. You are expected. The King has left instructions."

"Where are the Hunga?"

"Dead. The Orcs killed them."

Urial was surprised, and he instinctively raised his defences, creating a silver tinge to the air around him. Unphased, the Slave expounded.

"When the order came for the Wengo to answer the Sleepers Call – to place their allegiance with Amon Murn, there was tension. Many died. Amongst them the Hunga."

It did not matter to Urial that the Wengo were traitors or the Hunga waiting here were dead. It only mattered that the Mad King kept to the bargain.

"Where is the bell."

The slave reached into his robes and produced a small bell. It was crafted from a dull metal and intricately carved on its surface. It seemed ancient and was cold to touch. After passing the bell to Urial, the Slave also produced a metal tapper that he passed on ceremoniously.

"The Mad King said that only the bearer is safe when the bell is struck. Others must stand well back. He suggested covering their ears."

Impatient, Urial walked back to where Urath'a'tharack was placed. He ordered others back, and they obeyed. At the last moment, he shouted the instruction to cover their ears, and all did so. He held the bell forward and raised the tapper.

"Urath'a'tharack, I release you from your slumber."

Ding!

After a long moment, the Acolyte looked back at the slave, who stared back at him. He maintained the same simple smile that gave nothing of his thoughts away.

Ding!

After another long moment, Urial knew the situation for what it was. Nothing seemed right since landfall, and now he was the butt of this Mad King's joke. Turning, he reached out with his magic, grabbing up the slave, levitating the man roughly toward him until their faces were only a palm width apart.

"Where did the Mad King go?"

The slave was uncomfortable in the magics tight grip; his body bent backwards at an unusual angle, and heavy pressure was on his chest. Nevertheless, he was conditioned to withstand pain. He was also programmed to tell the truth.

"The King departed by ship twenty-four days ago."

"Does he have the bell?"

"He had a bell. It was much larger than the one he left for you. If you do not release me, the Colossi will attack."

Urial wanted to snap the slave in half, but he could not risk losing the body of Urath'a'tharack to the Colossi. So instead, he placed the slave back on the ground and ended his spell.

"I will find your Mad King."

There was no doubt in his voice. There was no doubt either that there was violence in his purpose.

DUSK

When dusk approached, both armies were battered, bloody, and exhausted. In places where the fighting was fiercest, bodies were piled high, and the Fesadi found few survivors amongst those struck down. The Fesadi healers continued to cart the wounded back to the hills for treatment as they did all day. In some places, the Southerners could claim victory. Where the Wengo fought the giants, it was victory enough not to have been overrun and slaughtered. On the other hand, the South was sorely beaten in the middle, where the Hunga raged.

The sky was purple behind the hills occupied by the Northerners, and red smoke issued from the Southerners' signal fires. Wherever there was a break in the combat, both sides retreated, intent to regroup during the night and resume the fighting when morning came. Some warriors were reluctant to move back to the hills, but there was nothing on the plains except stony earth and bloody corpses, making neither a comfortable nor safe bed.

Already Mannace was making changes. There were thousands of Belg amongst his armies, and he ordered them together as a unit. Tomorrow they would stand at the army's centre alongside the remnants of his Viletri elite. The Belg would provide the Hunga with a worthy challenge or even the giants if matched. Now that he controlled the skies again, those flying ships with ammunition would be his main strike force to combat the giants, and Mannace sent a Brula to summon the captains to discuss tactics. Unfortunately, only two colossi remained with the army. The intruder that aided them against the giants had gathered all the others and led them north. That was a significant setback and might be the Southerners' downfall in the day ahead.

Mannace learned of an attack at the northern end of the Mesah Long. It was a flanking manoeuvre intended to overrun their defensive positions from behind. However, it was the Spiders that saved them, intercepting, and routing the Amon Murn soldiers - trapping them in the woodlands to the North and dealing them a savage defeat. Many other updates and decisions needed his time, but Mannace was exhausted, needing to rest before the morning. For now, instead of sleep, Thog was shared amongst those that needed to be awake.

Clerks and messengers came to him with reports; rifle ammunition was utterly spent, although musket powder and shot were still in good supply. There was a food surplus, and Mannace ordered double rations for all soldiers. The order reminded Mannace that he also needed to eat, directing a clerk to bring him meat and fruit. When it arrived, he joined Jaal and Render, who sat near a fire on stools that they stole from *The Gull*. They were roasting pheasant. Jaal looked up at him.

"This is poor pickings for a last meal. Where is the wine?"

Mannace took criticism from the words, intended to be humour.

"Ha, you were in the worst of it. The South gave as good as they got today. You will eat again tomorrow night."

Render and Jaal looked at each other. It was clear to

Mannace from the way they shifted uneasily that they disagreed, but they left the topic aside. Jaal raised a concern.

"Athose went off with the Colossuses."

"Colossi."

"What?"

"More than one Colossus is Colossi."

"Hells' sake, Mannace, who gives an Orc's bollocks! They headed for the Tombstone. You need to send some Brula to find out where they are. Get the Elves to see if the Tombstone is still with Amon Murn or if the Colossuses, *bloody Colossi*, took it."

"Ok. I'll do that."

Mannace watched Render check his dinner by piercing it with a thin dagger, then place the meat back over the flame. He always liked his meat well seared.

"I hear you killed the Sorcerer."

"I had some help. I am starting to like Elves. They're more useful than they seem."

Jaal nodded, forgetting that he, too, was an Elf.

"Antiel is a giant bird now. A white Roc. When you meet with the captains of the ships, you should tell them not to kill him if they see him."

Render had their attention, and to satisfy his friends' curiosity, he told them the whole story of Churgwarthos' demise and how Antiel was transformed. By the time Render completed the tale, Mannace was finished his dinner and wiping his mouth on a cloth handed to him by an aide.

"Well, it seems that you are the Sorcerer now. Today we won the battle of the skies, and we have superior magic. We have our Sorcerer. Those advantages will make the difference tomorrow."

Jaal and Render shared another look. Mannace did not want to hear what Jaal might say. He preferred to keep his thoughts positive, so he would be convincing when he told his Generals and Captains that they were winning. If he believed it and they believed it, Mannace knew from experience that it would be true. He excused himself from his friends' company and returned to his army of clerks. They were waiting impatiently for him with their data and questions.

BROTHERS

The Mad King stood before the High Satar. The High Satar was not his usual calm self. The Mad King always rattled him.

"Don't do this, brother. There is no purpose to it."

"Why must there be a purpose?"

"You have always been a horse's prick. You're only happy when you're the focus of attention. When you are at the epicentre of chaos."

The High Satar could see that his words had no impact, so he changed tact.

"Nobody will know you have done this."

"Tyriah is dead. She killed herself. She was so bored that she chose the void over her life in this world. You are here, brother. You will be my witness."

"If you do this, then we will be dead. There will be nobody left in this world to tell."

"Your Gods will know."

"They will know you are a cock, a selfish man that despised his own life so much that he hated all life. A man so cowardly that he would make others pay the price for his shortcomings."

The Mad King heard enough. He raised the metal striker, and he hit the bell. He struck again because he was agitated, and he wanted this to be over. There was a deep rumble in the earth where he stood at the top of the hill overlooking the temples and city of Imbor. The ground shook so much that even the Colossus standing behind knelt on one knee and braced itself.

A crack appeared in the city below, widening quickly to be a great maw that swallowed buildings and people as it expanded. The growing orifice consumed the slope leading up to where they stood, temples toppling into its depths. Once the city was consumed, the maw spread out to take in orchards and farms. Behind the Mad King, the walls of the Grand Temple collapsed in on themselves, adding to the ear-splitting noise.

Before the trio, there was a gigantic wound upon the earth.

It took an eternity for the ground to cease shaking and for the noise of destruction to abate. There were other survivors, and their distant screams and cries carried up to where the Mad King and his brother lay shaken. As he raised himself from the ground, the King looked down into the vast abyss. Within the darkness of the pit was a spec of red light at the very edge of his vision.

The King perceived another noise, at first an echo of a wind or storm. Soon after, black shapes emerged from the gulf and hurried skywards. Demons. But they were only a forerunner, and the noise grew to be deafening. Then, as the clamour threatened to consume them, a vast blackness of shapes ascended, spilling into the sky, hiding the sun from view. In the chaos and darkness, nearby creatures flapped and screeched. The High Satar was chanting, unknowing if it was his ritual that protected them or if it was because of the King who opened this gateway between worlds. In just a brief time, millions of the flying hell-spawn were set free. Now, as the flow abated, restoring their view of the landscape, the brothers watched other shapes clambering out of the abyss, mostly human-sized creatures, with others as big as the colossus behind them – walking things of darkness and oblivion.

"An Age of shadow. Are you proud of yourself, brother?"

The Mad King ignored the words. It was done. The feeling of agitation at his brother for spoiling this moment was gone. He did not need to wait to see more creatures come through the portal. Perhaps there would be no end to their number. So, instead, he commanded the Colossus to take up the bell, and the trio made their way down the hill. They hurried away from the abyss that was once Imbor, and back towards the distant coast where the Ark awaited them.

DAWN

There was something new about this dawn. Mannace was not the only one to sense it. Today felt like the beginning of something, and his optimism sat better with him. He was confident when he addressed the generals, but as he faced those gathered, a shadow was expanding across the plain behind them. Soldiers looked and pointed to the blackness filling the sky behind the enemy camp. They witnessed enough demons to know that their swarm cast this shadow. But this was much larger than anything they dealt with over the last days.

"Get the soldiers back to the Rhalec towers."

The commanders needed no other instruction, quickly dispersing. Mannace could see the troops were not waiting for orders on the plains. Instead, they were already hurrying back to the ridgeline.

On the far side of the Mesah Long, the enemy moved too. It was too far to be sure, but their movement gave the sense of a similar panic in their camp. Soon, it was evident to Mannace that the armies of Amon Murn were under attack. Obscuring his view were tens of thousands of demons swooping over the field, many landing to feast off the dead. As the swarm drew closer, they appeared famished, tearing into battlefield carrion, and fighting amongst themselves for the best pickings. Men were still clambering up the slopes as the first demons made it to the hills. Musket shots echoed, but the screech of the hellish fiends soon drowned out all other noise. When the devils came in a swarm, the Rhalec released the tower's lightning. The sky went white with the raw power of it, cutting a swath through the demons' mass. Dekon Ruel and the War Priests called on their God too. Thunder joined the lightning, and beyond Mannace's expectation, they rolled back the demon mass. Still, in some places the creatures dragged soldiers off the slopes and into the sky or snatched up the stragglers that were too slow to retreat safely to camp. Then, they angled back to the Mesah Long and joined the feasting there. Some descended to consume their own dead at the foot of the slopes, ravenous, though Mannace expected the gruesome orgy would not satisfy them for long. In the sky, flights of demons moved in all directions, and it seemed that more were arriving from the west in a continuous flood.

At Mannace's insistence, the Alani reached deep into Amon Murn through the ways. They found the same horror; demons ransacking the landscape, killing, and destroying. Other reports arrived of incursions into neighbouring regions. Mannace struggled for breath as if the fates drew a belt around his neck that they kept wrenching tighter, intent that he should fail. But, without choice, Mannace put his ambition aside, drawing on common sense to be his strength and guide, one straightforward step after another. Pragmatism was his defence against the panic that threatened to devour them all. He commanded a withdrawal and sent messengers ahead to Angorok.

It was a long trek back to safer lands. The army did not bother to keep order as they fled down the single road that led back to the Veldaan. The Wengo followed a different fork toward their hills and mountains. The flying ships, particularly those with the most capable navigators, were used to ferry soldiers not only to Angorok but to Viletri and the distant bases in Arenland. The Elves were soon gone; they exited through the ways or into near-space.

Not everybody was so eager to flee the Mesah Long. The Remman chose to stay. They had honoured their commitment to Mannace to fight in the final battle, and now they were entitled to a heroic death. The Rhalec priests and warriors would not abandon their sacred towers. Instead, the Remman helped them move the defences further back along the ridges so that there was a much smaller area to defend. The War Priests stayed too. Their God and Dekon Ruel, their commander, would not release them from this battle; there was still an enemy to slay. Other warriors remained; devout followers of the War God and some that preferred to stand and die rather than escape. Bollo was there, with those Galandarians that were inspired by his courage or who were tired of running. Mannace left them the two Colossi, the surviving stone men, and the animated metalworkers. Most surprisingly, the Fesadi were still present, working alongside clerics from the Holy Lands. They cared for the wounded that were in no condition to move. It was no ragtag army. More than three hundred thousand veteran soldiers prepared their defences. Dekon was in charge; for him, this suddenly became a holy war.

Part 6:

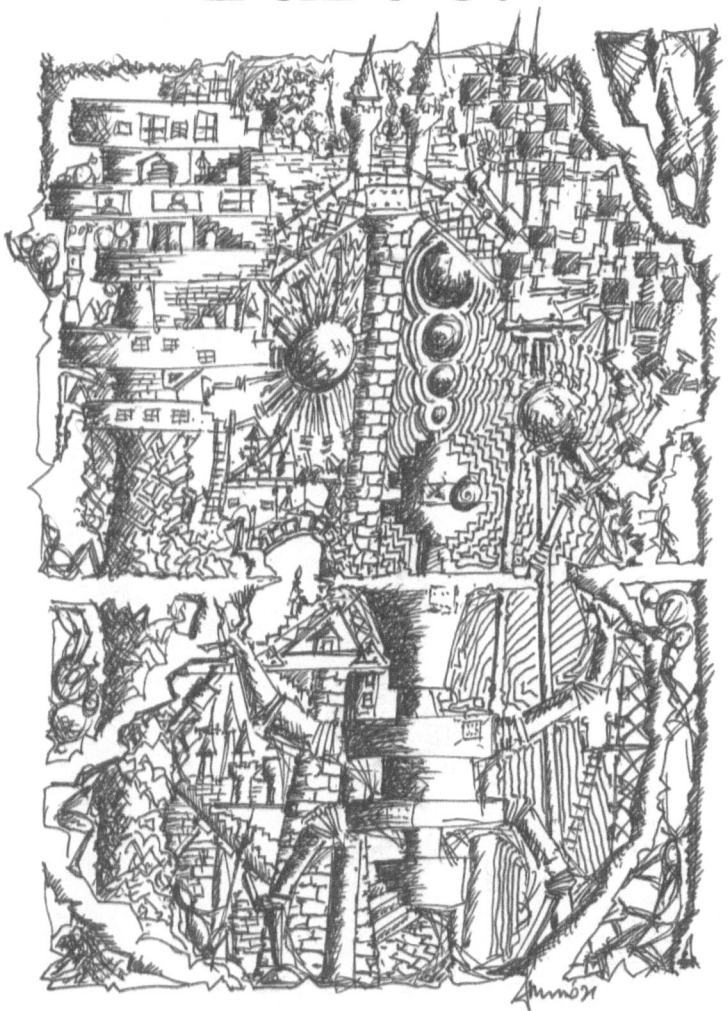

A New Age

A SHIFT IN POWER

During the retreat to Angorok, Mannace learned what he could about the demons. Nobody was controlling them as they did during the battle with Amon Murn. Instead, they seemed driven by hunger, with an appetite for carrion or anything with blood flowing through its veins. Where the demons attacked in massive numbers, they quickly overwhelmed his troops, and there was little the Southerners could do to stop the killing. Even when the musket men slaughtered them by the hundreds, it only served to fuel the frenzy and feasting. So, it was a relief to make it to the Veldaan capital with most forces intact.

Mannace reassigned the Rhalec towers protecting the Veldaan cities to the capital. They slowly arrived. Some civilians came with them, but most made haste to the Rhalec Portal. A stalwart few did not heed the warnings, though Mannace expected they would not be so bold if they saw the demons at work.

Malakai did his best to protect the Veldaan, but some cities were already in ruins, sacked by the rampant armies from the east and rebel raiders from the west. At least the portal, with the Rhalec's help, remained secure. Now, at Mannace's order, Malakai's horsemen protected the roads so that people could make their escape. To help with the task, army units returning from the Mesah Long and Sompher Gris reinforced the young generals' patrols.

Reluctantly, Mannace released the units of northern allies from his service. They remained unaware of the betrayal of their leaders, but they would know the truth soon enough, and the returning fighters helped spread the news of the demons. He hoped such information would motivate the enemy raging across Veldaan to return to their homelands.

Above the city of Angorok, as Mannace looked out from the keep's top parapet, he was joined by one of the Asari. Jayne, who stood nearby, gave the wizard a stern look to leave Mannace in peace, but the mage ignored his gesture.

"General, Angorok is blessed. I thought you should know."

"What does that mean, Elderlin?"

"It is a refuge against demons. We have experienced troubles with demons in the past, so a blessing was arranged. The High Satar came with other priests from Imbor, and they placed protections over the city. It worked against the Drutha."

"Will it protect us against the swarms?"

"It might."

"That is good news. Good news is in short supply."

"There have been hard times before. Perhaps not as tough as they are now."

The mage paused as Mannace turned back to his view of the city. Rather than leaving him in peace, the wizard's intuition was to stay.

"Can you not feel it, General. These events are a beginning, not an end."

Mannace turned towards the Asari, his interest sparked.

"I did not take you for an optimist, Elderlin. I do feel it, but I have eyes and ears. Look about you: defeat, terror, desperation. The Southern lands are lost. Veldaan is under assault. The war with the North is shattered."

Elderlin put his hands on Mannace's forearms and looked him in the eye.

"Those are things of an Age past."

The two men stood there, eyes locked for a short while until the Asari pulled back and nodded at Mannace. Then, he turned and walked back to the stairs.

Mannace sent word to Fitius to summon the Council. They would meet at Viletri for an emergency session. Mannace expected it to take several days to convene, even with the flying ships. Meanwhile, he focused his efforts on moving the population of the Veldaan to safety.

For now, Veldaan was free of demons, but the information Mannace received warned that neighbouring Islan was teaming with hellspawn. He conceived a plan to buy more time, requesting Casteel to join him. When she arrived, Mannace rolled out a map of the North on a table, wasting no time with chit-chat.

"Some demons followed us through Rockhome and down here into the Veldaan. But we have dealt with those. A much larger swarm passed through the gap and attacked Tubul and these parts of Islan. They could move west into Veldaan or South into the Sarang, even this way into Sompher Gris. I want you to make sure they go south, ideally south-east."

Casteel always did as asked.

"We will need more ships with class A navigators. At least four."

"This is important. For now, you can have six."

"Leave it with me, General."

Three days later, *The Bracadian* pulled into the Sky Tower at Viletri. Four Viletri guards were waiting for Mannace there. One ran ahead while the others escorted the leader to the Council Chambers. As he travelled between the two locations, Mannace was already suspicious. Now in the Chambers, only Fitius was there to greet him. There was not the usual busyness to suggest that others would be attending.

Fitius looked nervous, and Mannace's glower did not help his anxiousness.

"Mannace, I will get to the point. You have not been present as Governor for over two decades. During the last twenty years, I have kept the government running. The Eastern Colonies have grown considerably under my leadership."

Fitius took a moment to collect his words before sharing them. His nerves raised the pitch of his voice, and he was tweaking his right earlobe with his hand. Mannace was used to making people nervous, but Fitius was not one of those people in the past.

"I am the Governor now, Mannace. I meet regularly with the Emperor. I have his blessing."

Once he said the words, Fitius put his hands on his hips as he puffed himself up. His face took on a look of determination. Mannace never considered that Fitius might usurp him, but he already knew his mind.

"Soldiers are returning through the portal, Fitius, including many who have never seen the Eastern Colonies. Some will want to visit their families, but they must *all* understand that the fighting is not over. They are still needed."

Mannace wouldn't give Fitius the affirmation he was seeking, but he did not have the time to mess with him either.

"In the North, there is a new enemy. A horde spawned from the first hell that feasts upon the domain of men. They will devour the North and cast hungry eyes over the South, over Viletri and Arenland and the rest of it. I need to know you are committed to the fight, Fitius!"

An awkward silence followed. There was too much unsaid for Fitius to feel comfortable to respond. Mannace, though, knew he could bend Fitius to his purpose, and he took a step closer to the new Governor, slowing his speech so that each word was deliberate and intimidating. Of course, he wanted what he said to be menacing.

"Fitius, will you support the fight in the North?"

"Yes, Mannace. Of course. The Eastern Colonies remain committed to the fight in the North."

Mannace relaxed. He liked Fitius, but he saw too much of the demon bitch's influence in his actions to respect him. He would leave this conversation before letting those thoughts take him down a darker path.

"Give the Emperor my regards, Fitius."

Mannace planned other business in the city. He left it too long to set the Dwarf free from his cell, but he need not have worried; the Architect already extracted him from the dungeons and bonded him to projects where the Dwarf's knowledge could be of use. Mannace found Logthar in the Animators' Quarter, sitting on a three-legged stool huddled over a workbench. He wore a steel ring about his neck to mark a prisoner.

Logthar saw Mannace approach, but he did not raise his head from his work. Instead, Mannace watched him place a cog amongst a configuration of other components. Thirty years ago, Mannace would have found the work fascinating, but he did not have the patience or time now to show an interest. Rather, Mannace took a moment to remind himself of the Asari's advice; the past was the past.

"I need your help, Logthar."

The Dwarf flinched, but he stayed with the task at hand. He was securing the cog with a tiny pin. Once done, he looked up.

"We are enemies, Mannace."

He tapped the ring around his neck for effect.

"We are friends, Logthar. I need you to come with me. What happened is in the past."

"You waited a long time to show up, Mannace. I've almost forgotten why I came back."

"You pissed on our friendship. Good men died fighting

your kin. Men I called friends."

Logthar frowned at that last comment. It poked at the guilt he held for his actions. This man called Mannace before him, was not the same as the man he had known. This man possessed a deepened hardness to his features and cold steel in his eyes.

"All right then. Get this damned collar off me." Then, looking down at his work, he added, "I hate this intricate fiddling, always have. Don't have the thumbs for it."

"Then, why do it?"

"Why do you think! That bloody Architect is impossible to work with. He likes the sound of his own voice. Only has ears for his own ideas."

Mannace didn't want a scene, and Logthar did not attempt to lower his voice. He changed the subject.

"Logthar, A New Age has started."

"What the hells does that mean, Mannace? One day at a time, that's how life works. One bloody day at a time."

EVOLUTION

Nordan sensed the change. A shift in time. The death of an Age and the birth of another. It was not the climax he travelled here for.

Nordan and the Colossi arrived at the sea: a sandy beach with crystal clear waters. It was far enough from cities that few people were about, only a handful of fishers, far out on the water.

The Ancient stood on the beach, letting his mind relax, reaching out into the environment around him and then further afield. He would learn the truth of this new age. Was it indeed the time of Ancients reborn? It did not have that feel to it.

The wyverns that circled above spiralled slowly down to rest on the dunes. The Colossi, too, relaxed, standing and looking out to the sea. Hu set Athose down so that the Elf could stretch his legs and wash his face in the water. Athose paced back and forth, talking to those Colossi he knew and looking for those minor differences that could tell the others apart. Then, as he had done before, he gave names to those that did not have them.

A night passed, and still, Nordan did not move. Athose found a Beard Nut washed up on the shore and balanced it on his foot and head to pass the time. He tried to make conversation with his companions, but it was hard when it was just him talking.

A screech broke the silence in the bay. More noises followed. Demons appeared flying low over the dunes, and they hurled themselves at the wyverns as they slumbered and pruned. It startled the fantastic beasts so that they launched themselves into the sky. Even those not near the attack rose to circle and look back down at the ground. More demons were appearing, flapping, and searching the dunes. One noticed Athose, but as it dived at him, he was quick enough to raise his bow, piercing its chest with an arrow. As it fell, it screamed and writhed, attracting the attention of its kin, who swooped on it and tore at its black flesh. They saw Athose too, and several scampered and hopped across the ground to be at him. Hu put an end to one with a stomp of his foot, and he scooped Athose up to protect him. Another of the Colossi scattered the attackers. Hundreds more demons appeared amongst the dunes, but with the Wyverns taken to the air and the Colossi not constructed of flesh, they sped west along the shoreline. More were joining them all the time, so soon, there were thousands, swooping and bickering as they moved away.

Athose remembered there were cities and towns along the Markhon coast.

"Hu, Fungus, Norm, Bella, Scratch, follow them."

The named Colossi moved to obey Athose's instruction. Others followed their lead, and soon only the meditating Nordan and a single Colossus remained. The wyverns circled the group, staying high enough to be out of the demon's range.

Nordan was oblivious to the movement. He cast his mind much broader, and he did not like what he was finding. He saw the servants at the epicentre. Nordan hadn't attributed them such a pivotal role in events, believing them inconsequential. Some of the demons that arrived in this world bore names. They were names that fought the Ancients before, been their match, resurrected now to usurp the Ancients rightful place as lords over the mortal world. He understood their capabilities, what darkness they would bring. Nordan knew they would not forget the old struggles and their demise.

The Lord of the Colossi opened his eyes and returned his focus to the physical world. Beside him, there was a colossus, and in the sky, two wyverns circled. Demons lay dead on the sand. Much of his entourage was missing, though the Colossi were not light-footed, leaving deep impressions as they strode west.

Nordan moved out of the bay, crossing a small headland. Demons flapped about, and he passed groups of the creatures feasting on slaughtered livestock. Past the point was another long bay, ending in a small fishing village. Demons perched on rooves while others gnawed at the dead. They screeched at Nordan and the Colossus as they passed. The ancient was following a road now, passing more abandoned homes and slaughter. Finally, a port came into view, with long docks backing onto a walled fort with many dwellings surrounding it. The Colossi were there, standing amongst the houses, swatting at demons. Nordan watched as wyverns dived and swooped. They were magnificent beasts, such powerful and efficient killers. The demons were numerous, though, moving in swarms so that sometimes they obscured his view. He knew that these bat-things were just the forerunner to the potent hell-spawn that would come. It was time for Nordan and his underlings to depart.

As Nordan moved amongst the houses, demons circled about him, sometimes scratching, too frenzied to be rational. He ignored their pitiful efforts and instead reached out with his mind and compelled the Colossi to rejoin him. Some of them moved, but others continued to fight. Nordan had never been disobeyed. He compelled them once more. Another Colossus submitted, but the others continued their defence. As Nordan drew closer, it was apparent there were far too many demons for the Colossi to be successful. It was a futile and pointless pursuit. The boy was on the shoulder of one of the Colossus. He was an anomaly in the pattern, and Nordan understood now why the boy was dangerous. Best dealt with promptly.

Nordan strode up to Hu. The Colossus straightened, and Athose turned from shooting demons to face Nordan. He expected the leader of the Colossi would not be happy that he seconded the troop. Reaching out, Nordan opened his hand to scoop up the boy, but Hu's hand grabbed the Ancient's wrist and held to it tightly. Nordan was surprised to be challenged by one of his own. Then, raising his other fist, Nordan struck the Colossus a mighty blow.

As Hu lurched back, Athose ran down his arm and up the arm of his assailant. Drawing his short blade, Athose stabbed the Ancient, hoping that he might find a weakness. But, of course, there was none. A demon grabbed at the Elf and pulled him away. Another fiend caught hold of Athose's leg, hauling him into the air. Then a much larger shape assailed Athose. It knocked the wind from his lungs, and the shock of it left him senseless for a moment. He was in the grip of a wyvern, crushed by the monster's tight squeeze, and carried high above the fight at the port. Less concerned for himself, Athose looked down. Four of the Colossi were fighting Nordan and another of their kind. Around them, houses and demons were crushed or shoved aside as the creatures of legend clashed. It was a fierce, impossible brawl.

Athose was suddenly in the clouds, unable to see what was happening. The powerful grip of the wyvern threatened to push his guts through his mouth or out his arse, but he could still draw a small breath, enough for the moment to stay alive. However, a black dot in his mind was expanding, a void, eventually taking away all his thought and vision.

As he came awake, Athose was back on the sand. It was a relief to see Hu standing near him. Other Colossi and wyverns were present, looking out to sea or resting. Nordan and others of their number were absent.

"Where are they, Hu."

Hu looked down at Athose, then he looked up again and pointed out over the ocean. Athose sensed sadness in his friend's manner.

As he sat up, it seemed to Athose that his ribs might be damaged, but he could move and stand with an effort. He looked about at all those gathered.

"We should go to Regnorak."

PIGEON POST

Mannace gave Render the responsibility to invent a better way to communicate over long distances. It was a challenge that the Wizard kept at the back of his mind since they first came to the Blood Sea, but he was no closer to a solution. Now at the fourth gathering of The Muster, he put the challenge to others.

"We need a better way to communicate. To send messages and have them received. It should be scalable for the battlefield or between leaders of nations. It could send warnings or coordinate a campaign."

One of Elderlin's apprentices eagerly stepped forward. He was very young, perhaps in his twenties.

"We can do that. When Tyriah ruled over the Veldaan, each general had a box. We sent messages to the box. It's a complex spell, but it's reliable."

One of the Animators started talking over the young mage.

"What you want is like the navigator's stone; in two places at once. A message, or words, could exist in two places. That's high-tech, though; you'd need the Architect's help with that one."

The apprentice started his magic before the Animator finished his last sentence. With a loud *whoosh,* a candlestick on one table disappeared and reappeared close by. It clattered and fell, the candle rolling to the side of the table and dropping to the floor. The mishap didn't deter the apprentice's enthusiasm.

"It's simple transference. The challenging bit's where you can't see the destination. That's why we use a box that is prepared to receive the message."

Elderlin was nodding. The Animator, however, was determined with his approach.

"That's just a letter. What if two people wanted a conversation."

One of the Elven Spellweavers spoke over the top of the discussion.

"We can do that now. There are devices, three of them, that allow a gathering amongst the Elves. It happens in a place between worlds. We use it in conjunction with the paths."

The Animator was shaking his head.

"I hadn't finished. You want a *Real-World* solution. Something everybody can use."

Dekon stood on the podium in the War Room.

"Enough. Render, it seems that you are closer than you might have thought to your solution. Take who you need now and make it happen."

Render grabbed Elderlin, his apprentice, the Animator who talked, plus another Animator that always impressed him. They moved together into the adjacent library. Render believed Dekon was right, and the solution was already there. Wizards were often like that; they were a great resource of knowledge and ideas, but to access it and apply it to the real world, they often needed to be prompted with the right questions.

Just a week later, Mannace was happy with Render's solution. Twenty-six pairs of boxes could each send or receive messages over vast distances. Render was arranging the manufacture of more. He also employed the Animator's Guild and Students of the Architect to prototype new technology to provide even better options. The boxes were essential to Mannace's strategy. He tasked the Alani to get one of the boxes and paper to write on to the army at the Mesah Long. The pair of that box was with his clerks. He did the same for those nations allied to him; the Wengo, the Elves at the Hand, the Spiders, the Holy Lands, the refuge he knew existed at the Demonswar Range, Viletri, and with Fitius in Arenland.

Mannace asked the Alani to approach the Northern leaders. Not only those along the west coast but some of the nearby hostile nations. It seemed to Mannace that they would need to unify to survive. A new age indeed.

The last box, Mannace gave to Logthar.

"This is why I need your help, my friend. You are the only one that can do this. In the war that will come, Men and Dwarves share a common foe."

Logthar knew what Mannace was asking of him, but he was shaking his head.

"Logthar, something good can yet come out of the treachery of the Dwarves."

"Mannace, the Dwarves do not see it as a betrayal. On the contrary, to them, it was retribution. A cleansing. They have long memories and have taken back what was theirs."

It was not a point Mannace would concede.

"They slaughtered families, Logthar. You cleanse your hands, not a race, not children. Logthar, the Remman did not deserve their fate. Would you rather travel to the Mesah Long and give the Remman your excuses?"

That last point hit home for Logthar. Mannace did not know Logthar's part in that campaign. Therefore, he had no reason to suspect that Logthar knowingly killed the Remman King.

"I will do this, Mannace, but I will look like a fool if the demons make it no further south than the rift."

"Before you go, I will share with you what I know, and we will talk with the Elves about what they have seen. My clerks have estimated the demons' numbers. Those are figures that will make your Dwarf King pay attention."

"Queen Mannace. The Dwarves have a Queen."

"Tell your Queen then. Know that the Four Hells will soon be on her doorstep, and the only thing between her and them is the men whose families she slaughtered. So, Logthar, tell her whatever you need to, but let us forge a new beginning. Despite our history, in these desperate times, there must be an alliance between Dwarves and Men."

LAST STAND

While the Remman expected to die on the hills above the Mesah Long, the quest for a heroic death meant they would do their best to stay alive, to keep the attention of the demon hordes, and help to deplete their seemingly endless numbers.

Once the demons consumed the battlefield carrion on the plains, the creatures assaulted the Rhalec towers so ferociously that the priests could not prevent some from penetrating the defence. Those that made it through the blasting lightning, threw themselves upon the Remman and others, insane in their desire to kill and feed. The Remman employed their shields, as they would against arrows, to make a tight shell that kept the creatures at bay, finishing them with their spears and swords that they poked through the defence. The Galandarian warriors soon learned to do the same, while the Rhalec preferred to stay near the towers and use their muskets.

The first of the ground creatures arrived. The smaller ones were much like those with wings and could be killed with a blade. However, the more massive demons were formidable, requiring the Colossi and animations to drive them off. The hellspawn were of all shapes, some resembling men or animals, while others were of a form that made no sense; bulbous, or a mix of parts all in the wrong places.

One creature to arrive was a leader amongst them. It was a tall beast equal to the Colossi, black but with a yellow rash over its body. Its head was small compared to its torso, but its arms were extensive, ending in large claws that belonged on something even bigger. As it waved its arms and roared, the demon army became more organised and harder to contain. Finally, the Colossi moved forward to assail the enemy commander.

The beast did not back away from their attack. Instead, it charged and leapt, knocking a colossus onto its back, seemingly impervious to its flailing fists. The Other Colossus entered the melee from the side, grabbing the demon by one of its arms so that it could not escape, then punching at its head repeatedly. Eventually, the massive beast went limp. The Colossus pushed the demon's dead weight off its comrade. Revealed, the seemingly invincible Colossus was scared with deep rents across its chest and abdomen and was motionless; whatever forces that gifted it life dissipated. Demons flapped about them, chaotic again in their attacks on the surviving colossus and landing like flies on carrion to butcher and consume their fallen general.

Elves appeared nearby, too late to save the fallen Colossus. Spellweavers amongst the newcomers summoned a hail of ice to clear away the bat-like demons. Others performed a ritual over the dead enemy general. After checking the deceased Colossus, they disappeared as suddenly as their arrival.

The attacks against the encampment above the Mesah Long became less frequent. However, with the presence of greater demons, the hellspawn were becoming more organised, which made them increasingly dangerous. Mostly, the demons travelled and attacked by night, resting during the days.

When the Elves returned with supplies, they also brought news. The demons were gathering into armies within Amon Murn. The Alani referred to them as The Legions of Hell, seemingly endless numbers. It was becoming increasingly perilous to travel the ways, and when a sizeable warband did not return from there, the Alani ended the expeditions.

The Spiders also kept a vigil over Amon Murn. Like Nordan, Eya was there when the demons were at war with the Ancients. Unlike Nordan, though, she would stay in the North. As everywhere else, the flying beasts assaulted her forest, landing amongst the trees, scampering about, killing everything they could trap. Webs surrounding the Spiders domain were full of their kind. Eya did not know or care how her neighbours, the Elves of the Hand, fared. She expected the wild Elves would find it challenging when the demons appeared in more significant numbers and increased variety.

Jaal came to visit her. He was becoming adept at navigating the ways and finding new paths. He was intuitive and fearless, so she was not surprised that he possessed the knack for it.

"You only come when you want something, Jaal."

"Not this time Eya. I have come here to be away from Mannace. It is his fate to fail."

"Why is that?"

"Because he is trapped. He is bound to finish what he has started, but it will have no end."

"There always comes an end and new beginnings, Jaal. Time moves in cycles."

"How many mortal lifetimes would that be?"

The question was rhetorical, and Jaal didn't wait for an answer. Instead, he pursued a more pressing matter.

"Eya, do the ways extend beyond the Great continent, past the Eastern Colonies?"

"It is possible. I am not aware of any."

Eya wanted Jaal to be at her side, but she knew she would drive Jaal away if she compelled him to stay. The time he spent with the Spiderkin was the only time in the aeons she lived that Eya put her trust in another. Already he undermined that trust when he avoided his duties and conspired with those of the Light. Now he was talking about travelling further afield. Why should that make her feel so panicked? Eya did not see her children in the same light; to her, they were minions, low in *The Order* though necessary to expand and protect her domain. She allowed the Spiderkin to aid the South against the North because it kept her aligned with Jaal. It made Eya feel weak to need this Elf and entertain such nonsense. It stayed her hand, but she could sense in him the desire to be away from her, so why should she not be true to her character? Jaal was young; he barely touched on his darkness. Perhaps she should devour him and be done. For now, although it made her gut tighten, she played his game and let him live.

"You can rest here."

Jaal was clueless as to Eya's thoughts. He was pragmatic.

"I will help with the defences."

"That will be needed."

There was always that raw urge to murder this Elf standing before her. Sometimes when he slept, Eya would shift her shape and hover over him to test her will, but also because she loved the anticipation of the kill, the delight that came of being the predator, dominant and in control. Eya's thoughts and hunger distracted her from the conversation. It made her desire his seed too, to be fucked and impregnated. Her passions were suddenly rampant.

"What do you think, Eya?"

"You already know the answer, Jaal."

"Yes, Eya, of course, you are right."

"Lie with me, Jaal. I have had enough of talking."

FAMILY

It was not hard for Jaal to find the Druids. He learned long ago that nothing happened in the forest without the Elves keeping track of it, and when he walked into their domain, they knew to send Roanna to him. She followed Jaal for a while before revealing herself. For effect, Roanna distracted her father with a breeze, then came close by his side, almost whispering in his ear.

"Father."

If Jaal was startled, he hid it well. Instead, he turned to face Roanna so that their noses almost touched.

"Roanna. Daughter."

She moved a short distance before facing him. Another impulsive wind rustled the leaves across the forest floor.

"How is Eya. I hope she is well."

Jaal laughed. He appreciated sarcasm, proud that his daughter had wit.

"The Mother of Spiders sends her regards."

A songbird high above them gave a long chorus of chirps and whistles. It was echoed by a similar call further away.

More seriously, Roanna asked, "How are Vilera and Athose?"

"Vilera is a part of the Wizard's muster. She has taken an apprenticeship under one of the Veldaan Asari. I hear that she learns fast. Athose left the battle at Mesah Long in the company of the Colossi. I have asked Eya to look for him."

"She has her other uses then?"

"Why do you care?"

Roanna shrugged. She didn't know why she became rattled when Eya's name was mentioned. Perhaps it was because she was frustrated that Eya and the Spiders seemed intent on conflict. Roanna reminded herself of her mission, changing tact.

"Is there hope of peace between the Spiders and the Elves?"

"Perhaps you and I are the only ones who can see the value in peace. We have a racial trait; Dark Elves are pragmatists and logicians. So, it seems reasonable, doesn't it, that we should be allied against a common enemy? The Wild Elves are practical people, but they see the spiders as intruders, an infestation. Eya is a predator. She will always act with aggression."

Jaal knew the key to brokering peace, but he could not say it. Eya was not only the Mother of Spiders. Long before that, she was also the Mother of Elves. He expected Alani Elders to know that fact, but they did not speak it. It would be a betrayal to Eya for him to share that detail.

"The Spiderkin will do as I say. We can coordinate our defences against the demons. Can you promise the same for the Elves?"

"I will convince the Elves and the Fen."

"The Fen too. You have been making new friends."

"I've found friends to be more reliable than family."

Jaal smiled. He was enjoying his children.

Athose was startled by a wyvern screeching behind him. He was further surprised to see Jaal take a seat next to him when he turned.

"Athose. My son."

"Jaal."

They sat in silence, and Jaal took in the countryside. It was a remote area of low hills with clumps of light vegetation. Two of the wyverns behind him were eating cattle, so Jaal surmised the demons had not yet ransacked this place. It was Eya who had informed Jaal where to find his son.

Athose was curious, "How did the Battle at Mesah Long end?"

"The demons came. Now we are all fighting demons. They are everywhere."

Athose was reluctant to ask his father for anything, but he needed advice.

"Where should I go?"

Jaal thought a while before he answered.

"The Remman and Rhalec still fight at Mesah Long and would benefit from help from the Colossi. Mannace has an army at Angorok; he will need help too. The city of Colossus would welcome you back, but that is further away. One of the Colossus is dead."

At the last point, Athose stood and looked at his father.

"Who?"

Jaal did not know. Only Athose ever took the time to understand the subtle differences between the Colossi. Athose knew his father could not answer his question, so he returned to his place on the grass, and they sat in silence again for a period.

"How did the Colossus die?"

"I wasn't there, but I was told it was a demon. There are many types, some very powerful."

The breeze blowing across the hills was cold. Athose rubbed his arms to keep them warm.

"Roanna asked after you. I will tell her you are with the Colossi."

Athose was unsure what to say or ask, and when he turned again, his father was gone.

"Whatever."

The Colossi and wyverns waited for his command. He did not know how he became the leader. Perhaps it was because the Colossi could not talk. It was much more responsibility than he asked for, but he would do his best for them.

Athose and the Colossi were in a stretch of land that remained off the demons' route. As they moved southwest back towards the Mesah Long, Athose's band encountered other refugees; Giants, several thousand, were organising themselves in response to the wyverns circling above. The refugees drew wagons and carts into a circle to protect the families, while warriors took a vigil on and around the makeshift palisade.

Athose approached on the shoulder of Hu while he asked the other Colossi to remain at a distance. When he was close to the wagons, two of the giants came forward to confront him.

"I am Athose. This is Hu, and these are the Colossi."

The larger of the two giants had a broad smile.

"By the West Wind, an unexpected sight. Athose of the Arena. I have seen you fight in the city of Colossus. An Elf amongst Orcs, very entertaining. I am Thag of Rockhome. This is Gurad, our shaman."

"I remember the night the giants came to watch at the arena. Agro was worried you brought your own team."

Thag smiled, but it turned quickly to a frown.

"On the Long, the Colossi fought for the South, but much has changed in a short time. So where do we stand now, Athose who speaks for the Colossi?"

Athose shrugged, "I have heard that we all fight demons now."

Athose didn't know what else to say. Historically, the Wengo and Rockhome were allies, but he led the Wengo to fight for the South. While he deliberated, Gurad stepped forward, reaching up to place his palm on Hu's thigh. The shaman closed his eyes, and when he opened them, he looked at Thag.

"There is no malice here. This one, Hu, has light upon his soul."

"And the boy?"

Gurad looked up at Athose, who instructed Hu to set him down. Once upon the ground, Gurad put his hand on Athose's shoulder, and again the shaman closed his eyes. When he opened them, he looked concerned.

"Athose intends no harm."

"Then we should join forces. The Giants of Rockhome and the Colossi of the Wengo."

Athose had no intention of staying in this place.

"We travel back to the Mesah Long. There is an army still fighting there."

Thag knew that staying in this peaceful valley was only a temporary solution. Unfortunately, he did not have a better option. The Colossi and Wyverns would be powerful protectors.

"We will return to the Long."

THE LAST REMMAN

The Wyverns and Colossi led the way. Athose was not telling them what to do; they seemed to have gained independence since Nordan's departure, and they knew the way to their destination. The Wyverns scattered any groups of demons that got close, driving them away from the Colossi's path. As Athose spent more time amongst the great beasts, he could see that they were intelligent and social creatures.

When the group finally arrived at the Mesah long, it was during the day and at a time when the demon numbers were limited to clusters of scavengers picking over the bones on the plains. The travellers observed the allied camp on the distant hills and hurried across the plain to arrive at their destination before dusk. They passed by the wreckage of the War God's Thunder. Hu reached out and hit the iron mortar so that it clanged. It was the most human thing Athose had seen him do.

The body of Muri was still lying where it fell. Athose and Hu stood by the Colossus' lifeless form until darkness arrived, then moved to join the others at the camp. The giants were made welcome; neither the Remman nor Rhalec commanders were concerned with the old alliances.

The next day was another quiet one. The day after, Rhalec priests ventured onto the plain and were joined by more of their order arriving by flying ship. They commenced an elaborate ritual, and at midday, the Rhalec Portal appeared near the camp. It was a spectacular sight. Through it passed the Rhalec towers and soldiers, the war priests, plus some of the other warriors, including the animations. At Thag's request, the Giants also took the passage to safety. They and the Portal were gone by early afternoon; returned to the Fogmir far away.

Wasting no time, those that remained started a march east towards Amon Murn, to where they expected to find the origin of whatever malevolent power afflicted the land. They would fight the darkness at its source. The Remman all stayed. Bollo and his devout followers from Galandar swore oaths to continue the fight. Athose, the Colossi and Wyverns were there. Thag too. The big giant felt too much guilt to pass through the portal with the others of his kin. It was guilt for all those warriors that died and the families who were not saved. He did not feel worthy of being amongst the survivors. Rather, he trusted Gurad to settle the giants in the new land while he would atone for his shortcomings.

As they travelled east, the countryside they passed through was stripped bare of life. Bloody carcasses lined the road, and where they passed through towns. Flies and other insects abounded everywhere amongst the corpses. Occasionally they witnessed a bird or small animal scampering for cover. At least there was still some life in the land.

Sometimes small groups of demon scavengers assaulted them, fearless even against superior numbers and ferocious in their quest for flesh. But, again, the experienced soldiers quickly handled them.

After six days of marching, the Wyverns returned from their distant scouting, screeching a warning of a more substantial force ahead. They were within the borders of Amon Murn.

The Remman commanders moved the army quickly to higher ground. The hill they ascended was large enough to have several peaks along its ridgeline. There was a small forest of tall trees on one slope and grazing land on the others. The top was clear, and in a flattish area between two of the peaks, there were stone buildings, long abandoned and in ruins. At the base of the hill, flat, swampy land lay to the south. Hills blocked their line of sight in the other directions. It was rural countryside, and like everywhere else, rotting carcasses dotted the landscape.

The Remman made an early camp as dusk approached, eating a cold meal and talking. They were in good spirits. In the distance, the occasional roar or piecing screech would reach their ears from somewhere amongst the hills. It was getting dark when the bat demons were the first to appear above the terrain. This time they landed on the slopes and ridges watching the Southerners, moving only to make way for more substantial creatures that loped over the hilltops, herding them forward. Soon all the hills around the Southerners were alive with shapes flapping or crawling – no longer holding back, but instead speeding toward their position. On one of the neighbouring hills, two enormous demons crested a ridge, gigantic like the Colossus but misshapen so that they were vaguely humanish in form. One of them roared, and the hellish army increased its pace, surging up the slopes. More winged creatures, much larger than the bat demons, passed over their generals and screeched as they dove into the Remman ranks.

It was a weak moon that lit the night sky. Bollo, though, was blessed with Orcish vision, and he watched as the Remman took the brunt of the attack of the flying creatures. The more enormous beasts crashed against their shields, crushing warriors beneath their weight and tearing soldiers out of the formation with their powerful claws. The smaller bat-like demons joined them, throwing themselves at the shields, kicking and clawing the defenders. A halberdier near Bollo cut one of the creatures out of the air.

In a great whoosh of noise and moonlit shadow, Wyverns came like bullets out of the sky to scoop up the larger flyers and rend them apart with their talons and jaws. It left the relieved Remman to beat off the minor demons. With the threat quickly dealt with, the soldiers moved forward from the carnage, regrouping and steadying themselves to confront the shadowy hoard hurrying up the slopes. Bollo watched the Colossi move to be alongside them.

It was the stuff of legends, and Bollo roared as he looked to those followers around him. Then, raising his blades, he led the brave Galandarians in a charge forward. They kept pace with him, holding their halberds and spears and axes high so that when they met the demons loping toward them, they brought their weapons down upon them with all their strength. With the advantage of the slope, their attack cut a path through the enemy's mass. Bollo was in the thick of it now, always towards the front of the combat. He clasped a blade in his left hand and an axe in his right, finding the axe better for hacking through the tough demon hide. The Half-Orc quickly discovered his rhythm: stabbing, hacking, dodging. He quickened his pace, exhilarated by the noise of battle. The number of adversaries was boundless.

Bollo had acquired some Thog from a Two-Face Officer, the good stuff. Stepping back a moment, he let the halberdiers get in front of him, and he swilled the foul-tasting liquid. It burned in his throat and stomach, but already he could feel its potency in his limbs. He clenched his weapons and roared his death roar. He was invincible and insatiable, striding past those fighting and wading into the thick of the foe. Bolo's blows and mind were ablaze with the fire of the Thog. He would bash them all. Bash them to a bloody pulp.

Athose expended the last of his arrows, but he still held his bow to fend off the bat-things. The young Elf gripped Hu's ear with his other hand as he surveyed the battle from the Colossus' shoulder. Athose watched the Remman change their formation so that their shield wall was to the front and many ranks deep. Their line encircled the hill. It was a good thing they did as Athose spotted demons swarming around its base and ascending from all sides. The wyverns dived at the creatures, scattering some and pulling others up in the air before dropping them from a height.

A cloud passed before the crescent moon, reducing further the poor light so that Athose could see little for a time. When the moon reappeared and his vision adjusted, he tapped Hu urgently on the head and pointed. Massive demons moved down the adjacent slopes. There were more of them now, and they would soon be amongst the fighting. Hu strode towards them. There was no way above the din and in the darkness to signal to the others, but Athose hoped that more Colossi would see the threat and move to defend it.

As Athose passed by the Remman ranks, the fighting was intense. The elite warriors battled heroically. In some places, berserk hell-spawn grabbed the Remman shields to pull warriors out of the line. Further along, dark beasts climbed upon the mounds of dead and leapt amongst their prey. But, as always, the Remman were fearless and resolute. Deadly and efficient killers.

Closing on his target, three other Colossi joined Hu. Together they waded through the smaller creatures and did their best to avoid trampling the Galandarians before charging into the massive demons from the flank. The fiends turned to meet the Colossi's attack. One of them raised its three massive arms and waved crescent-shaped talons at the sky. As it did so, a thick shadow once more descended over the landscape. It was a suffocating void, much darker and colder than the night. Within it, Athose could only see a short distance. He felt Hu move beneath him, swinging and surging forward, but then there was a sudden jerk backwards, and the ground came rushing up to meet him. Athose did his best to leap free, hitting the ground hard, his head smashing against the earth. Dazed but looking up, Thag was towering over him, beating back long tentacles with his shield and blade.

One tentacle shot out of the darkness, and like a whip, it wrapped itself around the giant, pinning his shield arm and knocking the sword from his hand. Halberdiers came to cut at the thing, and then a figure leapt at it, burying his axe into the flesh so that the tentacle released its grip on the giant, withdrawing with lightning speed back into the void. Athose saw it was Bollo who wielded the weapon. Now the Half-Orc charged fearlessly into the enveloping dark. As Thag collapsed unconscious next to Athose, more Galandarians and several Remman ran past, following the crazed Orc. Dizzy from the wound to his head, Athose could no longer feel his body or see the Colossi. His eyes closed.

It was the second time Athose awoke amongst the Colossi and wyverns. Before he opened his eyes, he could tell that it was daylight and that the fighting was over. Scared of what he might see, Athose lay there for several minutes before lifting himself onto his elbows and taking his first peek at the scene about him. It was worse than he imagined. Athose was hauled back to the hill to a patch of grass, and all around him were the Remman and demon dead, some partly devoured. There were bodies for as far as he could see along the hillside. The Colossi stood amongst them, providing a solitary vigil. Athose took a moment to get his bearings, suddenly knowing where to look. As he feared, there were Colossi on the ground where they fought the leaders. He could see several of the heroic creatures and livery of the Galandarians there too - all in a great heap and tangle. When he looked behind,

Athose saw the unconscious Thag. The giant was breathing deeply, and his hand was twitching. A solitary Remman sat nearby.

"No scene for a boy to witness."

"I am no boy. I am older than many that died here."

The Remman shrugged.

"At daylight, the demons withdrew. Their general is not amongst the dead."

"Where are the other survivors."

The Remman shook his head, then nodded toward the giant.

Athose could see that Hu was standing further up the hill. The Colossus had a rent on his chest that extended down his arm and a dent to his hip. The young Elf was relieved that his friend was alive. His eyes blurred, but he took a deep breath to hold back the tear.

Out of the corner of his eye, Athose could see that the Remman was glowering at him. The man's voice was bitter and accusing.

"Boy, are you smiling?"

ANGOROK

Casteel did what was asked of her; she drew the demons south into Islan and the Sompher Gris. It bought time to evacuate the Veldaan, but it was disastrous for the people of these Northern territories.

Now she was determined to help these same people she put in peril. Where they could, the Blood Legion used their six ships to draw the demons away from the cities or disperse them into smaller groups that the troops and militias might handle. It was not hard for the navigators to lure the demons close and then shift their location to a safe distance away. Fortunately, the demons did not appear to learn or adapt, always following the ruse. They were driven only by their thirst for blood and flesh.

The Islani soon learned that the demons were less active during the day. As a result, soldiers and civilians became adept at moving about when it was light and finding places to hide when the evening came.

Most of the cities of Islan were under siege. Some were utterly ransacked, while others found some form of workable defence. The town of Skon was a bastion within the beleaguered nation, and Casteel aided the river city with supplies and information.

Skon withstood multiple assaults by the flying demons. When the creatures attacked, they were vulnerable to crossbow fire through the narrow windows of the residential towers, and after their first assault, the people of Skon nailed stakes into the roofs and hung slivers of wire between the buildings. Most importantly, the land-bound demons could not cross the river that flowed around Skon's formidable walls. For all their ferocity, they would not enter the waterway. The Blood Legion utilised the location as a base, returning to Angorok only to restock and keep Mannace updated.

Amongst the soldiers of Skon, The Ravista commander, Shamal Shamas, was the one to trust Casteel when she first approached the city, and he continued to be her best advocate. He was sociable and harboured an intent towards the Elf that went beyond a sharing of resources. Casteel liked his attention, and for the first time in many years, she let herself be pulled into a private place, away from her protectors. The crowded storeroom was not an ideal location, but she allowed this handsome man to lean her back across sacks of wheat and examine her undergarments with his dextrous hands. She explored him too, liking what she discovered and showing that she was also deft with her fingers. It was a moment bought amongst the chaos and a prelude to a passionate affair.

The Islani were inventive and inquisitive people. It was evident in their food and social lives, and even in this lean time of war, they congregated during the day to eat. At night, the Blood legionnaires treated themselves to delectable meals and an assortment of flavoursome liqueurs. The people of Skon were famous amongst the Islani for their Portett, dust made from drying and grinding a fungus found in the nearby forest. Mixing the powder with goat's milk and drinking it heightened a person's senses and reduced their inhibitions. As they became more familiar with the people of Skon, some of the legionnaires attended parties where Portett was shared, and orgies would ensue.

Malakai and his Clansmen were aided now by the Brula and other reinforcements from Mannace's army based at Angorok. They were still fighting groups of Churgwarthos' raiders across the broad Veldaan, though the Sorcerer was dead, and the demon's incursion usurped the war between North and South. Demon scavengers were becoming common, moving west from Islan and down from Rockhome. With Malakai's help, most of the southern population escaped through the Rhalec Portal before the mystical structure disappeared. The staunch remnant of Southerners and Veldaanians that remained made their defences in the cities or lived like nomads on the plains.

At Angorok, Mannace managed the campaign. He was calling it adaptive warfare. Half of his Southern army left through the portal with the civilians. Some others returned South to the Holy Lands. Aside from Malakai's deployments, Mannace garrisoned all remaining soldiers at Angorok. With Rhalec towers to protect it, Angorok was the safest place. The defences were tested once already by one of the Demon Generals. The horned beast threw his horde against the city, but the towers, Muster, and musket men repelled the assault. Rather than gather more strength and persist, the general moved on, passing into Islan, and was reported to be moving further South. Mannace was slowly identifying other demon armies and tracking their movements. It seemed that at least two other large forces were winding their way south toward the Rift. He put notes in the magic boxes to share what he knew with those that would listen. There were few responses, but Mannace expected a trusting alliance would take time.

The Alani Spellweavers left Angorok to join the Elves at the Hand to strengthen their defences against the demons and maintain a vigil over Eya's spiders.

Though drawn to her, the demons would not find Eya easy prey. She quickly summoned her allies, not just the spiders from The Hand or her lair near Viletri, but all her kind. They filled the catacombs deep beneath the forest, and they lurked, hidden in the ways. Jaal did not know. She continued to let him control the Spiderkin and work with the Elves.

The first of the greater demons to arrive at the forest's edge was too big to move amongst the trees. So instead, she lurked outside the woodland and sent armies into the Hand of Fengal to rampage and feast. Flying creatures leapt through the treetops while human-like shapes loped along the ground. When the first night fell, the general used her diabolical powers, opening portals through which great worms slithered, and the dogs of Nerbus came forth in their slavering packs. When the light of day touched the portals, they closed, but the new denizens remained. The she-demon raised her arms over the trees and bellowed; it was a mighty sound that rolled like a storm across the forest and demanded plunder. Her servants responded, scooping up carcasses and scuttling back to where their commander waited. Already carrion was being placed at their mistresses' feet. When there was a mound around her, she let her bulbous form relax over it as if she were taking a seat on a comfortable chair. When the pile increased, she feasted on the gruesome bounty, building her strength for the fight ahead.

During the next night, another of the high demons arrived. The two beasts screeched and roared at one another, and from the discord came an understanding. The new arrival faced the edge of the forest and spewed forth a spell of acid and rot with its jaw widened. Trees disintegrated, disappearing in a spray of green sludge. Other vegetation around it buckled and collapsed as if losing the will to remain standing. Before the monstrous creatures, a path expanded far into the forest, allowing them passage through the tall wood.

Although the demons were still far from where the Elves waited, the Druids sensed the forest's agony and the horrific extinguishing of life. Such an atrocity could not be left unmet. Tens of thousands of Wardens joined them from the Fogmir, journeying through the ways. All the Alani were there, amongst the Wild Elves or close by in near-space. A handful of Dark Elves aligned themselves with the Congress, each with their unique talents. They also kept allegiances to the Spider Mother as followers of the Order, so they gravitated towards Jaal and his troop. There were five hundred Spiderkin, and with their Dark Elven allies, they were a formidable fighting unit.

The Fen were not as keen as the Elves to take the attack to the demons, and instead, they gathered to defend their border. Likewise, the Rhalec wisely abandoned their river port, making haste for the safety of the sea.

After two days travelling through the Hand of Fengal and clearing the forest of the far-ranging demons, the Elves focused their attention on the primary enemy host. The demonic horde was immense and spread over a vast distance, systematically plundering and destroying. But now the forest itself was awakening, it was coming for them, and at dawn, the demons met with the full wrath of Fengal.

Roanna ran alongside two older Druids, Shasta and Meanfox. Ahead of them, a stag angled between the trees, and around the Druids, other animals loped and scampered. High above, branches were filled with birds; some perched while they waited for the Druids to catch up, while others darted ahead. They seemed manic, madly chirping and squawking. Unexpectedly, a long-tusked boar charged past Roanna. The young deer was there too, one of the three Ra-Anu that returned to Roanna after a time with the Fen, running alongside the dark druid as it often did. Amongst the animals, Wild Elves ran and hooted.

Demons were between the trees ahead, attracted to the noise, and once they saw the animals, they came hurtling towards them. From all directions, birds swooped, attacking faces, or pecking annoyingly at the demon's flesh. When the surprised creatures stopped to grab or bite at the avians, Roanna saw the Stag hit one of them at speed. The foul creature jolted backwards, and the deer shook its powerful neck to cast the demon from its antlers. Charging beasts knocked other devils from their feet or assaulted them with bites and claws. The surprised hell spawn fought back franticly, quickly turning the tide and would have scattered the animals if arrows from archers in the trees did not cull their number.

Roanna stopped, focusing her mind on the forest around

her. She reached out at the fiends well ahead, grabbing them, impaling them, and tearing them apart. When the threat felt overcome, Roanna jolted herself back into her body, running again to catch up with the others that were now well ahead. She passed her handiwork of demons tangled and broken on branches, leaping over one that a tree root had crushed. Fighting was all around her now, and unexpectedly a monster fell from a tree above, its wing slapping her on the face as it tumbled. An arrow fired by a warden pierced its skull, while yet another foul creature crashed down from the canopy, landing a short distance away. This one was alive, and an Elf tumbled with it. The warden was stunned after hitting the ground, bleeding from many cuts. Roanna lashed at the assailant, a branch whipping down to knock the winged creature aside. A wolf ran past Roanna and seized the demon by the throat.

Roanna whirled around. An impossibly long creature was behind them, weaving between the trees. The thing was like a black snake with a bear head. Elves were firing at it from above, and arrows stuck out of its tough hide. Suddenly the thing lurched up a tree; an Elf clutched in its powerful jaw. Meanfox saw it too, and Roanna watched the druid disable the beast with roots and vines. Roanna stabbed at it, sapling branches appearing from the base of a tree and impaling the creature through its thick skin. The spears snapped as the demon-thing writhed, but tightening vines subdued it, and it could do little harm.

As she ran on, Roanna found the stag kneeling with its forelegs on the ground. She could see that it was dazed and bloodied. Borrowing life from a large tree, Roanna shared it with the wounded animal. The stag jumped quickly and shook his head. Roanna could see the fear in its eyes, so she moved alongside it, stroking its head.

"You must return to the battle, brave guardian."

Touching the stags mind, Roanna guided the beast forward to charge amongst the trees. Then, for a moment, although there was still a great din, it was just Roanna and the Ra-Anu. The fawn looked up, and she leaned down to stroke it. The forest spirit's heart was racing.

"Fengal, give your creatures strength."

Amongst the thick of battle, the Spiderkin were efficient killers. Jaal led them as they surged ahead to slaughter the demons before the creatures could react. Like him, they mastered their talent of slowing time. It was so natural for them, being born to it. Even the more giant beasts, animal-like and spikes over their armoured hide, were easily handled. Jaal mostly stayed back from the fighting to watch and keep an eye for danger. Above, the Wild Elves were also at work, efficient marksmen against the flyers in the trees.

SPIDERS

The Elves were vastly outnumbered. When night cast its shadow over the forest, the demons arrived in immense swarms that overran everything in their path. Only the magic of the Druids, aided by the three Ra-Anu, stopped the creatures from surrounding and annihilating their entire force. The forest was exhausted, and the animals were dead, hidden or scattered. For the Elves, the night fighting became a desperate retreat, and it seemed to Roanna that they would run out of arrows and magic long before they ran out of enemy to kill.

The Alani sent assassins to destroy the demon generals in a desperate attempt to turn the tide. They ambushed and wounded the bulbous one, but the other proved immune to their attacks, slaying Elves with its infernal magic. The botched effort only succeeded in fuelling the devils' rage.

As the hours passed and with the generals feverishly driving them, the demon horde's pursuit of the Elves was relentless. The retreat of the Elves became a desperate rout.

A contingent of Wardens crossed the first of the narrow ravines that formed the fingers of the hand. A giant log that bridged the gorge was broad enough for twelve Elves to run alongside, dragging their wounded. They leapt over clumps of moss and were careful not to slip or trip on the long vines that hung from the bridge's rotted edges. The gorge was an excellent place to make a defence.

As thousands of fleeing Elves rallied at the ravine, Roanna was amongst the very last to cross the divide, turning when she was halfway. As the remainder of the Elves passed her, Roanna could already see demonic shapes come to the edge of the forest, screeching as they peered over the lip of the cliffs. They stared down fearfully at the raging river that cut a deep trench into the earth. Its white waters surged and roiled, powerful and loud. Some demons scrambled onto the log crossing, ravenous and desperate to catch up with the Elves. Rylla, who was amongst the Wardens, leapt onto the log to be with her adopted daughter. It was a long time since the two were last together, and it bolstered Roanna's resolve. The Ra-Anu rested at Roanna's feet. It attuned to the Druid, and through the forest spirit, Roanna connected to the power of the forest and could draw upon its full strength when needed. High above, giant crows circled, summoned by other Druids.

The Elves were fatigued, but there would be no better place to stop the demon army's advance. Wardens stretched out along the side of the Ravine, above the cliffs and in the trees. The Alani were still with them, but the Spiderkin retreated toward their territories.

As the demons charged across the log bridge, Roanna let her magic flow into the log, animating it so that the vines hanging from its sides whipped up to flay and tangle the attacking spawn, dragging them into the ravine. The young druid surged her energy through the ancient wood, lent to her by the forest, to stun or paralyse her foe. She was the wrath of Fengal, and as midnight approached then passed, the bridge did not fall despite the endless demon assault. Behind Roanna, her kin watched and rested, occasionally called on to dispatch solitary flyers.

A tremendous roar heralded the arrival of the demon's generals. Accompanying the commotion, an area of trees on the far bank disintegrated, and one of the fiends walked into the space its spell created. When its bulbous mate appeared next to it, they gibbered and bellowed, pushing each other. Then the bulbous one moved into the trees, breaking them to make her way, while the other turned to survey the opposite bank. Then, opening its mouth wide, it cast a putrid spell. A great stream of acid spewed across the divide from its maw, burning trees and sending the Elves scurrying. Those not quick enough screamed in agony.

The other demon leaned against a towering tree on the far bank. Under such an immense weight, the bole was uprooted and toppled to fall across the ravine. Demons immediately lept onto the wood to cross. Both massive beasts shifted along the bank, snapping the smaller trees to make their way, and toppling the larger ones to create other crude crossings. In response, giant crows swooped, and arrows took a high toll on those running across the logs. But still, in places, demons clambered to the other side, where the rested Wardens and Druids met them with fierce resistance.

Through the remainder of the night, the demons threw all they had across the divide, fighting tooth and talon against arrow and blade until, abruptly, the fighting ended. Roanna and Rylla saw it first; suddenly, there were no more demons waiting for others to pass on the bridges, and then, as the creatures perished to arrow and spell, the logs cleared. Only the two greater demons remained. Here at the crossing, the horde was dissipated. From her position on the bridge, Roanna shouted defiantly at the generals.

"Begone. Fengal has defeated you."

The bulbous demon angled toward the bridge where Roanna stood. It looked across at Roanna and her mother before leaning down to where the mighty log rested against the bank. A mighty hand reached underneath, grabbing a fist full of vines.

As the two Elves impossibly scrambled to reach safety before the log was wrenched from under them, the demon was abruptly lifted from the earth, grabbed up by some massive being without warning. Roanna glanced skyward just in time to see a creature of vast proportions; its many legs balanced on both sides of the ravine. Then, as quickly as it appeared, the monster stepped back into the night, disappearing with the demon in its maw. Rhylla was looking up too.

"A spider."

"That is what I saw also."

The remaining demon general turned and was hurriedly departing.

Later as they recouped, the Alani Spellweavers shared a theory about the spider. They recognized it, the same sensation they got from the great beast within the Ways. It was odd that the creature would strike now and in such a fashion. There was much to be explained. Although the enemy was defeated, there was little to celebrate in the Elves' camp. Many of their numbers perished, and they had no idea of the fate of Elves that fled in other directions. Those remaining here were wounded and exhausted, tended to by the Druids. The Alani stayed with them, out of fellowship, rather than retreating to their otherworld sanctuary. So many immortals died.

After a brief rest, the Fogmir Elves returned home through the ways while the Elves of the Hand walked back to their base alongside the Alani. As they drew closer to their groves, the number of spiders and webs in the trees increased noticeably, and within their inner sanctum, an infestation of arachnids touched every part of the forest. The returning Elves were anxious, especially when giant spiders were observed high in the canopy, spinning their webs and lurking. It appeared to be a trap, but the Wardens were compelled to move forward; this is where their people lived.

At the sacred sight of the giant trees, which formed the hub of their community, spiders of all sizes abounded. The Wild Elf residents, elders and children sat in their nests or workplaces. They were silent, waiting, terrified that anything they might do could invoke an attack from the arachnids that surrounded them. Of the six thousand Wardens that called this place home, only a quarter that number returned with this party, many of them carrying wounds. The Alani could bring as many as five thousand warriors to bear if a battle ensued. There were many more spiders, and it seemed that they already kept the population at their mercy.

Out of the shadows, Spiderkin appeared. There were groups of them, several hundred in total, and they watched the Elves menacingly. Roanna could not help but think that this was Eya's end game.

A unit of Alani appeared from near-space to surround a Spiderkin, who reacted - slowing time to move around the Alani. The Elves phased out and reappeared in more significant numbers a short distance away. Around them, the forest stirred, but it was the spiders, not Fengal, that edged forward. A fist-sized spider landed on one of the Alani, and he flinched dramatically in surprise, quickly brushing the creature away. Other arachnids were moving along branches or scuttling amongst the leaves. Above them, giant spiders unfurled, readying themselves to cast their webs or pounce.

Roanna stepped forward to say what she knew the other Druids would not.

"We will leave the Hand."

One of the Older Druids nearby was defiant.

"We will not. This forest is Fengal's domain."

Others echoed the Druid's words. Some readied themselves for combat, notching their bows or drawing blades. Finally, a voice from the shadows spoke.

"So be it."

THE RIFT

It was a curiosity. Four armies came together to be the most significant demon force Mannace was tracking. They ransacked cities as they crossed Islan and down through the Sarang. At first, it seemed that they might assault the Holy Lands; it made sense that the darkness would seek out the light. But then they disappeared at the rift. Unable to pass over it, Mannace could only assume that they descended into it, though he could not imagine their purpose. Of their number, only the flying demons remained above ground. After harassing Southern Veldaan and the Young Cities, the bat-creatures eventually regathered as a great swarm that headed south over the snow. Mannace immediately sent notes to keep those south of the Rift informed.

EaJa-KulAmani, revered BruEkNa of the Dwarves, stood before her generals, whom she hurriedly gathered in response to Logthar's warning.

"Commanders, you are called to the defence of the Core."

The generals who were unaware of any threat looked at one another to see if their comrades knew the information they did not. One coughed.

"The Four Hells have walked the earth before, and they do so again. Their armies descend into the Rift. They seek entrance into the domain of the Dwarves. They intend to take the Core."

Now there was a grumble and puffing of chests amongst her audience. However, none would talk until the BruEkNa finished.

"Do not doubt that we are under assault. News will come first from the outposts and then from the deep mines. Prepare your bastions. Protect your assets. We are, again, at war."

EaJa-KulAmani knew not to speak in half measures with the Generals. She could not let her uncertainty show through in her words. She needed them to act decisively.

"Go now. The enemy will be upon us."

When the BruEkNa turned to leave the hall, the Generals immediately commenced a raucous chatter. They asked many questions, and SinKayLas of the KinRa came forward to tell them what he knew, mainly speculation. Logthar, who stood next to the First Dwarf, turned and followed the BruEkNa. He was to stay close by with his box; the BruEkNa was interested in any other news from the North. He was forbidden, though, to respond to the messages.

Later that day, the first report from the undercities arrived. An outpost, deep and on the outskirts of the Dwarven territories, reported an encounter. Demons were in the old mines. It was rare but not unheard of for minor incursions into the Dwarves' territory by monsters or other underground denizens. But this was different, and the BruEkNa intuitively knew it for what it was, a prelude to war.

The massive swarm of flying demons was like a dark cloud high over the snow. The beasts screeched at the terror of being above the Ice, fearing that they might not be across its expanse before exhaustion forced them to land. There was little they were afraid of, certainly not death, but water in all its forms assaulted a raw nerve, evaporating their courage. A gigantic beast, a wyvern-like thing that was all heads and tails and wings, urged them forward. As their general, the demons obeyed it. Some faltered and dropped low as they grew tired, fighting with all their remaining strength before succumbing to the ice. As they landed, the beasts flailed and died.

After passing over the mountains and the land below turned from white to green, the swarm descended, carpeting the landscape with their dark forms. Though exhausted, the demons found the energy to chase anything that moved, ferreting out a bloody meal. Then they waited till night to move again.

Fitius always planned for the worst, and now he was justified to be so cautious, and to have covertly expanded Arenland's military. Brula scouts and patrolling flying ships brought news that demons were on his doorstep. It matched the reports from the North that the hell-spawn were heading in their direction. Arenland was well fortified against invasion, but that did not make it impenetrable, particularly against a foe that could fly.

The Overlord considered where he would make his defence. First, the northernmost city of Freyberg was the smallest of the nation's three metropolises. However, with the arrival of the refugees from the North, Freyberg's population increased significantly, becoming a base to expand into the frontier bordering the Icesleepers. Next, Ostoik on the coast was his industrial hub and vital to protect. Finally, his home city, Antigoth, Capital of Arenland, was the pinnacle of a modern city, to be protected at any cost.

All were within striking distance of the demons, but Fitius decided the battleground. While he ordered the populace to take sanctuary in any city or local fort, all available troops amassed at Freyberg. As with everything, the Arenlanders prepared with prodigious efficiency, and the flying ships drew the enemy into their trap.

Fitius looked down at his military from his Governor's Flagship as they took up positions in defence of Freyberg. Twenty-seven thousand riflemen deployed on the field before the city gates. Another ten thousand garrison troops and militia defended its formidable walls and narrow streets. Civilians armed themselves, ready to fight. There were more than three hundred thousand people here.

To the North, the twilight horizon was as black as midnight from the shadow cast by the enemy multitudes. Despite the clear warnings from Mannace, Fitius did not imagine that the swarm could be so large, potentially millions. He thought the reports were exaggerated until he witnessed the enemy numbers with his eyes. There were eighty flying ships arrayed to his left and right. While they were magnificent, Fitius was a realist, and he could see they would not withstand the coming assault. He sent orders for those with only Class B and C navigators to retreat to Antigoth. The rare Class A Navigators would transport their ships at the last minute. He did not want to alarm the troops below more than was necessary. Fitius, Governor of the Eastern Colonies and Overlord of Arenland, realised that the situation was hopeless. He gave his ship's captain the order to return to the Capital, and instantly Rangi brought the boat alongside the Overlord's docking bay. Fitius disembarked and hurried to his State Manor, where Saska dutifully awaited him.

"Have the demons been destroyed, Fitius?"

Fitius was usually unflappable. Now his movements were erratic, with panic on his brow and in his eyes. Saska helped him into a seat, giving him time to calm down. He did not have words.

"Fitius, is bad?"

The Overlord took a long breath, forcing himself to focus on the facts.

"It is bad … disastrous. At least a million demons, possibly many more. They will take Freyberg this night. They will destroy our army. After that, Arenland will be open to them."

"What High Priest say?"

"The high priest at Antigoth is a boy. The War Priests are

all in the North. The War God will not save us."

"Little faith, you. War God knows Arenland make flame alive, so now great furnace burn in north and west. The War God honour debt Arenland and Overlord."

Fitius was unsure if that was the case, but he summoned a servant and sent him to bring the temple priests to his manor. It gave him a small hope. However, he could not shake the suffocating sense of doom, knowing that his people faced impossible odds in Freyberg. He could take better measures with more time – not just as Overlord of Arenland, but also as Governor of the Colonies. As Governor, he still had much to do. He yelled at the door.

"Summon my Officials."

Fitius heard movement outside the room in response. He felt better for doing something, but the anxiety was consuming. Already men would be dying. Families would be dying. Fitius looked to Saska for affirmation.

"Antigoth will be next after Freyberg. So, we must make the best use of our time."

"Lead your people. Now, Fitius."

Saska was again her civilised self, but this conversation with Fitius pulled at her nerves. While her exterior was calm, a part of her wanted to strike him. To usurp him and make all of them do her bidding. So often, she felt that she was better than those around her. Incredibly, they forgot that they already had a demon in their midst.

Freyberg fell that night. The demons chased the flying ships, which led them towards Antigoth. It seemed that by the next evening the capital, too, would be consumed. Most civilians fled, making what haste they could for neighbouring lands, while those with wealth hurried to Ostoik, where they purchased passage by ship. The brave citizens that stayed in the city fortified their homes or assembled in government buildings. At Fitius' insistence, the garrison and militia already manned the walls and prepped their siege engines. The artillery corps took their position behind the defences. Flying ships transported things of invention and industry to safety that Fitius considered essential, his best industrialists and artisans amongst them. The vessels sped towards Lapthos in the desperate hope that the island would be a sanctuary from the demon infestation.

That night, when the demons descended upon Antigoth, Fitius was aboard his flagship to confront them. People precious to him were onboard the vessel, too, so that when the situation became hopeless, they would escape together. Antigoth's High Priest stood at the ship's prow, close enough to the city's walls that the defenders were looking up at him. The clergyman outstretched his arms, and he called skyward to his god.

"Greatest of Gods, God of War, cast down this Hells army, be our shield and our sword."

The evening sky auspiciously darkened further, and those on the ship and walls could hear the roar of horses' hooves and the clash of steel on steel. Ghostly figures appeared on the walls next to the living. They looked out at the approaching swarm, and they jeered at it, shaking their weapons in defiance. Further along the defence, more spectral shapes stepped onto the parapets. Fitius looked over the sides of the ship; in both directions, the walls were filling with dead warriors, come from the War God's halls to take a stand beside the living. At the front of his ship, the Priest looked triumphant, still holding his arms wide and staring up at the sky.

Out of the night, the demons were suddenly upon them. Fitius lost his view of the walls and city behind him, its lights hidden behind the mass of swooping shapes. In such overwhelming numbers, the feeling of hopelessness hit him like the strike from a hammer, and in desperation, the Overlord ran to the priest, yelling at him to get his attention over the din of the demons screeching.

"DO MORE!"

The horde roiled backwards with a sudden jerk, retreating on itself, and lifting away from the walls and buildings they assaulted. Their mass swirled about Fitius' ship, and those demons closest hovered and stared at those on deck. Fitius put his hand on the Priest's shoulder to encourage him further, but the young man looked back at him, perplexed.

Saska came forward. She was radiant and powerful. Fitius could see that her magic held the horde at bay. Everybody on board was drawn into her spell.

"All leave. Navigator, stay."

Rangi lowered the ship so that Fitius and others could depart onto the battlements. Even Fitius could not resist Saska's order.

A gigantic demon appeared amongst the others, landing heavily on the wall and clambering for a foothold. Many heads watched Saska, and one screeched, expecting her to understand. But, instead, Saska reached into its mind and bound it like the others. All of them, this collective of demons, this swarm that was one and many, were hers to dominate and control.

Her human visage was disappearing; still, Saska in outline, but not of this world. Using a mental command, Saska ordered Rangi to move the ship skyward. He obeyed, and the horde that stretched beyond vision, now wholly hers, followed.

More demons rose from the carnage to re-join the great swarm as the ship crossed over Freyberg. Within the city, after a day of gorging themselves, some hellspawn were so bloated that they laboured hard to stay in the air. Compelled to do as commanded, the demons crossed the mountains, snow, and rift. Saska was in their minds now, and she knew how to retrace their steps. The swarm felt like part of her, and as they journeyed, she drew others in.

Finally, Saska stood, transformed to her demon self, upon the hill overlooking the abyss that was once Imbor. There was a price for what she did; she had trouble remembering herself. Saska was bursting with wild and carnal thoughts. Insatiable cravings. Thirst for power. But she was also driven by human behaviours; she saved Fitius. Saved those others in Antigoth that were her wards - rescued them all from these demons and from her.

The portal to a darker world welcomed her; its stolen child returned.

TOMBSTONE

Vestig Gozer, General of the Thran, Champion of the Hunga, stood on the beach outside of Regnorak. He was waiting here until the burning stopped in the city, enough that he could return to examine it. He did not expect to find much amongst the charred ruins.

It was fortunate to have a priest amid the Hunga. Only the Eternal priests wielded the power to keep the demons away. Moreover, it allowed Vestig to travel Amon Murn and assess the poor state of his nation.

Frain stood beside him. The giant removed his helmet so they could talk.

"Why did they return here?"

In front of them on the beach was the wreck of a massive ship. It was run aground near the capital and attempted to unload its precious cargo. From what Vestig could tell from the carcasses littering the sand, demons slaughtered the crew and marines. Something massive broke the ship in two.

A great slab of rock was on the beach similar to the tombstone they transported west and into battle. This one was unbroken, and on reflection, it seemed more ancient than the one they held to be precious.

"They failed, as we have failed."

"If this stone holds Urath'a'tharack, we should take it. Protect it."

"What for?"

The giant did not know. They had all believed the ancient giant would rise to lead them. It seemed a lost cause now.

"At least we should take him somewhere safe, where we can find him if we need to."

Vestig was done with legends.

"We can find him here. Let the demons look over him."

Frain shrugged. If they were to take the tombstone, it would likely fall to the giants to carry it.

"Here is good."

The tide was coming in, and Urath's tombstone was already sinking into the soft sand. Frain leaned down and put his palm on it. He had no words. There was an orange sunset, beautiful against the calm ocean. Soon it would be night, and the demons would come again searching for food.

Political Maps

The North

Southern controlled Veldaan and The Young Cities. The nations of the
Northern Alliance under the supremacy of Amon Murn. The
independent territories of The Wengo Mountain Tribes, The Tangle,
the Hand of Fengal, and The Aghan.

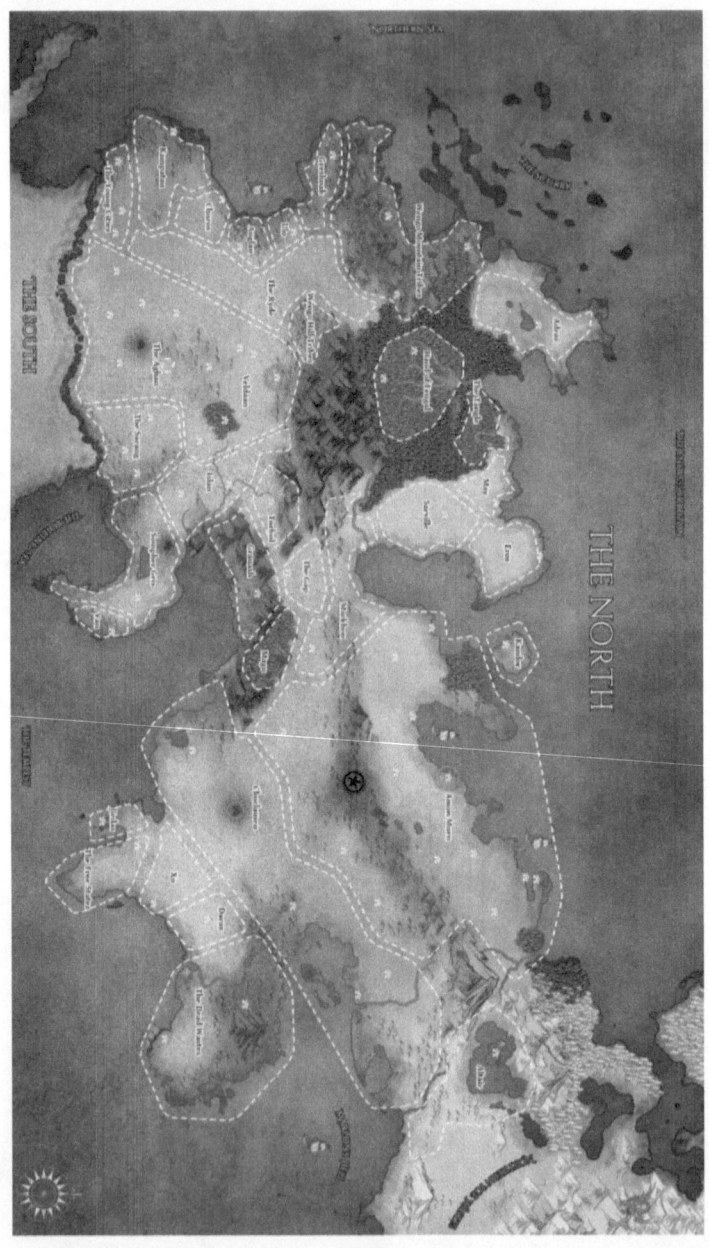

The South

The independent territories bordering the Frozen Wastes. The Eastern Colonies of Bracadia. The great expanse of The Dwarves. The autonomous regions of The Ark, Merin, Mongier, The Holy Lands, and Demonswar.

Topical Map

The Bracadian mainland, highlighting the locations visited by Fitius'
expedition.

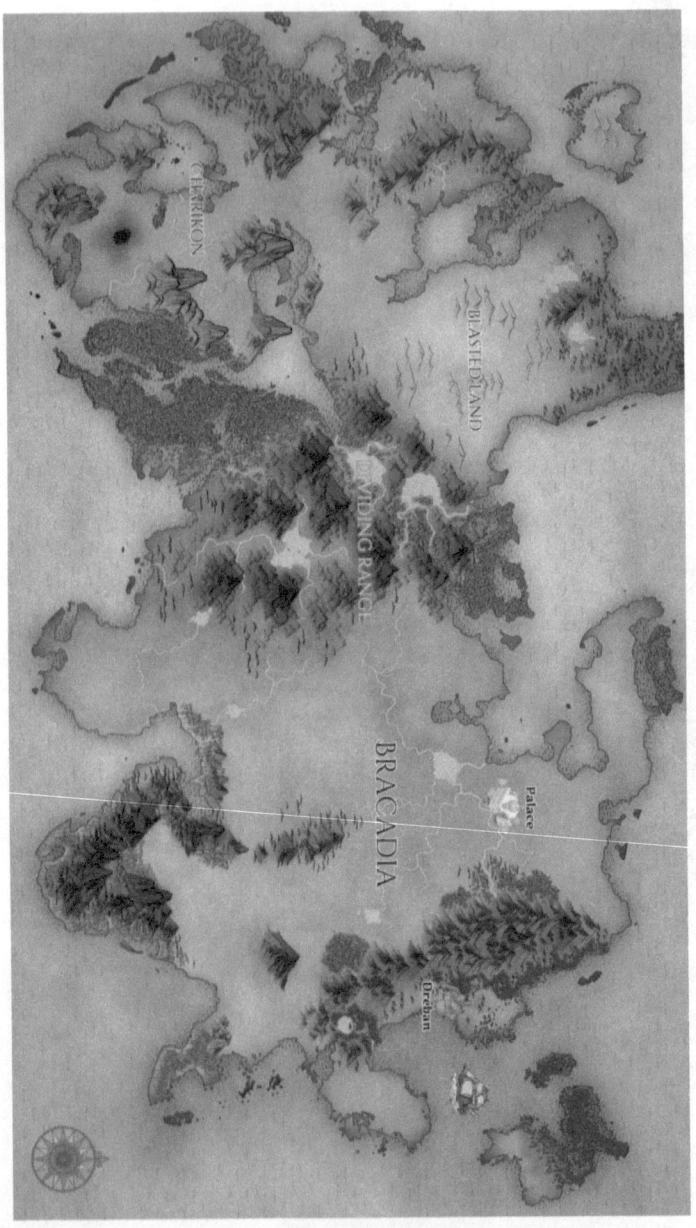

All maps produced using Wonderdraft.

Immortals Book 3: The Bracadian

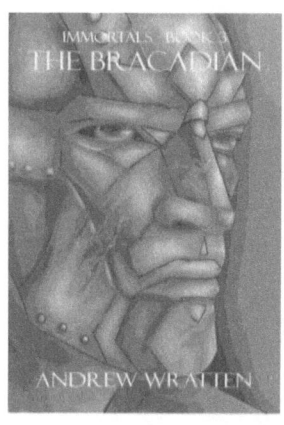

With the North gripped by devastation, and the South broken and abandoned, it was not the future foretold to the companions. It was *not* the destiny promised them.

Mannace, more broken than the lands he rules, must rebuild himself before leading others, else he will only steer his people to their doom. More than ever, the world that despises him depends on his fortitude to overcome the Northern threat. Mannace must save them all, alone.

Render prepares for Churgwarthos' vengeance, but the Elves who helped defeat the ancient Sorcerer have left the lands and cannot aid him. Hardened by ego not to run, Render will die fighting rather than acknowledge a superior foe.

Jaal, sworn to the Darkness yet loyal to his companions, must choose which side to take. His children, too, each cursed with the same contradiction, face tough choices and change.

But while some stumble, others rise. The Bracadian Emperor takes great interest in the innovation of his Eastern Colonies as a prelude to much grander expansion. He has declared an Age of Empire, and by his hand, he has the might to conquer the North and all other lands.

Far and wide, Darkness ascends. Not content to fight from the shadow, its agents grow bold, and armies drawn from the hells cast a heavy net over the North. As it has always been, Light confronts Darkness. What is known is not what it seems. And the impossible is asked of those with nothing left to give.

About the Author:

Andrew Wratten

I am a proud Kiwi, living in sunny Australia, with my beautiful Nigerian wife, Tessy, and our six amazing children. Family and friends mean everything ... and good food of course, and dogs, and embarrassingly, reality TV.

One day on the train to work, I took my fantasy daydream and boldly typed my first paragraphs. Since that time, I remain amazed at how the words reveal themselves and the tales evolve.

It is a wonderful process to shape a story, witnessing the plot unfold, unexpectedly twist, and surprise even me in its audacious conclusion.

The story belongs to the characters in it, and it is my job to help them be heard, understood, and celebrated for all their glorious traits and flaws. I am indeed a puppet of the Mad King, and like all the others in my books, I am dancing to his manic tune.

I hope others enjoy the characters, their triumphs, and their misadventures, as much as I do.

www.ingramcontent.com/pod-product-compliance
Lightning Source LLC
Chambersburg PA
CBHW020245120726
47904CB00001B/93